EVENTIDE

A Chief Mattson Mystery

(Formerly published as Dead by Sunrise)

Copyright © 2021 by R.L. Ryker

D1209105

Join my mailing list at richardryker.com for new releases, offers for free books, and more.

Books by R.L. Ryker

Brandon Mattson Mysteries
Eventide
Dark Forest
Silent Fool
Death Cap

Standalone Thrillers
Chasing Black Widow

Chapter 1

The midmorning sun breached the ragged cliffs above First Beach. Seagulls and crows scavenged the pebbled shore for wayward crabs. An incessant gale swept off the Pacific, the wet air heavy with the salty odor of kelp.

Brandon squinted at the dark, rolling ocean, his eyes following the whitecaps as they tumbled onto the log-strewn beach. There was something about standing at the edge of the continent, peering out into the seemingly endless horizon.

More time at the beach was one of the perks Brandon had considered before accepting the chief of police position in Forks. But this wasn't how he'd imagined his first trip back to the ocean.

"Over there," Officer Josiah Trent said, reminding Brandon he wasn't there to take in the scenery.

Fifty feet up the beach, Tribal Police Chief Simpson had his back to the body. A group of gawkers encircled him. Simpson waved his arms to prevent a lookie-loo from photographing the girl.

Off to the right, another tribal officer was interviewing a Native American woman in her thirties. She had her arms around two young girls. The woman pointed at the body.

"Find out what happened," he said to Josiah. "I'll check out the scene."

The spectators parted to let Brandon through.

"Thanks for coming out," Chief Simpson said.

Erik Simpson was in his sixties and had been a beat cop up in Port Angeles before moving back to the area. Technically, he was a member of the Hoh Tribe, about an hour to the south, but from what Brandon had heard, he had a good reputation in the Quileute community.

Simpson swatted another cell phone away.

Brandon turned to the bystanders.

"Did any of you witness what happened?"

All of them shook their heads, no.

"And were any of you here when the body was discovered?"

"We were the first to speak to the two girls that found her," a woman said. The man at her side bobbed his head in agreement.

"There's an officer over there. I need you to tell him what you saw. The rest of you—the show's over," Brandon said.

"And you are?" a man to his right asked.

Brandon hadn't had time to pick up his uniform and badge.

"I'm the police chief of Forks. Now beat it."

At that, the rest dispersed without protest.

Brandon hoped Simpson didn't mind him taking charge. "Were any of those schmucks local?"

"Hell, no," Simpson said. "Tourists."

Brandon kneeled next to the young woman.

"I appreciate you coming out," Simpson said.

It was Brandon's first day on the job. He'd planned to tackle the growing pile of paperwork on his desk, meet with his team, and initiate the process for hiring at least one new officer. A homicide investigation was not on his to-do list.

Brandon had spoken with Chief Simpson just after taking the job in Forks. He'd even encouraged Simpson to call anytime he needed a hand.

He hadn't expected that call to come so soon.

"How long has she been here?" Brandon asked.

"Got the call over an hour ago. EMS came and went."

"You're not convinced she drowned?" Brandon asked.

The girl's face was swollen, her eyes shut.

"There's a cut on her head," Simpson said, pointing to the woman's scalp.

The injury was about two inches long and wide enough to cause significant bleeding. There was no visible blood, but she'd been in the water.

"Did you turn her over?" Brandon asked.

"I didn't want to touch anything, just in case. The coroner is on her way."

The young woman wore a red and yellow bikini top and jean shorts. She had black hair and was probably Hispanic.

Something caught his eye.

"You got a pen?" he asked.

Simpson offered him a pencil.

"Only pen I got is a keepsake. You can keep the pencil."

Brandon took the pencil and slipped the girl's thick, wet hair away from her neck.

About an inch below her right ear, there were four puncture wounds.

"What the hell is that?" Simpson asked.

"Good question."

"Looks like a snake bite, but bigger."

"Human," Brandon said.

3

"No normal person has teeth that can do that," Simpson said.

Brandon stood, circling the young woman. "Any ID?"

"Not that I found," Simpson said.

"How long until the coroner gets here?"

"She's coming down from Port Angeles. The crime scene tech is with her."

Simpson considered the girl. "I'm hoping you'll take this case over, Brandon. I don't have the resources for a murder investigation. And I don't need a bunch of feds poking around here, either."

The reservation wasn't in Brandon's jurisdiction. But through a contract with the Clallam County Sheriff, the Forks Police Department covered the southwestern area of the county. And Brandon's department did have a shared jurisdiction agreement with the tribe.

"I'm not exactly flush with extra officers," Brandon said.

"But your experience as a homicide detective—"

"*Former* homicide detective," Brandon reminded him.

He'd left homicide behind for a reason—the endless hours, attorneys, dealing with death and crime scenes every day. Running a small-town police department wasn't a cakewalk, but it wasn't those other things, either.

"I'll lend you any support you need," Simpson pleaded.

There were aspects of the situation that would be over the head of any cop without homicide experience.

And besides, it was just one case.

"Alright," Brandon said.

"I owe you one."

4

"More than one, depending on where this goes. Can you do me a favor and let Josiah know I need to speak with him?"

"Will do," Simpson said.

While he waited, Brandon kept the girl company.

Despite the number of homicides he'd worked, Brandon had never lost sight of the fact that the victims were people. A son, daughter, or parent. Even the loneliest soul had someone who cared.

Whether they knew it or not, that was another story.

The girl was in her early twenties. Brandon's daughter, Emma, was back home in Seattle. She was just 15. Being a parent was hard, but being a cop and a parent, when you were daily reminded of the depravity of certain elements of the human race? Some days it was too much.

Josiah's form peaked the dunes near the parking lot. He jogged down the hill, stumbled as he reached the bottom, and sprinted to Brandon. He came up short at the sight of the young woman.

"I interviewed the mom and the girls who found her," Josiah said. His eyes darted away from the body.

"You might as well get used to it," Brandon said.

"What?"

"Seeing dead bodies."

Brandon considered Josiah's buzz cut and slight build. He was a local product who'd recently graduated from the Academy. His naïve eyes reminded Brandon of a kid in his first week of boot camp, not an officer investigating a crime scene.

"I'm not—"

"Here," Brandon said, waving him closer. Josiah edged forward.

He squinted at the girl's neck. "Bite marks?"

"You notice anything else?" Brandon asked.

Josiah glanced sideways at the girl. She was only a few years younger than him.

"Her muscles. They're stiff."

"Rigor mortis," Brandon said.

"That means she's been dead at least twelve hours. Less than twenty-four," Josiah said.

The kid had paid attention at the Academy.

"But she's been in the water for a while, so that changes everything," Brandon reminded him.

"Oh yeah, I remember that now," Josiah said.

"What do you think?"

"Me?"

"Yeah, I'm asking you."

Josiah stroked his chin. "The cut on the head means she fell or maybe was hit. And there's the bite, but some people are into that."

"Into what?"

"You know, all that vampire stuff. That's what we're famous for."

"Those are just books," Brandon said.

Brandon hadn't read the bestselling *Moonbeam Darklove* series that had transformed Forks into a tourist mecca. Teen angst and blood-sucking creatures weren't his thing.

He'd seen his fill of real blood and gore during his tenure as a detective with the Seattle PD.

"Have you seen the freaks we get around here?" Josiah asked. "Some of them, you know, dress up, act it out. It's a thing."

The world was full of strange, sometimes very sick, people. Brandon had never imagined them out there, far from the big city where most congregated.

If this was the work of a vampire-obsessed murderer, then Brandon had grossly underestimated the impact of the *Moonbeam Darklove* craze on his once-peaceful hometown.

Chapter 2

When the coroner arrived 20 minutes later, Brandon let Josiah get back to the station to write up his report. Simpson had one of his officers lead the coroner and crime scene tech to Brandon and the young woman.

"Lisa Shipley," the coroner said. "Traffic was hell."

Lisa was in her late thirties and had blonde hair with a purple stripe down one side. She wore khaki shorts, hiking boots, and a button-up shirt.

Brandon glanced at her bare ring finger.

"Road construction?" Brandon asked.

"Yep," she said, extending a hand. "This is one of our techs, Michael."

Michael was probably in his early sixties. He twisted the cap off his camera, eager to photograph the scene.

"Brandon Mattson, new chief of police over in Forks. Tribal called us in on this one."

"What do we have?" Lisa asked, pulling on a pair of gloves.

"Two kids found her washed up on the beach."

"Any witnesses?"

"No," Brandon said. "There's a gash on the crown of her head and a bite on her neck."

"Bite?"

"It looks human. But..."

Lisa moved in closer. "Vampire teeth."

"You've seen this before?" Brandon asked.

"Once. When I worked in Salt Lake."

Lisa stepped aside as Michael captured the puncture wounds.

"Let's take a peek at the rest of her," Lisa said.

Carefully, they tilted the girl onto her side.

Half a dozen scrapes furrowed the girl's back. The bottom of her bikini was torn but intact.

"Someone dragged her," Brandon said. He eyed the cliffs to the north and the outcropping of rocks at their base.

"After she died. There's not much bruising. Minimal livor mortis," she said, referring to the process of blood pooling under the skin when a body remained unmoved after death. That meant the young woman wasn't in one position long before she went into the ocean.

If she had been dragged, and especially if it occurred after death, that meant she was probably killed, and the murderer wanted to cover up what he'd done.

Lisa took the girl's body temperature. After making some preliminary notes, they prepared her for the trip to Port Angeles, where Lisa would continue her investigation.

They checked her pockets for a cell phone or any identification. There were none.

After they loaded the young woman into the coroner's transport vehicle, Michael got in and started the engine. Lisa closed the van's back door.

"First impressions?" Brandon asked.

"The watery conditions change all our assumptions."

"Right."

"I'll know more by tomorrow, but I'd say around twelve hours ago is a good start for the time of death. The scratches tell me someone dragged her after she died. Why there's a bite mark, I have no idea. That's your department. Motive and all that."

He liked Lisa. She knew her stuff but stayed in her own lane.

9

She snapped the blue latex gloves off.

"So, how's your new job treating you?" she asked.

"Considering this is my first day and I'm dealing with a potential homicide..."

"Welcome to Clallam County. It's not always this bad," she said, motioning toward the van where the young woman's body lay.

"You don't have to tell me." He patted his chest. "Forks born and raised."

"And you came back?"

"Long story. Divorce, family. All that."

"Maybe you can tell me about it sometime," Lisa said.

Brandon's response caught in his throat. Flirting wasn't his thing. At least it hadn't been for the past 10 years. He'd chalk that up to another reason his marriage had failed.

Lisa's cheeks glowed pink at Brandon's uneasy silence.

He tried to recover. "I can. I will. Sometime."

Dammit.

"I'll call you when I know more." She paused. "About the girl."

Brandon shook off the awkward conversation. There was plenty of work to do without complicating things so soon after his divorce.

With no missing person's report matching the girl's description, the bite marks, and a town full of wannabe vampires, it would take some time to get to the bottom of the case.

Once the public learned of the circumstances surrounding the girl's death, there would be a general hysteria about the undead or similar nonsense. That wasn't the worst of his worries, though. There could be a murderer roaming his turf. One brazen enough to leave a bite mark—meaning evidence, possibly even saliva—on a young woman's neck before tossing her into the sea.

Brandon climbed into his truck and slipped the key in the ignition. His phone rang.

It was Emma.

"Hey, sweetie."

"Hi, Dad. You ready to come back home yet?" she asked.

Brandon and his ex, Tori, had agreed on an every-other-weekend and all-summer parenting plan. Emma was almost 16 and spent little time at home as it was. It had only been two days and Brandon already missed the few minutes a day he saw his daughter.

"I get to see you in two weeks," he said.

They'd just gotten back from a father-daughter road trip to Yellowstone and the Grand Tetons. Unlike her mother, Emma loved the outdoors, camping and fishing.

"Why not now?"

"I've got to get the house ready, Em."

"But mom is driving me crazy."

Brandon knew better than to meddle in their mother-daughter conflicts. He'd tried to play peacemaker before, only to end up in the doghouse with both of them.

"You need to work that out with her."

"Alright," she said.

"Is there something else going on?"

Emma's best friend Madison had died in a car accident during the previous school year. She'd taken it hard but had been in counseling and seemed better the last several months.

It didn't help that Brandon's mother and brother had both passed in the last year, too.

11

Tori claimed Brandon had a hard time dealing with death. Brandon had grieved for both of them—especially Eli. Just because he hadn't resorted to self-pity and public weeping didn't mean he wasn't affected. He was a homicide detective. He knew how to deal with death.

In his own way.

Emma needed more than pat answers, so Brandon had done his best to be there for her, to listen.

"I'm fine," Emma insisted.

"You sure?"

"Yes."

"I love you, Emma."

"You, too."

Had he made a mistake leaving Seattle?

But in just two weeks, she'd be staying with him for the summer. Brandon wasn't sure how she'd stay busy in a small town like Forks. There wasn't much to do except get in trouble.

He reminded himself that Emma wasn't like him.

At the end of the summer, she'd head back to Seattle for her junior year of high school.

Junior year? It seemed like only yesterday he was teaching her to ride a bike.

Chapter 3

Brandon slowed his truck to 30 mph as he entered the city limits. Traffic rolled to a stop as a cluster of tourists crossed the two-lane road that passed for the town's main street.

A vinyl sign stretched across Forks Avenue read *Welcome to Forks, Moonbeamers* in maroon letters. The advertisement, swaying lazily under a slight breeze, announced the date of the upcoming *Moonbeam Darklove* festival.

The street cleared and Brandon took a right on Fifth and headed for City Hall and police headquarters.

He'd been on his way to the station to meet his officers when Simpson called him out to First Beach, setting Brandon's schedule back several hours. Now he was late for the mandatory meeting he'd scheduled.

He had spent the evening before rehearsing what he'd say to his team. Brandon had grown up in Forks, but after two decades he'd be a stranger to most in the town of 3,500 and—homegrown or not—he would have to prove himself to his new department.

A Native American woman in her fifties greeted him in the station's chilly reception area. Outside, the temperature had barely touched 70 degrees. She had the air conditioner on overdrive.

The woman looked up from her computer and pointed to the door. "Close it. I like it cold."

Brandon considered the woman's thick, woolen vest and long-sleeve shirt. The Hoh Tribe's symbol was embroidered on her vest.

"Then why—"

"Can I help you?" she asked.

"I hope so, seeing as I'm your new boss." He held out a hand. "Brandon Mattson."

She picked up a pair of glasses and slid them over her nose. A smile softened her eyes. "Sorry, Chief."

"Sue McDermott. Chief secretary," she said, standing. She shook his hand. "Only secretary, as a matter of fact."

"You been here long, Sue?"

"Long enough to know you're the prodigal son coming home."

Brandon bristled at the word *prodigal*. His parents had always opposed his move to Seattle. But that was 20 years ago.

"Look, Sue. I don't know what you've heard—"

"It's all right, Chief Mattson. No need to worry about me. In the meantime, I've got a few things for you." She was just over five feet tall and, due to her ample midsection, waddled as she crossed the room to a box sitting on a table.

"I've got a meeting with my team," Brandon said. "Can we do this later?"

"It won't kill them to wait." She winked at him. "Teaches them respect."

Sue rummaged through the contents and found his badge. "This is yours. Papers for HR in here too. Insurance, that sort of stuff. And here's your uniform." She stepped back, eyeing Brandon. "I guessed extra-large."

"That's about right," Brandon said.

"Good. No one smaller than extra-large should be chief of anything." She glanced at him. "In my opinion. Your key's in there too, and the code to the door—90210."

"Like Beverly Hills?"

Sue rolled her eyes before returning to her computer.

Seven officers were waiting for Brandon in the station's conference room. He stepped into the room, closing the door behind him. "I appreciate you all coming in."

Of the officers, the three he'd already met were Isabel Jackson, a reserve in her mid-thirties, Will Spoelman, an old-timer who'd let Brandon know he planned on retiring soon, and Josiah Trent, the officer that had helped him out at First Beach earlier that morning.

Then there was Neal Nolan, the only full-time officer to skip the *get to know the new chief* shindig the mayor had orchestrated two weeks earlier. Nolan was 42 years old, over six feet tall, and had the arms, chest, and waistline of a gym rat. They squeezed each other's hands, eyes locked just long enough for both men to establish that neither conceded anything. *Like dogs pissing on trees*, Brandon thought.

"I knew your brother, Eli," Nolan said. "He was a good man."

"I know," Brandon replied.

Eli had been an officer with Forks PD and an extra-duty sheriff's deputy. Early one Sunday morning, he'd pulled over a late-model Honda for speeding and expired tags. The occupants, according to detectives, were an unknown man and woman. They'd unloaded four rounds into Eli as he approached to ask for identification.

Brandon had viewed the blurry dashcam video a hundred times, memorized the license plate, the almost

15

indistinct shapes of his brother's murderers, the passenger pulling the trigger, leaving Eli to die by the roadside.

He had kept in touch with the detectives and, despite his frustration with their lack of progress, they'd assured him they knew what they were doing.

Eventually, Eli's murderers would be brought to justice. Brandon would make sure of it.

"They named the highway outside of town after Eli," Josiah said.

"I know that too," Brandon said.

"Hard reputation to live up to," Nolan added.

"That's why I'm not going to try."

No matter how well Nolan thought he knew Eli, they weren't brothers. And Brandon wasn't big on talking family business with strangers.

"What's going on out at the reservation?" Jackson asked.

Although Isabel Jackson was the department's newest recruit, she'd worked on the force down in Portland before relocating to Forks. Jackson's black hair was pulled back tight, revealing blonde streaks throughout. Freckles spotted her honey-toned cheeks. Brandon recalled reading something in her file about her family being from Cuba.

"Possible homicide," Brandon said. "A young woman." He glanced at the clock. He'd been twenty minutes late and he didn't want to waste his officers' time. He dropped the remarks he'd prepared for the team.

Instead, he focused on the one point he wanted to get across.

"I know you've all been overworked since Chief Satler's retirement. I hope to hire at least one additional officer soon. More if I can convince the mayor—"

"The overtime doesn't bother me," Nolan interrupted.

"Speak for yourself," Will said, retrieving a pouch from his coat pocket. He selected a toothpick and slid it between his teeth. "I'm getting too old for this."

"Like it or not," Brandon said, "We don't have the budget to keep everyone at time-and-a-half."

"If we have to hire, I got a buddy interested in the full-time position," Nolan said. "He's working down in Ocean Shores right now."

Jackson shifted in her seat. Was the reserve officer hoping to apply for the position?

"We'd be stupid not to hire him," Nolan said.

"Stupid would be hiring a man I've never met," Brandon said.

"When will the job be posted?" Jackson asked.

"As soon as I get the paperwork finished."

"You need help with the homicide?" she asked.

Nolan crossed his arms. "You're a reserve, Jackson. Not a detective."

Brandon's jaw clenched. "I'll assign duties to my officers based on the needs of the department. Regardless of reserve status." He turned to Jackson. "Josiah is working on his report. I'll add what I learned from Simpson. We'll know more when we hear back from the coroner. I'll let you know what help we need then."

"Got it," she said.

He turned his attention to where Nolan stood glowering at the back of the room. "As for the rest of you— get back to work."

Chapter 4

The mayor had scheduled a meeting with Brandon for six that evening. In the meantime, he caught up on the growing list of emails he'd already received his first day on the job. Then, he brought in a few things from his truck: a picture of Emma and a stack of books he'd never read but that would look good on the shelf.

When he finished, he skimmed Josiah's report. The only witnesses with any real information were the two sisters who had discovered the body. Not much to go on and still no ID on the girl.

The mayor's office was across the parking lot from city hall in a two-room portable. The newly hired mayor wanted separation from the rest of city government. Her receptionist had gone home, but the mayor's door was open. He found her at her desk, typing. Brandon tapped on the door.

Mayor Sara Kim rose to greet him. She wore a navy-blue dress with a candy-red scarf. Her smile was just like everything else about her—confident and commanding. He'd read about Mayor Kim in a couple of online articles. She was a first-generation Korean American hell-bent on making a name for herself. Just last year, she'd defeated Spencer Wilson, a man who'd been mayor for 16 years. She'd won by promising to attract more jobs and money to Forks through increased tourism. Mayor Kim had even convinced the city to make the mayor's job a paid position—a first for Forks.

"Brandon. Have a seat."

She motioned to an expensive-looking mahogany table. Mayor Kim settled into the chair next to him. She crossed her legs, the point of her bright-red shoe centimeters from Brandon's knee.

"You getting settled in?"

Brandon frowned. "Unfortunately."

Her eyebrows arched in a question.

"We had a suspicious death in La Push," Brandon said.

"Isn't that tribal land?"

"They asked for our help."

The mayor tapped her pen against the table. "Does the media know?"

She was a politician—of course that would be her first concern.

"Not that I know of," Brandon replied.

"A local?"

"Not sure yet. She's a young woman, early twenties."

He didn't mention the bite marks on the woman's neck or that it might be a homicide. As a detective, he'd learned to avoid sharing the details of a case until he got his facts in a row.

He'd wait until he heard from the coroner before sharing anything further with the mayor.

She pressed her hands together, the tips of her fingers pointing at Brandon. "You think I'm insensitive."

Brandon stared back without answering.

"My job is to make sure this town thrives," she said.

"What's that got to do with a young woman drowning?"

"Tourism, Chief Mattson. It's what keeps people working. And paying taxes. More taxes mean revenue to pay for more officers, better police vehicles—"

"I get it."

His stomach grumbled. He hadn't eaten since breakfast. Listening to the mayor lecture him about taxes and how the young woman's death somehow threatened the economy was making him lose his appetite. And if that happened, he'd really be in a bad mood.

"What did you want to meet about, Mayor?"

She leaned back. "You can call me Sara."

"Okay."

"I'm assuming you know who Tiffany Quick is?" she asked.

"She's the author of that vampire book."

"The *Moonbeam Darklove* Series," she reminded him.

"Right."

"She's a *New York Times* best-selling author."

"Not really my thing."

Emma had started the series but lost interest when it was clear the plot hinged on a kissy-face love triangle.

"You can't argue with success," she said.

Brandon's eyes caught on the framed *Northwest Business Woman* magazine photo on the wall behind her. A confident Sara Kim graced the cover, the declaration, "Bringing a Town Back from the Brink" beneath her.

"What's this got to do with the police?" Brandon asked.

"In two weeks, Ms. Quick will visit our town for the first time. She's the guest of honor at this year's Moonbeam Festival."

Brandon had read somewhere that, despite using the town as the setting for her bestselling series, the author hadn't stepped foot in Forks. She'd done all her research online.

"You're expecting a greater than usual number of tourists?" Brandon asked.

"That's right."

"Are you anticipating trouble?"

The mayor's forehead furrowed. "Fans of Tiffany Quick are no different from you or me, Brandon."

Except for the ones that don black capes and vampire fangs, he thought.

"I'll need to know locations and times of any events," Brandon said. "And the expected turnout. This will cost us in overtime."

"The festival is just two weeks from today. With the increased revenue from sales tax, overtime won't be a problem."

Taxes and tourists. She was a broken record.

"Okay. Anything else?"

"Just a reminder, Chief Mattson. If we keep the visitors to our town happy, our citizens benefit."

Brandon had dealt with his fair share of elected officials and the way they said things without actually saying them.

"Mayor, we'll get along a lot better if you're up front with me."

She pursed her lips, accentuating the frown lines that must have formed over years of worrying about how to get ahead of everyone else.

"I can appreciate that," she said.

They both stood.

"One more thing," she said.

"Yes?"

"Some officers in your department have a history of making our guests feel unwelcome."

"You have examples?"

"Overzealous enforcement of certain traffic laws."

"The law is the law—"

"Harassing some of our marijuana tourists."

Marijuana had only been legal in the state for a few years. People from across the country were no doubt flocking to the town to get stoned while dressed up as Count Dracula.

Brandon had noticed a marijuana store on the edge of town. Pot stores were legal, but some towns had made it nearly impossible for the sellers to set up shop within city limits. The fact that the store was able to operate in Forks meant the mayor must have supported it.

"With all due respect, Mayor, enforcing the law—for all citizens—is the responsibility of the police department."

"Understood. And you'll remember that you have a job here because I hired you."

"To enforce the law."

Brandon held her gaze for several seconds.

"Good enough. For now," she said, returning to her desk. "Good evening, Police Chief Mattson."

"Evening, Mayor," he said, but she was already back to typing.

Before he'd accepted the chief position, Mayor Kim had promised Brandon she'd stay out of his way, let him deal with the town's police business. Now, he wondered if she were capable of that. She was driven, and like many people with that trait, she would be blind to the idea that not everyone she met was aiming at the same target as she was.

Brandon didn't have the luxury of minding other people's business. He had enough to worry about, not just the everyday tasks like filling vacant positions and managing a department, but the potential murder case he'd just agreed to help solve.

Brandon stood in the parking lot and considered heading back to his office.

The paperwork would be there tomorrow. He climbed into his truck and started the engine.

When he'd left Seattle earlier that morning, he'd figured the biggest challenge facing him today would be pulling off his first team meeting as chief. Instead, he had a potential homicide and a mayor bent on inviting as many vampire-obsessed fans into her town as possible, no matter the cost.

Chapter 5

He picked up a burger and fries at the local drive-in and headed for home. QuickBurger had changed hands a few times since his high school days. Dick Meyer, the original owner, had left it to his daughter, who'd run the business into the ground. The newest owners were immigrants from East Asia, and they'd added spring rolls and Pad Thai to the menu.

Brandon had planned on dropping by his dad's house, but he was beat and needed food and sleep. He called his dad and left a message that he'd stop by another day.

Brandon pulled up to the 1940s craftsman he was renting until he could find a place of his own. The rent was cheap, less than a quarter of what a similar house would cost in Seattle. He unlocked the door, felt for the switch, and flipped the porch light on.

He passed through the living room where moving boxes were scattered haphazardly, most still taped shut. Pizza boxes littered the floor along with a few beer bottles. His buddies from the Seattle PD had helped him move and they'd made a night of it.

His mattress lay angled on the bedroom floor where they'd left it. He hadn't had time to set up the frame. Brandon fell onto the bed now, unwrapped the hamburger, and ate in silence. As much as he'd coveted alone time when he was married, Brandon still hadn't gotten used to the ear-ringing quiet of an empty house.

He picked up a book he'd been reading the night before. *Anton Chekhov's Short Stories.* Brandon had finished the volume half a dozen times but never grew

24

tired of it. He'd been introduced to Chekhov while playing the lead in a couple of high school plays. The dark realism of Russian literature—stories of everyday people battling for survival in a society that sometimes cared little for them—resonated with Brandon.

He tossed the hamburger wrapper and bag aside and popped his shoes off, falling asleep with the book propped on his chest.

Brandon's phone rang just after nine that evening.

"This is Mattson."

"Hi, Chief. It's Lisa Shipley."

He pinched the bridge of his nose. It took him a moment to remember where he was.

"The coroner," she said.

"I remember," he said, propping himself up on one elbow. "You got results already?"

"I have a few ideas, but that's not why I'm calling."

"Okay. What's up?"

"You know about the missing person report?" Lisa asked.

"I haven't heard anything."

"Apparently someone reported the young lady from the beach missing."

"They informed my department?"

"I'm looking at the report right here. It says it was sent to Forks PD this morning. We usually get a copy too."

If the report had arrived that morning—before the young woman's body had been discovered—why hadn't his officers told him about it?

Brandon heaved himself off the mattress and went into the kitchen to grab a notepad.

"What's the girl's name?"

"Lauren Sandoval. Hispanic, twenty-four. There's no picture. Just a call from her friends. Why don't you know about this?"

"Good question. Let me know what you learn about the cause of death."

"I'll have something tomorrow morning."

Brandon hung up and headed to the station.

He found the missing person notice on the fax machine. A man named Adam Cane had called earlier that day, said he and his girlfriend were camping out at Second Beach and when he woke up, she was missing. He'd left his cell phone number.

Second Beach was a popular ocean camping destination near La Push. In the summer, cars lined the road up to half a mile from the trail that led to the beach.

Brandon's officers better have a damn good explanation for why they hadn't connected the deceased woman on the beach with the missing person report. It was the part of leadership he hated the most—dealing with staff who didn't do their jobs.

He dialed the number Adam Cane had left with the report.

The young man answered. He was still camping at the beach with friends, waiting for news about Lauren. Brandon told Adam to meet him at the trailhead in half an hour.

Brandon contacted dispatch and had them instruct an on-duty officer to head to the Second Beach parking lot. On the way down, he called dispatch again, asking for a callback from the officer.

He received a call five minutes later.

"What's up, Chief?"

It was his most experienced officer, Will Spoelman.

"You heard about the body we found on the beach today?"

"Josiah told me all about it," Will said.

"Someone called in a missing person report this morning—about the deceased girl."

There was a short pause before Will said, "No one told me."

"So, you didn't know about this?"

"You think I wouldn't tell you if I did? Listen, Brandon—"

"I had to ask."

He should know better than to assume Will Spoelman would screw up something as simple as a missing person report. Brandon had known the officer most of his life. Will wasn't one to slough off his responsibilities.

"I was in for twenty minutes for your meeting. That's it. I started my shift half an hour ago."

Brandon hadn't memorized his officers' schedules yet, but Will probably knew who took the report in the morning. Will wouldn't rat out a fellow officer, though.

"I contacted the source of the report," Brandon said. "The girl disappeared at some point last night. He's still here with two of their friends."

"You notify family?" Will asked.

"Not yet. I want to check out the story first. The friends don't know about the girl's death."

Will grunted. "I hate this notification of death crap."

"You and me both. But as far as I'm concerned, if this is more than a simple drowning, these are potential suspects."

And if it was an accident, someone has a lot of explaining to do—considering the scratches on her back and the bite marks on her neck.

"Got it. I'm almost there," Will said.

"See you in five."

The highway to Second Beach was a two-lane road that dissected a few miles of farmland before nearing the Pacific, where it cut into a swath of coastal evergreens. It was well past sundown, but Brandon knew every curve and corner, even in the dark.

Brandon found Will parked on the side of the road just outside the entrance to the campground's gravel parking lot.

Adam Cane was waiting near the registration station. Campers were expected to place a site fee into an envelope and leave it in the drop box. A dull lamp at the trailhead did little more than color the area a lighter shade of dark. Adam stood under the lamp, hands in his pockets and hoodie shielding his eyes.

He stepped forward as Brandon and Will approached.

"Is she safe? You wouldn't be here—don't tell me you found her—"

Will pointed a furtive finger at Brandon, as if to say, *this one's yours, Chief.*

"Lauren's body was discovered this afternoon," Brandon said.

Adam's face contorted in confusion. "Body?"

"I'm sorry, Adam."

"No." He stumbled back, head swiveling in denial.

Brandon waited a moment. He'd done this countless times. If he was lucky, and that wasn't often, a chaplain was present to do the emotional heavy lifting. That wasn't going to happen out there in the middle of nowhere.

"We need to ask you a few questions," Brandon said.

Adam leaned back against the registration station and slid to the ground, his face hidden beneath the hoodie. "This isn't happening."

After a moment, Will slipped a hand under Adam's arm. "We know this is tough, kid, but we need your help. Up on your feet."

Adam pushed himself up. "Sorry."

"Go ahead and remove your hoodie," Brandon said.

Adam did, revealing a head of curly blonde hair and a clean-cut but acne-ridden complexion. His eyes were swollen and wet with tears.

"How did she die?"

"We're not sure yet," Brandon said before Will could reply. If this was a murder investigation, there was no point in giving away what they did—or didn't—know.

"Was she...hurt?" Adam asked.

"Right now we're focused on finding out what happened last night," Brandon said.

Adam sucked in a deep breath, gathering his wits.

"We were all hanging out, you know. Partying at our campsite. I fell asleep and she was gone in the morning."

"Why would Lauren leave?"

"I don't know."

"Did you have an argument?"

"No," he said. The defensiveness in his tone told Brandon that Adam understood the implication behind the question.

"Did she ever mention wanting to hurt herself?"

29

Suicide wasn't on the table, but Adam didn't know that. Brandon wondered if the young man would try to use it as an out to cover for anything he might have done.

"Not that I know of."

"What about your friends? Where are they?" Will asked.

"Down at the campsite."

"Alright," Brandon said. "Show us the way."

They followed Adam down the winding forest path that led to Second Beach. Will trekked behind Adam, holding his flashlight high. A slight breeze swept through stands of fir, cedar, and spruce, carrying with it the far-off roar of the ocean.

Brandon had hiked the trail a hundred times as a kid. In the winter, local teens used the beach as a favorite party spot. Back then, no cop would make the two-mile trek just to check on a bunch of kids out after curfew.

Tourists packed the beach during the summer months. Probably more so now since the *Moonbeam Darklove* craze.

The path led them up a slight incline, leveling out before a steep descent down a series of switchbacks punctuated by wooden stairs where the path would otherwise have been too difficult for many of the thousands of visitors frequenting the spot each year.

The trail landed in a patch of brush and a 40-foot-wide obstacle course of barren and blanched logs, like the mother lode of all driftwood had washed ashore.

Ahead of them, a waxing moon cast a silvery glow over the sand. One of the area's popular sea stack rocks rose off to the left. They scrambled across the moonlit timber graveyard that guarded the entrance to the beach.

Campfires dotted the sand like ancient beacons. You could pitch a tent anywhere, but people tended to spread out in a more or less even distance from each other. A layer of wood smoke swelled near the tree line, where most campers settled, far enough away from the shore that they'd be safe from high tide.

"Over here," Adam said.

They'd set up camp only 30 feet from the trail.

A weak flame flickered in a rock pit between two tents. They had pulled driftwood near the fire. There were two sitting logs, one on each side of the firepit. On one of the logs, a man and a woman leaned against each other. The man held up a lighter to a pipe. Despite the ocean breeze and campfire haze, the stink of marijuana wrinkled Brandon's nose.

"Hey, guys. The cops are here," Adam said.

The young man stood, lowering the pipe. The girl rose too, letting the blanket around her shoulders drop to the sand. She had short black hair and a Celtic knot tattoo on her right arm. Her arms were toned, almost muscular. She had the build of someone who might run a marathon—pretty much the opposite of the young stoner standing next to her.

"Where's Lauren?"

Adam saved Brandon the trouble of breaking the bad news.

"She's dead, Brooke."

Brooke dropped onto the log. The man with the pipe fell onto the spot next to her.

"No...it's not...I can't..." She buried her head in the man's shoulder.

Adam swept the back of his hand across his eyes. The other young man, Brandon noticed, wasn't reacting with grief. His blank stare told Brandon the man was either in shock or stoned out of his mind.

"You were close?" Brandon directed the question to Brooke.

She looked up, blinking through tears.

"Lauren was my best friend."

"I know this is difficult," Brandon said. "But we have a few questions. What are your names?"

The woman answered that she was Brooke Whittaker.

"And you?" Will asked.

"Justin Tate."

Justin's deep tan was evident even in the firelight. It was barely June and, being Washington State, a tan that early in the year meant the kid must fake and bake. The tan wasn't what held Brandon's attention, though. It was Justin's coiled, knotty hair. Dreadlocks. Another upper-middle-class kid going for the Bob Marley look.

"When was the last time you saw Lauren?" Brandon asked.

"When we all crashed last night," Justin said.

"What time was that?"

"It wasn't that late. We'd been partying all afternoon."

"So, you all went into your tents. Then what?"

"Isn't that sort of private?" Justin asked.

"We fell asleep," Brooke answered. Her eyes slid to Adam. "I don't know what Adam and Lauren did."

Adam shrugged. "Same."

"What time?" Will asked.

"I don't know."

"At some point she got up and left?" Will asked.

"I must have been sleeping," Adam replied.

They'd been drinking and smoking all day and turned in early, all at the same time. Went straight to sleep and, in the morning, Lauren was gone.

It almost sounded rehearsed.

"How did she..." Brooke started.

"We're working on that," Brandon said.

"Okay, but was she like, hurt or what? Or did she just drown?" Justin asked.

Brandon considered Justin for a moment. It might mean something that he'd mentioned drowning and the possibility of injury. Sure, they were by the beach, and drowning was a natural assumption. But injury? Not a question most people asked when learning their friend had died.

"Is there anything you want to tell us?" Brandon asked Justin.

Justin swept the question away with a wave of his hand. "No way, man. I'm just asking."

Brooke leaned away from Justin. "Do you know something?"

"He's just trying to mess with our heads." Justin pointed his pipe at Adam. "You're the one who was supposed to be with Lauren. She was *your* girlfriend."

Fists clenched, Adam cast Justin a murderous glare.

"Where are Lauren's belongings?" Brandon asked.

Adam motioned toward one of the tents. "In there."

"We'll need them."

Adam retrieved a duffel bag from the tent. "These are her clothes."

Brandon borrowed Will's mini flashlight and searched the tent himself. There was a backpack and two sleeping bags.

33

He called out to them. "Which sleeping bag was hers?"

"The red one."

Brandon rolled up Lauren's sleeping bag and rejoined the others. Because it still wasn't clear what sort of case they were looking at, everything she'd left behind was evidence.

"I'll need each of your phone numbers," Brandon said.

Will pulled out his notebook and the trio passed it around, recording their contact information.

"Did you find her cell phone?" Brandon asked.

"I tried calling it as soon as she was missing," Adam said. "It went to voicemail right away."

"Write down her cell number, too."

When they finished, he said, "Who of you knows her home address?"

"I do," Adam and Brooke said simultaneously.

Brandon offered the notebook to Adam. He scribbled a name and address.

"Her mom's name is Lily," Brooke said.

He handed the notepad back to Brandon.

Brandon would have to notify Lauren's parents. They might shed light on her relationship with Adam and her two friends.

"How much longer do you plan on being here?" Will asked.

"Are we suspects or something?" Justin asked, his voice tinged with agitation. It wasn't the first time Brandon had witnessed a potential suspect mask fear with faux anger.

"We may have more questions," Brandon said.

"We were going to leave tomorrow," Adam said.

34

"Don't you want to find out what happened to Lauren?" Brooke asked, the hint of an accusation in her voice.

"Don't be stupid," Adam said. "Of course I do."

"Dude, chill. She's upset," Justin said.

"We're all upset, moron," Adam replied.

Justin stood as quickly as his dope-filled mind would let him.

"Alright, boys," Will said, shoving an arm between them. "No reason to fight at a time like this."

"We'll be in touch," Brandon said. "And, Justin, you might want to lay off the weed."

"It's legal—"

"Not on federal land," Brandon said. The beach was part of the Olympic National Forest, meaning federal rules against using pot trumped any state laws. "I can call the ranger down here if you need a better explanation."

Justin lowered his pipe.

"Whatever."

Brandon and Will hiked back to the trailhead, Brandon hauling Lauren's belongings. Will led the way with his flashlight.

"Nice kids," Will said, the sarcasm hard to miss, even in the dark. "You think they're involved in her disappearance?"

"Adam seemed genuinely upset," Brandon said. "But that could be an act. The same goes for Brooke. She may not be as innocent as she seems."

"What about that kid, Justin?" Will asked. "He didn't seem too upset, except when he thought you might consider him a suspect."

"More important," Brandon said, "he mentioned drowning and asked whether the girl had been hurt. Either he's good at guessing, or he's trying to figure out how much we know."

"Which is not much, right?"

"Still waiting on the coroner's report," Brandon said. "She was found in the water, so drowning is likely. But there were scratches and bruises on her back."

"Josiah said something about bite marks," Will said, his usually confident tone suddenly uneasy.

"Right."

"Were they human?"

"Vampire."

Will twisted around. The glare from the flashlight momentarily blinded Brandon. "Are you shittin' me?"

"Hey," Brandon said, smothering the light with his palm.

"Sorry. Habit."

Will's wide eyes scanned the shadowy forest. Was the old cop trying to scare Brandon, or was he genuinely concerned about vampires invading Forks? Will shook his head as if to recover his wits. "Maybe this girl and her beau Adam were into that, you know, kinky stuff. Biting, handcuffs—"

Josiah had suggested the same thing. Apparently, those sorts of activities weren't as foreign to Forks as Brandon imagined they might be.

Will pointed the flashlight through the thick underbrush, then up to the forest canopy. "You know, there are some people, a group of locals, who get together and dress up as vampires. Some say they drink blood."

"Nonsense."

"So say you," Will said. Brandon sensed a hint of fear in the older man's voice.

Will swept the flashlight across the sea of trees one last time. "Let's go," he said. "This place freaks me out."

Brandon documented the items they'd taken from the campsite and placed them into evidence. Meanwhile, Will had done an online search of the girl's cell phone number, found out the carrier, and contacted the company to request phone call and cell tower records. Because he was able to frame the request as related to a missing person, the carrier had responded quickly. But the information they provided was limited—anything related to the full homicide investigation would require a warrant, and the response from the phone company would take days if not weeks.

Will learned the last call Lauren had made was to Sequim. Probably her mother's house, the day before she'd died. The cell towers showed her near the campground the night of her disappearance. The phone had gone silent around midnight.

It had probably died before Lauren's passing and been tossed into the sea with her.

Back in his office, Brandon flipped through the list of phone numbers he had in his notebook and found the 24-hour number for the ranger on duty at the National Park Service.

He informed the ranger they'd been doing some poking around, talking to witnesses about the girl who'd died on the reservation. Like the tribes, Brandon's department had a jurisdictional agreement with the Park Service, allowing them access to the huge swaths of land that encompassed Olympic National Park. Second Beach was one of those areas.

Lauren Sandoval's mother lived up in Sequim, an hour-and-a-half away. Brandon donned his Forks PD uniform for the first time and made the trek up Highway 101. As a detective, he'd been able to escape the starched shirt and buttoned collar. He wedged a finger between his collar and neck, loosening the material. More than his waist had grown in the past decade.

Before leaving town, Brandon pulled into an all-night gas station and purchased a 24-ounce cup of stale coffee. He picked up an overpriced bottle of antacids too. The only thing worse on his stomach than gas station coffee was the heart-rending job of having to inform a parent that their child had died.

He could have called the east county sheriff's deputy, or even the Sequim PD to do the notification. But this was his case and, to Brandon, that meant it was his responsibility to notify the family. In person, if at all possible.

It took a while to wake Lauren's mother, and when he delivered the news of her daughter's death, she was inconsolable. The best he could get from her was that she had no idea why anyone would want to harm her daughter.

Brandon gave Lauren's mother the coroner's contact information and said he'd be in touch. She would need to identify Lauren's body. Brandon still had questions for her, but she was in no shape to talk. It turned out the girl's father had disappeared years ago, so Brandon waited until the woman's sister arrived from Port Angeles to stay with her.

It was three in the morning when he opened the door to his mute and shadow-darkened home. He left the lights off, sensing his way down the hallway to his room where he found his bed on the floor and fell into a deep, troubled sleep.

Chapter 6

Lisa Shipley called Brandon at eight the next morning.
"What's up?"
"You got time to come up to Port Angeles?"
"You learn anything new?"
"I'm leaning homicide for sure," she said. "And possible sexual assault."
"I'll be up."
He'd have to delay on his first order of business—ripping his officers a new one for not letting him know about the missing girl, even after they learned about the young woman found on the beach.
He was about to step up into his truck when someone called out, "Brandon Mattson?"
Strutting toward him was a woman in her late thirties with chestnut brown hair and a wide, cherry-red lipstick smile.
"You don't recognize me," she said.
He didn't, at first. But as she neared him, her face registered in his memory.
"Misty Brooks," he said.
She wrapped her arms around him, holding him for just a second too long.
"I heard you were back." She playfully poked a finger into his badge. "Chief of police."
Misty's always-have-fun attitude was one of the many reasons he'd fallen for her in high school.
"We're neighbors," she said, pointing at a red and white craftsman across the street.
"Nice," he said. "How's Lee?"

Her gaze fell as she fidgeted with the buttons on her shirt.

"We broke up ages ago. I raised Micah on my own."

After high school, Brandon had left for the Army with a plan to come back home and marry Misty. But when he flew home for his first visit after boot camp, he didn't get the hero's welcome he'd expected. Misty was pregnant and engaged to Lee.

Micah must be the son they'd had together.

Brandon checked his watch. "I've got to be somewhere—"

She pursed her lips in a timid smile. "Well...it was good catching up. I'm right over here if you need anything."

"Okay."

Brandon turned to leave.

"Wait," she said, holding onto his arm. "What's your number? In case, you know, we need to talk."

He wanted to tell her she could call 911 if she needed to get ahold of him. Brandon wasn't interested in rekindling long-dormant feelings for Misty. Not now, still recovering from his own divorce.

In fact, not ever.

But maybe this wasn't about romance. Neighbors exchanged numbers, didn't they?

Against his better judgment, he gave her his number. She typed it into her cell and his phone buzzed.

Her eyes lit up again. "There. I sent you a text. Now you have my number too."

"Alright," he said. "See you around."

He watched her walk back to her house.

It had been two decades and Misty still had the same effect on him. It wasn't all good, either. Misty was a buzz and a hangover all at once.

Brandon called into the office and left Sue a message that he was heading up to Port Angeles. He pulled onto Forks Avenue, enduring the slow roll through what served as the town's business district. Mostly *Moonbeam Darklove*-themed tourist shops. Brandon slowed as he approached the Forks Diner. Something had caught his attention.

He pulled up to the curb in front of the restaurant. Someone had tagged the diner's road-facing wall. Unlike Seattle, where spray-painted scribblings covered more real estate than Starbucks, you didn't see much graffiti in Forks.

A blood-red symbol in the shape of an Egyptian ankh covered most of the ten-foot-high wall. Brandon had always been a history buff and he'd read about hieroglyphics as a kid.

An ankh was like a cross, the top a loop instead of a straight line. The one here, though, narrowed to a point, like a dagger. Three drops of blood dripped from the tip.

Probably a local kid. Or a publicity stunt meant to garner more attention for the upcoming author visit.

He thought about the bite marks on Lauren Sandoval's neck. Could the ankh symbol be related to the local vampire craze? If so, there could be a connection between the girl's death and the crimson paint dripping down the side of the diner's white brick wall. He'd follow up on the graffiti later. For now, Brandon had more earthly evidence to deal with.

It took Brandon an hour and 45 minutes to make the trip up to PA. If it wasn't a logging truck slowing traffic on 101, the two-lane highway between Forks and Port Angeles, it was a caravan of Sunday drivers and puttering motor homes.

He ought to be grateful for the respite from the endless gridlock that was the Seattle commute. But what was the point of being out in wide-open nature if you had to drive 35 in a 50 zone?

Lisa Shipley led Brandon to an autopsy room where Lauren Sandoval's body lay facedown on an exam table. Lisa pulled back the sheet, revealing the seven or eight deep, jagged scratches stretching vertically up the girl's back.

"X-rays showed four cracked vertebrae," Lisa said. "The pattern here is consistent with a tumble onto an uneven surface."

"And the scratches," Brandon asked. "You still think that's because someone dragged her after death?"

"Definitely."

"That rules out an accident."

"You mean maybe she stumbled off a cliff, and the tide swept her away?" Lisa asked.

"It's a longshot," Brandon said.

More like wishful thinking. If the girl's death was a homicide, that meant there was a killer loose in his town.

"Her blood alcohol hit .21, so yes, there's the possibility of an accidental fall. But these scratches are consistent with dead weight dragged across stone or a similar surface. Something else. I don't think she drowned."

"Her lungs?"

"No evidence of drowning. There's water in her lungs, but very little. Everything else points to death before submersion."

"Right. She fell or someone pushed her—"

"I'd guess a drop of at least twenty or thirty feet."

"Wait a minute," Brandon said. "What about the bite mark?"

"Like we thought. Puncture wounds from fake teeth."

"But a hell of a lot sharper than plastic," he said.

"It's hard to tell how much blood she lost from the bite. But based on the lack of bruising, my hypothesis is that she'd already expired by the time the bite occurred."

The murderer owned a pair of fake fangs. Not exactly a novelty in Forks.

"Any saliva around the bite?"

"We're searching for any DNA we can find from the attacker."

"Time of death?" Brandon asked.

Lisa considered the girl. "With the evidence we have, and considering how long she might have been submerged, I'd say she died yesterday between two and five in the morning."

"Okay, well. It sounds like I need to talk to my boss."

The sheriff would want to know about any homicide investigation. He'd update the prosecutor's office too.

"I'm not done yet," Lisa said. "I found semen in her vagina and on her undergarments."

"Signs of rape?"

"Inconclusive, especially—"

"Her body's exposure to water. Got it. How long will it take you to get the DNA back?"

Lisa snapped her gloves off and Brandon followed her out into the hallway.

44

"Didn't you say you worked in Seattle?" she asked.

"Yeah, so?"

"However long it took there, times two."

"Great. We have what appears to be a homicide, or at the very least, an attempt to cover up a death. And a body compromised by exposure to water, not to mention a bureaucracy."

"That's why you get the big bucks, Chief."

"Funny. Anyway, keep me updated."

"Will do."

Lisa leaned back against the wall, crossing her arms. "I'm sure the prosecutor will say I should have sent her to King County the minute I suspected foul play."

"I was a detective in Seattle for almost fifteen years. They have more equipment, more staff, for sure, but there's nothing that beats a good medical examiner."

She winked at him. "I'll take that as a compliment."

"Good," he said. "It was meant as one."

She was an attractive woman. Single, like him. They probably had a lot in common. He thought back to his conversation with Misty that morning. His high school sweetheart was now his neighbor. Why let his past with Misty get in the way of the future? That part of his life had ended—badly—decades ago.

Misty or not, Brandon had heard it was a bad idea to mix work and play. He'd been married most of his adult life, and so had never had the chance to experience the perils of dating a professional associate.

"Alright, have a good one," she said.

He wasn't two feet out the door when he realized he'd just dodged a bullet. The new chief of police asking the coroner out on a date his second day on the job? It was

45

the sort of thing that led to front-page stories in a town like Forks.

Chapter 7

Brandon called Sheriff Hart's cell to let him know they had a homicide case on their hands. Technically, the murder had occurred within Brandon's jurisdiction—the newly configured West Clallam region—but leadership got touchy when it came to homicide investigations.

He told the sheriff he thought he could manage the case—an argument bolstered by the fact that Brandon had more experience in homicide than all the other officers in the county combined. Sheriff Hart agreed, but with one caveat. He couldn't promise to keep the prosecutor off his back. When Brandon identified a strong suspect, the prosecutor would want to make sure to keep the case clean. They didn't want some back-country cop stepping all over the evidence.

Brandon wasn't a back-country cop, and he wasn't about to let a murder go unsolved in his jurisdiction.

On the way to Forks, Brandon contacted Dennison, a reserve officer on shift.

"I need you to get all the staff in the office by noon."

"Chief, it's already 11:15."

"Good. That gives them plenty of time."

"But not everyone's scheduled to work today."

"I want them all there."

"You sure? Everyone?"

"Do you hear any doubt in my voice?"

"No."

"Good."

He was coming across as an ass, not the impression he was hoping for. But his team's failure to communicate the missing person report was a big deal, especially in a small town. Miscommunication could be the difference between life and death.

The conference room was packed—every last officer had shown up.

Most were in plain clothes, except for those on duty. Then there was Josiah, his youngest officer. Brandon knew he wasn't on until the next day. But he'd donned his uniform, anyway. Will was there, bleary-eyed. He'd probably gotten off shift after midnight.

Neal Nolan stood in the back corner, leaning against the wall with his arms crossed.

Brandon cut to the chase.

"I know Chief Satler was a good man. He took care of this department for a long time."

Brandon took a moment to look each officer in the eye.

"And he wouldn't have tolerated half-assed work," he continued.

"That sounds like an accusation," Nolan said, still holding up the wall.

"It is a statement of fact," Brandon said. "Sometime before yesterday morning, a young woman disappeared out on Second Beach. Her friends made a missing person report. Who received the report?"

Brandon scanned the room, curious if the guilty party would fess up.

"I did," Nolan said.

"And what did you do with that information?"

"Nothing."

"Why not?"

"It wasn't a priority at the moment."

"What were you so busy doing you couldn't tackle a missing person case?"

Nolan uncrossed his arms. He scowled at Brandon. "I don't recall."

Brandon had to be cautious. Nolan had been a candidate for the chief of police position. Brandon wasn't sure how popular he'd been with the other officers. But if he was easy on Nolan, it would encourage similar sloppy behavior among the others.

"The young woman was found dead on the beach a few hours later," Brandon said.

A few officers shifted in their seats.

"You're saying not posting the missing person report led to her death?" Nolan asked.

"Could be," Brandon said. "But even if it didn't, this is the kind of negligence that lets the bad guys get away."

"I thought she drowned," Josiah said.

"We've learned a few things since

yesterday. We're looking at a homicide investigation."

Brandon explained what he'd learned from the coroner.

"They're sure she didn't drown?" Will asked.

"Like any of this, it's an educated guess."

"Is the Sheriff's Office sending someone down to work the case?" one of the reserve officers asked.

"We can handle this one."

"Because you're the seasoned homicide detective from the big city, right?" Nolan asked.

"No. Because this is our jurisdiction, and we are going to show the folks up in Port Angeles that we know how to do things the right way. That means doing the small stuff, whether you think it's priority or not."

All eyes were on Nolan.

He crossed his arms again and gave a tired expression.

"Who's covering the far west region today?" Brandon asked.

Isabel Jackson raised her hand.

"Who else is on?"

"Me," Nolan said.

"Jackson, head out to the beaches—La Push, Second and Third Beach—any and every campsite you run across. Record the names of everyone you interview, along with contact info. Take the picture from the missing person report. I'm sure Nolan knows where there's a copy." A couple of officers snickered at the remark. Nolan's neck burned crimson as Brandon addressed him. "Nolan, I want you to run a report on all the registered sex offenders in the area, then go pay each of them a visit. Ask where they were during the time the girl went missing."

"You think she was raped?" Will asked.

1

"The coroner found semen in her and on her clothing. And she was intoxicated. We need to consider all possibilities." He turned to Nolan. "Understood?"

"Yes, *sir*," Nolan said.

"I'm on in a few hours," Josiah said. "You want me to do anything?"

"Go ahead and start your shift early. Cover your regular beat but be on the lookout for any information about this girl."

"You need anything from me?" Will asked.

"Yeah, go get some sleep. You're making me tired looking at you."

While none of the officers seemed particularly inspired by his rant, Brandon was pleased with how it had gone. He'd been a team lead and supervisor of one kind or another for half his working life. One thing he learned about leading others—people might like you but have absolutely no respect for you as a leader. The cops under his watch would learn to like him—or not. But first and foremost, they had to understand that sloppiness wasn't an option. They were accountable to Brandon for their actions. In time, they'd learn to keep each other accountable too.

His office phone rang. It was Sue.

"Chief, the mayor would like to speak with you."

"Transfer her through."

"In person."

"She's here?"

Sue scoffed. "I'm pretty sure she wants you in *her* office."

He didn't have time to talk parades or famous author visits.

"It sounded important," Sue said. "Just saying."

"Got it."

Brandon left through the front lobby. On the way out, he glanced at Sue's computer screen, revealing a selection of shoes on the Amazon website.

"It's my fifteen-minute break," she said.

He didn't care if Sue spent her free time window shopping online. As long as she got her work done.

"I need the paperwork for my department-issued firearm."

He had been carrying his own Glock 27 since he'd arrived in town.

"Already done," she said. "Nolan was supposed to tell you yesterday. It's in the first lockbox on the left by the lockers."

There was no end to Nolan's incompetence. Or was it something else? More purposeful.

"If there's something didn't get done around here," Sue said, "it wasn't my fault."

She was probably right.

"Understood," he said, leaving her to Amazon. He paused at the door. "Sue, do you know any places around here that sell vampire teeth?"

She squinted at him. "Lord. Not you too."

"It's for an investigation."

She pressed her lips, considering him doubtfully. "Try Maryanne Tyler. She owns the Original Damsel and Dracula store down on the corner of Division and Forks Ave. I'm sure she'll find something to suit your fancy."

"Like I said, it's for an investigation."

"Whatever floats your boat." She cracked a wry smile. "Better not keep the mayor waiting."

He clicked in the code to the door.

"Hey, Chief," Sue said.

"Good job kicking their asses today. They needed it."

Brandon winked at her. "Thanks, Sue."

Mayor Sara Kim wasn't alone in her office when Brandon arrived. The mayor and another woman lingered over the conference table, scrutinizing several colorful posters—photos of Forks and the surrounding area.

"Chief Mattson," the mayor said. "This is Olivia Baker, our Minister of Tourism."

Brandon cocked his head. "I didn't know we had a Ministry of Tourism."

"It's part of our plan to revitalize Forks," Olivia said. She was young, probably in her mid to late twenties and wore a black skirt and teal top. A mini-me of the mayor. Olivia shook Brandon's hand. "Nice to meet you. We have some great ideas for the city. And the department."

What did the Minister of Tourism have to do with his police force?

Brandon considered the glossy photos on the table. "Look. I'd love to talk business, but we're working a case right now."

"Is this about the girl who drowned?" Olivia asked.

Brandon eyed her. "How'd you know about that?"

He hadn't made a public statement about the case.

"Small town," Olivia said. "Word gets around."

"Anything I should know?" the mayor asked.

Brandon glanced at Olivia before answering the mayor. "If you have a moment, I'd like to speak to you in private."

4

Olivia left them alone, but not before making sure Brandon knew she wasn't happy about being kicked out of her own meeting with the mayor.

Brandon closed the door behind her.

"The girl who drowned. We think she was murdered."

The mayor frowned. "Are you sure?"

"All the evidence suggests foul play, some sort of cover-up. That's how she ended up in the water."

The mayor slumped into the chair behind her desk. "Any suspects?"

"She had a boyfriend, a few friends. But we're not ruling anything out right now. I have my officers checking on campers, rustling up the local sex offenders."

She shook her head. "This is bad news."

"We'll catch whoever did this," Brandon said.

"Tiffany Quick is coming in thirteen days."

A festival meant tourists trampling all over his crime scene—an indefinite space somewhere between Lauren's campsite and First Beach. But that wasn't what worried the mayor.

"We can't have people scared that there's a murderer out there, Brandon," she said. "If word gets out about this, our tourism numbers will plummet. Ms. Quick might refuse to show, we'll have to cancel—"

"Well then," Brandon said. "I'd better get to work."

"Okay, but—did you hear about the graffiti outside the Forks Diner?"

"I noticed it, yes."

"What do you think it means?"

"Just some dumb kids, probably."

Or someone hoping to increase the town's reputation as a vampire mecca. Maybe the mayor's new Minister of Tourism.

5

"Okay," she said. "Keep me updated."

"Will do," Brandon said.

"Before you leave," the mayor said, "Olivia would like to discuss some of her plans—"

"I've got a homicide to solve. You do want your tourists to feel safe, don't you?"

"Obviously."

"Good," Brandon said. "One more thing, mayor."

"Yes?"

"Whatever I tell you about this case, keep it between you and me, okay? I don't need the investigation compromised."

She folded her hands, resting them on her desk. "You can trust me."

He wasn't so sure. If he wasn't careful, the mayor's obsessive focus on tourism and Tiffany Quick would screw up this case. As if it wasn't enough keeping his own officers in line, he'd have to do his best to keep Mayor Kim and her staff an arm's length away from his investigation, too.

Chapter 8

Back at the Fork's Diner, he found a pack of tourists huddled around the ankh dagger symbol. He would ask the owner to paint over the ankh ASAP. Graffiti attracted more of the same, and if tourists kept visiting the spot, Mayor Kim might set up a photo booth and charge admission.

As Brandon approached the group, a family of four asked him to take their picture next to the symbol. He did, albeit reluctantly. They thanked him just as a trio of attractive women in their early thirties, seeing Brandon in uniform, asked if he would pose with them in front of the ominous ankh.

This time he declined. The last thing he needed was a front-page photo of himself posing with a group of women next to potential evidence.

When the crowd had dispersed, he pulled out his cell phone and took a photo of the ankh. If it came up again, he'd research the meaning behind the symbol.

Brandon scanned the street. One block away on the corner of Calawah Way sat a placard advertising the Original Dracula and Damsel store, with the first letter of each word accentuated, spelling the word ODD. It was the store Sue had mentioned might carry vampire teeth.

The Original Dracula and Damsel was a touristy trinket store with refrigerator magnets and collectible figurines featuring both Forks the town and the vampirish books that had made it famous. Entering the shop, he was greeted by a life-sized cardboard cutout of one of the main characters from the film adaptation of *Moonbeam Darklove*. The movies hadn't been filmed in town, a fact that had upset locals hoping to score roles as extras.

A mom with two teen daughters and another couple in their twenties browsed the shop. Brandon waited while the couple purchased a pair of matching *Moonbeam Darklove* t-shirts. When they left, he approached the cash register.

"I'm hoping to speak with Maryanne."

"That's me."

She was in her late fifties, plump and wearing a white dress with a blue cornflower pattern. She didn't fit the part of someone who might operate a store specializing in vampire paraphernalia.

"How can I...wait, aren't you Buzz Mattson's son?"

"That's me," he said. Buzz was what everyone had called his father for as long as Brandon could remember. He'd earned the nickname during his 40 years working for a local logging company.

"Welcome back, young man. For a moment there, I thought I was seeing Eli's ghost."

Except Eli had been skinnier and taller. Brandon was pretty sure he didn't look anything like his brother.

"I appreciate that. I won't take much of your time. Do you sell vampire teeth?"

She paused, considering him. "Are these for your father?"

"What? Why?"

"He's a huge fan of the books. You didn't know that?"

"My dad? No. I didn't."

She frowned at him. "Hmm. I thought everyone knew that."

Brandon had been away a long time. There were people in town that knew his dad, and had known Eli,

8

better than Brandon. But Buzz Mattson, hard-nosed diesel mechanic, a fan of the *Moonbeam Darklove* series?

"This is for an investigation," Brandon said.

"No need to get huffy about it," Maryanne said. She pulled the key out of cash register and Brandon followed her to the back of the store to a large display of plastic fangs. Some were bone white, others stained with fake blood, and still others advertised that they would glow in the dark.

"Do you sell teeth capable of piercing human skin?"

Her face contorted. "God, no. That sounds dangerous."

"Any idea who might?"

She considered him for a moment.

"Didn't you go off to Seattle? To investigate murders?"

You might move away from a small town, but the gossip always outlived your stay.

"Homicide," he said.

The chime above her door rang as two young girls entered.

"Is that what this is about?" she asked.

"Look, I just need to know who sells the teeth I described."

She peered over his shoulder. "I have customers. But if anyone sold something like that, it would be over at the Darklove Damsel."

"That's another store?"

"Out the door, take a right, two blocks down. It's the creepiest place in Forks. She sells just about anything."

"Thanks."

A sign in the door of the Darklove Damsel indicated the store was closed. Brandon tried the handle. It was locked. Blackout curtains darkened the store's windows. Cheap tinted film peeling at the edges covered the door. The lights were off.

It was almost two o'clock. He'd take a late lunch and check on his dad, then return to the shop. If Maryanne was right, and this store sold more realistic vampire teeth, a list of customers who'd purchased the fangs could lead to Lauren's killer.

Brandon's dad lived on five acres a few miles outside of town. When Brandon was a kid, his father had kept a few cows out in the pasture and had managed about an acre of raspberries, potatoes, and assorted vegetables. Now, wild grass had crept into every corner of the property, a fire hazard in the dry summer months.

Despite his infrequent visits, Brandon loved his dad—in his own way. They hadn't always gotten along, and his father's inability to approve of anything Brandon did was one of the reasons he'd kept his distance.

Brandon pulled down the long gravel driveway and parked in front of the house. He knocked on the door. The television blared, some news channel reporting on events in the Middle East. Brandon stepped back off the porch and peered into the window. His dad was lounging on the couch, feet up on the table, his hands folded on his lap. Next to the couch, leaning against the wall was his dad's .22 rifle.

Since when had he kept his rifle in the living room? Brandon made a mental note not to startle the old man.

He tried the door. It was open.

Brandon's father pointed the remote at the television and lowered the volume from 63 to 60. "About time," he said.

"Hi to you too, Dad."

He mumbled a few words, unintelligible to Brandon, over the trio of Fox News pundits arguing on the television.

Brandon grabbed the remote and muted the noise.

"Make yourself at home."

The sarcasm was hard to miss.

Brandon teetered on the edge of the loveseat, considering the room. His mom's trinkets sat collecting dust on shelves older than Brandon, her sheet music still on the piano. She had died over a year earlier, Eli not long after that. At least she'd missed the tragic pain of losing her oldest son. Brandon's father hadn't changed a thing about the house since her passing. It was as if his mom had gone shopping in town and his dad was waiting for her to come back any moment with a car full of groceries.

A few logs crackled in the fireplace. Brandon checked the combination thermometer-barometer on the wall. Eighty degrees.

"You keeping busy?" Brandon asked, because he didn't know what else to say.

"Much as I can, being sick and all."

His dad usually had some ache or pain to complain about. Growing old wasn't something Brandon looked forward to. Your days measured by how long it had been since your last major medical procedure.

Brandon considered his father's thin arms and hunched frame. He'd always been taller, stronger, and tougher than Brandon and Eli. The kind of man most men in town wouldn't dream of crossing.

"What's wrong?"

"What's not wrong? I'm just biding my time. God's taking me any day now to be with Mom and Eli. Not that you'd notice."

Brandon shifted in his seat. Conversations like this were the reason he'd only seen his dad a few times since his mom's passing.

"Damn shame," his dad said, motioning at the television, "about the Middle East. I say, don't waste another American life. You never made it over there, did you?"

"No."

His father knew that.

Brandon had served his time in the Army, but by the time 9/11 happened, he was already an officer with the Seattle PD.

"Eli served in Afghanistan," his dad said. "And he chose to stick around instead of moving off to Timbuktu."

"You mean Seattle?"

"Same difference. How did you put up with all those damn hippies, anyway?"

"Seattle isn't a bunch of hippies," Brandon said. Most people there were normal, working-class folks. Not much different from the citizens of Forks. "I get it, Dad. I haven't been around as much as you would have liked."

"Didn't say that."

"I'm not Eli—"

"He died a hero." His voice wavered, and he cleared his throat. "Protecting his own people."

"Yeah, and he's not the only one," Brandon replied. "I haven't been sitting on my ass in the big city collecting welfare checks or whatever the hell you think it is we do over there. I've been working, protecting people too. Solving murders."

His dad scoffed. "Yeah."

"Not to mention, raising a daughter."

"You couldn't do that here?"

"No."

"Your daughter—my granddaughter—disagrees."

Emma visited her grandfather a few times a year, at most. How could he possibly know what Emma did or did not want?

"She emails me," his dad said.

"Emma?"

"Says she wants to live out here, that she hates the city. Why can't her mom move out here with you?"

"Because Tori and I are divorced."

He pointed to the bookshelf. "According to my Bible, marriage is for life."

Brandon had no desire to argue the theology of divorce with his old man. "When did Emma tell you all this?"

"Yesterday, day before."

"Don't encourage her," Brandon said. "It's bad enough already with me moving back here."

"I still say you and Tori—"

Brandon stood. He wasn't going to discuss his failed marriage with his father. They didn't have that sort of relationship.

"I'd better head back to work."

His eyes hovered over a book on the couch, next to his dad. He noticed Brandon staring.

"Book three of the *Moonbeam Darklove* series. I'm reading it again." He narrowed his eyes at Brandon. "Don't knock it till you try it."

Maryanne from the ODD vampire store was right.

13

"What's that for?" Brandon asked, pointing his chin at the .22 rifle.

"Protection," his dad replied.

"Against?"

"Vampires, psychopaths. The usual. In case the police don't get here fast enough. On top of that, I heard there's a new sheriff in town and morale is down."

"Really?"

His father chuckled. "I'm kidding you, son."

"And by the way," Brandon reminded him, "it's chief of police. Not sheriff."

He grunted. "You never did have a sense of humor."

That wasn't true. He just never liked his *father's* sense of humor.

Brandon headed for the Darklove Damsel store.

He tried to shake off the conversation with his dad. His father had never been a happy man. Why would he change now? Brandon cringed at the thought of his dad getting close with Emma. If his dad started throwing verbal jabs at Emma the same way he had Brandon...

He shook his head. Brandon wouldn't let it get that far. He'd ask Emma about the emails. It was bad enough, begging Brandon to let her move to Forks early. Now she had his dad on Brandon's case about it too.

This time the sign hanging in the window of the Darklove Damsel store read open.

Warm, incense-laced air swept past him as he opened the door. The only light in the shop came from an assortment of onyx black candles scattered across the room and three dim, stained glass lamps that dangled from a sable ceiling that matched equally bleak walls. He let the

14

door close behind him as his eyes adjusted to the cavernous atmosphere.

The offerings here were sparse compared to the shop he'd visited earlier. A few rows of bookshelves with information on the occult. A selection of tarot cards. A vampire-themed Ouija board was displayed on a table near the front door. The musky odor of incense itched his nose.

"Hello?" he called out.

"Be right there," a singsong voice responded.

A woman appeared from the shadows near the back wall of the store. She was tall, thin, and had made no effort to mask the crow's feet that graced her eyes. The dayglow yellow moon and stars peppering her silk dress were an oasis of color in a goth-inspired desert of darkness. Her blonde, curly hair was in a loose bun atop her head.

Her eyes scaled Brandon. "Good morning, officer."

"Afternoon. I'm hoping you can help—"

She slid forward. "Welcome, Brandon Mattson. I am Phoenix Weaver. You can call me Phoenix because I can see we will be fast friends."

"How did you know—"

Phoenix grabbed ahold of his hand and traced the lines on his palm.

He wrenched free from her grip.

"You don't believe?" she asked.

"No, I don't."

She flicked her fingers at him dismissively. "It does not make it untrue."

Why couldn't people just be normal? It was a question Brandon had asked himself a hundred times during his law enforcement career. There must be something human

15

about wanting to be different, and a certain percentage of the population would take the idea to the extreme.

"I'm investigating—"

"Yes, I know."

How would she know why Brandon was there? They'd never met.

"You expect me to tell you my powers of insight allowed me to foresee your coming. But I already know that cow Maryanne sent you. She said the police would be here to investigate me for selling dangerous paraphernalia."

Not exactly what he'd told Maryanne.

"Is that why you were closed earlier, so you wouldn't have to talk?"

"I don't know what you mean." She swept across the room to a faux Greek column with a crystal ball on top. She ran a finger over the glass orb.

"I have nothing to hide. I open late. My customers aren't morning people."

"Because they're vampires?"

"You mock the darkness because you fear it," she said.

"Isn't everyone afraid of the dark?"

To Brandon, fear was something to be confronted. Maybe owning a shop dedicated to the dark arts was Phoenix's way of dealing with her anxieties.

"You admit it, then?" she asked.

"Admit what?" He caught himself. He wasn't here to talk psychology, and he wouldn't get drawn into a conversation about ghosts and werewolves. "I'm here to ask if you sell teeth."

Phoenix drew a hand to her heart. "We may dabble in the occult, dear officer, but nothing as dark as human remains—"

16

Interesting place to go with a question about teeth.

"I mean vampire fangs. Like kids wear on Halloween."

"This is not a store for child's play. You should speak with Maryanne."

"These wouldn't be plastic," he said. "Hard enough to puncture skin."

"Do you mind if I ask why you are interested?"

"Like I said, it's part of an investigation."

"You have evidence of the undead?" She closed her eyes, breathed in through her nose, then exhaled slowly. "Real vampire activity has come to Forks."

Brandon couldn't tell if she was avoiding the question or if she really believed the nonsense she was slinging at him.

"Do you sell them or not?"

"You might check online." She sauntered to the front counter, resting her hand on a stack of tarot cards. "I've heard of such things, but that is all I know."

Was she hiding something?

Phoenix seemed to have a keen interest in the occult. Whether that was genuine or not, it was hard to tell.

"Tell me about the kind of person who would be interested in buying real vampire teeth."

Phoenix shuffled the tarot cards as Brandon spoke.

"People just like you and me, officer."

Brandon had never known anyone interested in fangs, plastic or otherwise.

"But some of us see things others do not," she said.

Phoenix flipped the cards, one at a time, onto the counter.

"What sort of things?"

"Spirits, creatures of the night. The undead."

"And you've seen these monsters?" Brandon asked.

17

"My gift is to see things yet to come. I have no real passion for the dark arts."

Brandon's eyes moved to the section of her store marked *Occult*.

Her gaze followed his.

"I sell *information*, officer. That does not mean I engage in those activities."

"Like those?" Brandon asked, glancing at the tarot cards she'd laid out.

"These are for you," she said.

"Me?"

"Don't worry. It's not all bad."

Brandon waved a hand at her. "Not interested."

It was time for him to leave.

But there was something else.

Brandon held up his phone, showing her the picture of the spray-painted ankh outside the Forks Diner.

"Do you recognize this symbol?"

She scrunched her eyes at the photo, studying it.

She shoved the phone away. Her voice quivered with genuine fear. "It is a vampire symbol. I don't want anything to do with this."

"How do you know it is a vampire symbol?"

"Do not ignore this," she said. "You must talk to Vasile."

"Who?"

"Vasile Anghel. The foremost expert on vampire activity in the northwest. And leader of the local Nightside Coven."

A coven? Wasn't that a thing for witches? She must have noticed his confusion.

"They're a group that gets together, celebrates all things vampire."

"By celebrate you mean—"

"I'll let Vasile explain," she said.

He jotted the name down on his notepad.

"Where can I find this Vasile?"

"He lives on some property outside town. It's where they meet."

"This is his real name?"

"A far as I know." She paused. "Please, you must take this symbol seriously. Talk to Vasile."

Brandon flipped the notepad shut. "Good enough."

He was at the door when she called out to him. "Officer, one more thing."

"Yes?"

"You must know there are dark forces at work in Forks."

As far as Brandon was concerned, murder always involved dark forces, if by that you meant rage, jealousy, and greed.

"And I do foresee family trouble in your future. An unexpected visitor."

Brandon stared back at her. She was drop-dead serious.

"I'll keep that in mind."

Chapter 9

Despite her weirdness and general obfuscation, Phoenix had given Brandon a lead. The bite mark remained the most distinctive clue so far. What sort of person would sink their teeth—real or not—into a corpse? Vasile might be able to answer that question. A quick check online revealed the vampire guru's location, right where Phoenix described it.

Brandon drove out to the address, a Victorian farmhouse with a nearby barn that seemed in good repair. Brandon wasn't familiar with the whole vampire-fan lifestyle. He'd once read an article about a similar group back east that engaged in bloodletting and sex parties. He eyed the barn. Could the same thing happen in Forks?

No one answered the door and after a quick scan of the property, Brandon left a note for Vasile to contact him.

On the way back, he gathered his thoughts. The vampire ankh and the conversation with Phoenix had him chasing secret societies and bloodthirsty psychopaths. As unusual as the bite marks were, they could be a distraction.

There were other, more common, clues to focus on, too. Lauren had been intoxicated. She'd had sex recently. Whether consensual or not, it wasn't clear. And she'd died from a fall from a high place. Because the body was dragged away from the scene of death, homicide was a fair assumption.

Right now, the only real suspect was Adam, her boyfriend, if only because the victim's partner was almost always a suspect. They'd have to follow up with Adam and

Lauren's friends about any specific interest in vampire lore.

Brandon called Nolan to see what he'd found out in his check of the area's sex offenders.

"No leads," Nolan said.

"How many do you have left?" Brandon asked.

"A few."

"Meaning?"

"Five or six."

"Keep working the list and let me know the minute you learn anything."

"Will do, *Chief.*"

Brandon hung up, willing himself not to get angry with Nolan. Not yet. He didn't have time to scrutinize everything Nolan did, even if he didn't fully trust the officer. The former chief had kept Nolan around for a decade. He must be useful for something.

Brandon called Isabel Jackson.

"Jackson here."

"This is Chief Mattson. How's it going at the campsites?"

"I've interviewed just about every site on the beach. There aren't many left."

"Are people leaving?"

"Yeah, the word's out about the girl. It's spooking some campers."

That was predictable. Brandon wouldn't want his daughter camping on a beach where a murder had occurred. Especially when the killer was still on the loose.

"What'd you find out?" Brandon asked.

"A few people said she looked familiar, but no one saw her the night she went missing. I ran across her friends too. It was a bit of a shock when I asked them if they'd seen the missing girl and they said they were the ones that contacted us."

"That's my bad," Brandon said. "I should have told you to avoid their site."

"I laid off once I knew who they were. I figured you wanted to handle them directly."

"Good."

"Although one of the group, Justin, gave me grief about re-traumatizing his girlfriend."

Based on the limited interaction he'd had with Justin, that sounded like something the kid would say.

"Anything else?"

"They are heading out this afternoon, back to Port Angeles."

Just yesterday, they were set on sticking around until they found out what had happened to Lauren. Why the sudden change?

"Have they left yet?"

"That was about an hour ago, but they hadn't started packing yet."

It wouldn't hurt to get a second glance at Lauren's friends before they abandoned what could be the scene of her death. They were most likely the last people, besides the killer, to see her alive. And now, with more definitive information from the coroner, he had more to work on than the first time he'd interviewed them.

The further you got from a murder, the more the human element contaminated the facts. Memories morphed based on news reports or conversations with other witnesses, and murderers had time to dig up alibis and fine-tune their stories.

"Don't let them go until I'm there."

Brandon arrived at the Second Beach trailhead within 20 minutes. Jackson stood watching the trio of Adam, Brooke, and Justin as they loaded their gear into a late model Ford Ranger. Brandon pulled in behind them.

Justin tossed a sleeping bag into the bed of the truck.

"We can't stay here. We're out of food," Justin said without looking at Brandon. He hauled an ice chest onto the tailgate.

"I need to know where you'll be over the next several days," Brandon said.

Justin pointed a thumb at Brooke. "Ask her. She knows."

"I have to get to work," Adam said. "We were only staying here because we thought Lauren might still—"

Adam broke off in a stifled cough. He wiped his eyes with the back of his hand.

"I'm sorry, son," Brandon said. He'd learned over the years to treat every grieving individual, suspect or not, the same. After a moment, he asked, "Where's your work?"

"A coffee shop up in Port Angeles."

"Which one?"

"Hurricane Ridge Cafe."

"Good. I expect we'll have more questions soon."

A lot depended on whose DNA they found on Lauren. If it belonged to Adam, that didn't tell them much. If the DNA was from another man, then he had to consider sexual assault prior to the girl's murder.

"I know it looks bad," Adam said. "I mean, leaving town."

"Do we need to get lawyers or something?" Justin asked.

"That's up to you," Brandon said.

Brandon noticed that Brooke wasn't saying much. That made sense considering her blowhard boyfriend.

"Brooke," Brandon said. "Let's take a walk."

He motioned for Jackson to stay put.

"You don't have to talk to him," Justin said.

"Frickin chill out," Adam said.

"You better watch your ass, Adam. You're suspect number one. It's always the boyfriend—"

"Enough," Jackson said, sounding like a mother scolding an out-of-control toddler in a grocery store.

Brandon led Brooke up the gravel parking lot, still in view of the others.

"We haven't had a chance to talk alone."

"Justin can be a jerk," Brooke said.

"I can see that," Brandon said. "Tell me. Were you close to Lauren?"

"Best friends."

"Is there any reason why she would wander off in the middle of the night?"

Brooke stared down at her feet.

"Is there something you're not telling me?" Brandon asked.

"I don't want to get anyone in trouble." She looked over Brandon's shoulder to where Jackson waited with Justin and Adam.

"Do you think this has anything to do with one of your other friends?"

"No," she said quickly. "I mean, I heard Adam and Lauren arguing the night she disappeared."

"About?"

Brooke slipped her hands into her sweatshirt pockets. "I couldn't understand them."

"You're sure?"

"I think so."

She was holding something back.

"Were they in their tent?" he asked.

"Yeah."

"And this was at what time?"

"Like twenty minutes after we all went to bed."

"When I visited your campsite, I noticed your tents were only about 10 feet apart. You're positive you don't know what they were arguing about?"

"I'm sure," she said. "You think I'm trying to protect Adam?"

"Maybe," Brandon said. Then, changing topics, he asked, "What was Lauren's interest in the occult?"

"Why?"

"We found bite marks on her neck."

"Weird," Brooke said in a matter-of-fact tone.

"You don't seem surprised."

She peered at Adam and Justin.

"I don't know anything about that."

"Okay. Did Lauren ever mention Adam hurting her? Any kind of domestic violence?"

"No."

"Unexplained bruises?" Brandon asked.

"I mean, I wasn't looking for anything like that."

"Do you know why anyone would want to kill Lauren?"

"No. She was sweet. A good friend."

"How long did you know her?" he asked.

"A few years. We met at work."

"Where was that?"

"The methadone clinic," she said. "Up in Port Angeles."

"She still worked there?"

"Yeah."

"And you?"

"No," Brooke said. "The pay sucks. I tried to get her to leave, too, but she's all into helping people. That was her thing."

Brandon cast her a sympathetic smile. "If you remember anything else, contact the department immediately. Officer Jackson says you're planning on returning to Port Angeles tonight?"

"That was Justin being stupid. I'm staying here in town with my aunt. I'm not leaving until you find out who did this to Lauren."

"And Justin?" he asked.

"He'll stay with me, no matter what he says." She crossed her arms. "So, what happens now?"

"Take Adam in for questioning."

"He's not a bad guy."

"I'll try to remember that."

When they rejoined the others, Justin was leaning on the tailgate of the truck smoking a cigarette. Adam paced several feet away, hands in his back pockets.

"Adam," Brandon said.

"My turn?"

"Yes, but we'll talk down at the station."

"Told you," Justin mumbled.

Brandon pointed a finger at Justin. "Put a lid on it, kid, or else—"

"That's police brutality," Justin said, waving his cigarette at Brandon.

"Yeah. Okay," Brandon said. He half expected the kid to pull out his cell phone to record the conversation.

Having worked an entire career in Seattle—one of the most politically correct cities in the country—Brandon knew how easy it was to get the police brutality moniker slapped on you by someone who didn't like cops. He'd learned to focus on the investigation and ignore the trash-talking meant to get a reaction.

"Let's go, Adam."

"Am I under arrest?" Adam asked.

"No, I'm just giving you a ride to the station."

Adam's eyes shifted to the police vehicle. "Alright."

With Adam tucked away in the SUV, Brandon took Jackson aside as Justin and Brooke finished packing their gear.

"You about ready to wrap up here?" Brandon asked.

"I didn't want to say anything in front of her friends, but I got a good lead," Jackson said.

"Tell me about it."

"I had just finished interviewing campers on the beach when I noticed the bulletin board with the reservation instructions," Jackson said. "I contacted the National Park Service office up in Port Angeles."

"What did you find out?"

"I had them send me a list of everyone who registered to camp on Second Beach during the night Lauren went missing. He emailed it to me and I'm going to get to work comparing it to my list from today. Anyone I didn't catch, I'll contact to see if they spotted Lauren."

"Good work, Jackson."

"Thanks."

It was smart thinking, the kind of tactic other officers could learn from.

"You're just a reserve here in Forks. How come?"

"I was full-time down in Portland."

"And?"

"Marriage, kids. I have two little ones. We relocated here because of my husband's family. He works from home most of the time. I've been a stay-at-home mom for the past seven years."

"And now your kids are in school."

"Right. And my husband has lost a few contracts here and there. We need the money."

"What did you do in Portland?"

"Patrol most of my career. I finally made it to detective when we moved."

"Sorry."

It wasn't easy making detective. Some officers worked for over a decade before passing the exam and getting the promotion. Others never made it or weren't interested, resigning themselves to life as a beat cop.

"Being a mom is number one for me. But I'm ready to get back to work full time."

"You know, we have an opening. In case you're interested."

"I was thinking about applying," she said.

"Not promising anything. Just consider it. You do good work."

Brandon led Adam to the department's only interview room. He offered Adam coffee or water. He asked for water. The kid was genuinely scared. But that didn't mean a thing.

Guilty or not, most people found a visit to the police department uncomfortable, especially when they were there to be interviewed as part of a murder investigation.

Stuck in the air-tight interview room, the reek of stale campfire smoke stung Brandon's eyes. Adam probably

28

hadn't showered in a few days. It made sense that the kid wanted to get back home. But Brandon wanted another shot at him away from his friends and under the revealing lights of the police station.

Brandon set a digital recorder on the table between them. "I'm recording this."

"Okay."

He had Adam state his name and date of birth.

Brandon slid the waiver-of-rights form across the table and read Adam his rights.

"Am I a suspect?" Adam asked.

"Right now, we're just gathering information. The rights are for your protection and mine."

Adam signed the document.

"How long have you and Lauren been dating?"

"About a year or so. We met at my work."

"That's the Hurricane Ridge Cafe?"

"Right."

Brandon knew the place. Its name came from the Hurricane Ridge area inside the northern boundary of Olympic National Park. The coffee shop in Sequim was about half an hour from Port Angeles.

"Tell me what happened the night Lauren died."

"We spent most of the day in town, then at the beach. Drank some beers."

"How many?"

"Me? Five or six."

"And Lauren?"

Adam's chair scooted back an inch from the table. "I wasn't paying attention. She could drink, though."

"She worked at the methadone clinic?" Brandon asked.

"Lauren was a recovering addict."

With a blood alcohol of .21, recovering addict wasn't the term Brandon would use.

"But she still drank?"

"She didn't see it as the same thing," Adam said.

That sounded like something an addict would say.

"When's the last time you and Lauren had sex?"

"Ah..." his cheeks flushed, either out of embarrassment or guilt.

"These are questions I have to ask."

"Okay. The night she disappeared."

"What did you two fight about that night?"

His eyebrows furrowed. "Who said we fought?"

"You did, didn't you?" Brandon pressed him.

"I don't...I don't remember. I was pretty out of it."

"You do remember the sex, though?"

"Um, yeah."

"Was the argument before or after?"

"The sex? I don't know. I don't think we argued."

The night Brandon first interviewed Adam, he'd denied arguing with Lauren. So far, he was sticking to his story.

"Okay, you had sex. Then what?" Brandon asked.

"I passed out. That was it until I woke up and she was gone."

"You didn't get up to piss? Not even once, after all that beer?"

"Not that I remember," Adam said.

There sure were a lot of holes in Adam's memory.

"Were you angry with Lauren?"

"No. Why would I be? She was great."

"Did you ever hit her?"

"Of course not."

30

"Were you and Lauren into...kinky stuff?" Brandon asked.

"What?" Adam's face reddened again. Either this kid was embarrassed easily, or he was a good actor.

"We found bite marks on Lauren's neck."

"What? How?"

He seemed genuinely surprised.

"Good question. Is that the sort of thing you and Lauren were into?"

"Biting each other?" Adam asked.

"Were you?"

"No. Definitely not," Adam said.

"Would you be willing to provide a DNA sample for us?"

"Ah. Sure. But why?"

"It will help with the investigation. During the autopsy, we found semen. We just need to make sure we're covering all of our bases."

"Will it tell you if it's mine?" Adam asked. "The semen, I mean."

It wasn't a question most men thought to ask about a girlfriend who had just died. "Why wouldn't it be?" Brandon asked.

Adam folded his hands on the table. "No reason."

"You'll do it?" Brandon asked.

"Alright," he said. "I don't have anything to hide."

Everyone had something to hide. The question was, did it have something to do with Lauren Sandoval's murder?

Brandon left Adam alone in the interview room. Jackson was at the copy machine printing out her report.

"You know where the DNA kits are?" Brandon asked.

She pointed. "I think in that cabinet over there."

31

They were right where she said they would be. There were only two left.

"We need to order more of these."

"Sometimes I get the feeling this place is hoping crime won't happen," she said.

Adam signed the DNA consent form and Brandon collected the cheek swab sample. He sealed the kit and prepared to send it to the crime lab. Meanwhile, Jackson took Adam's prints.

Before Brandon returned Adam to his car, he caught Jackson in the hallway.

"Do me a favor. Tell Nolan I want background reports on all three of these kids." Nolan was due back soon from his visits to the area sex offenders. His shift ended about the same time as Jackson's. "I'll need it by tomorrow morning."

She cast him a doubtful frown. Apparently, Brandon wasn't the only one who'd noticed Nolan's reluctance to do anything beyond the minimum work.

"Will do," Jackson said.

Back at the campground, Justin's truck was gone and there were few cars left in the parking lot. Brandon got out and opened the door for Adam.

"Where are you staying?"

"My stuff's already in my car. I'm headed back to Port Angeles."

"Tell me your address again."

He did, and Brandon recorded it in his notebook and let Adam go.

The future didn't look so bright for the innocent-faced young man. His girlfriend had been murdered and, according to her best friend, he'd been arguing with her hours before her death. Did Adam suspect Lauren was cheating on him? If so, Adam had the world's oldest motive for murder—jealousy.

Chapter 10

Brandon tossed a TV dinner in the oven and pulled a beer from the fridge.

He opened the tracking app on his phone to check on Emma. Brandon and Tori had installed the app a couple of years earlier. Some people might call occasionally checking on your child's location helicopter parenting. Brandon had grown up in a world where you left with your friends Saturday morning and the rule was you had to be back by dark. In the hours between, your parents had no idea where you were.

Brandon's years as a homicide detective had exposed him to the darker side of humanity, a world where monsters did horrible things to innocent people.

According to the app, Emma was home. He called her number.

"Hello?"

It was Tori.

"Where's Emma?"

"In her room. I confiscated her phone."

"Why?"

"Because she is being a snot. Teenage girl stuff. I'll get her for you."

"Everything all right?" Brandon asked.

"With me, or Emma?"

He'd meant Emma, but he knew Tori had been tackling some tough cases recently. It didn't help—or maybe it did—that their divorce had been finalized just two months earlier.

"How's work?" he asked, sticking to the impersonal. Anything else would lead to a different conversation—one about their relationship.

"The usual. Criminals and slimy defense attorneys."

Tori was a prosecutor for King County.

"Public defenders?" he asked.

"No. I'm working a sexual assault case involving a couple of prep school kids from the east side—kids whose parents can afford a top-notch defense team. How's Forks treating you?"

"Two days and I already have my first murder," Brandon said.

"Wasn't the goal to get out of homicide?"

"That was the idea," he said.

"Well, you could come back home..."

Time and again, they'd tried to make the marriage work. But they'd grown apart. That wasn't reason enough to end a marriage, in Brandon's opinion. But Tori was done, and in the end, had insisted on going through with the final paperwork.

Until she changed her mind, asking Brandon to give their relationship another chance. He did, and they went through the cycle half a dozen times until, finally, Brandon refused to delay the proceedings, needing some sense of his future. He was done waiting, wondering whether Tori wanted to make it work or not.

The brief moments of passion that sparked between them weren't enough to hold them together. They'd even tried counseling, but that only seemed to make things worse. Brandon had sunk his life into his work, and so had she.

At least they had Emma.

"I'm not ready to come back yet," Brandon said.

Yet? Why had he used that word? What he wanted to say was, we tried this, we care about each other and always will, but it's over.

"I know," she said. Then, her voice suddenly devoid of emotion, she said, "I'll get Emma."

A few seconds later, Emma picked up the phone.

"Hey, Dad."

"How's it going, sweetie?"

"Hold on, let me close my door."

Brandon waited.

"Okay. I can have some privacy now."

Why did she need privacy to talk to her dad?

"I can't handle Mom—"

"Because she confiscated your phone? That's what good parents do—"

"Not that. All we ever do is argue. She's always mad at me."

He downed a drink of beer while Emma talked. It always ended the same—both Tori and Emma unhappy and expecting him to play the role of peacemaker.

"Maybe you ought to go do something fun together. Like you used to."

"I can't wait until I get to stay with you," she said. "It's only two weeks away."

Brandon recalled the conversation with his father.

"I heard you've been talking to your grandpa."

"Email mostly. I like him. He's chill."

Chill was the last word Brandon would use to describe his father. Maybe the word meant something different nowadays.

"There's not much to do out here," he reminded her.

"Grandpa has a farm. And there's the cool vampire stuff. I've been checking it out online."

An image of the bite mark on Lauren Sandoval's neck flashed across his mind. He wasn't about to let Emma get involved in Forks' vampire craze.

"How are you doing in school?"

"Okay, I guess."

"You guess?"

Emma had been an 'A-' to 'B+' student most years. Before her best friend died in the fall, she'd had straight As.

"I miss Madison."

"I know, sweetie."

"And I don't have any other friends here," she said.

"You do—"

"You always say that, but I don't see the point of being here anymore."

Brandon's stomach clenched. What did she mean *not be here*?

"Emma—"

"I mean in Seattle, Dad. I can tell you're freaking out."

"That's my job. To worry about my daughter."

"Gee, thanks," she said, but he could hear the smile in her voice.

"Anything exciting happen so far?" she asked.

"Not much," he said. He didn't like discussing the darker side of his work with Emma.

"Liar," she said.

"What is that supposed to mean?"

"Grandpa told me about the girl who died. It was murder, wasn't it?"

"Emma..."

"You're not thinking of telling me to stay in Seattle until the case is solved?" she asked.

That was exactly what he was thinking.

"I need to know it's safe—"

"Dad, I live in Seattle. How many murders are there per year in King County, compared to Forks?"

He wasn't about to engage in an argument about crime statistics with Emma. It was a personal passion of Emma's—crime mapping, studies on prevalence rates by zip code.

"I get it," he said. "But I'm still your dad."

"And I'm your daughter, and I know how to take care of myself."

Probably the same thing Lauren Sandoval thought.

"Okay. But we're not done talking about this," Brandon said. "And there will be rules."

He imagined her eyes rolling. She was a good kid. But having her here during the investigation would make things more...personal. The quicker he solved this case, the sooner he could move on with being a dad—and chief of police.

They talked for a while longer about home and school and, eventually, he said goodnight. Brandon surveyed the kitchen and then the living room where the unpacked boxes stood stacked on top of each other. He'd have to get the house ready for her at some point. He still had time, though, and there was a murder to solve.

Brandon woke up around five in the morning. It was Sunday, supposedly his day off. Hadn't he dreamed of sleeping in on the weekends? No on-call work or cases to review, no witnesses to shake down. Yet his mind had kicked into gear well before dawn, scrutinizing evidence from the Lauren Sandoval case.

He boiled water and made himself a cup of instant coffee—the best he had until he bought a proper coffee maker. He'd left his espresso machine with Tori and had gotten used to getting coffee on the way to work. There was an espresso stand on the way into town, but he wasn't in the mood for conversation—no matter how friendly the barista.

Brandon made his way to the backyard, where he leaned back in one of a pair of weatherworn lawn chairs. As he watched the sun peek over the foothills, his thoughts turned to the future.

Emma would be there in less than two weeks and he'd told himself he needed to get back into the habit of attending Sunday morning services. They'd gone as a family for years—until the divorce. He didn't want Emma to give up on church, and it wouldn't do any good if Brandon didn't follow his own advice.

Maybe next week.

Brandon tossed his coffee—it was bitter as hell—into a rose bush outside his back door.

He showered, got dressed, and headed down to the Forks Diner. He hadn't eaten there since returning to town, but the café had a reputation as the best breakfast diner on the west side of the county.

It was just past six and the parking lot was already half full. Brandon parked on the street near the spray-painted vampire ankh. The blood-red symbol reminded him he still needed to locate Vasile, the vampire coven leader.

Inside the diner, there was a group of road construction contract workers at the bar, three or four guys and three women wearing safety vests. At least Brandon wasn't the only one working on Sunday. The waitress who was refilling their coffees looked up at Brandon.

"Look who's all grown up," she said.

Brandon checked over his shoulder to make sure she wasn't talking to someone else.

"Brandon Mattson," she said, setting the pot of coffee on the counter. The construction workers twisted in their stools to gawk at him.

The woman was in her fifties. Her name tag read Tammy, and that's when he remembered her. Tammy was the older sister of Brandon's high school best friend.

"How's Mark?" Brandon asked.

"Doing great. Married, couple of kids. He moved to Spokane a while back."

"Good to hear it," Brandon said.

"Hey, everyone," Tammy said to anyone in the general area who might listen. "This here is our new chief of police, Brandon Mattson. So be on your best behavior."

A few people in nearby booths waved, welcoming him back to town. The group at the counter—most likely out-of-towners—generally ignored Tammy's proclamation. One of the workers, however, locked eyes with Brandon. The man snorted sarcastically before turning his back on Brandon.

Some people didn't like cops. Brandon got that. But it didn't mean you had to act like an ass.

"Come on, Brandon, I'll get you a booth."

Tammy grabbed a menu and led him to the back of the restaurant where there were still open seats.

Brandon was about to sit down when he noticed someone in the booth across the aisle staring at him.

It was Misty.

She smiled. "You can join me if you want company."

He took the seat across from her. Tammy handed him a menu.

"Coffee?"

"Sure."

Tammy left them and Brandon asked, "You already order?"

"Just now. I'm in no hurry."

There was an awkward silence, the kind that props up between two people that have only had one conversation in the last 20 years.

"How's it feel being the big cheese in town?"

"Ask me in a month," he said.

"Hard time getting settled in?"

"I've got a mayor who doesn't care about anything but some author coming to town—"

"Those books bring in a lot of tourists," Misty said.

"Don't tell me, you're a fan?"

She bit her bottom lip. "I might have read them."

Brandon rolled his eyes. "You too?"

"I'll deny it if you tell anyone."

"Even my dad's read them," Brandon said.

"Maybe you should give it a try."

"No thanks, teenage angst isn't my thing. Even when it involves extraterrestrial beings."

"Not extraterrestrial. Undead."

"Whatever."

Tammy returned and took his order—a Denver Omelet.

"You got any green Tabasco sauce?"

"Sure thing, Chief."

"Thanks."

When Tammy left, Misty said. "Speaking of teen angst, I hear you have a daughter."

"She's fifteen. I guess I should be thankful there hasn't been much drama with Emma. Not yet, at least."

"Lucky you," she said with a hint of sarcasm.

"Your son?" Brandon asked.

"Micah is twenty-three. Sometimes he's got his head on straight, other times—well, let's just say I hope you don't ever see him in your line of work."

"He's had trouble with the law?"

"Close to it, but I've been able to catch him a couple of breaks."

Brandon didn't like the sound of that. By the time a young man was in his twenties, he ought to be past the stage of needing his mom to bail him out of trouble. And how exactly was Misty catching him a break? Did she know someone on the force? Or the courts?

It wasn't his business.

They made small talk while Misty finished her eggs and toast. Brandon's omelet arrived and Tammy refilled his coffee. Misty talked while Brandon ate.

She motioned to Brandon's ring finger. "Sorry to hear about your divorce."

Brandon finished his omelet, chasing the last mouthful with a gulp of hot coffee.

"No secrets in this town," he said.

"You know better than that. Besides, when a handsome man comes into town, of course the ladies are gonna want to know if he's eligible."

Brandon wiped his mouth, trying to think of a good response. What was Misty getting at?

"Thanks," he said.

Misty steered the conversation to town gossip as she recited the fates of every friend, or enemy, they'd both had at Forks High School. Eventually, she got around to talking about her work. She'd recently been promoted to supervisor at a company providing in-home caregiving.

42

That made sense. Misty had always been the type that gravitated toward people in need.

Maybe that was why she'd left Brandon—unlike the father of Misty's child, Brandon wasn't a needy, teat-sucking loser.

"I've applied for a manager position," she said. "Down in Aberdeen."

"You'll have to move."

She wrapped her fingers around the mug of coffee. "If I get the job. I mean, I'd need a reason to stay here, otherwise..."

Brandon realized Misty was staring at him.

"So, are you?" she asked.

"Am I what?"

"Eligible? Back on the market."

"Uh, I hadn't thought about it."

"Well, don't keep the ladies in suspense too long."

It was one of those moments between a man and a woman where the man isn't quite sure what the woman means. Was she directing her comments at him for her own sake, or was she really concerned about the welfare of the town's single women?

"Right now, I'm focused on work, and my daughter. She'll be moving here soon."

"I can't wait to meet her."

"Yeah," Brandon said.

"Unless you don't want me to."

"No, not at all," he said.

She slipped her hand over his. "Good. We are neighbors, after all."

"Well, look here. I didn't know you two knew each other."

Officer Nolan stood an inch from their table, thumbs hooked into the front of his duty belt.

Misty pulled her hand back. "We go way back. High school."

"Isn't that nice," Nolan said with a smirk.

Something about the tone in Nolan's voice made Brandon want to knock him on his ass.

Nolan squeezed in next to Misty. She didn't budge.

"You two know each other?" Brandon asked, his eyes resting on Misty.

"We're together," Nolan said.

Misty's eyes bolted away, landing outside the window.

Nolan propped his arm on her shoulder. "Isn't that right, honey?"

"Yes."

Great. Brandon's least supportive officer was dating his ex.

Brandon studied the check. Tammy had left both orders on the same ticket. He slid out of the booth and picked up the bill. "Nice talking to you again, Misty."

"Wait," Misty said, eyeing the bill. "You don't have to pay for mine."

"No worries," Brandon said. "I'll get it. For old time's sake."

He gave Nolan a wink before heading to the counter to pay the bill.

Chapter 11

Brandon spent the next hour catching up on emails. Most were reminders from human resources. Do this, don't do that. Sign here, and here, and...

It was a wonder they didn't ask you to swear on a Bible that you'd read all five hundred pages of the personnel manual and promise under penalty of hellfire that you—and your employees—would abide by every rule.

It wasn't the Sunday morning he'd hoped for, but the idea was to get his mind off his interaction with Misty.

That she was with Nolan made things easier—or at least it should. If she was dating someone else, that ought to keep her from getting the wrong idea about her relationship with Brandon. Except she'd been pretty forward at the diner—until Nolan showed up.

Maybe he'd been reading too much into her actions.

Brandon opened his email. Half the officers, including himself, were already behind on their annual trainings. How could he be late when he'd just started?

Sue, the department's secretary, had sent him a stack of applications she'd received from HR. Will was retiring soon, and they'd have to replace him. He flipped through the names but didn't recognize any. One person who hadn't applied was Isabel Jackson, the reserve officer who'd proved to be a good investigator.

A calendar reminder popped up on his screen. He had an appointment with the mayor in 10 minutes. What kind of person scheduled a meeting on a Sunday?

He clicked on the invitation and noted that the meeting had been sent to him just 20 minutes earlier.

Brandon was tempted to hit the decline button. He had work to do, and whatever the mayor wanted to talk about wasn't as important as the homicide investigation.

He closed the screen, neither accepting nor declining the meeting. Not wanting to ruffle too many feathers this early in his stint as police chief, he'd give her five minutes of his time.

"Chief Mattson. Glad you could make it," the mayor said as he entered her office.

She stood and Olivia followed her lead. A man Brandon didn't recognize sat at the table.

"I don't have much time," Brandon said. "On such short notice."

"Understood."

"Working the homicide case, Chief?" the man asked him.

Brandon's eyes shifted from the man to the mayor. One day was the longest she could keep quiet about the investigation?

"This is Ted Nixon. He's a writer for the local newspaper," the mayor said.

"It's a weekly, more frequent when needed," Ted said. He remained seated. "I cover the area for the Port Angeles Times too."

"Okay," Brandon said.

"And before we get any further," the mayor said, "I'm not the one who spilled the beans."

"Then who did?" Brandon asked.

"Private sources," Ted said. The reporter was a few years younger than Brandon. He had sandy blonde hair thinning on top. His balding hairline was accentuated by the forest green clerk's cap he wore, the kind with the tinted visor.

"You want a comment? Here it is—no comment."

"That's not why we're here," Olivia said, casting Ted a warning. "Today is about Tiffany Quick's visit and the Moonbeam Festival. It's less than two weeks away."

"Then why the reporter?" Brandon asked.

"Ted is our partner in promoting the event," the mayor said.

"Look. As Mr. Nixon here mentioned, I have an investigation to run."

Ted chimed in, "Word on the street is that there's a darker connection—especially with the recent appearance of vampire symbols."

"You know of more than one?" Brandon asked.

"Not yet," Ted said.

"Good. And I already said I'm not commenting on the case."

"Ted, let's focus here," Olivia said. She strolled over to Ted, resting a hand on his shoulder.

"Chief Mattson," Ted said. "Just so you know how things work around here. I am used to a certain level of access to the inner workings of our local government. That includes public safety."

"And just so *you* know, Ted, I'll give you a statement regarding the case when I am ready."

"Okay, again, not why we're here," Olivia said, her voice rising half an octave.

"Send me a report on any plans for the festival and I'll review them with my officers for any public safety concerns," Brandon said.

Brandon moved toward the door.

"Wait!" Olivia said, holding her hands out. "What about the uniforms?"

"Uniforms?" Brandon asked.

"Maybe later, Olivia—" the mayor started.

"It will only take a minute," Olivia said. She rustled through a pile of papers until she found the one she was searching for. Brandon gazed longingly at the door.

Olivia glided over to Brandon.

"Here it is," she said, holding up a colored pencil sketch of a silver police badge. The words Forks and WA were emblazoned across the top and bottom. Vampire fangs formed the centerpiece of the badge, the words *Vamp Patrol* emblazoned below the upper teeth.

"What is this?"

"Special edition badges. For Tiffany Quick's visit," Olivia said.

"No way in hell," Brandon said.

Ted tittered. Brandon narrowed his eyes at the reporter. What was so funny?

"We would only want your officers to wear them for one weekend," Olivia said. "Then we'd auction them off—"

"Not happening," Brandon said. "Look, miss...tourism czar or whatever you are. I'm sure you're a great PR person. But PR has nothing to do with being a police officer—"

"It does have to do with being a police *chief*," Ted chimed in.

Brandon stared Ted down for several seconds until he glanced away. The last thing Brandon wanted was to get on the wrong side of the local press, but his officers were not going to wear toy badges.

48

"Fine," Olivia said, her lips pouting. "But I did have an idea for a purple sash—"

He'd had enough.

Brandon was halfway across the parking lot when the mayor caught up to him.

"Brandon."

"Mayor?"

"She means well," Mayor Kim said.

"Possibly, but that's irrelevant. We don't need a fashion designer."

"I'll talk to her," she said.

"Good."

"Before you leave...any news about the girl?"

"We're following all leads, waiting for more information from the coroner," he said.

"How is her family doing?"

"Her mom was devastated. I need to follow up with her, learn what I can about the girl."

She nodded, a look of concern on her face. "I do care about the community, you know."

"Not just tourism?"

She exhaled. "The truth? Yes, we're worried about the effect this will have on the festival. A quick resolution lessens the likelihood that Tiffany Quick cancels."

Brandon's private phone buzzed. It was Tori.

He let it go to voicemail.

"This author," Brandon said. "You think she'll stay away because of one murder?"

"This is more than a visit. She's considering writing a sequel to her series. If we can convince her to make Forks the backdrop of her new series too—"

"My goal is to make sure we have a quick—and accurate—resolution, Mayor Kim."

"You know what's funny?" the mayor asked.

"What's that?" Brandon said, glancing over his shoulder, toward the police department. He had a list of things to do, and none were getting done.

"Olivia thinks the recent events—"

"A young woman's death," he reminded her.

"Will somehow positively affect tourism. Especially the vampire angle."

Was she seriously suggesting the town make money off of Lauren Sandoval's murder?

"I mean," the mayor continued, "I don't agree with her. It's a horrible thought—"

"Good morning, mayor," he said and left her staring after him.

Back at the station, Brandon found Nolan in the bullpen.

"Morning, Chief," Nolan said, pouring powdered cream into a cup of coffee.

Did Nolan know Brandon and Misty had been an item back in high school? If he did, it would make it that much harder for them to get along.

But Brandon was Nolan's boss, and whatever Brandon and Misty had had in the past was irrelevant when he was on the clock.

"You finish the rounds with the sex offenders yesterday?" Brandon asked.

"Yes, and it was pretty much a waste of time."

"All of them denied involvement?"

"Right."

"Alibis?" Brandon asked.

"Yep."

"All of them?"

"That's what I said." Nolan stirred the creamer for half a second and tossed the plastic spoon in the trash. "Look, Mattson. I didn't graduate the academy yesterday, and I'm not some reserve like Jackson—"

"Jackson's a good cop," Brandon said.

"My point is you don't need to nitpick everything I do."

That was for Brandon to decide. Nolan had shown himself to be lazy, at best. Bordering on negligent.

"What about the background check on the victim's friends?"

The night before, Brandon had asked Jackson to pass along the message to Nolan he should do a background check on all three of Lauren's friends. By the blank expression on Nolan's face, it was obvious he hadn't done what Brandon had asked.

"What checks?"

"I asked Jackson to tell you. Last night."

"Well, she didn't," Nolan said.

Brandon looked to the desk where Nolan usually sat. On top of Nolan's notebook, next to his keys, was a note from Jackson with Brandon's instructions.

"I just saw that," Nolan said. His face flushed scarlet with anger and he moved to leave.

Brandon stepped in front of Nolan. "I don't know how things worked around here before," Brandon said. "But I will not put up with bullshit. Especially lies."

"Just because you came in here riding on Eli's coattails—"

"What?"

"Everyone knows you only got this job because of your last name, because of Eli's reputation."

"I'm here because I earned the job. You didn't."

51

Nolan was still pissed he'd been passed over for the chief position. Brandon would be too. Except Brandon wouldn't be such an ass about it.

"I need to trust my officers, and I hope you'll learn to trust me. If neither of those can happen, I suggest you find another department."

"You're threatening to fire me over a note?"

"I'm telling you that what I've seen so far from you is sloppy police work. This town deserves better than that, and so do your fellow officers."

Nolan's gaze was cold, resentful. "I'll get started on those background checks. Sir."

Brandon had his butt in his chair for less than two seconds when there was a tap at his office door. Brandon motioned for Will to come in.

"Anything new on the Sandoval girl?" Will asked.

"I wasted half the day yesterday searching for vampire fangs like those that made the bite on the girl's neck," Brandon said. "I have to follow up on some sort of vampire high priest living on a farm outside of town. I'm sure it'll be a dead end."

Will shifted in his seat. "I wouldn't take that stuff lightly. Some people believe in vampires. Any idea what the graffiti at the Forks Diner means?"

"I talked to two of the shops. They weren't much help. Except for the lead on the vampire guy."

"You talked to Phoenix?"

"Yeah. She's...interesting."

"I'm surprised she couldn't tell you more about the symbol. She's known for her interest in the occult. Some churches in town have been trying to get her shut down."

"I don't think they need to bother. She doesn't seem to have many customers as it is."

"So," Will said. "I, ah, heard you and Nolan."

He must have been down the hallway, waiting for Nolan and Brandon to wrap up their conversation.

"Yeah, well, he's not too happy with me being chief," Brandon said.

"I wouldn't worry about Nolan," Will said. "He'll get over it. Or he won't."

Brandon considered Will. "Why didn't you apply for the chief position?"

"Too old. Other reasons, too." He pointed a thumb toward the common area, where Nolan was now.

Brandon clicked his tongue. "I hear that."

He leaned forward. "Is it true that people think the only reason I got the job was because of Eli? I mean, because of the family name?"

Will took his time considering the question, and that was answer enough.

"You were qualified for this job. I've seen your resume, heard about the cases you solved."

"How?"

"Eli couldn't shut up about you. Always bragging about his little brother."

Brandon held back a smile. Eli was that way—liked to build Brandon up.

"I'll tell you this. It doesn't matter one damn bit what people think about you. What matters is how you handle this job. You belong here. Prove it."

Will was right. People would have their opinions. What mattered was results.

He had made it his goal to lead by example, to motivate people on his team by teaching them why their jobs were important. But every once in a while you had to be a hard ass. He didn't like it, but he accepted that responsibility when he took the job. Either Nolan would straighten up, or he'd leave. Hopefully, of his own volition. Firing a cop was hard enough. Doing it in a small town where everyone knew everything—that was near impossible.

Chapter 12

Brandon had just finished reviewing the evidence they'd gathered so far when Jackson came rushing into his office.

"Chief! Good news."

"Alright. Catch your breath."

She took the chair across from him.

"What's up?"

"I was going through the list of campers I got from the park service—the ones who had registered but had left by the time we started our investigation."

"Right."

Calling the campers who had already vacated the site had been Jackson's idea.

"I was on my fifth call and got someone who said they saw Lauren Sandoval," she said.

"You're sure?"

"This guy, Edward Voss is his name, was headed to his car around midnight to get an extra blanket. Apparently, his wife complained it was too cold and—"

"This was the night Lauren disappeared?"

"Exactly. He was headed to his car and noticed a girl in her early twenties trying to get into a truck."

"Probably Justin's," Brandon said.

"And after trying the handle, she gives up and heads for the road and starts the trek into town."

"He's sure she was headed to Forks?"

"Yep. And I emailed him a copy of the missing person photo. He's sure it was her. He said she seemed pretty out of it, like she'd been drinking."

That was consistent with Lauren's blood alcohol level.

"Did you do a background report on this Edward Voss?" Brandon asked.

It wasn't uncommon for criminals to revisit the scene of the crime, especially in cases involving murder under such unusual circumstances.

"No criminal record. No arrests," she said.

The 14-mile road between Second Beach and Forks was a stretch of farmhouses and forest. Had Lauren planned on making the long trek into town on foot—in the middle of the night?

She might have misjudged the distance, being from out of town—and intoxicated.

"Okay, we move the investigation to Forks. Did anyone see her in town? On the way to town? How'd she get there?"

"I'll start asking around," Jackson said. "But it's a long shot. Not much is open that late."

"Good point. I want you to focus on the stretch of road between the beach and Forks. Start at the parking lot where she was last seen and check each house."

Most of the properties on the road were five acres or more, so it shouldn't take too long to cover that many homes.

"Got it."

After she'd gone, Josiah poked his head into the room. "What's up with all the excitement?"

"We might have a lead. Lauren Sandoval was seen hiking into Forks, alone."

"What do you need me to do?" Josiah asked.

"Canvas the shops. Start at the north end of town. I'll take the south side. Any information, anyone who has any idea of her whereabouts. Ask if they have any outward-facing video cameras they might let you take a look at."

"Got it," Josiah said.

Half an hour into his search, Brandon had interviewed three store owners—long shots for sure. A feed store, a hair salon, and a boutique wine shop. They would have closed for the evening by the time Lauren wandered into Forks, if she'd made it that far. None of the shops he interviewed owned cameras.

His next stop was Bar-B-Que Pete's. Back in the day, the building had been a greasy spoon restaurant. After a recent remodel, the place had the feel of a suburban sports bar. They weren't open until lunch on Sundays and the parking lot was empty, so he made a note to come back later.

Brandon got back in his SUV and pointed it toward downtown. He'd never considered how many businesses there were in a town as small as Forks. Rather than wasting the morning on long shots, he'd try a few high-value targets first. His eyes landed on the Jackpot Gas Stop and Convenience Store a few blocks up.

He knew the store closed late. Brandon and his buddies from Seattle had grabbed beer there the night they helped him move in.

He parked behind the gas station and circled the building, checking for cameras. He found one, just above the main entrance.

Inside, he surveyed the store for other cameras. He spotted one in the far corner, above a sign that read *Restrooms for Customer Use Only.*

There was one patron, a guy buying a hotdog and a pack of smokes. Brandon waited for him to leave and approached the counter.

The cashier was a woman in her fifties. Her ginger hair was in a sloppy ponytail, as if she'd pulled it back a day ago and left it there.

"What do you need?" she asked brusquely.

"Do you have other cameras besides that one?" he asked.

She considered him, slid something around in her mouth. Maybe candy or gum. He could almost taste the mint on her breath.

"No," she replied.

Brandon squinted at the nametag on her wrinkled, food-stained gas station uniform.

"Tell me, Ruby, do you always work the morning shift?"

"I come in whenever they need me. Too much, if you ask me."

"Even graveyard?"

"Sometimes," she said. "I'm here nine or ten hours, sometimes longer, until whenever the owner feels like showing up."

"On the night of June 21—that was three nights ago counting last night—did you work then?"

"What day?"

Ruby's eyes were as glazed over as a sugar-dipped donut. She'd gotten lost in a mind fog, and it didn't appear she would find her way out any time soon. It was hard to tell if this was her normal state or if she needed a couple of days to catch up on sleep.

"Thursday," Brandon said. "Going into Friday morning."

"What's this about? If someone made a complaint, you need to talk to the owners."

"You've had complaints before?" he asked.

She shifted her weight from one leg to the other, crossing her arms.

"No."

Brandon took that as a yes.

"I'm investigating the disappearance of Lauren Sandoval."

Ruby blinked. She'd found her way out of the fog.

"You know her?"

Ruby's expression slackened. "I might have heard the name."

"When?"

"I keep to myself—come to work, go home and sleep. I don't bother nobody. What do I have to do with some missing girl?"

Brandon unfolded the photo on the counter between them. Ruby's eyes passed over the picture.

"She's been murdered," Brandon said.

Ruby was hiding something, and Brandon had to decide which tack to take, good cop or bad cop. Ruby seemed the kind of person who'd respond to the more direct approach.

"This is a homicide investigation, Ruby. And I'm sure you don't want to get in the way of finding out who murdered this young woman. How do you know her?"

"I don't—"

"The truth," Brandon said.

She stared back at him, her eyes redder than they were a moment earlier.

"She came in here, okay. Got beer. I didn't want to say anything."

"Why not?" he asked.

"Because she was pretty out of it. I mean, you can't tell nowadays, with all the weed people smoke, if they're drunk or high or both."

"We're talking Thursday night, after midnight?"

"Yeah."

"Who was she with?"

"No one. I mean. Once she was in the store."

"Before that?"

She shrugged. "I don't want to get no one in trouble."

Brandon never quite understood the concept of hiding the truth from the cops, especially when it involved a murder.

"I understand wanting to protect—"

"I'm just saying, I'm no narc." She took a good look at Brandon. "You're new around here?"

"No."

"I've never seen you before."

"I grew up here. Now answer my question."

She glanced out the window at the parking lot. He worried she might clam up. If she was protecting someone, she needed to know the consequences.

"What's your last name, Ruby?"

"Walker."

Brandon pulled out his notepad. "Your home address?"

"Why do you need to know that?"

"You may be the last person to see Lauren Sandoval alive. You are a witness in this investigation."

"I said I didn't know her."

Brandon's phone buzzed in his pocket. He checked the incoming number. It was Emma. He'd let Tori's call go to voicemail earlier.

"I'll be right back," he said.

Outside, he answered the call. "What's going on?"

"Mom is being—"

"Look, I can't deal with bickering right now."

Couldn't they figure out things on their own? Just this one time.

"Dad, I can't stay here any longer—"

"You need to finish school. Two weeks, okay?"

"Yesterday was the last day of class."

"I got to go," he said, hanging up.

Brandon slid the phone into his pocket and stepped back into the store.

"Okay, Ruby. Your address?"

She gave him her address. He'd follow up with the store owners later to make sure Ruby was being honest.

"Now tell me, who was with Lauren before she came in the store?"

Ruby moved the candy around in her mouth until it settled in her cheek. "A tow truck dropped her off, out by the curb. That's all I know."

"Which tow company?"

"I don't know. How was I supposed to know I'd be part of some murder investigation?"

"Was there a logo?"

"I didn't look," she said.

"I'll need to check the video. Inside and out."

She glared back at him. "The cameras don't work. Haven't for years."

Brandon held her eyes for a moment. Ruby blinked and looked away.

"I'll get a warrant, then," he said.

"Go ahead."

"You sold her beer. What kind and how much?"

61

To Brandon's surprise, Ruby answered the question. "Six pack, Coors Light."

"That's all?" he asked.

"Yes."

"And she left with the tow truck driver?"

"No. He was gone by then."

"So, she just walked away."

"Yep. That way." She pointed north, toward downtown.

Josiah was canvassing that section of town. Hopefully, he'd found at least one business with active video surveillance.

"Anything else?"

"Like what?" she asked.

"Did the girl say anything?" he asked.

"Nope. Just bought the beer and left."

Brandon studied Ruby's expression. A sheen of sweat covered her face. She was more worried than she should be if the only interaction she'd ever had with Lauren was to sell her a six-pack of beer.

She seemed to notice Brandon's scrutiny. "Too bad about the girl. I hope you catch whoever did this."

"Me too," he said. "Call us if you remember anything else."

Despite her reluctance, Ruby had been some help. Lauren had been dropped off by a tow truck driver. There couldn't be many towing businesses in the west county.

He contacted Josiah and Jackson and told them to meet him near the hospital, on the west side of town.

Josiah had come across two businesses with cameras. One had already written over Thursday night's recording and the other's footage showed no sign of Lauren. Jackson hadn't garnered any useful information from her interviews with homeowners on the road from Second Beach.

Based on the information he had gained from Ruby, Brandon instructed Josiah and Jackson to check into any towing businesses in the west county area and interview all drivers with access to a tow truck the night Lauren disappeared.

Brandon took a trip down to Second Beach to survey the area again. Lauren had purchased beer in town the night she went missing. Was she murdered on the way back to the beach? Or had she made it to the campground before she was killed?

On the way, he kept his eyes on the edge of the pavement for any sign of trash, especially discarded beer cans. There was a chance Lauren had started back toward the beach but had been forced into a vehicle.

It was hard to imagine Lauren, intoxicated as she was, making the 14 miles to Second Beach on her own. The forensics indicated that she'd fallen, probably near the beach, and been pulled into the water shortly thereafter.

Brandon parked at the trailhead and grabbed his evidence collection kit out of the back of the SUV and made the hike down to the beach. He was grateful the former chief had ensured the department had kits that included a backpack for hauling evidence out of the middle-of-nowhere locations in which his officers might find themselves.

The first thing he noticed was how few campers were out. Rain was in the forecast—already, gray clouds loomed over the endless horizon that was the Pacific Ocean.

The campsite where Lauren and her friends had stayed was abandoned now. The fire pit contained little of interest. Remains of burned-out logs and cigarette butts. One crushed can of Miller Lite blackened by soot. Not the brand Lauren had bought.

A search of the marram grass surrounding the site didn't reveal any clues. Second Beach was home to several rock formations called sea stacks. Remnants of the former, higher coastline, these monoliths were popular with tourists and locals alike. Most were vertical on all sides, providing a challenge for all but professional level rock climbers.

The one Brandon considered now, the one closest to Lauren's campsite, had a more forgiving incline. He'd scaled it as a kid, and most healthy adults could make it to the top, as long as they were willing to leave behind any fear of heights.

Brandon stood at the base of the sea stack. Even here, jagged rock rose a few inches above the sand. This flat, hard surface extended from the larger stone pillar by several feet on each side.

If Lauren had fallen, then been dragged away across a rough stone, it was likely someplace like this sea stack. Bluffs towered over the north end of the beach, jutting out into the ocean where the shoreline ended abruptly. But those cliffs were nearly impossible to scale, and it was unlikely Lauren could have climbed that high, considering her state.

He made a circuit around the stone formation. When the tide came in, the sea would encircle the rock. Even now, Brandon had to step over shallow pools left behind by the previous high tide. Some pools showed signs of life—sea anemones, small crabs, and an abundance of sea kelp.

Any biological evidence like hair or blood would have washed away along with Lauren's body.

At the western edge of the sea stack, his eye caught a glint in one of the pools. A tiny silver chain lay tangled in a clump of black mussels. Brandon took a picture with his phone—it was most likely part of a necklace. He slipped on a pair of gloves and tugged gently on the chain, revealing a small pendant. The pendant was dull white, possibly porcelain, shaped like a crescent moon.

He snapped another picture, this time focusing on the pendant, still connected to the chain, although the clasp appeared broken. At first glance, there didn't appear to be any hair or skin on the necklace, but he'd leave it up to the forensic team to determine what hidden clues the trinket might hold. He placed the necklace and pendant in an evidence bag.

After he'd finished checking the area, he made the trek up the sea stack. It hadn't rained for some time, but the stone was slick, moistened by the sea spray that doused the ancient geological formation with every high tide.

He pulled himself up onto the highest point, a narrow plateau about 10 by 20 feet. Brandon came up on the ocean-facing side of the rock and stood on the edge now, peering down at the jagged stone 30 feet below.

The Pacific Ocean rumbled in the distance, its roar interrupted by brief gusts that nudged Brandon back from the cliff. His eyes rose to see massive waves swelling offshore. Smooth and dark, their pace appeared deceivingly slow.

He followed the waves as they approached the shore where they grew more intense, if smaller, finally crashing onto the wet beach.

This could be the last place Lauren had stood before she died. But she wouldn't have seen the ocean then. It had been hours before sunrise, and her injuries indicated she'd landed on her back.

Waves brushed the rocks below, only to retreat a moment later.

The tide was coming in and before long the sea stack would become an island. Brandon turned to leave, but something caught his eye.

A black plastic bag.

He knelt down. Inside were six beer cans. He used a pen to open the bag more.

Coors Light. He checked for a receipt but didn't find one.

He photographed the bag from a few different angles.

The beer could have been left by anyone, but if this was the place where Lauren plunged to her death, DNA from those cans might tell him who she was with when she died.

Brandon pulled out a larger bag and carefully placed the evidence inside, then checked and double-checked the top of the sea stack for other clues. Not finding any, he gathered his pack and descended the rock.

Back at his vehicle, Brandon contacted the crime scene techs up in Port Angeles.

Brandon would meet a tech halfway between Port Angeles and Forks. The sooner they got to work testing for any DNA or fingerprints, the better.

It was becoming clear to Brandon that whatever happened to Lauren occurred near her campground. Second Beach was National Park Service territory, so he'd have to keep them updated. He'd give Police Chief Simpson at the Quileute Police Department a call too, letting him know the murder most likely occurred somewhere off the reservation. Simpson wouldn't be disappointed to learn the case had moved out of his jurisdiction. No small town or Tribal Department wanted to deal with a case like this.

Brandon met the tech up at the west end of Lake Crescent, 30 miles north and east of Forks. He completed the chain of evidence paperwork and handed over the necklace and beer cans.

On the road back to town, he listened to Tori's voicemail. As he expected, she was upset at Emma. They'd had another blowup. He called her back, but her phone went to voicemail. He left a message.

They'd probably figure it out on their own. These rows usually lasted a couple of days, then they were back to getting along.

Brandon recalled Phoenix Weaver's ominous warning—something about family trouble in his future.

It was a good thing he didn't believe in that nonsense. Everything would be fine.

He hoped.

Chapter 13

Brandon had asked Nolan to run background checks on Lauren's friends. When he returned to his office that afternoon, he found the report on his desk. The write-up was comprehensive—Nolan had actually done a good job.

Brandon flipped first to the page describing Justin Tate. Not that Justin had a clear motive in Lauren's murder, but the kid's attitude toward the police irritated Brandon, and part of him hoped to find something less than impressive about his past.

He wasn't disappointed.

Two years ago, Justin had been charged with attempted rape. The charges were eventually dropped. Nolan had learned the victim was the same age as Justin, and while initially alleging sexual assault, she later claimed it was consensual.

The victim's name was Brooke Whittaker—Justin's girlfriend and Lauren Sandoval's best friend.

Despite the alleged assault, Brooke had stayed with Justin.

There were no other charges or convictions in Justin's record. Brooke's record was clean, as was Adam's.

Could Justin have sexually assaulted and killed Lauren?

She'd had intercourse before she died. Someone had most likely shoved her off a sea stack and then dragged her body into the ocean. Justin was strong enough to do both.

Proximity and a history of accusations weren't enough to arrest him. He needed to take the information he had and interview Lauren's trio of friends again.

It sure would help if the crime lab would get him the DNA results back. If Justin was the murderer, Brandon knew where to find him, for now. If not, that meant the killer still hid among the thousands of anonymous faces that passed through Forks every year.

With the Moonbeam festival approaching, the number of people in the town would double over a two-day period. Meaning more places for the killer to hide—and more victims to prey upon.

Brandon contacted Brooke and Justin and asked them to come down to the station.

The sexual assault allegation by Brooke against Justin could be important. As was the new evidence that Lauren had made it into town the night she passed. Brandon was beginning to believe she'd died after having drinks on the sea stack. Whether she'd been drinking alone—or not— during those final minutes could be key to solving the case.

Brandon interviewed Brooke first.

He'd just hit the record button when Brooke asked, "What did you find out about Lauren?"

"We're still waiting on a few things," Brandon said. "I was hoping you could help me answer a few questions."

She leaned back in her chair, crossing her legs. "Okay."

"When was the last time you saw Lauren?"

"Right before she went into her tent. With Adam."

"You didn't hear from her again?" he asked.

"Not at all."

"You said before you heard her and Adam arguing."

"Right. But I didn't see them," she said.

"How long did the argument last?"

"I don't know."

"And it just stopped? The arguing, I mean."

"It got quiet, I guess," Brooke said. "Maybe I passed out."

Brandon stared at the blank legal pad on the table between them. Brooke was holding back again. Was she protecting her boyfriend?

"Why are you asking me all of these questions? It's not like I know who killed Lauren."

He wished he believed her.

"We have evidence that Lauren made it into town in the hours before she died."

Her eyebrows furrowed. "That's like ten miles away."

"Fourteen," Brandon said.

"How did she get there?"

"Did Lauren ever say anything about a tow-truck driver?" he asked.

"No."

"Anyone that bothered her? Creeped her out?"

She shook her head, no. "You think someone kidnapped her in Forks?"

"We know she bought beer at the gas station."

Brooke scoffed. "That's a shocker."

"Why?"

"Lauren hated the lady that works there."

"You know her name?" Brandon asked.

"No. She has red hair. She's mean. Maybe in her fifties."

The description matched Ruby, the cashier who'd sold Lauren the beer.

"What was Lauren's issue with this woman?"

"She was a dealer, messing with Lauren's clients. Lauren was a drug counselor."

"Right. You mean Lauren thought this woman sold to her clients?"

"Yeah."

Ruby, the cantankerous cashier, was a dealer? The late-night shift at the local gas station wouldn't be a bad gig for someone hoping to distribute drugs in a public but anonymous location.

"Did Lauren have any evidence of this? Did she ever tell the police?"

"Nah, just what the clients told her. We confronted her one time," Brooke said.

"We?"

"Yeah, Justin and I used to work at the clinic too. Justin still does. But one time, there she was, down the street in her car waiting to deal. We all went down and warned her to get out of town before we kicked her ass."

She read the disapproval on Brandon's face. "Or, you know, called the police on her."

"Right."

"You think this lady had something to do with Lauren's murder?" Brooke asked. She leaned forward, her hands on the edge of the table. "If that's true, she might target Justin and me."

"Right now we don't have proof Ruby has harmed anyone."

Brandon might downplay Ruby's involvement in front of Brooke, but it was beginning to sound like Ruby had been dishonest and at the very least withheld information.

"Did you all ever climb the sea stacks on the beach where you camped?"

"I hate heights. Lauren and Adam might have."

"Okay."

"Why?" she asked.

71

"Just part of the investigation."

Best friend or not, Brooke was still a suspect. And Brooke would likely share anything she learned about the investigation with Justin.

"You accused Justin of rape. Is that right?"

The color drained from her face.

"No. I mean. I took it back. It was a misunderstanding."

How could rape be a misunderstanding?

"But you made the accusation. And you're still with him."

"So?"

"Has Justin ever hurt you?" Brandon asked.

"Justin would never hurt anyone."

Yet she somehow felt the need to press charges against him.

"Have you ever suspected Justin had any interest in Lauren?"

Brooke's jaw tightened, and now all the color flooded back at once.

"No."

She slid back from the table and crossed her arms.

"You're making it out like Justin had a thing for Lauren then killed her or something."

"Just asking questions," Brandon said.

"Why? Do you have some sort of evidence—did they have sex?"

"I can't answer that right now," Brandon said.

"Well, it's not possible. Justin was with me all night. And before that too. He wouldn't do that to me."

He abandoned that line of questioning. Any further inquiry about Justin would garner the same defensive response.

Brandon pulled his phone out and scrolled to the picture of the moon pendant. "Did Lauren have a necklace like this?"

She bit her lower lip. "It doesn't look familiar."

"Alright. That's it for now."

Brooke was silent on the trek back to the waiting room. Brandon brought Justin back.

"Do I need a lawyer?" Justin asked before sitting down.

"Have a seat, Mr. Tate," Brandon said. "Whether you obtain an attorney is up to you."

"Am I a suspect?"

"Should you be?"

Justin shook his head as if the question offended him but took the chair across from Brandon.

"Brooke and I didn't do anything wrong."

"Then you have nothing to worry about," Brandon said, leaning back in his chair. He flipped through the notebook he'd brought with him. The notebook was blank, but inside there was a copy of the one-page report Nolan had left him. Brandon considered the report for a while before glancing up at Justin.

"Your girlfriend accused you of rape?"

Justin's right eye twitched. He swallowed hard. "I don't know what you're talking about."

"We're the police, Justin. You don't think we keep records?"

He waved a hand at Brandon. "That was nothing. She made a mistake."

"Made a mistake telling the police what you did, or made a mistake like it never happened?"

"It never happened, okay?"

73

"Then why stay with her? Someone who said something like that about me—"

"Whatever. You're a cop. No one ever says bad stuff about cops."

That, Brandon thought, was one of the top 10 stupidest things he'd ever heard.

"Did you rape her or not?" he asked.

"Brooke? No, man."

"Anyone else?"

"I ain't like that."

"You willing to take a lie detector test, Justin?"

"Hey, screw you, man. You said I wasn't a suspect."

Brandon wasn't seriously considering a lie detector test. Not at this point.

"I didn't say whether you were or weren't," Brandon said.

"What does this have to do with Lauren? Isn't that why I'm here?"

"What really happened the night she disappeared?" Brandon asked.

"We already told you—"

"But now it's just me and you. I want to hear your side of the story."

"We had a few drinks, went to bed," Justin said.

"What about Adam and Lauren?"

He spread his hands out dramatically. "How am I supposed to know?"

"Did they argue?"

"Like I said, not my business what other people do."

"So, they didn't?"

Justin shrugged. "Can't say."

Wouldn't Justin have heard the same argument Brooke did? If Justin and Brooke were colluding, they weren't doing a very good job of it. The argument was a key piece of evidence against Adam, and they couldn't agree if it had even occurred.

"After you all went to bed, did you leave the tent at any time between then and when you woke up?"

"Yeah. I got up to go piss a couple of times."

"You didn't see her then?"

"Nope."

Brandon leaned forward, elbows on the table. "Tell me, Justin. What kind of person was Lauren?"

Justin frowned, and for just a moment, Brandon caught a glimpse of sadness in the kid's eyes. Justin stared at his hands. "Lauren was pretty sweet. A good person."

"How long have you known her?"

"About a year. We worked at the clinic."

"What's your job there?"

"I'm an SUDP trainee—substance use disorder professional—basically a drug counselor. I'm working on my license."

Brandon recalled the first interaction he'd had with Justin—the kid had been cradling a pipe, already stoned, and probably drunk, too.

"You help people with addiction problems?"

"It's a job."

Apparently being an addiction counselor didn't require one to live a sober lifestyle. Not to mention the charge of sexual assault. But he hadn't been convicted, so it wouldn't be on his record.

"And what does Brooke do? Is that how she knew her too?"

"Brooke's a personal trainer. It's why she has such a nice—" He glanced at Brandon. "You know..."

"Okay," Brandon said. "Just one more question."

"Yeah?"

"Did you murder Lauren Sandoval?"

Justin's expression remained stoic. "No."

Justin and Brooke hadn't been gone for more than 10 minutes when shouting rattled the relative silence of the police station. Out in the hallway, Josiah led the intransigent man into the interview room.

Jackson appeared a moment later.

"What do we have?" Brandon asked.

"Tow truck driver," Jackson said.

"The one who dropped Lauren off at the gas station?"

"Yep. Though he didn't admit it at first," Josiah said.

"Did he refuse to come in?" Brandon asked.

"No," Jackson answered. "Josiah insisted on the cuffs."

"Why?"

Jackson pointed a thumb at Josiah. "You'll have to ask him. I'm just a reserve, remember?"

Something had pissed her off. Or someone. Mild-mannered Josiah?

"I'll get started on the first part of this report," she said. "We checked on four drivers and...I'll let Josiah tell you the rest of the story."

Josiah had just finished cuffing the driver to the table.

"Name?" Brandon asked Josiah.

Before he could answer, the man said, "My name is Garrett Zornes. I told him I would talk."

"After you lied to us," Josiah said.

"Uncuff him," Brandon said.

Josiah moved closer to Brandon and whispered, "Nolan says never trust a suspect uncuffed."

"Is Nolan your supervisor?"

76

"No."

"Then do it."

Josiah uncuffed the man. Zornes mumbled something about police brutality.

"Mr. Zornes," Brandon said. "I understand you gave Lauren Sandoval a ride to the convenience store on La Push Road the night she disappeared."

He nodded.

"What did you do when you found out she was missing?"

"I didn't know. I don't get out of the house much."

"You're a tow truck driver," Josiah said. "Do you think we're stupid?"

Brandon raised a hand to silence him. There was a time to be a hard-ass and a time not to. It wasn't something you learned in the academy. Knowing which approach to take took experience and intuition. What skills Josiah might have developed in his brief time on the job had been tainted by Nolan's negative influence.

"You gave her a ride, dropped her off. Then what?" Brandon asked.

"That's it. I went home."

"Chief," Josiah said, "Can I speak to you for a moment?"

They went out into the hallway.

"He's not telling you the whole story."

"That's usually how it goes," Brandon said. "You've got to keep your cool. Playing it rough won't get you anywhere."

"But—"

"Tell me what you know."

77

"We checked with the owner of the company," Josiah said. "This guy was the only one on-call during the time she was killed."

"But the drivers have access to the trucks twenty-four-seven. How do you know it wasn't one of the other guys using the truck off-duty?" Brandon asked.

"The owner has a GPS system on these trucks. He pulled up the history and it showed our guy here at the gas station."

"Then what?"

When Josiah didn't respond, Brandon continued. "According to the GPS, where did he go after the gas station?"

"Home. But here's the thing. At first, he totally denied having any contact with the girl at all."

"Okay. The GPS says he went home for the rest of the evening?" Brandon asked.

"I know what you're thinking, but he could have taken the truck back to his house, pulled the girl into another car, and then to the beach."

"What's his other car?"

"I'm not sure," Josiah admitted.

Josiah followed Brandon back into the interview room.

"Mr. Zornes. You admit now that you dropped the girl off?" Brandon asked.

"Yes."

"Tell us where you found her."

"I was coming back from my buddy's house on the rez. It's by the beach."

He meant the Quileute Reservation.

"Your friend's name?" Brandon asked.

"Randy Troxel. A few other guys too. We were playing poker."

"Okay, and you were on your way home—"

"About a mile past his house, I see this girl sort-of swerving on and off the side of the road. Like there was something wrong with her. I pull up to her and ask if she needs a ride. She got in and right away I could smell the booze."

"Did she appear hurt?" Brandon asked.

"No. Just...pretty buzzed."

"Can you describe her appearance?"

"It was dark, but, you know, she was pretty. Young."

"What was she wearing?"

"That was the weird thing," Zornes said. "All she had on was shorts and a windbreaker."

"What else? About her clothes, I mean."

Lauren had been wearing a yellow and red bikini underneath her shorts. The only way he'd know that was if he'd seen her without her clothes on, meaning, in Brandon's estimation, during a sexual assault.

"Ah, no. Like I said, it was dark." He cleared his throat. "I asked her if she wanted me to wait—if she needed a ride home. She said no, she didn't."

"So, you left her there?" Brandon asked.

"What was I supposed to do?" Zornes asked.

"What did she talk about?"

"She said she needed more beer. Something about men being useless, stuff like that. It wasn't easy to understand her, the way her speech was slurred. I'm hard of hearing in this ear too." He pointed to his right ear.

"Anything else?"

"No...wait. Before she got out, she looked in the window of the gas station and saw Ruby and said something about her being a real bitch." He chuckled. "Can't say I disagree."

This corroborated Brooke's assertion about Lauren's dislike of Ruby.

"Did she say why she thought that?" Brandon asked.

"Nah. Just said that and a few more cuss words and got out. Didn't even say thank you."

Brandon looked to Josiah. "Any questions, Officer Trent?"

"Yes. Mr. Zornes, the first time we contacted you, you claimed you hadn't been out. Now you admit that you were and that you had contact with the girl. Why did you lie?"

"I didn't want my wife to find out," Zornes said.

"That you were with the girl?"

"No. That I was out playing poker. My wife goes to bed early, which leaves me time to go out and spend a few dollars on beer and betting with my buds." Zornes considered Josiah. "You aren't married, are you?"

"Why would that matter?"

Zornes cocked his head with a grin. "Just sayin'."

Brandon tried his best not to laugh.

"You're free to go," Brandon said. "We'll be in touch."

He was pretty sure Zornes had nothing to do with Lauren's disappearance, but he wouldn't rule it out. The information about the relationship between Ruby and Lauren was concerning. If Ruby was dealing to Lauren's clients, and Lauren had threatened Ruby, there was room for motive.

Brandon directed Josiah to go finish the report with Jackson. Jackson had several more years' experience than

Josiah, including a brief stint as a detective. He hoped some of her wisdom would rub off on the young officer, maybe even counteract Nolan's influence.

Back in his office, Brandon checked his cellphone for messages from Tori or Emma. He clicked the power button. His phone was dead.

As he plugged the phone into the charger, his eyes caught on a note taped to the bottom of his computer screen. It was a reminder from Sue—telling him to review the resumes and applications they'd received for Will's position.

Brandon logged into the human resources website where he could check for new applicants. He hadn't been impressed with what he'd seen so far. Supposedly, the county's HR department screened out unworthy applicants. They even performed the basic physical tests before sending the applicants along.

Realizing the overtime gravy train was coming to an end, Nolan had lobbied for Brandon to hire one of his friends—Steve Chilton.

Chilton's background wasn't bad—he had some experience as an officer—but being Nolan's buddy wasn't a positive in Brandon's book. Especially if Chilton had anything like Nolan's approach to police work.

Brandon clicked on the list of names and there was a yellow highlight indicating a new application. He smiled at the name.

Isabel Jackson.

She'd decided to apply after all. He wanted to let her know he was glad she'd applied, but he had to avoid any semblance of favoritism, especially in front of Josiah.

Josiah was a good kid, but Brandon wasn't sure how close he was to Nolan. The last thing Brandon needed was an ethical complaint from Nolan about unfairness in his hiring practices.

As if on cue, Nolan swept past Brandon's office.

Brandon stepped to his door.

"Nolan. You got a minute?"

Brandon returned to his desk. Nolan ambled into the office, leaning his back against the doorjamb.

"Good work on the background checks," Brandon said.

He'd gotten off on the wrong foot with Nolan. Truth be told, he hadn't done a bad job on the report. "I appreciate you contacting the prosecuting attorney, too, to check in on Justin Tate's charges."

"Just doing my job. Like I have for ten years now."

Nolan trained his eyes on Brandon's computer screen. "You doing interviews soon?"

"I hope to," Brandon said. "My first priority is this case though."

"You know, we're not all country bumpkins here. We know how to investigate," he said.

"Understood, but property crimes or DV cases aren't the same as homicide. The case has to be airtight."

Nolan's jaw clenched. "Anything else?"

There was no point in pretending to like Nolan, but the fact was, he was still one of Brandon's officers. "You have ideas about this case?"

"I've been kept in the dark, how could I?"

It was a fair statement.

"Okay," Brandon said. "We'll debrief in five minutes. That work for you?"

Brandon grinned at the surprise on Nolan's face.

"I guess," he said.

Brandon gathered Nolan, Jackson, and Josiah in the station's bullpen. The bullpen had several file cabinets, a kitchenette, and desks for the officers. There was a conference table in the middle of the room. Brandon had brought the whiteboard from his office and set it up on top of the filing cabinet.

He wiped the whiteboard clean and began summarizing the case.

"A young woman, twenty-four years old. Found on the next beach over from her campsite. Scratches and fractures consistent with a fall from a high place, onto her back. She was dragged, presumably directly into the water. Bite marks on her neck, probably from vampire fangs. Metal or some other hard substance. Had intercourse shortly before death. Unsure if consensual. Awaiting DNA results."

"How much longer for the results?" Nolan asked.

"Not sure. Any day now if we're lucky, and that's being hopeful." He turned back to the board. "One of her friends, Justin, has a previous charge of sexual assault against his girlfriend, Brooke. Garrett Zornes dropped her off at the gas station, where she purchased beer and headed back toward the campsite. Some information suggests Lauren and Ruby didn't get along. Despite the distance between town and the beach, Lauren somehow made it back."

"And you think you've found where she was killed?" Jackson asked.

"Maybe. The beer cans match the brand she bought. The necklace—Brooke says she doesn't think it was Lauren's."

"It seems obvious," Nolan said, resting his arms behind his head. "The boyfriend did it."

"Because they argued?" Jackson asked.

"Yeah. I mean, they fought, he took her out at some point and killed her."

"The argument was hours before she died," Brandon said.

"So? I've argued with women longer than that," Nolan said. "Time doesn't heal all wounds."

"And does that make you guilty of homicide?" Jackson said.

Nolan let his chair rest on the floor. "Not the same thing. I'm not a murderer."

"Adam is a suspect, for sure," Brandon said. "But we don't have enough to pin him down."

"So, what's next?" Josiah asked.

"Tomorrow I'm heading up to Port Angeles to see if I can talk to Lauren's mother. I'll pay a visit to Adam, too."

"You need company?" Jackson asked.

Nolan rolled his eyes.

"Sure," he said. He asked Nolan, "You feel like coming up with me tomorrow?"

Nolan waved dismissively. "My day off. I've got lots to do."

Brandon tried to hide his relief. "You working tomorrow, Jackson?"

"Yes," she said.

"We'll leave at nine." Brandon turned to Josiah. "You and Will continue asking around town if anyone laid eyes on the girl the night she died. Oh, yeah, and get ahold of Ruby and see what she's willing to share about her beef with Lauren. Don't focus on the drug dealing. Just press her about Lauren knowing her from Port Angeles."

Brandon scanned the schedule board. He needed to get to work filling Will's position before he found himself down an officer in an already overworked department.

Brandon was already taking over too much of the investigation—work that detectives would manage in most departments. But a full-time detective wasn't in the budget, leaving Brandon as the only person on the force, besides Jackson, with true detective experience.

With the evidence from the sea stack and Ruby's history with Lauren, the number of threads to track was growing, and he'd need every officer available to work the case. He'd have to trust those under his command, including Nolan, even though every bit of intuition he had told him it was a bad idea.

Chapter 14

Brandon picked up takeout on the way home. If he kept eating like this, he would have to ask Sue to get him a new uniform. Not only a new shirt but a larger pair of slacks, too.

By late afternoon, the clouds had cleared, and it was a warmer than usual June evening in Forks. Brandon had the idea to enjoy watching the sun go down, so he grabbed two beers and his dinner and parked himself on the front porch.

He was halfway through the beef teriyaki and fried rice when a glint of orange sunlight flickered across his eyes. Someone had opened a screen door across the street.

Misty stepped out onto her porch, made like she was about to sit down, but then noticed Brandon. It was a bad attempt at pretending she didn't know he was out there.

She crossed the street, a beer in one hand.

"You look lonely," she said, hesitating at the edge of his lawn. "You want company?"

Honestly, he wouldn't mind being alone.

He shifted over as Misty squeezed herself into the narrow spot between Brandon and the porch railing.

"How's the new job?"

"Great," he said, folding the teriyaki container shut. He reached back for his beer and held it up to his mouth. Empty.

He opened the other bottle.

"Hard day, huh?"

"Working a case."

"The girl from Sequim?"

He looked sideways at her. She was so close that it was impossible to make eye contact. "Did Nolan tell you about that?"

She took a sip of her beer. "No."

He didn't believe her.

"If I said yes," she asked, "what would you do? Fire him?"

"I can think of plenty of reasons to fire Nolan."

He regretted the words as soon as they left his mouth. He shouldn't be discussing personnel issues with the girlfriend of one of his officers.

"He's not a bad guy."

Brandon swallowed a long drink. "I never said he was."

He wasn't interested in talking about work.

"Sorry about the diner the other day," she said.

"What about it?"

"Neal acting all weird like that. He can be—"

"You don't need to explain." He thought about it for a minute and then said, "But why didn't you tell me you were with Nolan?"

"I was going to—"

"Never mind," Brandon said. "It's not my business."

Had he misread her at the diner? It seemed to Brandon she'd been flirting. Reliving the past, asking Brandon if he was available.

"Hey," she said, resting her hand on his knee. "Forgive me?"

"For?"

Even in the twilight, he was drawn to the deep, dark hue of her brown eyes. *Brown Eyed Girl*, that was the song he used to sing to her.

She was too close.

"For everything," she said. "All the dumb things I ever did."

He'd been watching her lips. Now, his eyes rose to meet hers, and it was like they were 18 again, sitting on her mom's front porch.

Why did everything remind him of an old song?

Because he was getting older. Too old to waste time.

He leaned in.

It was just like when they were kids. When Brandon went off to boot camp and by the time he got back, she was with someone else.

After all those years together.

And now she was dating Nolan.

What was he thinking?

When their eyes met again, he couldn't let go of her gaze.

Screw it. Why not relive the past, just tonight?

His lips had just brushed against hers when a car rounded the corner onto his street. He pulled back, looking to see who it was.

The car drove slowly, deliberately, as if searching for something. It edged up to Brandon's truck. There were no driveways on his street, so everyone parked next to the curb.

Two figures approached. He stood, setting his beer down behind him.

"Dad!"

Emma sprinted to the porch, wrapping her arms around his neck.

"What are you doing here?"

His eyes rose to Tori, several feet behind Emma.

"We've been calling you all day," Tori said.

Brandon patted his empty pockets. He'd forgotten his personal cell at work, plugged into the charger. He had his department phone, but Tori and Emma didn't have that number yet.

"That still doesn't explain why you're here."

Tori stopped short, her eyes landing on Misty.

"Oh. Hi."

"Hi," Misty said.

"I guess that explains why you didn't return my calls," Tori said.

Misty stood. "I'd better get going."

All three watched Misty cross the street to her house.

"Getting to know the neighbors?" Tori asked.

"I already knew her."

Tori's eyebrows rose in twin arches. "Really?"

They were divorced now. Who cared if he dated? And he wasn't dating anyone, so—

"Ah. I get it," Tori said. "That must be the infamous Misty."

Like most men, Brandon had made the mistake of sharing too much about his exes.

"Knock it off, Mom," Emma said.

"Don't talk to me like that. I've had enough of your disrespect."

"Dammit," Brandon said. "Will someone tell me what's going on?"

They both stared back at him.

"Alright. Come inside."

Brandon closed the door behind them.

"This is what I've been trying to tell you," Emma said. "We don't get along."

"She said she would hitchhike if I didn't take her. I caught her walking toward the highway."

Brandon pointed a finger at Emma. "Not okay. Not even close to okay."

"I wasn't going to actually do it."

Tori sighed, crossing her arms.

"You were supposed to bring her in two weeks," Brandon said. "I'm in the middle of a homicide investigation."

"What's new?" Tori asked dryly.

"And the house isn't ready."

Emma scanned the room, taking in the moving boxes, empty takeout containers, and cans of soda and beer. "Looks fine to me," she said.

Brandon took Tori's hand. "We need to talk."

Outside, Brandon asked, "What's going on, Tori?"

"I can't do this anymore. She hates me."

"Emma doesn't hate you."

Tears welled in her eyes. "You don't know."

Tori slid a hand over her face, folding her arms across her chest.

"She's just upset," he said. "A lot happened this year. Her friend died. We got divorced."

Tori glanced across the street toward Misty's house. "You seem to have moved on."

There was a sadness in her voice. He should be angry with her for driving Emma all the way out here without warning. But they'd raised Emma together for 15 years. Not long ago, Emma and Tori had been best friends, and Brandon had felt like the one left out.

He wrapped his arms around Tori. She leaned into him.

"I'm sorry," he said. "I'll take care of her. A little separation might make things better."

She sniffled. "Absence makes the heart grow fonder, right?"

"Right."

She pulled back. "I'll try to get ahold of myself. I have her things."

They unloaded the car while Emma explored the house. When they finished, they found her in the living room watching a Food Network show.

"Tell your girlfriend I'm sorry," Tori said.

"She's dating one of my officers."

"Oh," Tori said, a glint of relief in her eyes. "Well, anyway."

"You sure you don't want to stay here tonight?" Brandon asked. "It's late, and it's a four-hour drive back home."

Tori's gaze slid down the hallway to Brandon's room, his bed on the floor. "I'd better not."

She walked over to the recliner where Emma had already settled in. Tori bent to hug her. "Love you."

"You too," Emma said, her attention locked on the television.

"Take care of her," Tori said.

"I will."

Brandon thought back to Phoenix Weaver's tarot card warning about family trouble and an unexpected visitor. Her accuracy was uncanny, coincidence or not. Whatever Phoenix might say about Brandon's future, he hoped she was wrong about her other prediction—that there were dark forces at work in Forks.

Brandon shook his head. He didn't have time to speculate on the existence of the occult in his jurisdiction.

He had a daughter to raise, a department to manage, and a murder to solve.

Chapter 15

Brandon let Emma have his bed and he slept on the recliner. His neck and back were stiff by the time he heaved himself out of the chair at 6:30 the next morning. He left Emma 20 dollars and a note telling her she could order a pizza for lunch. There were eggs and bread she could use to make herself breakfast.

He didn't want her wandering around town alone, but just in case, he made sure she had the pepper spray he'd bought her back in Seattle. Emma didn't know Forks, and even small towns had areas that were better to avoid. Not to mention, there was a murderer on the loose.

Brandon and Jackson arrived in Sequim around mid-morning. The plan was to interview Lauren's mother and then head to Adam's work and ask him a few follow-up questions, considering the new evidence they now had. If they had time, they might stop by Lauren's former employer, too.

Jackson drove, giving Brandon a chance to call Lisa Shipley to get an update on the DNA results.

"Any chance they'll expedite the report on the semen found with Lauren?" Brandon asked Lisa.

"I'll check with the lab."

Clallam County used the state patrol crime lab, so Brandon knew it was out of Lisa's hands.

"I won't hold my breath," he said. "Anything you can do helps."

"Speaking of holding your breath, I'm still waiting for you to tell me about why you came back to Forks."

Brandon recalled the conversation they'd had on the beach the day they found Lauren. He glanced at Jackson. He wasn't about to set a date with the coroner in front of one of his officers.

"Yeah. Sure. That'd be great. I gotta go. I'll call you later."

She paused. "Okay."

Brandon hung up.

"What was that about?" Jackson asked.

"Just getting an update from the coroner."

"Hmm."

"What?" Brandon demanded.

He tried to ignore the glint in her eye. "The exchange at the end there was a little awkward."

Brandon pointed ahead. "Keep your eyes on the road. And mind your own business."

Jackson turned back to the road, making no effort to hide the smart-ass smile crossing her lips.

Sequim was about 20 minutes east of Port Angeles, part of the Olympic Rain Shadow. It was a popular West Coast retirement community for Californians fleeing expensive, overpopulated cities for life in the beautiful Pacific Northwest—sans the rainfall. The difference between Forks and Sequim was striking: 119 inches of rainfall per year in Forks versus 16 in Sequim.

While the influx of retirees from across the west helped the tax base, not all locals were happy about the newcomers. The easiest way to spot an out-of-towner was the way they pronounced the city's name. Outsiders would ask about see-quim, pronouncing the name as it was spelled; but the correct pronunciation was squim, like squid with an 'm' at the end.

Lauren's mother lived in a remodeled turn of the nineteenth century two-story, dark blue with a white picket fence surrounding a healthy patch of grass. Rose bushes lined the inside of the fence, the flowers in their full glory, red, white, and pink.

It was too happy a picture for what Lauren's family must be going through.

Brandon knocked on the door and Lauren's mother, a Latina woman in her forties, answered. She considered their uniforms, then seemed to recognize Brandon from the night he'd notified her of Lauren's death. Without a word, she led them to a room with a couch and two chairs.

Brandon and Jackson sat on the couch, Lauren's mother across from them. On the wall were photos of Lauren, ranging from baby pictures to elementary school, junior high, and prom. Brandon knew from his previous visit that Lauren's father had left the home when Lauren was 15. The family hadn't heard from him since then.

"Mrs. Sandoval," Brandon said. "This is Officer Jackson."

Her eyes were swollen, raw with grief.

"I want to say again how sorry we are about Lauren," Jackson said.

Mrs. Sandoval's vacant gaze seemed stuck on the cushion between Brandon and Jackson.

"I talked to the coroner when I identified Lauren," she said.

Brandon hoped Lisa Shipley hadn't shared too much. Facts were facts but could be misinterpreted by the public.

"She said Lauren didn't drown. That she had fallen and was—"

There was a tissue box on the table next to the couch. Jackson pulled two out and handed them to Mrs.

Sandoval. She wiped her eyes and took a deep breath, forcing the words out. "That she was already dead by the time she went into the water."

Mrs. Sandoval eyed Brandon. "Is that true?"

"It would seem so, yes," he said.

They were all silent, the dull, lonely ticking of the clock on the mantel the only sound in the room.

After a moment, Mrs. Sandoval said, "Lauren was a beautiful girl. Smart. The kindest person. Always wanted to help people. That's why she became a counselor."

"She worked at the methadone clinic?" Jackson asked.

"Lauren counseled addicts there. It's not just doling out medication, you know? They do help people. Talk to them. That was her passion."

"Did Lauren ever struggle with addiction herself?" Brandon asked. Lauren had consumed a significant amount of alcohol the day she died.

"In the past, when she was younger."

"How long ago?" Brandon asked.

"After her father left. She started drinking, and worse. But she got clean. Went to school."

It seemed Lauren's mother was unaware of Lauren's ongoing struggle with alcohol abuse. Like many addicts, Lauren had probably worked hard to hide the truth from her family.

"How well did you know Adam, Lauren's boyfriend?" Brandon asked.

Mrs. Sandoval peered at Brandon, then Jackson. "Did he do this to her?"

"We're just starting our investigation, Mrs. Sandoval."

"You suspect him?"

"Is there a reason you believe Adam might hurt Lauren?"

96

"I met him once or twice. He seemed like a nice young man. Strait-laced. But I'm her mother. I should have known."

She began sobbing.

After a few moments, Jackson said, "This isn't your fault."

"Was there anything about Adam that concerned you?"

She neatly folded the tissue. For a moment, Brandon figured she must not have heard him. Finally, she answered, "No."

"Anyone else? An ex-boyfriend?"

"Everyone loved my Lauren."

"What about at work? One of the clients?" Jackson asked.

"Sometimes people would get mad at her. Like if she had to report them for relapsing. There are rules, you know. If someone is on probation."

"No specific threats?"

"No," she said. Then, "Wait. There was a woman. A drug dealer trying to sell to her clients. Lauren confronted the lady, told her to stay away from the clinic."

The story about a woman selling drugs near the clinic confirmed what Brooke had said about Ruby.

"Did anything come of that?"

"Lauren was furious, threatened to report her to the police. I don't know what happened after that."

"Anything else that might be helpful?"

She shook her head. "I'm sorry."

"I want you to know we have every officer involved in this investigation."

"Tell me, what do you know about what happened to my daughter? I have to know."

Brandon weighed how much to reveal. He imagined what it would be like if Emma had been the victim, and how he'd feel being helpless, waiting for a stranger to bring his daughter's killer to justice.

"The coroner is in charge of finding any clues left with Lauren when she died. We think she might have been pushed off a cliff or one of the sea stacks."

"Why would someone do that to Lauren?"

"That's my job to find out. We've been interviewing her friends. Adam, Brooke, and Justin," Brandon said.

"Who is Justin?"

"Brooke's boyfriend."

"Oh," she said.

"Have you met Brooke? I gather she and Lauren were close."

"Once. A couple of months ago," Mrs. Sandoval said with something like a sneer.

"You didn't like her?" Jackson asked.

"She reminded me of a snotty rich girl."

Interesting observation. Brandon wouldn't have characterized Brooke that way.

"Okay. And we do know at some point during the night Lauren went from her campsite into town."

"Alone?"

"It appears that way, but she did get a ride. We're not sure what happened between then and when she was found."

"Was my daughter raped?" she asked in a matter-of-fact tone. "The coroner wouldn't say."

"We'll have to leave it up to the coroner to determine that."

98

There was no need to go over the presence of semen or the DNA evidence with the girl's mother. They were still waiting for results.

He changed the topic. "Take a look at this for me," he said, pulling out his phone. He clicked on the picture of the necklace he'd found at the beach.

"Did you ever see Lauren wearing this?"

"No. That's not hers."

"Not familiar at all?"

"No. Sorry."

"Okay. That's all for now. Please let us know if you think of anything else."

"Thank you," Mrs. Sandoval said. She fixed her eyes on Jackson. "You said you wanted to help me. Then find the person who did this to my daughter."

"We will," Brandon said, halting just short of a promise.

Chapter 16

"Where to now?" Jackson asked.

"Lunch. Then I'd like to have a few words with Adam. And I want to follow up on this lead about the dealer."

"You think it's Ruby?"

"Sounds like it."

Brandon had asked Will and Josiah to contact Ruby and ask her about her history with Lauren. He called Will and asked if they'd been able to get ahold of Ruby. They'd gone out to her house, but no one answered. He told them to keep trying.

Brandon and Jackson stopped for lunch at the Taco Time in Sequim.

He ordered a taco salad because it sounded healthy. But he knew it wouldn't fill him up, so he got a deep-fried burrito to go with it. So much for losing weight.

He hadn't brought any of his workout equipment with him to Forks. It had been in storage for years thanks to an annual membership at a local fitness club. But that was back in Seattle. He'd have to find a gym, or his health would go down the crapper.

At least he'd had enough self-control to forgo the mexi fries.

Jackson ordered a soft taco and while they ate they made small talk about her family.

"My father is from Cuba," she said.

"Your mom?"

"Blonde as Marilyn Monroe," she said. "Crazy as her too. I still love her, though."

"You stay in touch?"

"I go back to Florida when I can afford it. My husband, he's supportive of me visiting my family."

"But he'd rather stay home?"

"Right," she said. "Mostly, I miss the food, the culture."

"Not much Cuban cuisine in Forks," Brandon said.

"Or anywhere in this corner of the country." She pointed a finger at him. "One time, I asked someone if there were any Cuban restaurants in the area. You know what they told me?"

"What?"

"They said, 'we have Mexican. Isn't that the same thing?'"

Brandon laughed, almost choking on his bean burrito. He took a drink of water. "I saw your application."

"I should have told you I applied."

"I was happy to see it. You're sure this is what you want to do?"

"Be a cop?" she asked.

"Go back full time. I mean, you talked about missing your kids."

"Am I being interviewed right now?" she asked, the tone in her voice suddenly harder.

"No—"

"Because you can't ask bullshit questions like that. You know that, right?"

"Like what?"

"About a woman's family, whether she's pregnant."

Was she pregnant?

He waved a hand at her. "Just making conversation, Jackson. This has nothing to do with your application."

She was right, he should know better. In fact, he shouldn't be talking to her about the job at all.

Brandon's phone buzzed. There was a text from Emma: *There's nothing to eat.*

He replied: I left you $20. Did you see my note?

A minute later, she wrote: *Sorry. LOL.*

He smiled. "My daughter."

Jackson took the last bite of her soft taco, wadded the paper wrapper into a ball, and tossed it on the table. "I didn't mean to get so pissed," she said. "It's just...people make all kinds of assumptions about women being cops. That's bad enough, but then you have babies and everyone thinks you should retire."

Brandon nodded in agreement, not wanting to say anything else to set her off again.

"I do have doubts," she continued. "It's not the same as before I had kids. Back then, all I cared about was making detective. Catch the bad guys no matter what, no matter the risk. Now, with kids, I have someone else to protect."

"I get it," Brandon said. "Things were different after we had Emma. It reminds me of that story, *The Shot.*"

"The what?"

"*The Shot.* It's a story by Alexander Pushkin."

"Never heard of him," she said.

"He's the father of Russian literature."

"Oh, well. I'm sure everyone knew that—except me. You sure you grew up in Forks?"

"Don't knock my hometown. Some of the smartest people I know live there. Smarter than a lot of know-it-alls I met in Seattle."

"So, what brought you back here?"

"My dad's all alone now," he said. It was more than that, but that was the pat answer he'd prepared for anyone who asked. "That, and it's good to come back home."

"Your brother Eli was a big deal in the department."

"Everyone loved Eli," Brandon said.

"You get along with him?" She stared back at him. "I mean, it's okay if you didn't. I come from a big family, sisters, brothers, cousins. Always someone fighting."

"He was my brother." Brandon paused. "Look, it's not that I didn't think he was the greatest guy on earth. I did. I don't like talking to other people about it."

"Sorry. I shouldn't have—"

"No. It's fine. I've got to get used to it. They named a stretch of highway after him, for God's sake."

"It's a big deal when an officer dies in the line of duty," she said.

"They never solved Eli's murder."

She was silent, and Brandon said, "But I will find out who murdered my brother."

"You've been working on his case?" she asked.

"Not officially, no. But I've reviewed the evidence. Unofficially."

"The less I know, the better. For now. I am just a reserve, after all." She forced a smile, obviously trying to lighten the heaviness of the moment. "You were going to tell me about the Russian guy."

"Right. Pushkin wrote this story about a young man who thinks he owns the world, can do what he wants to whoever he wants. One thing leads to another, and he challenges a man to a duel—with pistols. Back then, in Russia, it wasn't like the Wild West here in America. The duelists took turns."

"Damn."

"Right? So the older gentlemen he'd challenged let the kid go first, and he misses. Now it's the old man's turn to take a shot. What does the kid do? Sits there, eating cherries out of his hat like he doesn't give a damn if he dies or not. Anyway, the old man decides he'll reserve his shot for later."

"You can do that?"

"Hell if I know, but that's how the story goes."

"It ends there?"

"Years pass, the kid grows up and falls in love. Is about to be married."

"He has something to live for," she said.

"Right. And that's when the old man appears and demands the right to take his shot at the kid. Did I mention the old man was a sharpshooter?"

"Did the kid run away?" she asked.

"Nope."

"The old man killed him?"

"Missed on purpose. The point is, things are different when you have something to live for. It's the same whether you're a man or a woman." He slid their trays off the table and threw the trash in the garbage.

Back in the car, Jackson said, "You asked Nolan to come up with you today first, before asking me."

"Yep."

"Why?"

"I'm trying to get him on track. And avoid any semblance of favoritism," he said.

"Toward me?" she asked, failing to suppress a smile.

"I've given you a lot of leeway, and responsibility, on this case. Nolan, not so much. No doubt he'll have plenty more to say when I don't hire his buddy."

"Well, I'm still applying, whether Nolan likes it or not," she said.

"That's good news to my ears," Brandon said. "But you never heard that from me."

Adam worked at the Hurricane Ridge Café in Sequim. It was the middle of the day and except for the chic decorations and aroma of espresso, the place could have been an old folk's home. The average age of the customers had to be at least 65. Like most of the cafes in Sequim, Hurricane Ridge was a standard hang out for the older generation, a place to tell war stories or complain about the state of the world.

Retirees lounged around tables, as many women as there were men.

No one was in line.

The barista greeted them. "Can I help you?"

"Quad Americano. Twelve ounce," Brandon said. He scanned the room for any sign of Adam. He had claimed he was a shift manager.

"You want something?" Brandon asked Jackson. "It's on me."

"I'll get my own. Thanks."

"Suit yourself."

They waited for their drinks at the end of the espresso bar. When the barista handed him the Americano, Brandon asked. "Is Adam in today?"

"His day off," she said. The woman was in her mid-thirties with short black hair in a sort of bob. Brandon didn't normally like short hair, but she was definitely attractive. Maybe it was her smile.

"Thanks," he said, smiling back at her.

"You're up from Forks," she said, glancing at his uniform. "Is this about Adam's ex-girlfriend?"

"Ex?"

She frowned. "Lauren. Too bad."

"Tell me, what's your name?" Brandon asked.

"Stacy. And you?"

"Brandon."

Brandon waited while Stacy worked the machine. Jackson had ordered a latte. The rush and gurgle of the steam made conversation impossible.

A minute later, she poured Jackson's drink and set it on the counter.

"Adam was pretty upset by Lauren's death?" Jackson asked, grabbing her latte.

"Well, yeah," Stacy said. "I mean, despite what happened."

Brandon and Jackson glanced at each other.

"I said something I shouldn't have," Stacy said.

"Not at all," Brandon said. "Do me a favor. Give me your name and number."

He passed her one of his business cards. He'd found them in the box Sue had given him his first day.

"Write it down on the back of this," he said.

"Is Adam in trouble?" Stacy asked.

"We're hoping to learn everything we can about Lauren and her friends."

"Okay." She scribbled her number on the card.

"Why did Adam and Lauren break up?" Brandon asked.

"They were always on again, off again. But this time I figured it was over. Adam believed she was cheating on him. You didn't know any of this?"

"That's why we're asking," Jackson said.

Stacy looked askance at Jackson before turning to Brandon.

"They were supposed to go camping," Stacy said. "Adam decided not to go, but then at the last minute, he changed his mind."

106

"Why?"

"Adam tried to make things work, despite his suspicions. He's a great guy. Too nice, if you know what I mean."

"Why did Adam believe Lauren was cheating?"

"Something about emails on her phone."

"He was spying on her?" Jackson asked.

"You'll have to ask Adam..."

"Did he say who Lauren was with?"

"I don't think he knew. Or at least he didn't tell me."

"He trusts you?" Brandon asked.

"I'm just one of those people that, you know, everyone thinks they can share their secrets with. It's a gift—and a curse."

Brandon handed her another business card. "Call me—for any reason."

She winked at him. "I will."

As they headed for the car, Jackson said, "She seemed nice."

"Yep."

"Kind of flirty, but nice. Maybe not as nice as the coroner..."

"Alright, knock it off," he said.

"Just sayin'."

Chapter 17

Adam lived in a one-story apartment complex a couple of miles from the café. The layout was more like a trio of fourplexes. Few buildings in Sequim stood higher than one story, except the old Victorians and a handful of brick structures left over from the turn of the nineteenth century.

Adam was in unit A3. Brandon gave the door three loud raps and waited.

"Chief Mattson from Forks Police."

The door opened. Adam stood there, skinny arms and legs sticking out of a sleeveless t-shirt and a pair of baggy shorts, the appearance of a young man who never worked out but didn't eat much either. His blonde curls were pressed against one side of his head as if he'd just woken up.

"You can come in," he said, his voice raspy.

The place had an open concept—if that term could be applied to an apartment smaller than a two-car garage. The living room and kitchen were one room and shared the same linoleum floor. Straight ahead down a narrow hallway, the bathroom door was open. The bedroom must be back there too. The place was clean. No dirty dishes, no clothes thrown haphazardly about.

Adam didn't ask them to have a seat.

"You have a maid?" Brandon asked.

"No. Why?"

"Your place. It's tidier than I'd expect."

Adam forced a chuckle. "You mean because I'm a bachelor in my early twenties? I like things neat. Organized."

He was a control freak. Good to know.

"You live alone?" Jackson asked.

"Always have," he said. "What's this about? Did you find out something about Lauren?"

"How come you didn't tell us you and Lauren had broken up?" Brandon asked.

Adam's arm twitched, his eyes set on the front door. For a moment, Brandon thought the kid might try to make a run for it. But something held him there.

"We didn't break up."

"But you were going to," Brandon said.

Adam stood silent for several seconds. They were giving him a chance to tell his side of the story. He wasn't doing himself any favors hiding the truth from them.

"It's not the end of the world if you broke up with her," Jackson said, her voice taking on a calmer, more soothing tone. "But the more you talk, the better it will be for you. Do you want us to trust you, to believe what you've told us?"

"Yeah."

"Then you need to tell us everything," Jackson said.

Adam ran a hand across his cheek. He hadn't shaved in a couple of days. A sign of stress for someone as clean-cut as Adam.

"I planned on ending it. After the camping trip," he paused. "Unless..."

"Unless things improved?" Brandon asked.

"Yeah. I mean, we'd split before and got back together."

"Why did you want to break up with Lauren?" Jackson asked.

"I...this is going to sound really bad."

"You let us decide that," Brandon said. Jackson shot him a warning glance. She clearly didn't want Brandon stepping all over her good-cop routine.

"Trust me," Jackson said. "You're going to feel a lot better when this is out in the open."

Adam sat down in one of the two wooden chairs at his kitchen table.

"Sometimes, Lauren would stay the night. One time, I checked her cellphone. I don't know why I did it."

"You knew the password?" Jackson asked.

"I'd watched her enter it a hundred times."

"What did you find?" Brandon asked.

"Emails. From some guy. About how they'd hooked up."

"Did you confront her about it?"

"Not at first. I mean, I didn't want her to know I'd been spying on her."

"But you stayed with her?" Brandon asked.

"I tried to forget about the whole thing."

Adam had let Lauren walk all over him. But that didn't mean he wasn't a murderer.

"What happened when you confronted Lauren?" Jackson asked.

"She denied everything. Said what I saw was an old email from a previous boyfriend. Before she'd met me."

"But the dates on the emails—" Jackson said.

"She had an excuse for that. Said she'd forwarded them to herself."

"Why would she do that?" Brandon said, asking the obvious question.

"I don't know. I just wanted to move on."

"Meaning stay with her," Brandon said.

"I guess."

"What did you two argue about the night she disappeared?" Jackson asked.

"I already told you all. Nothing, or at least I don't remember."

Brandon considered Adam. He wanted to believe the kid was telling the truth—that he was just a pushover who'd been duped by his girlfriend and whoever had killed her.

"You don't know who the emails came from?"

"No. There wasn't a name. Just a bunch of letters and numbers."

"We've learned that Lauren hitched a ride into Forks before she died," Brandon said.

"After we fell asleep?"

"Sometime after midnight," Brandon said. "You didn't notice she was missing?"

He shook his head, no. "What the hell was she doing? Was there someone with her?"

"Another man?" Brandon asked.

Adam backtracked. "Anyone. I mean, maybe Brooke and Lauren went out or something."

"She was alone. Someone dropped her off at the gas station."

"And whoever gave her a ride back—that's who killed her?" Adam asked.

"We don't know that," Brandon said.

"You're sure you didn't see her come back?" Brandon asked.

"I didn't."

"You didn't hear anything? Voices? Arguing?" Jackson asked.

111

"No."

"We think she might have fallen or been pushed off the sea stack near your campsite," Brandon said. He watched Adam's face, but it remained as vacant as before. "When she came back, she drank beer with someone, up on the rock."

"Who?"

Crimson envy tinged his freckled cheeks, rage boiling beneath his friendly, passive demeanor. Adam might be a pushover, but like all red-blooded men, there was a breaking point.

"I know this is hard for you," Jackson said, using her tone to soothe him. "But we just don't know yet. That's why we're asking questions."

Brandon tried not to roll his eyes. They needed Adam to crack, not reveal his inner hurts.

"You think you know who she might have been with?" Brandon asked. "Another man?"

Adam sucked in a breath, stared down at his feet. "I don't know."

When he looked up again, the rage was gone, stuffed back into the dark place where Adam hid his anger from the world.

They weren't getting anywhere. On a hunch, Brandon asked, "Can I use your restroom?"

Adam glanced toward the bathroom as if considering the request. "Sure."

Brandon made his way down the hallway, briefly glancing into Adam's bedroom. The bed was unmade, but the room generally sparse and clean. On the wall above the bed was a framed vintage movie poster. The movie, *Blood of the Vampire*, reminded Brandon of the old black-and-white B-rate flicks he used to watch Saturday nights when he was a kid. A woman lay on her back, neck exposed, terror writhing her face as a vampire crept closer. The byline started, *"No woman alive is safe..."*

Brandon went into the bathroom and waited a minute, flushed the toilet, ran the water as if washing his hands, and came back out.

He paused at the bedroom door, directing a question at Adam. "You a fan of vampire flicks?"

"Ah, no. That poster was Lauren's."

"She decorated your bedroom for you?"

"Lauren gave it to me."

"So, you tacked it to the wall above your bed," Brandon said.

"Yeah."

"One more thing," Brandon said, pulling out his phone and scrolling to the photo of the necklace found near Lauren's body. "Does this look familiar?"

He took the phone from Brandon and studied the necklace with the crescent moon pendant. "Uh. Sort of. I'm not sure. Why?"

"Did Lauren ever wear it?"

"I don't think so. I mean, I didn't pay attention to everything she wore."

"Alright," Brandon said, taking the phone back. He handed him a business card. Jackson did the same. "Call either one of us if there's something else you remember. And don't plan on any out-of-town trips. Understood?"

"Yes."

In the SUV, Brandon said, "We got crossed up back there."

"How so?"

"I know the good cop, bad cop thing can work—"

"That's not what—"

"You were being easy on him, I wasn't. That works, sometimes. But if I'm trying to break someone, it doesn't help if you step in and act like his mother—"

"That's not fair."

"Maybe not. But he was getting pissed. Did you see the rage?"

"I guess."

"I think you did, and you didn't like it, so you tried to cover it up, tried to make him feel better. That's not your job. If he needs a counselor, he can go find one—"

"Okay, damn. Get off my back." She paused. "Chief."

He wanted to say more, but she didn't need a lecture. He'd gotten the point across, and that was good enough.

On the way to the methadone clinic in Port Angeles, they compared notes.

"Give me your impression of Adam," Brandon said.

"He hasn't been totally truthful, until now."

"You believe he doesn't know who Lauren was cheating with?"

"I think he honestly wanted to believe she wasn't cheating at all," Jackson said. "But then again, I *was* acting like his mother."

The sarcasm bit at Brandon. He shouldn't have made the mother comment.

"Alright. I'm sorry," he said. "Let's move on. Give me a summary of what we know so far."

"Adam and Lauren have a rocky relationship. She disappears while camping with Adam and two other friends. Last seen buying beer, alone. Probably drank the beer with someone she knew out on a sea stack. Someone with a motive to kill her."

114

"You think the bite mark means anything?" Brandon asked.

"It definitely means something; I just don't know what. My first thought was it's some sort of kinky thing, connected to sex. But the coroner said the bite occurred after she died. You mentioned a poster in Adam's bedroom."

Brandon described the poster.

Jackson shook her head. "It doesn't feel right. It's too simple. And he's not acting guilty. I know, all perps don't act guilty and sometimes the easiest answer is the right answer."

"Exactly what I was about to say."

"That's why I said it first."

The clinic was about half an hour away. They drove in silence for a while, until Jackson said, "Maybe the bite mark has more importance than we think. I mean, there is that whole vampire symbol thing everyone's talking about."

Brandon wasn't convinced the graffiti had any connection to Lauren's murder.

"I need to follow-up with this guy Vasile—some sort of vampire expert. Not that I take any of that seriously. But he might give us a lead on where we might find the fangs we're looking for."

"Sounds interesting," she said.

"Nothing like a freak show to muddy up an investigation."

On their way from Sequim to Port Angeles, they passed a furniture store, reminding Brandon he needed to get a bed and dresser for Emma.

"You mind if we stop here for a sec?"

"Don't go there," she said. "They're overpriced and they use cheap materials."

"You know a better place? I need someone to deliver."

"In Port Angeles. I'll show you."

He was glad she'd moved on from being pissed about the mother comment. He needed Jackson on his side—she'd been supportive of Brandon, so far. Not to mention, she was a good investigator.

Jackson directed him to a warehouse furniture store in Port Angeles. Brandon purchased a bed and dresser. Upon hearing he only had a recliner in the living room, Jackson talked him into buying a couch and love seat too.

"What if you ever have company over?"

"As if," Brandon said.

"And if you want to watch TV with your daughter? You only have one chair."

"Good point."

The final purchase was enough to qualify for free delivery. They were in and out of the store in under 30 minutes.

The site manager for the methadone clinic where Lauren had worked wasn't in, but they were able to talk to a shift supervisor.

The supervisor, a woman named Cynthia, was newer and hadn't known Lauren long.

"Lauren was a lead too, but more on the counseling side. I'm in charge of the methadone distribution."

"Did Lauren ever mention feeling threatened by the clients?"

"No. But again, we didn't talk much. If there's a threat by a client, we have a protocol for that. Not that Lauren was a fan of following the rules."

"What do you mean?" Jackson asked.

"A while back, we had some trouble with a dealer targeting patients."

It sounded like the stories they'd heard about Ruby.

"What did Lauren do?" Brandon asked.

"Found out where the lady was parked, two or three blocks away. Threatened to turn her in. At least that's the rumor."

It was another confirmation of Brooke's claim that Ruby and Lauren had it in for each other.

"What became of the dealer? Did Lauren call the police?"

"I don't know."

"You said, 'she,'" Jackson said. "This dealer was a woman?"

"So they say. The clients I mean. I'm sure Lauren had good intentions. But you can't go targeting dealers." She considered Brandon. "It sounds like she was trying to do the police's job for them."

Brandon ignored the jab. "Anything else?"

"That might help you in your investigation? No. Except, well, I can say she didn't keep the best of company."

"Her friends?"

"Shady characters if you ask me," she said. "One of them works here—when he shows up."

"Is his name Justin?"

She nodded. "Justin Tate."

"What about a young man named Adam?" Jackson asked. "Her boyfriend."

"Boyfriend? Never heard of him."

"Any other friends?"

Brandon was thinking of Brooke.

"Look, I'm new here—"

There was a knock at the door and a staff member poked her head in to ask Cynthia a question about a client asking for an exception to dosing rules. Cynthia seemed to take that as her cue to end the conversation.

Brandon passed her his card and they left Cynthia to her work.

They were mostly silent on the way back to Forks, and Brandon thought Jackson had fallen asleep. He appreciated the time to think through the case. Some things didn't fit—like the necklace. Both Adam and Brooke—the two people closest to Lauren—suggested the necklace didn't belong to Lauren. It could be a coincidence it happened to be near where Brandon had found the beer cans. Of course, that she had bought those specific cans was an assumption. He wouldn't be sure until he heard back about any DNA or fingerprints.

Then there were the bite marks. Adam had a vampire poster on his wall, but so did a lot of other people who frequented Forks. Adam had motive—Lauren had been cheating on him. But unlike Justin, Adam had no history of assault.

The dealer Lauren had confronted was obviously Ruby. Was she angry enough at Lauren to murder her?

Ten miles outside Forks, dispatch sent out a call about a break-in at the Darklove Damsel store—the shop owned by Phoenix Weaver. Will responded that he would take the call.

"Drop me off at the Darklove store," Brandon said.

"It's just a burglary. I'm sure Will can handle it," Jackson said.

"He can, but I already interviewed the owner about the bite marks."

Jackson dropped him off in front of Phoenix's shop. Will was already inside.

"Hey, Chief," Will said.

"Don't mind me," Brandon said.

Phoenix glanced at Brandon before continuing. "I haven't taken full inventory yet, so I don't know everything that's missing. But at the very least, several tomes on the occult. All of my vampire books."

"All?"

"Well, at least the more serious ones."

"Any reason why you're calling just now?" Will asked, "At three in the afternoon."

"I keep my own hours," Phoenix said. "I know my customers, and it makes no sense for me to open up at seven in the morning."

"How did they enter?" Will asked.

"Back here."

Phoenix led them through a black curtain to the back of the shop. The small storage area was mostly empty.

The door handle to the rear entrance had been smashed off.

"It was like this when I got here," she said.

"Looks like someone took a sledgehammer to it," Will said.

"Yeah, and they didn't have good aim," Brandon said, pointing out the scratches and dents where the object, whatever it was, had slammed the door but not the handle. The disfigured metal doorknob was on the ground a foot away.

"You smell that?" Brandon asked.

"Spray paint," Will responded.

Brandon stepped back. A few feet away, on the back wall of the shop, someone had used spray paint to form the same dagger ankh found outside of the Forks Diner. Crimson paint dripped down the brick wall. It was still fresh.

"Was this here when you came in earlier?"

"I would have noticed that," Phoenix said, her voice full of fear. "It is the symbol of the vampire." She eyed Brandon. "Did you talk to Vasile?"

"I haven't had time—"

She latched onto Brandon. "I warned you, officer—"

"Ma'am, he's not an officer," Will said. "He's the chief of police."

She narrowed her eyes at Will. "The undead respect no rank."

Brandon lifted her hand off his arm. "Your friend Vlad is on my list."

"His name is Vasile."

"Why would these vampire people target your shop?" Will asked.

"I don't know. I haven't done anything against their kind."

"You think Vasile did this?" Brandon asked.

"I did not..." Her voice broke. "Don't tell anyone I said that."

"Okay, Miss...Phoenix," Will said. "We're going to check around a bit more. We'll let you know if we have more questions."

When Phoenix had gone, Will said, "Did you see that? She's terrified of this Vasile fellow."

"It seems so."

"But why?"

"Your guess is as good as mine. You've got to admit. She's a little off her rocker," Brandon said.

"I say she's afraid and there must be a reason."

"Okay," Brandon said, wanting a change of topic. He'd heard enough of vampires for one day. "Let's take a look around."

They searched the alley. There was no sign of a discarded spray paint can.

"Ask around at the local hardware shops," he said. "There can't be too many folks buying red spray paint in a town this small."

"You want prints?" Will asked.

"Off the back door, yes. I'll trust your judgment about inside. The problem is, there are customer prints all over the place in there. Was there any cash missing?"

"She said no."

"Okay. I'll let you finish up here."

Brandon started down the alley.

"Brandon," Will called out after him.

"What's up?"

"This vampire stuff," Will said. "You know, the symbols, the bite on the neck. People stealing books on dark magic. You think it's connected?"

"To Lauren Sandoval's murder?"

"The symbol is the same as the one at the diner. I mean, it's possible some vampire freak is out to get people."

"The problem is," Brandon said. "I don't believe in vampires."

"That don't stop some people from acting like one, though."

Finding out who was behind the ankhs could be the break that led them to Lauren's murderer. Whether they were a vampire enthusiast or someone posing as one didn't matter to Brandon, as long as he caught the killer before they struck again.

Chapter 18

Brandon hiked the half mile to the station, entering through the front door.

"There you are," Sue said. "There's someone waiting for you."

He looked at the empty reception area.

"She's in your office."

Sue let a stranger into Brandon's office?

"Before you get all miffed at me, just...go see."

Brandon shook his head and headed back.

He found Emma lounging in his chair, her feet propped on his desk.

"I got bored," she said before he could ask why she'd showed up at his work.

"So, what, they arrested you?"

He pointed to her feet and she slid them from the desk.

"I was looking for you," she said. "Sue told me I could hang out here."

"A police station isn't the best place for kids."

"Yeah, it's really boring."

Jackson popped her head in the door.

"Hi, Isabel," Emma said.

"Is there anyone you haven't met?"

"She was bored, so—"

"I heard."

"We owe her three dollars," Emma said.

"We? For what?"

"It's on me. Don't worry about it," Jackson said.

"We went out for ice-cream," Emma said.

"Thank you," Brandon said to Jackson. To Emma, he said, "Out of my seat. I have work to do."

"Come on out here and I'll show you what police officers do for fun," Jackson said.

"What is it?" Emma asked.

"Writing reports."

Brandon answered a handful of emails, ignoring several from the mayor and her henchwoman, the Minister of Tourism.

He deleted a reminder about a presentation to the city council. He didn't have time for planning committees, public relations get-togethers or, God forbid, uniform design meetings.

Jackson had sent him a draft report of their visit to Sequim and Port Angeles. He had a few additional notes, but otherwise, the summary was thorough and well written.

Brandon switched off his computer. He found Emma in the common area with Jackson and Sue. Emma was speaking to a woman in a vampire cape.

The vampire spun to Brandon. It was the mayor. She plucked a pair of plastic fangs out of her mouth.

"Chief Mattson, I just met your daughter."

"I see that."

"She's a lovely young lady."

"She gets it from her mom," Brandon said.

Next to the mayor stood Ted the reporter and Olivia.

"What is he doing in here?" Brandon asked, motioning to Ted.

"Oh, calm down, Brandon. We were hoping for a photo of me and the officers."

"Wearing that?"

"It's part of our promotion for the Moonbeam Festival."

"Come on, Dad," Emma said.

"I'm not taking a picture with a role-playing—"

"I'll do it," Jackson said. "My kids would think it was great."

It never hurt to show the police in a positive light, considering the way the media usually covered law enforcement. In Seattle, there was a whole department dedicated to public relations.

"Fine. But not in here."

"In the lobby then," the mayor said.

On their way out, Ted caught up to Brandon. "Hey, Chief, any comment on the Sandoval girl?"

"Ongoing investigation. No comments."

Ted grimaced. "Is Neal Nolan in?"

Brandon followed Ted's eyes—studying the schedule board.

"Hoping for a leak on the case?" Brandon asked.

"Just wondering."

Brandon extended his arm toward the door.

"Out. Now."

When they had all gone, Brandon said to Sue, "No unauthorized visitors in this area. We've got confidential information on open cases in here."

"It's the mayor, what am I supposed to do?"

"Call me if you have to. I'll take care of the mayor and her entourage."

As he pulled up to the curb in front of the house, Brandon realized he hadn't gone grocery shopping. Between Emma's surprise appearance and the investigation, he hadn't even thought about dinner.

125

Brandon had just slid his key into the lock when they heard Misty calling out from across the street.

"Hey! You all hungry?"

He'd planned on catching up with Emma and talking through their plans for the summer.

"Totally," Emma said before Brandon could stop her.

Misty crossed his lawn, a casserole dish nestled in one arm, a bag of tortilla chips in the other.

"Enchiladas," she said. "My recipe."

Brandon must have had a thoroughly ungrateful expression because Misty said, "You don't have to take it."

"You should have dinner with us," Emma said.

"You sure?" Misty asked, looking to Brandon.

"Come in," he said. "We didn't have plans anyway."

Brandon spent most of the next hour listening to Misty and Emma talk. Mostly Misty asking questions and Emma giving long, drawn-out answers about her favorite movies and television shows.

Brandon's phone rang. It was Tori. He got up from the table and walked into the living room.

"Hey."

"How's my daughter?" she asked.

"So far, so good."

"Figures. She's a saint for you."

"Give it time," Brandon said. "Hold on."

Back in the kitchen, he held out the phone. "It's Mom."

"What does she want?" Emma asked.

Brandon gave her a cold stare.

"Take it."

Emma snatched the phone and fled to her room, slamming the door.

Misty stood, picking up their plates.

"You don't have to—"

"I do have domestic skills," Misty said. "At least let me show you I can cook and clean."

"Together, then," Brandon said.

It didn't take long to wash and dry the few dishes they'd used. Misty dried her hands and tossed the dishtowel at Brandon. "How's your investigation going?"

"Lots of new leads."

"You think it has something to do with the vampire symbol out at the diner? People are scared."

"Understood, but there are other things to consider. Evidence from the beach. A woman she'd argued with at the convenience store."

"What woman?"

Brandon caught himself. He'd fallen into old habits, like when he'd come home and talk through cases with Tori. But Tori was a prosecutor, and someone he knew he could trust to keep quiet.

"I can't say..."

"It's not Ruby, is it?"

Brandon stared back at her, and she said, "Sorry, I should know better than to ask—"

"Does Nolan share information about cases with you?"

Her face grew hard at the mention of Nolan. "No. Never."

He didn't believe her.

"He's not like that," she said.

"Good to hear. Because I won't tolerate leaks coming from my department. I have to be able to trust people..." Their eyes met for the briefest moment. "...trust the officers under my command."

Brandon and Misty stood at the bottom of the porch. The night air was chill, and he was close enough to sense Misty's welcoming warmth.

"Thanks for dinner," he said.

"It's not like I have anyone to cook for nowadays." She stepped closer. "Sorry about the whole Nolan conversation."

"It's over," he said. "We can agree to disagree."

"Brandon," she said, resting her hand on his chest. "About us—"

"This isn't a good idea," Brandon said.

"What about the other night?" she asked.

They had almost kissed, would have kissed, if Tori and Emma hadn't shown up.

"I'm recently divorced. You're with someone. One of my officers."

And there was no proof that what had ruined their relationship the first time wouldn't ruin it again.

"I know, but—"

"Things could change, I know," Brandon said. "But they haven't."

He took her hand. "Thank you for dinner. And by the way, I'm glad you're my neighbor. Let's keep it that way."

Her eyes studied his face as if judging how far she should press the issue. She let go of his hand.

"Goodnight, Brandon."

Back in the house, Emma was still in her room, chatting it up with her mom. Brandon listened for a moment. Emma giggled, describing her encounter with the vampire role-playing mayor of Forks.

He smiled. It was good hearing them get along again.

Brandon had warned Emma she'd be bored hanging around Forks during the day. There was a library, and she was a voracious reader, but that would get old too. He encouraged her to make friends, knowing how difficult that would be in a small town where you didn't know anyone. Not to mention her dad was a cop, and Brandon was very selective about Emma's acquaintances.

Brandon called his dad from the landline.

"Mattson here," he answered.

"It's Brandon."

"I know who it is. I have caller ID."

"What do you think about Emma coming over tomorrow?" Brandon asked.

"You want me to babysit?"

"She's almost sixteen. It's hardly babysitting."

His dad grunted.

Brandon knew it would be a mistake asking his dad to watch Emma. All he was asking was for the old man to spend the day with his granddaughter.

"Fine. Send her over," he said.

"We'll be there at eight if that's not too late," Brandon said.

"You working banker's hours now? That's practically lunchtime."

Brandon swallowed hard, holding back the handful of replies that came to mind. He needed his dad to keep an eye on Emma. At least for a few days until things settled down. If that meant putting up with his father's jabs, so be it.

"Alright, then. Eight o'clock."

Brandon sank into the recliner and propped his legs up. His thoughts turned to Misty. It was strange, living across the street from her after so many years.

Was he being too careful? What if she broke up with Nolan? Maybe they weren't that serious. There were no rules about dating someone a fellow officer, or even a subordinate, used to date.

But that still didn't make it a good idea.

His attraction to Misty was more about the past than anything he knew about her today.

He'd moved on a long time ago. But forgiveness didn't mean making the same mistake twice. Maybe she'd changed. But he had, too.

One of these days he'd get around to asking Lisa Shipley out. Maybe it would go somewhere. Maybe not. At least it would be a fresh start. No baggage or old resentment to worry about.

He drifted off, listening to the sweet, peaceful tones of Emma getting along with her mother.

Chapter 19

Monday morning, Brandon dropped Emma off at his dad's house and headed for work.

He flipped his office light on. Josiah had left a manila folder on his desk with a sticky note. *Chief, check this out. Good info.*

Brandon slid his finger into the folder to open it.

"So, what do you think?"

It was Josiah.

"Aren't you here a little early?" Brandon asked.

Josiah's shift started in half an hour.

"I wanted to get moving on this, ASAP."

"I just picked this up, so why don't you tell me—"

"I interviewed about every business in town. Then, I tried the bus station. That's when I ran into old Jim Daniel."

Brandon hadn't known Josiah for long, but the kid seemed pretty excited.

"I don't know who that is," Brandon said.

"He's a homeless guy—drifts between Forks and Port Angeles. Mostly keeps to himself."

There was a public transit station just outside downtown. The bus went one place—to Port Angeles. It was a good deal for those who worked in Port Angeles or vice versa, but it also meant an increase in homeless folks who otherwise wouldn't have made the trip.

"Jim tells me he saw the girl in the wanted poster—Lauren."

"When?" Brandon asked.

"The night she disappeared."

If Josiah was right, that meant Jim was the only other person besides Ruby to see Lauren in Forks.

"Why come forward now?"

"Jim's not exactly a fan of law enforcement."

"What's his record?"

"Drug convictions. Trespassing," Josiah said.

"No assault? Crimes against individuals?"

"You think he's involved?" Josiah crossed his arms, leaning against the door jamb.

"It's not uncommon for a perp to come forward."

"I don't think Jim would do that," Josiah said. "He doesn't drive, so how would he get her to the beach?"

"Right, but we don't want to rule anyone out." Brandon motioned Josiah toward the chair in front of his desk. "Tell me what Jim told you."

Josiah sat on the edge of the seat, leaning forward. "First off, Jim says he recognized Lauren from the methadone clinic up in Port Angeles. He's a client there, has been for a while. He saw the tow truck driver drop her off that night and watched her go into the store."

"Did you tell him about the driver, or did he say that on his own?"

"On his own," Josiah said.

Like any murder case, there could be hundreds of tips, most useless, fueled by the distorted facts the public had heard or read about.

"But here's the thing," Josiah continued. "After she left the store, she got into a different truck with two men."

"At the gas station?"

That's not the story Ruby told. She said Lauren left on foot—alone.

"Right."

"You get a description?"

Josiah shook his head. "No luck, but he did say they were in one of the road construction trucks. They came from the Forks Inn, across the street."

Workers assigned to local road projects often stayed in town for days at a time. Forks and the surrounding area were too far from home for most contractors.

"She got into their truck willingly?" Brandon asked.

"Not sure, but there were two men," Josiah said.

Why would Ruby want to protect a couple of out-of-towners? Did it have something to do with her drug-dealing? Or was there a deeper connection between Ruby and these men?

"Which direction did they go?" Brandon asked.

"Down La Push Road. Toward the beach."

"We need to interview those workers."

"So we're headed to the Forks Inn?"

"First, the gas station. I take it you weren't able to locate Ruby yesterday?"

"Not at home or work," Josiah said.

"I want to know why she never mentioned these guys picking up Lauren," Brandon said. "And Josiah, good work."

The outside door opened, and Nolan strode past Brandon's office.

Brandon stepped into the hallway.

"Hey, Nolan."

He cocked his head at Brandon. "Yeah?"

Brandon looked up at the clock.

"You're late," Brandon said.

"I'm sorry," Nolan said, his tone making it clear he wasn't sorry at all. "I wanted to spend a few minutes with my lady friend. Seems she was busy last night."

Had Misty told Nolan about dinner with Brandon and Emma?

"Take care of your personal business on your own time," Brandon said.

"Like I said. Sorry. I'll make it up to Misty tonight." He winked at Brandon and continued down the hallway.

Bastard.

It shouldn't bother him. What did he care about Misty's personal life? The past was over, and old feelings were just that—old and feelings. They didn't mean a thing.

Brandon and Josiah drove together to the gas station where Ruby worked.

The day before, Brandon had asked Josiah and Will to check in with Ruby about her relationship with Lauren. But she had called in sick to work. And if she was at home, she wasn't answering the door.

People got sick, and sometimes they weren't home when you stopped by.

But they had learned a few things about Ruby and Lauren. Not only did they not like each other but Lauren had confronted Ruby for trying to sell drugs to patients at the methadone clinic. At some point, Lauren had threatened to turn her in—or worse.

None of that explained why Ruby would fail to divulge that Lauren hitched a ride back to the beach from the two men in the truck.

Brandon could have visited Ruby's work alone— technically, he didn't need Josiah there. But he wanted the young officer to learn. Sure, he would have gotten the basics at the academy, but dealing with a murder investigation, the stakes were higher, and the defense would be more likely to target the way you handled everything from evidence to interviews.

When they arrived at the store, there was no sign of Ruby. That was no surprise—she worked the night shift. Brandon approached the counter, Josiah a few steps behind him.

The man at the cash register was in his late forties. By his appearance and accent, Brandon guessed he was Pakistani.

"We're hoping to speak to a manager," Brandon said.

"I'm the owner. My wife and I."

"Chief Mattson," Brandon said. "We had a few questions."

"Yes, I've heard of you."

"How's that?"

"In the newspaper." He pointed to a stack of papers near the door.

Josiah picked up a copy of the Forks Journal Extra. His eyes widened. "Front page news. Wow."

The headline proclaimed New Chief Puts Homicide Skills to Test. The byline read, Chief Cares Little for Local Tourism Efforts but Wants to Nab Bad Guys.

"That S.O.B.," Brandon said.

"It says here you and the mayor don't see eye to eye on the importance of tourism," Josiah said. "And there's a bunch of details about the girl's death."

"What sort of details?"

Josiah passed him the paper. Brandon scanned the article. The majority was fluff, Ted Nixon's attempt to dramatize Lauren Sandoval's murder. Mostly guessing. But there were a few facts—things Brandon didn't want public. Like the bite marks. And an anonymous comment referencing Ruby and her "less than friendly relationship with the victim."

How the hell did he know that?

Brandon handed the paper back to Josiah. "Are you aware of any leaks in our department?"

Josiah looked him square in the eyes. "No."

Dammit if he couldn't trust anyone. How was he supposed to run an investigation with some hack reporter spilling info to the community—including potential suspects? He'd track down the source. His first guess was Nolan and his connection to Ted.

"Mr.—"

"Kayani."

"This is about Ruby Walker and a young woman who visited your store on the night of June 9," Brandon said.

Mr. Kayani glanced at the newspaper rack. "You mean the girl who was murdered?"

"You had no idea she'd been here?"

"Of course not."

"Ruby and I chatted a few days ago about the girl," Brandon said.

"She did not tell me."

Brandon pointed to the security camera on the back wall.

"Are those active?"

When Brandon had spoken with Ruby, she had claimed the video system was broken.

Mr. Kayani looked up at the camera.

"Of course."

"And you still have footage from last week?"

"Yes. It is all stored digitally." He motioned to Brandon. "In my office."

He led them back to a tight room with a table, a desktop computer, and one chair. They stood behind him as he logged in.

"What date and time do you need?"

Brandon told him the time and date of Lauren's disappearance.

"I'll start at twelve a.m."

Mr. Kayani pushed play. The screen split between an outside camera and the one above the restroom. Ruby sat behind the counter reading a magazine. Five minutes later, she drifted outside and smoked a cigarette.

"Fast forward a bit," Brandon said.

They watched as Ruby's figure puffed her cigarette in double time, then reentered the store.

"Wait," Brandon said. Mr. Kayani paused, then moved back a few frames.

"There." Brandon pointed to a spot on the left edge of the frame. Headlights swept over the screen. The vehicle remained offscreen. A moment later, Lauren Sandoval appeared and the lights drifted away, leaving the parking lot in darkness again. That would be Garrett Zornes, the tow truck driver, leaving.

Lauren ambled into the store, glanced at Ruby, then shook her head before stumbling down an aisle. For about a minute, Lauren studied the beer section, wavering before the refrigerator like a sleepwalker.

Ruby came around the corner and said something to Lauren, but Lauren waved her off.

Finally, she opened the door and grabbed a six-pack of Coors Light. Lauren took the beer to the counter and pulled out a wad of cash.

The conversation soured as Ruby slid the six-pack away from Lauren and pointed toward the door.

"The girl appears intoxicated," Mr. Kayani said. "Ruby is doing the right thing."

Lauren pointed a finger at Ruby. Then, suddenly, she fought to free the six-pack from Ruby's grip. Ruby shoved her back. Lauren stood there for a moment, said something to Ruby. It was impossible to tell, but she had the demeanor of someone delivering an ultimatum.

Then, a white pickup truck pulled into the parking lot, right up to the front of the store. There were two men in the cab.

Inside, Lauren handed Ruby a wad of money. Ruby counted it, placing one bill in the register, pocketing the rest with Lauren too drunk to notice. Ruby pushed the six-pack and receipt to Lauren.

"I can't believe this," Mr. Kayani said. "Not only is she giving alcohol to a drunk person, she's keeping the change for herself."

"Didn't card her, either," Josiah said.

What had Lauren said to Ruby? The argument verified the animosity between the two.

"These must be the workers Jim Daniel told me about," Josiah said.

One of the men entered the store, holding the door for Lauren as she exited. She was about to move offscreen when the man who'd stayed in the truck motioned for her to come over. She paused, made a slow, drunken turn and stumbled over to him.

He got out of the truck and closed the door. He was in his early thirties, bald but with a wild, unkempt beard. A little on the heavy side. Leaning against the cab with his arms crossed, he struck up a conversation with Lauren. They both laughed at something the man said.

Inside the store, his friend bought beer and a can of chew.

Brandon recognized the men. They'd been with the road crew at the counter talking to Tammy when Brandon had breakfast at the Forks Diner on Sunday morning.

The man who had bought the beer got back in the truck. His friend motioned for Lauren to come with them. She stood, considering their offer. He tapped her on the arm, motioning again. Lauren relented and he made a gesture as if he wanted her to get in first. She shook her head, said something, and the man got in, leaving Lauren to squeeze in next to the passenger door.

The truck sped out the parking lot, taking the road that led to the beach.

Brandon checked the time on the video monitor: 12:17 a.m. The coroner had estimated the time of death somewhere between two and five.

Inside the store, Ruby stood at the window, watching the whole thing.

"What does this mean?" Mr. Kayani asked.

"It means we need to have a word with Ruby, again."

"Do you recognize that truck?" Josiah asked.

"They are the workers that stay at the hotel. They buy beer and food at night. Coffee in the morning."

"Thank you," Brandon said. "When does Ruby work next?"

"Tonight, if she doesn't call in sick. But I will tell you, I don't think I'll be keeping her after this."

"Understood," Brandon said. He pointed at the screen. "Do you mind if we get a copy of this?"

"It's all yours."

"I'll come back with a jump drive," Josiah said.

"Do us a favor," Brandon said to Mr. Kayani. "Don't mention this to Ruby. Or anyone else."

"You have my word," he said.

Chapter 20

Brandon and Josiah regrouped outside.

"This looks bad for those guys," Josiah said, motioning toward the Forks Inn. "What did the coroner say about semen?"

The young officer was ready to book the two men for rape and murder. It was possible they'd just discovered how Lauren had made it back to the beach in the hours before her death.

They might have identified her killers, too.

But nothing was certain. Yet.

"The coroner said semen was present," Brandon said. "But we've got a bunch of evidence to consider. The video is important. But just one piece."

Josiah shrugged off Brandon's cautious attitude.

"Now what? Go find out who those two guys are?"

"I'll head over to the hotel," Brandon said. "See what the manager has to say. You get a copy of that video."

"You know about the Forks Inn, right?"

"I haven't been here in twenty years, Josiah. So, unless you're telling me it's still the best place to celebrate prom without getting busted, no, I don't know."

Josiah laughed.

"Worse. Prostitution. We have calls here and there, made a few arrests, but no proof management is involved. The old chief said the owner was probably getting a cut."

"And the contract workers?"

"It's a cheap hotel. Most of them stay there."

"And the room service has more to offer than food, apparently," Brandon said.

"I think *service* is all they offer."

Brandon crossed the street to the Forks Inn. The parking lot was empty except for a few sedans and two minivans. No sign of the truck they'd seen in the video. Probably the crew was already at work—hopefully, they hadn't left town. It would be a lot easier if the two men who'd taken Lauren were still in his jurisdiction.

Josiah's excitement about the lead was well-placed. But even if you knew who committed a crime, it didn't mean a thing until you had compelling evidence. If they found DNA from one of these men with Lauren, or even the beer cans on the sea stack...

He was getting ahead of himself. He had to treat this like any other case—not like he was the new chief of police with a hell of a lot to prove in a short amount of time.

The hotel was a modest two-story building with a pair of matching wings that spread out from a central lobby. The gray, peeling siding could've benefitted from a fresh coat of paint—a decade ago. The roof had sprouted a garden of moss, and the ground-floor windows could claim more mold than a middle school science class Petri dish.

The lobby was just as depressing. The carpet had worn through on some spots, and the mid-eighties decor hadn't changed since Brandon's high school days.

Brandon rang the front desk bell.

A girl in her late teens emerged from behind the curtain that separated the lobby from a back office.

She smiled at Brandon. "Hi."

"I need to talk to the owner."

"Okay," she said. The girl twisted her head. "Dad!"

A man in his early fifties with peppered hair and stubble swept through the curtain, his voice agitated.

"What?"

The scent of marijuana radiated from the man's blue and yellow tropical-themed shirt.

The man caught sight of Brandon's uniform. "*Great.*"

"Beat it," he said to the girl.

She scowled. "So rude."

"Just...go."

The girl disappeared back behind the curtain.

"If you're here to harass me about—" the manager said.

"A young woman was murdered about a week ago and we have evidence that some of your guests were involved in her disappearance."

"Oh." He seemed almost relieved.

"Your name?" Brandon asked.

"Benjamin Frey. People call me Big Ben."

"You been in town long, Ben?"

"Moved up about six years ago. From California."

"You operate a prostitution dive down there too?"

The man rapped the counter with his index finger. "You don't have a shred of evidence—"

Brandon held up a hand to quiet him.

He'd just wanted to put the man on notice. "I'm looking for a list of contract workers who were staying here on June 9."

"We get a lot of workers," he said.

"And you know who they are."

"You want me to share private information on my guests? You know what will happen to me?"

"I know what will happen if you don't give me the information. This is a murder investigation. And if, as part of the investigation, we uncover your involvement in certain other activities, say prostitution—"

"Okay, chill, man," he said, holding up his hands. "What do you want to know?"

"Names and the companies they work for. Everyone who stayed here that night."

"It will take a minute," he said.

"If it helps, they were driving a white pickup."

Frey left Brandon in the lobby and returned a few minutes later with a piece of paper. "Only two white trucks were registered here. Both with Apex West Engineering."

"What's that?"

"They do surveying."

"Where?"

"I have no idea. Are you done with me now?"

"One more question. You have video cameras?"

"No."

"Why not?"

"Too expensive," he said, glancing sideways at Brandon.

The real reason probably had more to do with moments just like this when the police came around searching for evidence. If the Forks Inn was being used for prostitution, he'd want to make sure there wasn't proof.

"That's enough," Brandon said. "For now."

Brandon checked the hallway and the exterior of the building for any cameras. He didn't find any. Frey was telling the truth.

Imagine that.

Back at the station, Josiah stood at the copy machine printing out still frames from the gas station video. Across the room, Jackson was checking out something on her computer. She'd just started her shift.

"I updated Jackson on what we learned," Josiah said.

"Good. The men who picked Lauren up at the gas station worked for a company called Apex West," Brandon said.

Jackson swiveled in her chair. "They're up on 101. Reinforcing the hillside. It's that road-widening project that's been going on for months."

They'd driven through the construction zone on the road up to Port Angeles.

"I'm getting ready to go up that way if you want me to check on anything," Jackson said.

There were more than enough threads to follow, including Ruby, and—as much as he didn't want to waste the time—Vasile, the vampire guru. Right now, the two men from Apex West were their best lead on what happened to Lauren in the hours—and minutes—before she died.

"Sure, but not alone," Brandon said, studying the shift board. "Where's Nolan?"

"He's out on patrol," she said, her voice less than enthusiastic. She knew what was coming next.

"Tell him to meet us at the construction site. We're all going to check this out."

"Alright," she said. The lack of enthusiasm was meant to send a message. He'd heard it, loud and clear. As far as Brandon could tell, Jackson and Nolan didn't get along. Nolan could be an ass. But if she had a shot at being a full-time officer, they would need to learn to work together.

An hour later, Brandon and Josiah pulled off the highway near the construction site. The road had been widened for a long stretch, and that meant removing part of the hill to the right. To prevent erosion, they'd planted grass over the fresh soil. A glowing, emerald green blanketed the hill.

A few workers directed traffic, alternating between "slow" and "stop." They'd excavated a large trench along the side of the highway. A crane was lowering a drainage pipe into the trench.

Jackson and Nolan arrived a few minutes later, parking behind Brandon.

When the four were together, Brandon held out the still frame shots from the gas station. "We're looking for either of these two men. Consider them dangerous until we know different. One—or both—of these men may have killed Lauren Sandoval."

Seeing the police officers, one of the workers approached.

"What's up?"

"Are you the foreman?" Brandon asked.

"That's me."

Brandon showed him the pictures from the convenience store.

"You recognize these two?"

He flipped through the photos.

"That's Derrick Green," he said, pointing to the image of the man who'd entered the store.

"And that one?" Brandon asked, holding up the other picture—the man who'd convinced Lauren to get in the truck.

"Yeah," he scoffed. "Doug Nevins."

"You've had trouble with him?" Brandon asked.

"Both those guys, yeah. Doug's a piece of work if that's what you mean. What's this about?"

146

"Just asking a few questions. Where are these two now?"

"Over there. Derrick's in the backhoe." He pointed. "And Doug..." he motioned north. "Down the road, holding up the sign. Over on the right."

Brandon stood out on the highway and saw the man, who had his back to them. He was about a quarter-mile away on the other side of the construction zone.

"Got it." Brandon spoke to Jackson and Nolan. "You two, go question Doug Nevins. I want to know everything—what they did after leaving the store, what time they arrived back at the hotel. We'll compare stories. If you sense anything off-kilter, detain him. Understood?"

They both nodded.

The foreman followed Brandon and Josiah over to the backhoe. Along the way, he called another worker over.

"I need you to take Derrick's place."

The foreman motioned Derrick over.

Derrick climbed down and pulled his gloves off.

"What's up?" He was doing his best not to look at Brandon and Josiah.

"We have a few questions," Brandon said. "It shouldn't take long."

"Let me know if you need anything else," the foreman said, then left them alone with Derrick. The man was about five-foot-six, with arms like a gym rat. His baseball cap was on backward, but he flipped it around now, revealing a Seahawks logo.

Brandon showed him a copy of the still shot of Derrick at the gas station. "This is you?"

"Yeah."

"And this is you in the truck with your friend Doug?" Brandon asked.

"I guess."

"You guess or it is?" Josiah asked.

"It is."

"And the girl?" Brandon asked.

"It was Doug's idea."

"What was Doug's idea?"

"Picking her up."

"Yet, you went along with it."

"We didn't do jack to her," Derrick said.

Josiah positioned himself off to the side and slightly behind Derrick in case he tried to bolt.

"You understand the girl you picked up—she was murdered."

A streak of genuine fear crossed his face. He didn't know.

"What happened that night?" Brandon asked.

"We were just getting beer, something to eat. I came back out and Doug was talking to some chick."

"What did she say to you?"

"She was talking about camping, how she needed a ride to the beach."

"What did you want in return?"

He held up his hands. "It wasn't like that."

Josiah stepped toward Derrick, reaching for his cuffs.

Brandon motioned him off. Not yet.

"Mr. Green, we have DNA evidence—"

"Hey, go ahead," he said. "Take my DNA. I got nothing to hide."

Brandon considered him for a moment. Was he bluffing?

"Okay, so you took her to the beach."

"Hells no. That bitch started freaking out. I mean, probably because of Doug, but—"

148

"*Why* was she freaking out?"

"I was driving, man. But if I had to guess, Doug was trying to cop a feel—"

"And she told him to stop."

"Right."

"You kept driving."

"No, I mean. I didn't have time to do anything. She opens the door like she's about to bail. I slammed on the brakes and she bolted. At first, Doug got out too, but she said something about pepper spray and Doug got back in."

If Derrick was telling the truth, Brandon should be talking to Doug Nevins. Either way, he would have to get Derrick down to the station and get an official statement.

"And you left her there. Alone?"

"What was I supposed to do? She didn't want a ride anymore."

"Then what?"

"We went back to the hotel. I was sort of done with all that, so I took a couple of beers and crashed in my room."

They had separated after letting the girl out of the truck. That meant neither of them had an alibi.

"And Doug? What did he do?"

"Hell if I know what that crazy bastard did. He said he was going to crash, too."

A crack of gunfire rang out from down the highway where Jackson and Nolan were interviewing Doug Nevis.

Brandon pointed at Derrick. "Stay here."

Brandon rushed toward the gunfire, Josiah on his heels.

"Shots fired!" Jackson's voice called out over the police radio.

Another gunshot echoed through the construction zone.

149

The foreman waved at Brandon, pointing up.

"The hill!"

Brandon spotted Nolan and Jackson scrambling up the hillside after a man in a bright orange safety vest.

Doug Nevins.

Jackson slipped but caught herself in the muddy, newly seeded grass. She was only about 20 yards behind Nevins. Nolan trailed Jackson by several feet.

Brandon motioned to Josiah. "Follow me."

They sprinted after Nolan and Jackson.

The peak of the hill was the edge of a thick, new-growth forest. Nevins lunged into the woods, a pistol in his right hand.

Jackson and Nolan were sitting ducks once Nevins gained cover.

"Around to the right," Brandon said to Josiah, directing him to the far boundary of the forest, in case the man headed that direction. Brandon veered to the right too.

Nolan had passed Jackson now and waded into the thick brush at the forest edge.

More gunfire.

Had Nolan been hit?

Jackson had reached the tree line but pulled back, taking cover.

Brandon and Josiah were in the trees now, about 50 yards south of Jackson.

"Stay even with me," Brandon said to Josiah. "No crossfire."

Josiah nodded.

Josiah positioned himself south of Brandon and they moved in.

Brandon spoke into his radio. "Jackson, Nolan. Are you injured?"

They both responded, no.

"We are several yards south of you—to your right. Drive him toward us."

"10-4."

If they weren't careful, Nevins would use them for target practice. The trees were thin conifers planted in recent decades. But the brush was shoulder-high in some places. The uneven terrain made it impossible to advance quietly in the thick underbrush.

Gunfire clapped against the hillside again, echoing through the forest. Brandon held his breath, listening. He scanned the area to the left, where he expected Nevins. He hoped the last shot was Jackson or Nolan edging Nevins toward Brandon and Josiah.

Another shot rang out. Then, a wild rustling of underbrush.

Brandon made eye contact with Josiah and motioned for him to stay put.

He waited as the commotion headed his direction.

Brandon crouched, scanning the sloping hillside.

Then, through the brush came the reflective glow of the safety vest. The idiot hadn't even thought to take it off.

Nevins trudged ahead, parallel with the tree line, no longer climbing upward. Waist-high in the undergrowth, he was even with Brandon now, about 30 feet further up the hill.

Brandon raised his weapon. Nevins' eyes caught on Josiah, several feet to Brandon's right. Brandon glanced Josiah's direction.

Josiah aimed his Glock at Nevins. Nevins ducked his head, lifting his hand above the brush, pistol ready to unload.

Josiah had lost sight of him.

"Drop it!" Brandon said.

Brandon had half a second to decide. Would Nevins choose to die, or give himself up?

Nevins froze. Gun pointed at Josiah, his head swiveled to Brandon.

"Shit."

"Last chance, Nevins," Brandon said.

Nevins dropped the pistol, shoving his hands up in surrender.

Brandon stepped forward, weapon trained on Nevins.

"Cuff him, Josiah."

Brandon notified Jackson and Nolan to stand down. They'd secured the suspect.

Chapter 21

Hours later, after getting an official statement from Derrick Green, towing Nevins' truck for evidence, collecting Nevins' gun, and transporting him to the Forks Jail, they headed to the station.

Josiah was convinced they'd caught Lauren's murderer. Running away from the police was a clear giveaway you'd done something wrong.

Meanwhile, he'd shot at two police officers. That was enough to hold and charge him.

Back in his office, Brandon regrouped with Jackson and Nolan.

"What happened? From the start."

So far, he'd only gotten a summary of their interaction with Nevins.

"We approached the suspect. He had his back to us," Jackson said.

"He noticed us and threw his flagger sign at Jackson. He bolted through some parked trucks and up the hill."

"Who fired first?"

"I did," Nolan said, leaning back in his chair. "Jackson had a shot but didn't act."

"My first goal was to apprehend the suspect. Not shoot him in the back," she said. "I was five feet behind him. I could have caught him."

"He had a weapon," Nolan said.

"You didn't know that until after you shot at him," Jackson said.

"Wait," Brandon said. "If Jackson was pursuing Nevins and you were trailing Jackson, you shot past Jackson at the suspect?"

"I had a clear shot."

And with one misstep, he could have killed Jackson.

"But you were *behind* her, and she was five feet from Nevins?"

Nolan tapped his holster. "I'm confident in my marksmanship."

"You put a fellow officer at risk, Nolan."

"That's bull, Mattson. I probably saved her life." Nolan leaned forward. "Even after Nevins went for his pistol. Jackson had her chance."

"I followed procedure, ordered him to drop his weapon," Jackson insisted.

There were times when talking didn't make sense. But so far, Jackson's approach seemed reasonable. If Nevins hadn't pulled his gun yet...

"Except you froze," Nolan said. "It's no good telling a perp to stand down when you can't even pull your gun."

Jackson's eyes fell on Brandon. "I admit, I fumbled for my firearm. But not because I froze."

"So, the guy fires a couple of shots," Nolan said. "It's a damn good thing he can't shoot worth a shit. Or someone would have got killed. That's when he got into the forest. As for me, I know I did the right thing. I didn't piss my pants just because—"

"Shut the hell up," Jackson said.

Nolan stood. "I'd better get working on my report."

"Do that," Brandon said. "And after that, take the rest of the week off."

"What?"

154

"I'm giving you two days unpaid leave. Shooting past Jackson was stupid and reckless. And at that point, there wasn't any indication of a weapon. You should have tried to apprehend him first, especially if Jackson was that close."

Placing Nolan on leave was the right thing to do. But he'd pay for it when he heard back from the union, and there would be a pile of paperwork.

"You're making a mistake, Mattson—"

"*Chief* Mattson. Or *sir* if you prefer," Brandon said.

"This is crap. Eli would have done the same thing. He wasn't afraid to use force—"

"My brother has nothing to do with this. He's not here. I am."

Nolan crossed his arms. "Is this because you're pissed that I'm with Misty?"

"I'm not even going to respond to that. Now get out of my office while you still have a job with this department."

Nolan narrowed his eyes at Jackson and shook his head as if all of this were her fault.

Nolan moved to leave.

Brandon said, "Something else. That reporter was in here yesterday asking for you."

"Ted? So what?"

"And today there's a front-page story about the investigation."

"And?"

"If I find out you're the one leaking to the press, I will have your badge. Permanently."

With Nolan gone, Brandon asked Jackson, "What really happened?"

"You mean when I froze?"

"You just said you didn't freeze."

"I don't know," she said.

"This your first time in a shooting situation?"

"No," she said quickly.

"You need time off? A break?"

"You going to tell me this is because I'm a mother now, that it was different when I didn't have kids?"

"Nope."

"Like that Russian story about the guy and the bowl of cherries?"

"I can't say what you're thinking. But people make mistakes. If you froze, okay, but it can't happen again."

"You think I should have shot him as soon as he pulled on me?"

"Depends," Brandon said. "You have to use your judgment."

"Well, if you believe Nolan—"

"I don't give a damn what Nolan thinks," Brandon said.

She smiled. "Thanks."

"Will this screw up my chances at getting on full time?" she asked.

"Not with me. But I can't do anything about what your fellow officers think."

It was his first week on the job as chief of police and already he was facing a murder investigation. It should be no big deal—he'd been a homicide detective for over a decade, even supervised a team. But those were professional detectives, not beat officers with relatively little investigation experience trying to make a name for themselves.

The problem was, he couldn't do it all himself. That meant he'd have to learn to trust his officers. But first, they'd have to learn to work together without killing each other.

Josiah knocked on the door jamb.

"Hey, good job today," Brandon said.

"Thanks," Josiah said. "Guess what?"

"What's up?"

"Doug Nevins is a sex offender. He's wanted for failure to register."

"Bring him to the interview room," Brandon said.

Brandon and Josiah sat across from Nevins.

"Water? Coffee?" Brandon asked.

"Screw you."

Brandon read Nevins his rights.

"You know why you're here?"

"Because some dumbass cop tried to shoot me."

"Hadn't they told you to stop?"

As much as Brandon disagreed with Nolan firing on Nevins at that point during the pursuit, he wasn't about to express his frustration with Nolan in front of the suspect. Any error in judgment by an officer, no matter how unrelated to the offense in question, was the sort of thing a defense attorney would jump on.

"I don't remember," Nevins said.

Brandon locked eyes with Nevins.

"You're familiar with the young woman found dead on the beach?"

Nevins scoffed. "No."

"That's interesting, because you picked her up the night she died."

"Not sure what you're talking about."

Brandon tapped his fingers on the table.

"We have video, Nevins."

157

Nevins tugged on his handcuffs as if to remind himself: yes, you really are screwed.

"The girl jumped out and we left her on the side of the road."

"Then what?"

"Derrick took me back to the hotel."

"Right, but what did you *want* to do?"

Nevins' gaze rose to meet Brandon's.

"You wanted to go back after her, isn't that right?" Josiah asked.

"It don't matter what I wanted to do. I went to my room and crashed. That's all."

"Did anyone see you after Derrick left?" Brandon asked.

Nevins' eye slid to the door, then Brandon. "You think I killed her."

"All I want is the truth, Nevins. What happened?"

"I already told you."

"And if I say we have video of you heading back to the highway alone after Derrick left?"

There was no such video. But Nevins' eyes widened, all the blood draining from his ruddy complexion.

"That doesn't mean I found her. I was just getting some fresh air."

Brandon fought to mask his surprise. It had worked.

"And when you found her?"

"I didn't...I want an attorney."

"You sure? Because we were doing so well, with you finally deciding to be honest—"

"I want an attorney."

That was Brandon's cue to halt the interview.

"Anyone in particular?" Brandon asked.

"Yeah, the kind that prevents me from having to answer stupid questions about crap I didn't do."

Brandon motioned to Josiah. "Take him back to his cell and have the jail staff contact a public defender."

"I didn't do nothing," Derrick insisted as Josiah led him away.

An hour later, Josiah was back in Brandon's office. "He's in CODIS," Josiah said.

Convicted sex offenders' DNA was collected and stored in the CODIS database, making it easier to match evidence from unsolved crimes to criminals in the system. Having a DNA sample on file would make it easier to match Nevins to the semen found with Lauren.

"I think it's obvious he killed Lauren Sandoval," Josiah said.

"He's a sex offender, was last seen with her hours—or minutes—before she died. And he'd made statements about wanting to go after her even after she fled," Brandon said. "It sounds good, but it's not enough—yet."

If Nevins' DNA matched the semen found with Lauren, it would be an easier—but not guaranteed—conviction. If not, they had a lot of circumstantial evidence. For the time being, they didn't have anything putting Nevins at the scene of Lauren's death. And the person last with Lauren had likely downed a few beers with her. Based on Lauren's initial reaction to Nevins' advances, Brandon couldn't imagine her sharing a drink with him.

"You're not going to charge him?" Josiah asked.

"With evading arrest and attempted murder of a police officer? Sure. Let's see what forensics gets out of his truck."

This wasn't harassment or burglary. Not even armed robbery came close. The greater the charges, the more the defense would push back. Brandon had to be sure.

"But—"

"There are other suspects we need to clear."

"Like the boyfriend?"

"And Ruby and anyone else who happened to be around Lauren that night. The defense will ask us who else we considered. We have to show due diligence."

"Okay. So now what?"

"No one's been able to find Ruby for the last couple of days."

"Out to her place?" Josiah asked.

"Let's go."

Chapter 22

Ruby lived south of town in a wooded area about half a mile off the main highway. To get there, you traveled down a long gravel road punctuated by a mobile home or trailer every hundred feet or so. Ruby's lot was the fourth one down, but Brandon had Josiah park several feet back so they could approach on foot.

The case against Ruby was weak. But she had motive. She'd been selling drugs. Lauren had threatened to call the police. And Ruby had lied about the video cameras at the gas station, claiming they didn't work.

Why had Ruby hidden that Lauren had left with Nevins and Derrick Green? Hopefully, Ruby would be able to shed more light on Nevins and what he did—or didn't do—the night Lauren was murdered.

"What if she's not home again?" Josiah asked.

"We'll take a look around." Brandon motioned for Josiah to follow his example and walk in the knee-high grass lining the gravel road to avoid announcing their arrival.

Brandon slowed as they approached Ruby's plot. The trees thinned, and from the road, they could see her car, an old Buick Park Ave with faded gray paint. The trunk was popped.

The screen door swung open and Ruby flew out of the house with two large paper bags, one in each arm. She dropped the bags in the Park Ave's trunk and rushed back inside.

Brandon remembered what Brooke and the others had said about Ruby dealing.

"She's leaving," Josiah said.

"I want to know what's in those bags," Brandon said. "Come on."

They crouched, edging ahead carefully.

There was a clanking of dishes from inside the house. Brandon paused for a moment, then sprinted to the car.

The paper bags were open. Inside were clothes. Women's socks and underwear.

Just then, Ruby emerged, carrying a large suitcase.

She was halfway to the car before she noticed them.

"Hi, Ruby. Going somewhere?"

Her eyes widened with panic as they shot from Brandon to the open trunk.

"I'm taking a little vacation. That's all."

She tossed the suitcase in the trunk, on top of the bags.

"You're not trying to hide anything, are you?"

Ruby slammed the trunk shut.

"Why would you think that?"

Josiah responded first. "Maybe because you withheld information in a murder—"

"I told you everything I know about the girl."

"Except the part where you argued with her," Brandon said.

She opened her mouth to deny the statement, then thought better of it.

"And that small detail about her leaving with two men."

"We have the video from the store," Josiah said.

"So?"

"You said the cameras didn't work."

"I thought they didn't. That cheapskate Mr. Kayani—"

"What were you and Lauren arguing about?" Josiah asked.

She crossed her arms, leaned back against the trunk.

"Maybe Lauren was going to snitch," Brandon said.

Ruby scoffed. "About what?"

He pointed his chin at the trunk. "Selling."

Ruby shoved her hands into her pockets. She was trying hard to appear calm.

"I don't know what you're talking about."

"We know you were selling up in Port Angeles," Brandon said. "And we know Lauren threatened you."

Ruby stood there, staring at her feet. She was probably weighing her options.

"We have witnesses," Josiah said.

She glanced up at him. "To what?"

"Everything we just talked about," Brandon said before Josiah could say more. It didn't help them to be specific about what they did or didn't have.

"You gonna try to bust me for dealing?"

"Right now, we're here to talk about the girl," Brandon said.

Ruby scratched at the gravel with the tip of her shoe. "Ok, we argued."

"About?"

"That little brat liked to talk big. Accused me of selling to her clients."

"You weren't?"

"No comment," she said. Then, "But how would I know who her clients were, anyway?"

"You parked down the street from the methadone clinic."

"It's a free country."

"And dealing is a felony," Josiah said.

"Anyway, she and her friends were always harassing me."

"What friends?" Brandon asked.

"That boy she was with, and some other girl."

She probably meant Justin and Brooke.

"The night of Lauren's death, you sold her beer even though she was obviously intoxicated."

"I wasn't going to. But then..."

"She threatened to go to the police."

"So I gave her the beer."

"Then what happened?"

"I told you—"

"We have the video, Ruby," Brandon said.

"Then why ask me?"

"We're giving you a chance to tell the truth. For once," Josiah said.

Ruby's eyes rose from his feet to his face. "You're a little young to be a cop, aren't you? Boy."

"Not too young to arrest your ass—"

Brandon put a hand up to silence Josiah. "Tell us what happened. Or we will be taking you to the station."

"Like you saw in the video, the little slut got into the truck with some guys."

"You know the men?"

"They come in, sometimes."

"You were trying to protect them," Brandon said. "That's why you didn't tell me Lauren left with them."

"They didn't do nothing wrong. They're good people."

"One of those 'good people' just tried to kill two of my officers."

Ruby stared back at Brandon, considering his statement.

"That has nothing to do with me."

"I'm not so sure about that," Brandon said. He pulled a notebook out of his back pocket and jotted a few things down.

Ruby looked back to her house. "Can I go now?"

"After Doug Nevins and Derrick Green left, did Doug head out later, by himself?"

Ruby might be the only person able to provide an alibi for Doug Nevins during the time after the two men had let Lauren out of their truck.

She didn't respond.

"You had a good view of the Forks Inn, right?"

"I guess."

"And you watch everything. The video showed that."

"So what?"

"Did Doug Nevins leave the hotel again and head back toward the beach?" Brandon asked. "The truth."

"I guess."

"You guess or you saw it?"

She paused, likely considering the consequences of snitching on Nevins.

"Yes."

It was confirmation that Nevins had left the Forks Inn after dropping Derrick Green off. Nevins has gone out after Lauren—alone.

"Okay, good. He left the hotel a second time, by himself. What time did he get back?"

She stared over Brandon's shoulder, toward the road. This was probably the last place she wanted to be right now.

"Tell us the truth, Ruby, and we'll do our best to keep you out of this."

"I don't know exactly."

"Give me an idea."

"What time did Doug and Derrick leave with the girl?" Ruby asked.

"12:17," Brandon said, recalling the time from the video camera.

"The first time, after they took the girl, they were gone like twenty minutes."

"So, they were back around 12:40."

"Probably.

"And then Doug Nevins left alone."

"I don't know if it really was him—"

"Okay, you saw the truck leave."

She nodded, yes.

"How long was he gone?"

"Doesn't the hotel have a video?" she asked.

"I need you to tell me," Brandon said, leaving the question unanswered. She was more likely to be honest if she believed they could catch her in a lie.

"Right before 1 a.m."

Nevins had wandered out alone for less than 20 minutes?

"How do you know?" Josiah asked.

"Because I'm off at one. He got back and then my replacement came and I went home. That's it."

"Anything else you're not telling us?"

"No."

Twenty minutes was barely enough time to make it out to the Second Beach parking lot.

Brandon slid his notebook into his back pocket.

"If you leave town, Ruby, you need to stop by the station and tell us where you're going."

She stared back at him. "But—"

"You want to stay out of jail, do what I say."

On the way back to their car, Josiah said. "She's hiding something."

"Right, but what? It could be she doesn't want us to find out about her dealing."

"Maybe that's why she's protecting the contract workers—if they are her customers," Josiah said.

"True," Brandon said. "But more importantly, we have an issue with the timeline."

"What do you mean?"

"If Nevins was back to his hotel by 1 a.m. he probably didn't kill Lauren Sandoval. The time of death is between two and five."

"Time of death—isn't that sort of a guess?"

"It's an estimate. And from what I've seen, our coroner Lisa Shipley knows what she's doing."

"Okay, maybe Nevins went back out again after one."

"Possible. But we don't have evidence of that, and it convolutes the timeline." Brandon visualized himself on the stand, positing that Nevins had made not one, but three trips out that night. It would be too much for a jury to swallow. "We'll have to wait for the results from the DNA."

Was Nevins a scumbag and potential cop killer? Sure. And Brandon would go out of his way to make sure the prosecutor followed through on keeping Nevins in jail for a very long time.

But that didn't mean he killed Lauren Sandoval.

Did someone else nab Lauren on the way back to Second Beach? If she'd been picked up around 12:17, then exited the car shortly after that, that still left 10 or so miles of drunken stumbling.

Then, she made it up the sea stack, had a few more beers, and was killed.

If it wasn't Nevins, who had given Lauren a ride to the beach?

Brandon made a call to the prosecutor's office, updating them on the case, including the recent developments with Nevins. They agreed, as much as everyone hoped Nevins was their man, there just wasn't the evidence to move forward with murder charges yet.

And then there was Ruby. Initially, she'd lied about the contractors and Lauren. Why? It was too soon to rule out the others too—especially Lauren's boyfriend, Adam. He'd known she was cheating on him, and that meant he had a motive to kill her.

Brandon wouldn't hold his breath waiting for the DNA from Lauren, or the later request for DNA and fingerprints from the beer cans he'd found. Most cases were solved through good, old-fashioned detective work. The forensic evidence provided a guide and helped rule out certain suspects. They had a lot of work left to do on this case, and now he was down one officer, thanks to Nolan's antics.

Chapter 23

At five o'clock, Brandon met his dad and Emma in the police station parking lot. They were waiting for him next to his dad's truck.

"So," Brandon asked, "how did it go?"

"Good," Emma said.

"See, Brandon. I'm not half the monster you think I am—"

"I never said you were a monster."

"You thought it."

"Okay. Anyways—"

"I told you," his dad said, elbowing Emma as if they were enjoying an inside joke.

Emma smiled. "What are we doing for dinner?"

"We'll pick up something from the store," Brandon said.

Emma hugged her grandpa and Brandon moved to leave, but his dad asked, "How's work? I heard you had some excitement today."

"How did you hear that?"

"Police scanner."

People still listened to scanners?

"I didn't know you spied on the police."

"Course I do," his dad said, holding up his cell. "I've got the scanner app on my smartphone. You think I want to lose another son?"

Listening to a police scanner wouldn't save anyone's life. Still, his father's expression of concern surprised him. It made sense, though, considering what had happened to Eli.

"Was anyone hurt?"

"No," Brandon said.

"Did you get the killer?"

"Not sure yet. It's complicated."

His father waved a hand at him. "I know, big shot detective stuff."

Brandon laughed. "Something like that."

"I do watch *Forensic Files*, you know. I'm not totally ignorant."

Most everyone figured they were an expert on forensic evidence, thanks to a plethora of true crime shows and podcasts.

His dad crossed his arms. "Look, take care of yourself. Okay?"

"I will."

"And watch your back. Not everyone in that department likes you."

"Because I'm not Eli?"

"That's part of it."

"Well, if they expect me to live up to his name—"

"People liked Eli because he was one of them."

Meaning Brandon wasn't.

"All I'm saying," his dad said, "is that you could learn a few things from Eli. Try being more down to earth."

Brandon's favorite topic—how different he and Eli were.

A spark of anger flickered in his chest. He'd confronted his father about the comparisons to Eli, and it had gone nowhere. There was no point in tilling dead ground. Brandon's eyes moved to Emma, waiting by his truck. He clicked the key fob, opening the door for her.

"Thanks again for watching Emma."

"I'll be out of town tomorrow," his dad said. "Got a doctor appointment in Port Angeles."

"Everything all right?"

"Annual checkup. That's all."

"Okay," Brandon said.

His dad got in his truck and drove off without another word.

Brandon shook his head. He'd probably never figure out his father. He'd always been a hard man. It was something Eli had been more forgiving about than Brandon, but then again, Eli was the favored son. His dad would never let Brandon forget that.

Brandon and Emma picked up groceries on the way home. They were both starving and agreed to keep it simple—spaghetti, salad, and garlic bread.

Brandon's stomach tightened as they rounded the corner to their street. He hoped to avoid a repeat of the night before when Misty greeted them with her homemade casserole. Brandon wanted time alone with Emma. He parked the car, glancing across the street at Misty's house.

She wasn't likely to come over any time soon. His last words to Misty were a rejection of her advances. It wasn't that he didn't want her around but rekindling a relationship with everything going on in both their lives. Not a good idea.

Half an hour later, Brandon and Emma sat down at the kitchen table.

"There you go," he said. "Noodles and spaghetti sauce separated."

"You remembered," she said, smiling.

"Hard to believe, I know. It's been what, a whole week?"

"Almost two weeks. Do we have parmesan?"

"I'll add it to the list," Brandon said.

A few minutes into the meal, Brandon said, "You talk to your mom today?" The last time he'd heard Emma and Tori talking, things were going well. No arguing.

"Yeah. For a few minutes."

She sounded non-committal.

Brandon knew better than to press Emma about her relationship with her mom.

"So how did it go with Grandpa today? Be honest."

"Fine. He showed me lots of old pictures."

"Ah, family photos. Exciting."

"Mostly ones of you."

"Really?" Brandon didn't know there were that many photos of him.

"Then he took me out to lunch. We went to the shooting range too."

"The what?"

"Don't be mad. You used to take me too—"

"I wished he would have asked me."

Emma slurped a noodle, the sauce sticking to her nose.

They both laughed.

"Some things never change," Brandon said. He was thinking of a picture of Emma—one of his favorites. She was three years old, a plate full of spaghetti in front of her, sauce covering her wide, innocent smile.

Now she was almost 16. Soon she'd be out of the house, and out of his life. No, that wasn't true. Emma and Brandon had always been close. She'd visit him when she moved away, right?

"Grandpa is gone tomorrow," Brandon said. "What are you going to do all day?"

"I don't know."

"I like you being here," Brandon said. "But I warned you. This is Forks we're talking about. You can walk from one end of the town to the other in 10 minutes and be bored out of your mind."

"If I lived here during the school year, I'd have friends."

"We talked about that, Em. It's not an option."

"Why not?"

"Because your school is in Seattle, all of your friends—"

"What friends?"

They'd had this conversation a dozen times. Part of being a parent, he'd learned, was patiently repeating yourself, hoping someday your advice would sink in.

"You have friends."

"Had friends, like Madison."

"I know it's been hard for you—"

"I don't want to talk about it."

They finished dinner and Brandon took their plates to the sink. He turned to Emma.

"Okay, but I'm worried about you."

"You're fine with me making friends here, during the summer?"

"Depends who it is."

"My overprotective-cop-dad tells me to make friends but then needs to approve anyone I find."

Brandon picked up a piece of garlic bread and pointed it at Emma. "You're a smart girl."

He ripped off half of the bread in one bite.

Emma rolled her eyes.

"If I'm so smart, why can't I choose my own friends?"

"Okay, fine. But be careful. I don't know where you'll find anyone to hang out with around here, anyway."

"Misty seems nice."

Brandon swallowed hard, the bread sticking in his throat.

He took a long drink of water.

"She's a little old to be your friend."

"That's not what I mean. Didn't you guys used to date? She seems...interested in you."

Brandon and Tori had split less than a year earlier, well before the divorce was finalized. It made no sense for Emma to suggest Brandon date someone other than her mother.

"That was a long time ago. We were different people."

Emma wiped the corners of her lips.

"Do you still love Mom?"

Brandon stared back at her, a dozen different answers rolling through his mind, each one with potentially negative consequences.

"I will always love your mom. We had something special—"

"But you're not in love with her?"

"Em, love is more than feelings."

She stood, taking both of their plates. "Never mind."

"Emma, we should talk about this. About the divorce. If that's what you need—"

"No Dad, I don't need more counseling or family meetings about why you and Mom can't live together."

Brandon stood. "Just remember I'm here for you to talk to."

"I know."

174

They did the dishes together in silence. When they finished, Emma asked him if he wanted to play cards. He did, and for the next hour she was back to her normal self, as if the conversation about the divorce had never happened.

He had to admire the resiliency of the teenage spirit. But her question about Brandon and Tori revealed something deeper—her desire for Brandon and Tori to reconcile. It was normal for kids to want their parents to get back together. It didn't mean it was a good idea, though.

Parenting was hard enough while married. Being a single parent for half the year was going to be twice as challenging. He'd have to watch his interactions with Misty. Brandon needed to focus on Emma first and his job second. He had enough on his plate without adding a new relationship to the mix.

Chapter 24

Brandon left Emma asleep in the morning, with a note that the furniture was due to arrive sometime before noon. There was plenty of food for lunch and breakfast, thanks to their trip to the store the night before.

Brandon was at the station by seven, hoping to get an early start on emails. He had told the city's human resources department to schedule interviews for the full-time position.

He wouldn't mind replacing Nolan too. The problem was, he only had two good candidates. One was Jackson, the other Neal's buddy, Steve Chilton.

Brandon had asked Will to sit in on the interviews with him. Will had been with the department longer than anyone, and the other officers respected him.

Around eight, Sue came in and reminded him he still hadn't finished his HR intake, so he spent the better part of the morning filling out retirement and insurance paperwork and taking mandatory online trainings about sexual harassment and IT security. Stuff he'd done a thousand times before. Still, half a day of lectures wasn't a quarter of what they dragged officers through in Seattle.

He called Emma at noon. The furniture had arrived, and she had already unwrapped the couch and set up her room. He reminded her he'd be home late. Jackson's interview wasn't until almost eight o'clock in the evening. Something to do with Jackson not being able to get a babysitter until then. Brandon wanted to ask her why her husband could watch their kids, but decided it was better to mind his own business.

Emma reassured Brandon that she'd be fine, she could make her own dinner. If she was bored she'd hang out with Misty. Not what Brandon hoped to hear, but it wasn't the worst she could do in a town like Forks, where sometimes boredom led to bad choices, even in the best of kids.

Will showed up half-an-hour before the first interview. They were supposed to review the applications, but Will wanted to argue the Seattle Mariners' chances of making the playoffs. It had been years since they'd made it to the postseason and old-timers like Will still dreamed of a run like the team had made back in '95.

He must have read the disinterest on Brandon's face. He'd been going through the case in his head while Will recapped Ken Griffey Junior's pre- and post-trade stats.

"Anything new on the Lauren Sandoval case?" Will asked.

"Still waiting on the DNA," Brandon said.

"You think it belongs to the guy we busted at the worksite?"

"Nevins admits he went looking for Lauren," Brandon said. "But the timeline doesn't fit. Ruby said he was back at the hotel by 1 a.m."

"And Lauren died after two," Will said, tossing the interview file on Brandon's desk. "Maybe Ruby's lying. Wouldn't be the first time."

"And then there are the beer cans and necklace I found on the beach."

Despite Brandon's assumption that the evidence from the sea stack was connected to Lauren's death, there wasn't hard proof of that, yet.

"It could be Nevins, could be any of her friends. The other thing is," Brandon said, "I don't see Nevins as the vampire biting type."

There was a knock at Brandon's door. Sue popped her head in. "Your interview is here. Twenty minutes early."

"Tell him we'll be out in a few."

Sue lingered, then leaned forward, speaking in a conspiratorial tone. "He seems like a nice fellow."

"Okay," Brandon said.

"Well dressed and well-spoken too."

"Sue, I get it. I'll let him know he can use you as a reference."

She straightened, her lips tightening. "I was only trying to be helpful."

Brandon sighed. "I apologize, Sue. Thank you and we'll be right there."

She raised an unforgiving eyebrow, then left without another word.

Will chuckled. "You better watch out for her. She has influence in this town."

"Her and everyone else," Brandon said. He slid the folder containing the applications to Will. "Take a look at his info. We only have a couple of minutes."

Sue was right, Steve Chilton was a nice guy. He was prepared and had even worn a jacket and tie. There were twelve standardized questions—ones developed by HR and the former chief. To Brandon, the interview forms were near useless. You got to know a person by asking follow-up questions.

When they'd finished the formal questions, Brandon asked, "Steve, I noticed you've moved around quite a bit, changing jobs at least once a year."

"That's right."

"Why is that?"

"I was working over in Thurston County, but I wasn't getting enough shifts, so I took a job with Tumwater PD."

"For how long?"

"About eight months," he said. "I moved down to Chehalis after that. I had some conflicts with the lieutenant in Tumwater."

"What sorts of conflicts?"

"We didn't see eye to eye."

Brandon leaned forward.

"Would you care to elaborate?"

"I just...I don't know what else to say. I don't want to disrespect a previous supervisor."

Will leaned over and whispered in Brandon's ear. "He's not a suspect. He's applying for a job."

"As a cop," Brandon said, loud enough for Steve to hear.

"After that, I went to Ocean Shores PD."

"And would you be willing to share why you made that change?"

"My mom died, and I wanted to be closer to my father," he said, eyeing Brandon.

"Sorry to hear that," Brandon said. Now he felt like an ass for asking.

But he didn't need a flake on his team. He was already dealing with the likes of Neal Nolan.

"And now that my father has passed away too, I'm not interested in sticking around Ocean Shores."

"Why here?" Will asked.

"I don't know if you know, but Neal Nolan is a buddy of mine. He's spoken highly of this department."

That must have been before Brandon arrived.

Brandon opened his mouth, but Will spoke first. "That's great. Neal's a good guy."

A good guy? He was on unpaid leave for almost shooting a fellow officer.

"Alright, Steve. We'll be in touch."

Steve stood, shaking hands with Brandon, then Will. "Not to pressure you," Chilton said. "But I've got an interview up in Port Angeles tomorrow and—"

"I'll make a decision by the end of the week."

Will showed Chilton out.

A minute later, Will closed the door, falling into the chair where Chilton had been sitting earlier. He crossed his arms, staring at Brandon. "Admit it. You don't like him because he's friends with Nolan."

"I don't need someone who'll leave town the second he gets bored with Forks—because you know as well as I do, it's hard enough to keep people around here."

"He had good reasons for leaving each job."

"You have to admit, there's a pattern there," Brandon said.

"Yeah, so he quit to return home after his mom died—"

It was an obvious reference to Brandon's situation. His mother had passed away, leaving his dad alone. Brandon held up a hand. "Okay, I get it. Just score the interview sheet."

They sat in silence, each scoring their own questions.

"There," Will said, tossing the sheet of paper across the table. "Not that it will make any difference."

"I am open to any and all candidates. Even an officer whose *buddy* happens to be on unpaid leave."

Will leaned back in his chair. "About that. I mean, did you really have to put Nolan on leave? It's not like any of us can afford to miss work."

"I should have fired him."

Why was Will taking Nolan's side? Of all the officers, he figured Will would be the one to understand the importance of decision making when it came to discharging a weapon.

"He nearly shot Jackson."

"That's not how Nolan explained it."

"I interviewed both of them."

"And it was he-said, she-said, right?"

"He admitted shooting past Jackson. That's problem enough. Not to mention firing on a suspect who, at the time, he believed was unarmed and near enough to capture."

Will pulled out a toothpick and stuck it between his teeth. "You're the chief."

"Yep."

Brandon stood, thinking the conversation over.

"I'm just saying," Will said. "Nolan could be a good officer."

"I'm still waiting for any evidence to support that—"

"And don't forget, this is a small town. You might be used to big-city politics, but things are different here. Each decision means more."

"So, firing Nolan would be a bad idea?" Brandon asked.

"Not saying good or bad, just that it would have more consequences than in a larger department. Not only for the police but the whole town. Nolan is well-liked around here. People listen to him."

"Then maybe they should have hired him to be chief."

Will removed the toothpick and pointed it at Brandon. "Ah, knock it off. Nolan would be a horrible chief."

"So, what are you saying?"

"I'm saying be careful. Everyone's watching you right now." Will stood. "Alright. What time is Jackson's interview?"

"Seven-thirty," Brandon said.

"See you then."

Brandon eyed Will's scoring sheet. He'd given Steve 52 points. Brandon had only awarded 40, and he figured that was being generous.

He had to remember—Jackson wasn't a shoo-in. If she bombed, it would be near impossible for Brandon to make the case for hiring her instead of Steve Chilton.

Brandon's radio scratched.

"Chief, you there?"

Why was Sue calling him on his radio?

"What's up?"

"We've got a situation out here."

"Out where?"

"The parking lot."

What sort of situation, he wanted to ask, but he doubted he'd get an answer. Sue was probably still miffed at him for his comment about Chilton.

He dropped the interview packets off in his office and headed for the lobby.

"You have a bunch of hooligans out there screaming at each other," Sue said. "And before you ask me why I asked *you* to respond, it's Ruby Walker and the kids who were friends with the girl who died."

Outside the police station, a car and a truck were parked haphazardly, the driver's door hanging open on each.

Ruby pointed a finger at Justin's chest. Brooke stood by Justin's side.

"You son of a bitch," Ruby said.

Justin noticed Brandon's approach. "Officer! I need some police protection here."

"What the hell is going on?" Brandon asked.

"This crazy lady followed us through town," Brooke said. "We didn't know what to do, so we drove here."

Brooke squinted her red eyes at him. Either Brooke had severe allergies, or she was stoned.

The pungent odor wafting off her told him it was the latter. He eyed Justin's truck.

"They got me fired," Ruby said.

"It's your own fault," Brooke said, stepping toward Ruby. "And you're probably the one who killed Lauren."

Ruby sneered at Brandon. "This is your fault. You going around telling people I had something to do with this."

"Alright, calm down. What's this about?" Brandon asked.

"This bitch and her boyfriend went in and said I threatened the girl who died."

"Her name was Lauren," Brooke said. "You should know that, considering what you did to her."

Ruby pointed at Brandon. "You told everyone I killed her. That's why I got fired—"

"No, I didn't," Brandon said. He turned to Brooke. "How do you know she threatened Lauren?"

183

The video evidence showing the argument between Lauren and Ruby wasn't public.

"She's been threatening her for years," Justin said. "Ever since Lauren busted her selling to our clients."

Brandon and Jackson had heard the same thing at the methadone clinic. Ruby had already admitted that she believed Lauren was harassing her, although Ruby denied selling drugs. This wasn't new information to Brandon, but why were Brooke and Justin antagonizing Ruby now?

"She deserved to get fired," Brooke said. "She killed my best friend."

"That's a lie," Ruby said. "And I'm the one getting harassed here. By *you* two and the police." She stepped toward Brooke. "And you know what, you little piece of crap—they arrested someone else today. The man who picked her up on the way to the beach."

Dammit if the entire investigation wasn't being leaked.

"Who told you that?" Brandon asked.

"I got friends," Ruby said.

Brandon hoped it was the other construction workers—not one of his officers—who'd shared that info with Ruby. If Ruby was selling to the work crew, they'd keep her informed of what happened.

He considered the three miscreants. "I want you to stay away from each other," Brandon said. "If I have to get a court order, I will."

"Aren't you going to arrest her?" Justin asked.

"For what?"

"Murder," Brooke said.

"We are considering multiple suspects," Brandon said. Including all of Lauren's friends.

"Then for harassing us, dude."

184

Brandon turned to Ruby. "Do you promise to stop following these two around?"

She pulled out a pack of cigarettes, lit one, blew the smoke in Brooke's direction. Brooke thrust out an arm to swipe the cigarette out of Ruby's hand. Justin held her back. "Chill, babe."

"I'll leave them alone if they leave me alone," she said.

"Good," Brandon said. "Now, all of you, get out of my parking lot."

Brandon faced Justin and Brooke.

"By the way, smoking marijuana in a motor vehicle is illegal. You're in my jurisdiction now. This is your final warning."

Ruby hadn't done herself any favors by going after Lauren's friends. She'd already lied to Brandon about the contract workers. And if she kept harassing Brooke and Justin, Brandon would have to do something about it.

Brandon had just sat back down at his desk when Sue poked her head in. "Don't forget. You've got that presentation at six-thirty."

"What presentation?"

"The one the mayor emailed you about a few days back. I reminded you yesterday."

"You did?"

"You calling me a liar, Chief?"

Brandon eyed Sue. He had no recollection of the conversation.

"Right there, on your desk."

She pointed to a sticky note tacked to the bottom of his computer screen. Brandon peeled it off. It read: *Reminder, 6:30 council meeting. Mayor called.*

"She called?"

"When you were at lunch."

"Next time notify me in person. Better yet, call me."

Sue crossed her arms. "How am I supposed to know how you want things done if you don't tell me?"

"I'm telling you now."

"Fine," she said and walked away.

"Wait," Brandon said.

She shuffled back to his office.

"Yes."

"Look, Sue. It seems like we're getting off on the wrong foot."

"Hmm."

"Maybe I don't do things the same way as Chief Satler—"

She cast him a sarcastic smile. "I noticed."

"I need your help to do my job right."

"Okay," she said.

"Are we good?"

"We agree that you need me to do your job, yes."

She wasn't making this easy.

"What do you need from me, Sue?"

"Right now, I need you to let me go home and make dinner for my husband," she said. "But if you mean, what do I need to do my job? I need you to trust me. I've been doing this a while. Just like everyone else around here."

Brandon crossed his arms. "You had a problem with me sending Nolan home, too?"

"Not for a second. That man is an ass. Good riddance to him."

He was glad to hear someone agreed with him.

"It's only for a few days. He'll be back soon enough."

"You do know he's the one slipping information to that Ted guy from the newspaper. Been doing it for years," she said.

"And Chief Satler didn't care?"

"He picked his battles carefully. Just like you should." It was good advice.

"And relax. No one's liked by everyone." She winked at him. "Not even me."

Brandon chuckled, waving a hand at her. "Have a good dinner."

He scrolled to the original email from the mayor, telling him about the presentation that evening. Now he remembered reading the email. At the time, he figured he'd wing it, not worry about slides or handouts, the usual stuff people did at these sorts of political gatherings. Now he wished he'd put some effort into the presentation.

It wouldn't be the first time in his career he'd have to BS his way through a situation.

Chapter 25

Brandon slid into the back row of the large conference room that served as the Forks City Council's meeting chambers. The city council members were at the front of the room at a few long tables, facing a half-full room of citizens.

Mayor Kim sat at the center table.

Relief crossed her face as Brandon entered the room.

A local pastor said an opening prayer and led the pledge of allegiance. This was followed by public comments. Landowners complaining about utilities. A young mother worried about drug activity on her street. Brandon made a note to follow up with the woman about her concerns.

The final public comment was from an older gentleman claiming that it violated the separation of church and state to have a pastor pray before each meeting.

"Mr. Galbraith," the mayor said, "as we do every meeting, we'll make note of your concern."

"Thank you," he said into the microphone. "And God bless you."

Imagine that.

The director of public works gave an update on plans to repave Forks Avenue. After that, there was a brief presentation on the new math curriculum at the high school. Brandon had always had a hard time staying awake in math class. By the sound of it, the new curriculum was just as boring.

"Thank you, Principal Howard," Mayor Kim said. "And now our chief of police Brandon Mattson will share his vision for the department. And I'm sure he'll have lots to say about how the department will ensure a safe Moonbeam Festival."

Her eyes landed on Brandon for the briefest moment. "Just a reminder to everyone, the festival is in nine short days."

Brandon approached the microphone.

"Thank you, mayor."

"Chief Mattson," one of the council members interrupted him. The man was in his early fifties, wearing a tan suit jacket and forest green tie. He looked familiar—maybe a local insurance agent? "We want to express our gratitude for your willingness to accept the chief of police—"

"Thank you—"

"And I think I speak for all of us when I say how blessed this community is to have your family, not to mention your brother Eli who gave his life for the citizens of this town in the line of duty—"

"Thank—"

"And that's why we want to take this moment to announce our plans to unveil a monument to Eli Mattson to be a permanent fixture at Tillicum Park."

The council member leaned back from his microphone.

Brandon stared at the man for probably way too long.

"Great. Thank you."

The five council members and Mayor Kim waited for Brandon to say more.

"And, ah, my family is grateful for your gratitude."

Grateful for your gratitude?

Brandon never had a problem with surprises while working a beat or solving a homicide. But for them to expect him to stand up there and talk about Eli without any preparation—why hadn't the mayor given him a head's up? How many of these schmucks were prepared to discuss a loved one they'd lost? In front of a bunch of strangers.

It was a public meeting, not a group therapy session.

"Let's move on to Chief Mattson's presentation," Mayor Kim said.

Brandon explained that he had no presentation, but he did have plenty to say about his plans for policing the community now that the department would be, through contract with the Sheriff's Office, covering a wider area.

He went into detail about his staffing patterns and that, after replacing Will, he'd be hiring another officer in the coming year. Just to throw the mayor a bone, he highlighted the importance of the upcoming Moonbeam Festival and told the council he was in ongoing discussions with the mayor about details of his safety plan for the event.

Everything he said was accurate if a little inflated to fill up his time on the agenda.

"Are there any questions for Chief Mattson?" the mayor asked, surveying the room.

"I have several."

Brandon twisted around to face Ted, the reporter from the Forks Journal Extra.

Brandon gripped the edges of the podium and forced himself not to shake his head in disgust. This guy was a parasite. He'd already gotten info from inside the department, most likely from Nolan. Now he was hounding Brandon publicly.

"Any updates on the murder investigation, Chief?" Ted asked.

"Not at this time," Brandon answered.

"How can we know your department is doing enough to ensure the safety of this community?"

"That's my job."

"How can you do your job without one of your most experienced officers?" Ted asked, clearly referring to Nolan.

Brandon wouldn't take the bait.

"Officer discipline is an internal matter."

Ted smirked. "Chief, is it true you're dating Officer Nolan's ex-girlfriend?"

Ex-girlfriend? The last Brandon had heard, Misty was still with Nolan.

Brandon tried to ignore the collective gasp from the crowd at Ted's obvious accusation.

"No. I'm single, Ted. And as bad as your investigation skills are, I'm sure as hell glad you're not working for me."

The room erupted in laughter.

Ted's face burned red, but he continued. "Still, Chief—"

"Ted," Mayor Kim interrupted.

"I have a few more questions—"

"That's enough," she said, eyes boring into the recalcitrant reporter.

Ted stood for a few seconds before sinking back into his seat.

"Thank you, Chief. That will be all. Up next, we have a report from Sally Metzger on the city's efforts to increase recycling."

Brandon eyed Ted on his way to the exit, but Ted pretended to be writing in his notebook. It was probably for the better. One sour look from Brandon and it would be all over the papers that Brandon had threatened him.

Where did he come off, asking Brandon about his personal life? Who the hell cared if he dated Misty?

Outside, Brandon loosened his tie and the top button on his shirt. The truth was, no matter where you lived, people cared about dumb crap like who was dating who, especially if it involved men or women in leadership.

He thought about Ted and his prying into Brandon's relationships. Brandon could deal with local gossip about himself, as long as they left Emma alone.

The moment Ted's scribblings affected his family— Brandon would take matters into his own hands, chief of police or not.

Back in the office, he texted Emma and she said she planned on hanging out with a girl she'd met in town. Having pizza at her house. That took care of dinner, and he should be relieved that she'd found a friend. She was getting older. He'd have to learn to trust her more, even if he considered the rest of the society a potential risk to his daughter.

Will and Jackson arrived at the office at about the same time, 15 minutes before Jackson's interview. Brandon kept the process formal, considering Will's previous comment about Brandon's bias against Steve Chilton, the only other interviewee. Then there was the accusation by Ted at the council meeting. No doubt someone would weave Brandon's supposed relationship with Misty into his decision to hire Jackson.

To Brandon's relief, Jackson's interview went well. She answered every question thoroughly and professionally.

She had more experience than Chilton, despite a hiatus to raise her young children. Jackson had even been a detective, an important skill in a small town that didn't have the budget to hire a proper detective team.

"How did you score her?" Brandon asked Will after Jackson had left.

"Fifty-seven."

"That's higher than you scored the other guy," Brandon said.

Will slid his chair back, clasped his hands behind his head. "Yep."

"So, you won't give me any crap about hiring Jackson?"

"Nope."

"You sure? I need you on this, Will. People trust you."

"She's got my vote, hands down."

That was all he needed to hear.

"Thanks, Will. I'll send out an email after I let her know."

"Can I go home now?" Will asked. "I got two steaks and a bottle of pinot with my name on it waiting for me. I might even share with my wife."

Brandon smiled. "Get out of here."

Brandon had just made the full-time offer to a very ecstatic Jackson when his phone rang. He didn't recognize the number.

"This is Brandon."

"Chief, this is Josiah Trent."

"Josiah. Aren't you on duty?"

"Yes, sir."

"Why are you calling me on my private cell phone?"

"Your daughter, Emma..."

"What about her? Josiah—"

"She's fine, Chief. I'm taking her home now. I wanted to give you a heads up."

Brandon grabbed his keys and headed for the parking lot.

"Keep talking."

"We had a noise complaint," Josiah said.

"This early? It's barely nine."

What did this have to do with Emma?

"It was pretty loud. Lots of yelling and um..."

"Get to the point, Josiah."

"Alcohol."

"You're telling me my daughter was drinking?"

"No. She was not, as far as I can tell. I didn't do a breathalyzer or anything like that." Josiah paused. "You want me to take her home, right? Not down to the office."

"Yes. Home. Tell her I'll be there soon," he said.

"10-4."

"Wait," Brandon said.

"Yeah?"

"Who were these people she was with?"

"That's the interesting thing..."

Not what Brandon wanted to hear.

"That kid Justin and his girlfriend."

"Her name is Brooke," Brandon said. "How many people?"

"About nine or ten. Not counting your daughter, I mean. They were all over twenty-one."

"Thanks, Josiah. And not a word of this—"

"I wouldn't do that—"

"Not even to Nolan. Do you understand my meaning, Josiah?"

194

There was a pause. "Yes, sir."

Chapter 26

Josiah and Emma were waiting on the porch when he arrived.

Brandon dismissed Josiah and followed Emma into the house.

"What the hell were you thinking?"

Emma glanced at her bedroom door.

Brandon pointed toward the kitchen. "In there, now."

Emma sat down at the table, her eyes fixed on the floor.

"I'm sorry," she said.

"Are you aware that one of the men—and I mean *men* because those were all adults—at that party is a suspect in a murder investigation?"

"Who?" she asked.

"His name is Justin."

"Him? He seemed really nice."

"You think every murderer looks and acts mean—"

"No."

"How much alcohol did you drink?" Brandon asked, slipping all-too-easily into interrogation mode.

"None."

"Yet you were surrounded by alcohol for—what—how many hours?"

"They had just started drinking," she said.

"And you had none?"

Tears welled in Emma's eyes.

"No. Why don't you believe me?"

"Let's see, a fifteen-year-old at a party—"

"And all teens are drunks, right?"

He wasn't going to let her twist this back around on him.

"Not what I said."

"You don't trust me."

"After tonight? No."

His words hung in the air, but in the meantime, he had a chance to gather his thoughts, let his heart rate slow.

"Why were you there?"

"I was in line at the grocery store and some girl started talking to me. She asked me if I was new to town and she said she was too. Her name was Brooke."

Brandon pressed a thumb into his temple. He glanced at the top of the fridge. He was out of ibuprofen.

"You told me to make friends," she said.

"Justin and Brooke are adults. If they want to drink, that's their choice. You, on the other hand, are a child."

"I'm not a child—"

"Fine. You're a minor."

"Why did the police have to come, anyway?"

"That's what happens when people play loud music, create a disturbance, and generally act like idiots."

"It wasn't that bad—"

"It was that bad," Brandon said. "and I could arrest the whole group of them for offering booze to a minor."

"They never offered me anything," Emma said. "They just wanted to hang out."

What happened to the smart, sassy, and very un-gullible daughter he'd raised? Justin was a pothead loser, and Brooke, well, he questioned her judgment for being with someone like Justin. Neither of them was the kind of person he wanted his daughter around.

"I thought you were smarter than this," Brandon said.

197

She narrowed her eyes at him. "You want the truth? I was trying to help."

"Help with what?"

"The murder investigation," she said.

"Oh, no. Don't even go there. My daughter is not getting involved—"

"You said you thought I was smart. Now I'm too stupid to stay out of trouble?"

Technically, she'd just proven that by getting picked up by the police.

"What were you hoping to do? Get a confession?"

"What if I did?" she asked.

"Did you?"

She frowned. "No."

"Did you learn anything besides the fact that Justin and Brooke drink and smoke pot?"

She stared back at him, defiant.

"Tomorrow, you're going back to Grandpa's."

She crossed her arms. "Fine with me. It's boring around here, anyway."

"You're saying you want to go back to Seattle?"

"You can be such a jerk sometimes." She stood. "Can I go to my room now?"

"Yes."

She paused at the doorway, sniffling. "I set up the furniture."

Brandon glanced into the living room.

"Thanks."

"You're welcome," Emma said, and the way she slowly closed the door broke his heart. He wanted to be mad at her, but the truth was he was afraid. She'd gotten mixed up with some of the last people to see Lauren Sandoval alive.

Emma spent the next day at her grandpa's house, saying hardly a word from the time she woke up until Brandon dropped her off. When he picked her up that evening, she was a little more talkative, granting him a few words in response to his attempts at conversation.

Had he overreacted? It was his job to keep her safe. Maybe he should have said it differently, but that didn't mean he was wrong. He was reminded of Tori's words to him during one of their many arguments. Sometimes, being right isn't the point. It's the relationship that matters.

But didn't he have a good relationship with Emma?

Emma had begged Brandon to let her come live with him.

He wouldn't take that for granted, though. Kids grow up and, at some point, they stop giving you the benefit of the doubt.

Brandon took time at dinner to apologize for the way he'd confronted her, admitted he could have said things differently. He even told Emma he trusted her.

Her response was a grunt and a head nod. She'd come around, eventually.

He hoped.

Friday morning, Nolan was waiting for Brandon outside his office. It was his first day back from involuntary leave.

"Chief."

"Nolan," Brandon said, sweeping past him.

"You got a sec?" Nolan asked.

"Have a seat," Brandon said. He motioned toward the hallway. "You want to close the door?"

"I'm fine with it open," Nolan said.

"What's up?" Brandon asked.

Nolan leaned forward. "I heard you hired Jackson instead of Steve Chilton."

Nolan had just returned from three days without pay and the first thing he wanted to do was gripe and moan about who Brandon had brought on board to replace Will.

"You need to get over whatever it is you have against Jackson," Brandon said, thumbing through the pile of mail on his desk.

"It's not what I have against her. Steve is way more qualified."

"Actually, he's not."

"I disagree," Nolan said. He leaned forward, edging his chair closer to Brandon's desk. "But since you brought it up, I do have concerns about Jackson. The way she froze—"

"We're not covering this again," Brandon said. "It's over."

Nolan's chair shot back as he stood.

"You made the wrong decision."

It had been less than five minutes and Brandon already wanted to fire Nolan. He really didn't like the officer—for good reason. He'd risked the life of another officer and, if Brandon was right, leaked info about the murder investigation.

"I'm beginning to think I made the wrong decision about letting you come back to work."

Nolan scoffed. "I've been here ten years."

"And I can end that in ten seconds."

Nolan started to speak but thought better of it.

"You're covering the west precinct today," Brandon said.

The west area was mostly farmland, sparsely populated even by Forks' standards. To Brandon, the further away Nolan was from town and his friends in the press, the better.

When Nolan had gone, Brandon picked up his office phone.

He should call Sheriff Hart—maybe he'd have some advice on how to deal with Nolan. At the very least, he would give the sheriff a heads up regarding his concerns about the recalcitrant officer. That way, if or when Brandon did fire him, it wouldn't come as a total surprise.

Brandon set the receiver back down. He'd handle this himself. And if Sheriff Hart was like everyone else familiar with the department, he'd push back against Brandon's concerns.

The last thing Brandon needed was the sheriff on Nolan's side.

Mid-morning, Brandon received a call from Lisa Shipley.

He realized he hadn't talked to her since Monday when he'd been in the car with Jackson. He'd promised to call her back.

"I emailed an updated report, but I figured I'd call and let you know what the crime lab found," she said.

"What's the news?"

"We found Doug Nevins' DNA profile in CODIS."

Brandon had updated the coroner about the case when they'd found out Nevins was a registered sex offender, meaning his DNA was on record.

"And?"

"No match to the semen we found with Lauren Sandoval."

"Dammit."

That made the case against Doug Nevins even weaker. He'd given the girl a ride, dropped her off in the middle of nowhere. That was it. The prosecutor wouldn't touch this one.

"They didn't find any blood in his truck. A couple of strands of hair, but nothing else," she said.

"And we already know she was in the truck, so no news there," Brandon said. "Alright, thanks for the update."

"I'm not done yet," she said. "We got a hit on the semen."

"Who?"

"One match was for Adam Cane."

"That was quick," Brandon said.

"Yeah, don't expect such rapid results every time."

Brandon knew better than that. Even with testing done at the state level, things took much longer.

"Okay, Adam was Lauren's boyfriend. But you said one match. Was there another?"

"Justin Tate. Another CODIS hit."

Brandon thought back to the accusation Brooke had made against the young man—the allegation of rape she later retracted.

"Your initial report indicated no signs of sexual assault," Brandon said.

"Right," Lisa said.

"And that hasn't changed?"

"No, but it doesn't mean it didn't happen," Lisa said.

She was right. Not all assaults left evidence.

"Okay. We know Lauren had sex with Adam and Justin."

He couldn't rule out that Justin and Lauren were seeing each other. Adam's coworker had said Adam worried about Lauren cheating. Adam had confessed—then tried to minimize—those concerns.

"How does this line up with other evidence you've uncovered?" Lisa asked.

"Adam suspected Lauren was with another man. Even to the point that he considered canceling their camping trip."

"Did Adam know it was Justin?" she asked.

"Hard to tell. The two men don't get along, though."

"Makes sense," Lisa said. "What's next?"

"I need to interview Justin, see if he wants to be honest about what happened with Lauren."

"And Adam?"

"I'll get a read on how much he knows," Brandon said.

He'd have to involve Brooke too. It was her boyfriend, after all, that was sleeping with Lauren—her best friend.

"Thanks, Lisa. I appreciate you pushing this."

"Keep me updated," she said.

"One more thing," Brandon asked. "Any news on the beer cans from the beach? Prints or DNA?"

"Prints, nothing usable. As for DNA, we found saliva and we're waiting. Like I said though—"

"Things take time, I know."

"Right," she said. "Talk to you—"

"I know I said one more thing. But there's something else."

"What's up?"

"You want to go out sometime?" he asked.

It had been in the back of his head to ask her all week. There was silence on the other end and he wondered if she was still there.

"I thought you weren't interested," she said.

"Yeah, I was in the car with an officer the last time we talked. So, how about I meet you in Port Angeles?"

"I'm out of town this weekend, but back by Sunday."

"Sunday night?" Brandon asked.

"Let's do it. I'll email you my personal number."

They ended the call and a minute later, an email popped on his screen. Lisa's contact info and the name of a steakhouse in Port Angeles. Seven o'clock Sunday. She was taking the initiative. He liked that.

Brandon called Sue and told her he needed her to relay a message to Will and Jackson. Both were on duty until afternoon. They were to contact Adam, Justin, and Brooke and escort them to the station.

Brandon had brought a few cans of soup to work and opened one now. He scrounged around the station's kitchen for a bowl but couldn't find one. Instead, he poured the soup into a mug with a faded D.A.R.E. drug prevention symbol.

He stood watch at the microwave, briefly hypnotized by the carousel's slow spin. Sue interrupted him.

"There you are," she said. "There's a man on the phone by the name of Vaseline or something like that."

"Vaseline?" Brandon asked.

"Exactly. What kind of weirdo calls himself Vaseline?"

"What does he want?"

"Said you left a card at his house, told him to call you. And I had to wonder, what's the chief doing visiting a guy with a name like—"

"It's *Vasile*," Brandon said. "Hungarian or something like that."

"If you say so."

He grabbed his soup from the microwave. "Transfer him to my office."

Brandon answered. "This is Mattson."

"Vasile Anghel here," the man said. Despite his foreign-sounding name, there was no hint of an accent in his voice. "You asked me to call."

"I heard you might help with a case I'm working on," Brandon said.

"I don't see how."

"It involved vampire lore. You're an expert," Brandon said. "At least that's what people say."

Brandon guessed Vasile was the kind of guy who liked his ego stroked.

"Indeed."

"You're home now?"

"Just for today. I leave for a conference in Japan tonight."

"I'll be there in half an hour."

Brandon disconnected.

His first priority was to interview Justin and Adam, considering the recent DNA evidence. But the vampire angle, fantastic as it was, had to be considered. There was the bite mark on the girl's neck. Not to mention the graffiti. There could be no connection at all, but if he ended up on the stand, the defense attorney would call him out on any unexplored leads. And as off-the-charts weird as the vampire aspect of this case was, it had to be covered.

Vasile was waiting for Brandon in front of the large barn that stood several feet from his midnight blue Victorian three-story.

"Vasile," Brandon said. "Is that your real name?"

Vasile had black hair slicked back and a devilish goatee. But his resemblance to a character from a B-rate horror movie ended there. He was about 40 pounds overweight and wore a yellow short-sleeve button-up shirt, khakis, and leather sandals.

He stifled a laugh as he imagined Vasile in a scarlet and black velvet cape.

"If you are asking if it is the name I was born with, no."

"Why the change?"

"To honor my Transylvanian heritage," he said.

"Your birth name?"

"Gordon Banner."

He was right, Vasile was a much more interesting name.

Brandon recorded the name in his notebook.

"So, Vasile," Brandon asked, "you operate this group that deals with vampire culture?"

Vasile sighed. "The Nightside Coven."

"Coven. That sounds sort of creepy."

"I wouldn't expect you to understand," Vasile said, his eyes resting on Brandon's badge.

"Why not?"

"By nature, cops are conformists."

"Okay."

"And we are not," Vasile said.

"Tell me. Who is *we*?"

"Vampire enthusiasts. People of the night."

"So, what, you dress up like Harry Potter and drink Bloody Marys?"

206

Vasile rolled his eyes. "Thank you for proving my point. Is there a reason for these questions? Have we done anything wrong?"

"That's what I'm trying to find out, friend."

Brandon pulled out his phone and scrolled to the photo of the graffiti outside the Forks Diner. "Does this look familiar?"

Vasile took the phone and held it out an arm's length.

"Ah," he said, smiling.

"I'll take that as a yes."

"It is a vampire symbol."

"It's an ankh, right?" Brandon said, referring to the ancient Egyptian symbol.

Vasil's lips twisted in an appreciative grin. "I'm impressed."

"We police may be conformist, but we aren't entirely ignorant."

"This ankh has been modified to include the dagger point. This one seems to be giving the impression of dripping blood. Nice touch, by the way. It's been a sign in the community for decades."

"Is it possible a member of your coven could have done this?"

He shrugged. "Possible? Maybe."

"Why would someone paint this symbol?"

"I have no idea," Vasile said.

It was becoming obvious Vasile wouldn't go out of his way to help Brandon.

"Okay. Another question. Is there anyone around here who sells vampire teeth? Not the plastic kind kids play with. Sharp enough to penetrate skin."

"Nothing you'd find in those chintzy tourist pits in town, no."

"But they do exist? Metal, maybe?"

"Porcelain."

"And they fit in the mouth?"

"The fang smith—"

"What?"

"Fang smith, a crafter of vampire teeth. Anyway, the smith takes a mold of the customer's teeth. The mold is used to fit the fangs for the customer."

It reminded Brandon of the process for getting a mouthguard when the dentist had told him he'd been grinding his teeth at night.

"There are dozens of models. You can choose the number of fangs, length of the canines or incisors—"

"And they pop them in and walk around with these all day?" Brandon asked.

"They stay on with denture cream, but you take them out for eating."

Brandon pictured a group of twenty-somethings in black capes applying Fixodent in the bathroom mirror before a night on the town. There was no end to the lengths some people would go to be different.

"These fangs—they're sharp enough to draw blood?"

"Possibly." There was a twitch of excitement in the man's voice.

Brandon's eyes followed his thoughts, landing on the large barn.

"Is that something your coven encourages? Drinking blood?"

Vasile waved a hand at Brandon. "No. Not at all. We don't condone that here."

"Others do, though?"

208

"Some covens have been known to indulge in the life-giving practice of blood consumption. Always voluntary, of course."

Something in Vasile's voice told Brandon that the man was more familiar with the practice than he wanted to admit.

"You mean people volunteer to give blood for drinking?"

Brandon imagined a mobile blood donation center, victims reclining in comfortable chairs while Vasile and his friends waited impatiently on the receiving end of an IV, crimson goblets in hand.

"It happens. Not here, though," he said, hastily.

"What's the barn for?" Brandon asked, pointing his chin that direction. He'd noticed there were no signs of horses or livestock. And the surrounding pasture was covered with tall grass. Another sign there weren't any animals.

"Just storage," Vasile said, his eyes avoiding the barn. "It came with the property."

"And what do you do for a living, besides running a coven?"

Vasile narrowed his eyes at Brandon. "I'm an IT professional. Programming. I work remotely. Is that everything?"

"Almost. I'll need a list of everyone in your coven."

Vasile leaned away from Brandon. "For what?"

"In case we need to interview anyone connected to a case we're working on."

"What sort of case?"

"Murder."

Vasile, if he'd been out of town for the past few days, wouldn't have heard about the case.

"What's it got to do with my coven?"

"A girl was found dead with a bite mark on her neck."

Vasile stroked his goatee. "Oh, come on. You don't think—"

"Are you going to give me the list of names or not?"

"Don't you need a warrant for that sort of thing?"

"Not if you give it to me now," Brandon said. He lowered his volume so Vasile had to lean in to hear him. "I could get a warrant. Trust me, it's not that hard in a backwoods place like this." Brandon wasn't sure if that was true, but it sounded convincing. "And when I do, the warrant will include a search of every inch of this property."

Brandon had done his own research on these vampire groups the night before, after Emma had gone to bed. Some were into raves, Ecstasy, and other activities Vasile claimed hadn't occurred on his property.

"Ok. Fine. It won't be of any help, though. No one in my coven is capable of murder."

After over a decade in homicide, Brandon was convinced there were plenty of people capable of committing murder, no matter what their friends or family—or coven leader—thought.

"You let me decide who's a suspect or not. Just get me the list."

Five minutes later, Brandon left with a printout of an email distribution list for Vasile's vampire group.

Brandon drove to the end of the driveway and scanned the roster. Vasile's grand coven was 15 people strong, at most. None of the names were familiar. Except for one.

Ruby Walker.

It was hard to imagine the crusty, cantankerous cashier participating in any social activity, much less one involving a bunch of wannabe vampires.

There could be a drug connection—Ruby peddling opiates to the coven members. But that wouldn't require Ruby's involvement in the cult.

For the moment, he had to accept that Ruby was somehow involved in Vasile's subculture. But if Ruby was guilty of murder, why did she lie about Nevins' involvement with Lauren? Why not lead the police right to Nevins?

He'd follow up with Ruby about her involvement in Vasile's coven, and have his officers check out the others on the list for any connection to Lauren's death.

Brandon's phone rang. It was Sue.

"Will's got the two kids here—Justin Tate and Brooke Whittaker."

"I'm on my way."

Chapter 27

Will had found Justin and Brooke at her aunt's home, where they were both staying.

Brandon let Justin stew in the interview room for about 15 minutes before heading in with Will. Brooke waited in the main lobby. Brandon took the time to update Will on the DNA evidence indicating both Adam and Justin had sex with Lauren.

They took the two seats across from Justin.

Brandon asked Justin to sign the waiver-of-rights form. As far as Brandon was concerned, the kid was a suspect. To his surprise, Justin signed the form without asking for an attorney.

"Did she fight back?" Brandon asked.

The abrupt question had the desired effect. Justin's smug grin crumbled like the façade it was, revealing a scared kid who wanted nothing more than to be far, far away from Brandon and anyone in a police uniform.

"What are you talking about?"

"Don't act stupid," Brandon said. "It will just make things worse. And if you have more than one girl in mind, you're in deeper than I thought."

Brandon and Will stared at each other and then both moved as if to stand up.

"Ok, wait," Justin said. "Lauren..."

Justin paused as if to make sure he was going in the right direction. Brandon didn't give him any indication one way or another.

"We'd been together for a month. Or more. It was totally consensual."

"How long had you been having sex with her?" Brandon asked.

"Same. I didn't count the number of times if that's what you mean."

"Hard to keep track between her and your girlfriend?" Will asked.

Justin glanced at Will before looking away without a word.

"And the night she died?" Brandon asked.

"I didn't know she would die, man. Otherwise, I wouldn't have..."

"This young girl is dead and you're more concerned about leaving evidence?" Will asked. There was a genuine disgust in his voice.

"Not like that. I mean, am I a suspect in her murder now?"

"You already were," Brandon said.

His chin trembled. "I didn't do anything. I swear."

"Tell us what happened that night."

Justin pushed his chair back and buried his face in his hands. Brandon waited, letting the silence weigh on Justin.

A minute later, Justin lifted his head.

"We all partied like we said. Then later, I don't know, like after everyone passed out, I went to go take a piss. When I came back, Lauren was awake, smoking a cigarette. Out by the campfire."

"And then what?"

"We went for a walk and then...you know. It wasn't the first time we'd done it, so it wasn't any big deal."

Brandon tapped his pen on the table.

"Was this before or after Lauren headed to town?"

"It had to be before. I mean, I'm pretty sure it was before midnight."

"Did you and Lauren climb one of the sea stacks?" Brandon asked.

"No."

"You're sure you didn't go up and have a beer with Lauren?"

"Not at all. After we, you know, did it we came back and said goodnight and we both went to bed."

"And that's the last time you saw her?"

"Yeah," Justin said.

"Tell me, bud," Will said. "Do you feel bad at all about Lauren's death?"

Justin looked from Will to Brandon, as if to ask Brandon to have Will back off.

"I do." He slid the dreadlocks out of his face. "She was a nice girl."

"Not nice enough for you to leave Brooke?" Brandon asked.

"Brooke's my girl. You know what I mean, right? I was just playing."

"Does Brooke know about you and Lauren?" Brandon asked.

Justin's eyes went wide. "Hell no. You won't tell her, will you?"

"Why not?" Will asked.

"If she finds out she'll never forgive me."

"You've done this before?" Brandon asked.

"No. I mean, Brooke doesn't know."

"So, you have but haven't got caught."

Justin ran his hand over his face.

"You're aware we have your DNA in the system, right?" Brandon asked.

"I guess."

"And you know why."

"That was all cleared up, man. I didn't do anything wrong."

"You were accused of sexual assault," Brandon said.

"Yeah, but Brooke dropped the charges. She was just mad at me because she figured I was playing around behind her back."

If Justin was telling the truth, all he was guilty of was being a two-timing, good-for-nothing boyfriend.

But even if he had consensual sex with Lauren, that didn't rule him out. Sex wasn't the only motive for murder.

"The DNA evidence will come out during the trial after we catch whoever did this. In the meantime, it's up to you to come clean with Brooke."

Justin stared at his hands.

"What about Adam?" Justin asked.

"What about him?"

"I mean, if he knew about me and Lauren, wouldn't he want to kill her?"

"You have evidence he murdered Lauren?" Brandon asked.

"No."

"Did Lauren ever say she felt threatened by Adam?"

"That wuss? No. She could probably kick his ass." Then, as if realizing he'd just blown his own theory about Adam, he added, "But he could have. I mean, isn't jealousy a good motive for murder?"

"There is no good motive for murder," Brandon said. He stood. "One more question. You ever been into the vampire culture?"

"Like what?" Justin asked.

"Dressing up, wearing teeth."

"You mean like cosplay?"

"Cosplay?" Brandon asked.

"Costume play. Like Comic-Con."

Brandon had heard of Comic-Con. They'd come to Seattle. Thousands of barely clad men and women dressed like anime characters, superheroes, or whatever they found at the local thrift shop.

"You're into that?" Will asked.

"That's for nerds, man," Justin said.

"How about Adam?"

"I don't know. He is sort of a nerd."

"Brooke?"

"Hell, no," he scoffed. "I wouldn't date no chick into that stuff."

"That's enough for now."

Will escorted Justin to the waiting area, then led Brooke to the interview room. Outside the door, Will spoke to Brandon.

"He could have done it," Will said.

"Maybe."

"It's clear he didn't give a damn about the girl. Or any girl for that matter," Will said.

"Agreed, but being a complete ass doesn't make him a good suspect for murder."

"Well, someone ought to knock some sense into him."

Brandon tilted his head. "How long until you retire?"

"Not soon enough."

They interviewed Brooke next.

Brandon had just closed the door when she asked, "What did you ask Justin? Is he in trouble?"

Brandon looked to Will.

216

"We'll leave it up to your boyfriend to tell you what we discussed," Will said.

Brooke stared at Will for a long time, as if trying to decipher the hidden meaning behind his statement.

"Was Lauren ever interested in anyone besides Adam?" Brandon asked.

"No...I mean, before Adam, she'd had a couple of boyfriends."

"No one recently?"

Brooke's jet-black hair was cut short on the sides, but her bangs were long and leaned over her right eye. Her hands trembled as she swept the bangs aside.

"No," she said.

"How long have you and Justin been together?" Will asked.

"Almost three years."

"How are things between you?"

"Fine. Why are you asking me these questions?"

"Just curious," Will said.

"Shouldn't you be going after Ruby?" She pulled her feet up into the chair and sat cross-legged. "I mean, she's the one who wanted Lauren dead."

"That's a serious accusation," Brandon said.

"Well, it's true. She threatened Lauren. Everyone knows that."

Brandon pulled out his phone, found the photo he was looking for, and held it up.

"Does this look familiar?"

The color drained from her face. It was a strange reaction, considering Justin had made it clear they had no interest in the vampire subculture.

After a few seconds, she said, "That's the graffiti in town. Justin and I were just talking about that."

217

"What about it?" Will asked.

"I don't remember. It was like, something about how weird it was."

"Do you know what it means?"

"No idea," she said, her eyes avoiding the picture.

"Not into that sort of thing?" Brandon asked.

"What sort of thing?"

Brandon slid his phone into his pocket, ignoring the question.

"We'll be in touch," he said. She'd already made it clear she wasn't interested in revisiting her accusations of sexual assault against Justin. She had gone out of her way to avoid saying anything negative about her wayward boyfriend.

"Are you going to stop her from doing this again?"

"Who?"

"Ruby, obviously. Because Justin and I aren't safe—"

"We're following every lead," Brandon said. He motioned toward the door. She was free to go.

Brooke stood.

"By the way," Brandon said, "I'll remind you not to invite underage teen girls to parties where you happen to be drinking and doing dope."

Her eyes widened in genuine fear.

"Especially when the underage girl is my daughter," Brandon said.

Will led Brooke back to the lobby. When he returned, he asked, "What the hell was that about?"

"What?" Brandon asked.

"The underage teen girl thing."

"Justin and Brooke invited Emma to the house where they're staying. Josiah responded to a noise complaint and Emma was there."

"Damn."

"By the way. Don't mention that to anyone," Brandon said.

"I've been doing this for how many decades, and you don't think I know how to keep my mouth shut? You know how many of the previous chief's kids I had to deal with?"

"Emma's not like that."

"I know that," Will said. "But keep your eye on that Justin kid. There's something about him..."

Chapter 28

Brandon shot off an email to the prosecutor's office, letting them know Doug Nevins' DNA didn't match that found with Lauren Sandoval. Nevins was being charged with resisting arrest and attempted murder of two police officers. Based on the information they had now, it appeared Nevins fled because he figured they were there to bust him for failure to report as a sex offender.

That, at least, narrowed the list of suspects. But that didn't rule out someone they hadn't come across yet. Anyone could have picked Lauren up on her way back to the beach. Considering her level of intoxication, she might have agreed to share a couple of beers with just about anyone.

That she'd had sex with both Adam and Justin was telling, but it didn't point to either man. They both had motive. Adam, if he knew Lauren had cheated on him. Justin had a history of accusations of assault against him. But was he willing to kill to keep his affair with Lauren a secret?

Brandon had asked Jackson to follow up with the police in Port Angeles if she wasn't able to get ahold of Adam by phone.

There had been no sign of him at home or work.

And what about Brooke? Lauren's best friend by her own report. Had she learned of Justin's most recent tryst?

Then there was Ruby. Brandon had no reason to like the woman. She had lied to him, acted as obstructionist as possible, and on top of everything else, she was a dealer. She had a clear motive to kill Lauren—considering the girl's threats to turn her in. And now he had proof she'd participated in Vasile's blood-sucking cult. Ruby might have owned a pair of fangs like the ones that made the marks on Lauren's neck.

Bite marks like that were usually part of some sort of fetish. Ruby didn't fit the mold. Then again, he would have never guessed she was part of a vampire coven.

A reminder popped up on Brandon's computer screen. He had an appointment with the mayor.

Ten minutes ago.

Mayor Kim and Olivia Baker were on opposite sides of the mayor's conference table, a map of the Moonbeam Festival stretched out between them.

"Nice of you to show," the mayor said.

Brandon ignored the jab. They were lucky he showed at all.

"I hope this isn't another attempt to change the way my officers dress. I don't have time for this today—"

"A hot date?" Olivia asked, her lips in a teasing smile.

Olivia had been at the public meeting where Ted had made the insinuation about Brandon and Misty.

Brandon's cold stare was enough to change her mind about pursuing the question further.

"Okay, well, as you might recall," Olivia said, "there are only six days until the Moonbeam Festival—"

"And Tiffany Quick has expressed concerns," the mayor interrupted, "about the ongoing murder investigation."

"What does Tiffany Quick have to do with my investigation?"

"She's concerned for her safety."

"I see. Then tell her to avoid camping on Second Beach."

221

"This is serious, Brandon."

"I know it is. That's why I'm spending all day every day working on this case."

"If she doesn't feel safe—" Olivia started.

"I can't change how she feels, Ms. Baker. All I can do is solve Lauren Sandoval's murder."

"You do know there's been another case of vampire graffiti?" Olivia asked.

"When?"

"Someone reported it this afternoon."

"Reported it to whom?"

"The newspaper," Olivia said. "It's the vampire symbol, but this time there's a message, too."

"And?"

The mayor found the picture on the Forks Journal website and twisted her laptop to Brandon.

The photo showed an abandoned house. He'd seen it before but couldn't place it. Blackberry bushes and knee-high grass framed a weathered craftsman. The vampire ankh covered the home's front door. Next to the door, in the same spray paint, were the words *More Will Die.*

"Where is this?"

"Over on Elm Street."

"Why contact the newspaper instead of letting the police know?"

"Maybe they don't trust you're doing enough," Olivia said.

Mayor Kim raised a hand to silence her.

"What does it mean?" the mayor asked.

The vampire symbol paired with the warning of more deaths solidified the connection between Lauren's murder, the bite on her neck, and the cult aspects of the vampire community.

Was it the killer, tipping their hand there would soon be another victim?

"I'll go check it out," Brandon said.

"Any updates on your investigation?" Mayor Kim asked.

She noticed Brandon glance at Olivia.

"You can keep it general," the mayor said.

"You've heard about Doug Nevins, the contract worker staying at the Forks Inn?" Brandon asked.

"Right," the mayor said.

"Evidence suggests it wasn't him."

"What about this Ruby person?" Olivia asked.

Ruby had been right about one thing. Rumors around town suggested she was the one responsible for Lauren's death. Those assumptions were based on the enmity between Ruby and Lauren. So far, Ruby's involvement in the coven wasn't public.

"Isn't it true she had it in for Lauren Sandoval?" the mayor asked.

"Did they have their disagreements? Sure. Would she have murdered someone? I don't know that."

"I'd say it was stronger than a disagreement," Olivia said.

Brandon eyed her. "You seem to know a lot about Ruby and Lauren."

He was confident Nolan had leaked information to Ted. For the first time, he wondered if Olivia was getting info from Nolan too.

Olivia was silent.

"Any other suspects?" the mayor asked.

"All of her friends."

"Her friends?" the mayor asked.

"Things aren't always as they appear," Brandon said. "And Lauren might not have been as good of a friend as she seemed."

Mayor Kim crossed her arms. "What you're trying to say is Lauren was sleeping with the other boy—what's his name?"

He'd underestimated the power of women's intuition—again. How the hell did she figure that out?

"DNA doesn't lie," Brandon said. "There is the possibility it wasn't consensual."

Brandon's eyes landed on Olivia, her mouth agape in surprise. He knew he'd said too much.

"This is not public information," Brandon said, locking eyes on her. "Is that clear, Olivia?"

She stared at the table, her expression suddenly blank.

"Olivia?" the mayor asked.

Olivia's head swiveled. "Sorry. Yes. Totally private."

Brandon didn't like the way Olivia reacted to the news that Justin and Lauren slept together. Besides being fodder for town gossip, the information wasn't directly relevant to Olivia. So why the reaction?

Next time the mayor asked for an update on the case, he would stick to generic answers. Brandon wasn't sure who to trust—Nolan might not be the only one leaking information to the media.

Out in the parking lot, Brandon called to check on Emma.

"I already dropped her off at home," his dad said.

"We agreed you would keep her until I was off."

"It's almost six, Brandon. I got plans for tonight."

224

What plans could his father possibly have? The man had been a hermit for as long as Brandon could remember.

"Vampire book club meeting at the library."

"I thought you already read the series. What more could there be to talk about?"

"There's more than one series, you know. It's a whole genre. Romance, mystery, suspense. All with vampires."

"Romance?"

"I didn't say I read that kind of vampire book," his dad said. "At least I don't read that commie Russian stuff you like."

"Chekhov, Tolstoy, Dostoyevsky—"

"Exactly."

"Were all pre-revolution," Brandon said.

"You don't think they read Marx?"

Brandon had no interest in debating nineteenth-century Russian politics with his father. In fact, Brandon despised just about any conversation involving politics. With his father or anyone else.

"You're not part of one of those covens, are you?" Brandon asked.

"Coven? Like for witches?"

"Vampires," Brandon said.

"You don't actually believe in vampires, do you son? Because this is fiction we're talking about."

"Never mind."

"Anyway, Emma's safe at home." There was a pause. "She told me about getting in trouble."

Of course she did.

"You mean because she was in a house with alcohol and probably pot too?"

"Don't be too hard on her, Brandon."

225

Buzz Mattson, the general, dishing out parenting advice?

"Yeah, because you were so easy on Eli and me—"

"She's a smart kid."

"And we weren't?"

"I'm just saying. She knows what she did was wrong. You got to show her you trust her."

"Okay, Oprah," Brandon said. "Thanks for the pep talk."

"Remember, you weren't so innocent yourself."

"That's what I'm worried about," he said.

"But you turned out okay."

"You know, that's the nicest thing you said to me all day."

Or ever, Brandon thought.

"Ah, hell, I got to go."

"Bye, Dad."

On his way home, Brandon headed to the house on Elm Street. The front door was locked, and, to Brandon's surprise, none of the windows had been smashed out. The spray paint was dry. He took a photo of the vampire ankh and threatening message. He did a quick search of the sticker bushes and knee-high grass but found nothing.

Returning to his truck, Brandon noticed a woman across the street watching him. He headed over to her house.

She was mid-forties, wearing a tank top and shorts. She sat on the top step, a cigarette in one hand, her cell phone in the other.

"You the one who called this in?" he asked.

She pointed her phone at the abandoned lot. "I noticed it this morning."

226

"No idea who did it?"

"Kids play over there all the time."

"How old?"

"Grade school. Too young to do that."

Brandon had seen elementary kids do worse than tag an abandoned home.

He handed her a business card. "Next time, call me instead of the newspaper."

She glanced up at him. "People say the cops won't do anything."

"People who?"

She thought about it, then shrugged her shoulders. "The newspaper."

"Don't believe everything you read," Brandon said.

She took a drag of her cigarette and held it in for a long time before letting the smoke escape.

"People say it's those vampire freaks." She pointed a finger at him. "They drink real blood. Most of all from virgins. Like that girl on the beach."

Brandon didn't see the point in revealing Lauren's sexual history just to make a point.

Back in his truck, Brandon peered through the passenger window at the foreboding message, *More Will Die*.

Was it the work of one of the vampire-obsessed locals?

It could be a copycat. A bored local kid, so starved for attention that they'd inserted themselves into a murder investigation? Or was it the killer? The strange symbol, the ominous warning, and even the public nature of the statement—Brandon had encountered those before—were the traits of a serial killer.

Chapter 29

Brandon pulled up to the curb in front of his house. Emma sat on the front porch. She wasn't alone.

Misty waved at him and he tried to hide his disappointment. Brandon sighed. He was tired and wanted to relax and spend time with his daughter.

"Dad! You're finally home."

"What are you doing out here?"

"I forgot my keys."

"Emma—"

"Don't be too hard on her, Brandon," Misty said. "You used to do the same thing."

If one more person told him to be easy on Emma...

"Can Misty stay for dinner?" Emma asked.

"I don't know," Brandon said. "I'm beat."

"Your dad's tired," Misty said. "It looks like he needs some shut-eye."

"Please, Dad? It's boring around here."

"You mean I'm boring?" Brandon asked, smiling.

He unlocked the front door. "Fine."

Emma pecked Brandon on the cheek. "Thank you."

"You don't have to do this," Misty said.

"It's not a problem," Brandon said. He let Misty in the house and checked the street one more time, just to make sure no one was watching. He imagined Ted capturing an image of Misty entering Brandon's house and posting it all over the local news websites.

"Let's just order pizza," Brandon said.

"I can make something," Misty said.

"No," he said. "Pizza is fine."

"You didn't like my casserole?" she asked, casting him a playful smile.

"It was excellent. Everything I hoped for."

"See if I ever bring you another welcome-to-the-neighborhood dish," she said.

Emma returned with an armful of board games. "Which one first?"

"I need to change. You two decide," Brandon said.

Brandon changed into shorts and a t-shirt and called the local pizza delivery joint. When he came back into the living room, Misty and Emma were setting up Monopoly.

"After this, we can play Risk," Emma said. She frowned at Misty. "Dad always wins."

"We'll see about that," Misty said.

Brandon flipped on the stereo. A blast of his favorite metal band, *Iron Maiden,* filled the room. He lowered the volume a notch.

"Ugh," Emma said. "Turn it off."

"This is classic Maiden," Brandon said. "Their first album. They were still on their first singer back then. Before Bruce Dickenson joined—"

"It's cheesy," Emma said.

"Your dad's favorite back in the day," Misty said. "I think it made him feel tough."

"I was tough," Brandon insisted.

"It's still cheesy," Emma said. "Play the *Civil Wars.*"

"I like them," Misty said.

Brandon found the folk band on his phone and connected to the stereo's Bluetooth. Despite his interest in old-school metal, he was a fan of a variety of music styles, including folk—Emma's favorite.

It was midnight before Misty convinced Emma to give up on her ever-dwindling chances at winning Risk. Like Monopoly, the game rarely ended in less than a few hours. In high school, Brandon and his buddies had played games that spanned days.

Brandon walked Misty to the edge of the lawn.

"That was fun," she said.

"Yes. A little late for me, but fun."

"Past your bedtime, old man?"

Brandon looked askance at her. "If I recall, you are, what, three months older than me?"

She tapped him on the arm. "It's not nice to ask a lady her age."

"My apologies," Brandon said.

Then he asked a question that had been eating at him since the city council meeting, when Ted had implied Misty was no longer with Nolan.

"What's going on with you and Nolan?"

She slid closer. "Why do you care?"

Brandon leaned away.

He'd wanted to know about Misty and Nolan because...he didn't know why.

"I care about the well-being of my officers," he said, trying to mask the sarcastic smile forming on his lips.

"That's not what Nolan says."

"Really? What else does Nolan say?"

"Sorry," she said. "I shouldn't have said that."

After a moment, she said, "This case is taking its toll on you."

"Yeah, well, that happens when you have a killer loose in your town."

"And they threaten to kill again," she said.

Brandon eyed her.

"It was on the paper's website. The new graffiti. More will die—"

"Right."

It was hard to keep track of who knew what.

"People are saying Ruby Walker did it."

"Rumors, nothing more."

"You're probably right. That's part of living in a small town." She paused. "Is that why you left?"

He searched her eyes. Did she really not know? She was the reason he'd left. How could he come back when they'd been together for so long, Misty pregnant with another man's baby?

That wasn't fair. Misty was just one of several reasons he'd moved on from his hometown.

"Rumors and false leads are part of the job," he said, avoiding her question. "People take one fact—like someone's involvement in a secret group—and act as if the person had a smoking gun in their hand."

"Who is part of a secret group?" she asked.

He held up a hand. "No one."

"C'mon," she said. "I won't tell anyone."

He'd said enough.

"I need to get back inside," Brandon said. "Thanks for coming over."

He turned and ascended the front porch.

"We're taking a break," Misty said, calling out after him.

Brandon took the bait. "Huh?"

"Nolan and me. We're taking a break."

Brandon considered her answer. He'd asked her about her relationship with Nolan. In the moment, he'd wanted to know, almost had to know. But now, after the conversation about Nolan and the case and the rumors going around town, it didn't seem important.

"Ok. See you."

It was an uncomfortable end to the evening, but he didn't have much else to say. Despite the rumors, he wasn't romantically involved with Misty, hadn't been for two decades. Why should it matter to him who she dated?

Taking a break. Whatever that meant. It sounded like something a 20-year-old would do.

Back in the house, Emma was waiting for him.

"Did you kiss her?"

"What?"

"You know, a goodnight kiss?"

"Emma—"

"Not even a peck?"

"If I didn't know any better, I'd think you were trying to set me up with that woman," Brandon said.

"What's wrong with her? She seems nice—"

"Your mom and I—"

"Aren't ever going to get back together," she said, an icy tone suddenly infusing her voice.

"Come here," Brandon said, sitting down on the couch.

She settled onto the cushion next to him.

"Your mom and I loved each other for a very long time. We still love each other."

"Then why did you get divorced?"

They'd talked about this before, but he knew it would take time for everything to sink in. Even now, it still bothered Emma. It made sense. Brandon hadn't fully recovered from the end of his marriage, either. Tori had been all he'd known for most of his adult life. As much as they'd argued, been so different, she was the constant in his life, the one he knew, or thought he knew, would always be there.

"I know," she said. "It's not simple. Adults don't always get along, blah, blah—"

"Hey. It doesn't change that both of us love you," he said.

"I know."

Emma yawned.

Brandon pulled her into a hug. "You need to get to bed."

"I don't have anything to do tomorrow," she said.

"Maybe you should ask around about work. Earn some money for a car—"

"I'll just hang out with Grandpa."

"I don't know," Brandon said. "If it were me choosing between work and Grandpa, I'd choose work."

"Haha," she said.

"And," Brandon said, "I don't need a girlfriend."

"Guys don't do good alone, Dad."

"Says who?"

"I read it on a relationship blog."

"So it must be true."

"Whatever, Dad. Besides, if you refuse to let me live here with you and Grandpa the whole year—"

"What about your mom?"

"She's too busy most of the time."

"It's not because you're not getting along with her again?"

"We're fine," she said. "We talked today. So why can't I live here?"

"We already went over this," Brandon said. "The school here is way smaller than the ones in Seattle."

"Can't you at least think about it?"

"Goodnight, Emma."

She rolled her eyes and headed for her room.

"Love you too," he said.

First thing in the morning, Brandon checked in with Will and Jackson regarding Adam. They still hadn't had a chance to interview Adam now that they had the DNA evidence suggesting both Adam and Justin had slept with Lauren.

They had called his work and cell numbers, and a deputy had checked his apartment. No sign of him.

He'd also heard from his team about the other individuals on Vasile's list of coven members. Unlike Ruby, none had any direct connection with Lauren, and each claimed to have an alibi for the night of her death.

About mid-morning, he got a call from Josiah.

"Chief. You won't believe this."

"Try me," Brandon said.

"I've been talking to every hardware store from here to Sequim."

"About the spray paint?"

"Will checked around town, but he said if I was bored, I could snoop around Port Angeles," Josiah said. Brandon chuckled. Will, the old-timer, had gotten Josiah to help him investigate the graffiti—an assignment Brandon had given Will.

"And?"

"I found a place up in Port Angeles. They'd sold about five cans over the past month. Two of them were purchased by the same person. I even went up and verified it, checked their video to confirm the most recent one."

"Who bought the paint?"

"Justin Tate."

"You're sure?"

"It's on video. And he used a debit card. Pretty stupid."

"Indeed. And great work on this. Pick him up. Go with backup." Brandon searched through the case file until he found the address where Justin and Brooke were staying.

Brandon read the address to Josiah.

"Question," Brandon said. "Was Justin alone in the video from the hardware store?"

"Just him."

"Got it."

Justin Tate, the kid who denied any interest in vampire lore, was potentially the one who'd painted the ankh—and the warning about more murders. Justin had motive—he didn't want Brooke to discover his affair with Lauren. Now, it appeared he was the one behind the recent bout of graffiti.

And the bite mark on Lauren's neck was clearly done by someone interested in the vampire subculture. Or at least trying to hide behind the veil of suspicion the bite—and the graffiti—would create.

Half an hour later, Josiah called back.

"He's not there."

"What about the girl?"

"Brooke was there with her aunt. They both said Justin went out last night and never came back."

"Now what?" Josiah asked.

"Send out an APB. Is his truck missing?"

"Yes."

"Okay. At least we know what he's driving."

Now he had two suspects missing. Adam and Justin. Both men had slept with Lauren the night she was murdered. Both men had motive. And one of them—Justin—had sent a message to Forks that Lauren's murder wasn't the last.

Chapter 30

Early that afternoon, Brandon received notice that they'd found Justin's truck a few miles outside of town. He'd been headed north on Highway 101 away from Forks. A quick scan of the area revealed Justin's body hanging from a noose tied to the lower branch of a big leaf maple.

Brandon arrived just as Josiah pulled up behind him.

Nolan had been the first officer on the scene.

"You call the coroner and crime scene techs?" Brandon asked.

"Not yet," Nolan said. "Didn't know if that's what you wanted me to do."

It was basic procedure. Even Nolan should know that. Nolan's passive-aggressiveness better not have screwed up his crime scene.

"Call them now."

Nolan headed to his vehicle to make the call.

Brandon studied Justin's lifeless body from a distance. His feet were about four feet off the ground. His arms were unbound, his head tilted to the right, held in place by a rope that led to a branch less than a foot above.

Long brown dreadlocks covered his closed eyes.

"You think he did this out of guilt for killing the girl?" Josiah asked.

"No," Brandon said.

"Then why?"

"Don't assume that the obvious answer is the right one."

"Someone killed him?"

Brandon edged to the left, keeping his distance from the body.

"There," Brandon said, pointing at a deep laceration just behind Justin's right ear. The blood had spilled down his neck and onto the back of his t-shirt.

Nolan returned. "Coroner's on the way." Then, noticing Justin's injury for the first time, he said, "Damn. Who did that?"

"Good question," Brandon said.

"Hey," Nolan said. "Check this out."

He strode over to a clump of weeds not far from the tree.

"A shovel." He bent to pick it up.

"Don't," Brandon warned him. "I want the techs to get here and document everything."

Nolan stepped back carefully.

"Who would want to kill him?" Josiah asked.

Brandon updated both officers on the DNA results.

"Adam might have killed him for cheating with Lauren," Josiah said.

"Possible," Brandon said.

"That means he could have killed Lauren too."

"What about the woman?" Nolan asked.

"Brooke? Again, possible. Justin was her boyfriend, and Lauren was cheating with him."

"Not the girl," Nolan said. "I meant Ruby. I heard she wanted Lauren dead...her friends too. Because they were going to turn her in—and they got her fired."

Brandon considered Justin's lifeless body. Like Lauren, too young to die. His eyes narrowed as they caught on two puncture holes, just above the noose.

He moved to the side for a better view.

"What?" Nolan asked.

"Another bite mark."

Josiah hooked his thumbs in his duty belt. "I bet it's someone connected to that vampire cult."

"What about Ruby, she into that stuff?" Nolan asked.

Brandon's better judgment told him not to mention what he'd learned about Ruby's involvement with Vasile. Nolan would assume the worst. But he didn't like hiding information from his officers.

"There is evidence Ruby is connected to a local vampire coven," Brandon said.

"Like what, bloodsuckers?" Nolan asked.

"Not necessarily. I had a talk with their leader. Ruby was on the list of names he gave me."

"See, this is what I'm saying," Nolan said, pointing a finger at Brandon. "She's our murderer. Ruby's got motive—we already knew that. Now we find out she's one of those vampire freaks—"

"Hold on," Brandon said. "Let the crime scene techs do their work first, then we can decide what to do next. In the meantime, we need to talk to Adam and Brooke."

"And Ruby," Nolan said.

"Yes, and Ruby."

Brandon would wait for the coroner. He sent Josiah to check in again with Port Angeles for any sign of Adam. He told Nolan to go find Brooke and take her down to the station. Under no circumstances should he reveal anything about what had happened. Brandon hoped to gauge Brooke's reaction to the news of Justin's death.

Brandon stayed out of the way while Lisa and the techs gathered evidence.

Once the techs gave him the okay, Brandon examined the tree where Justin had been hanging. The rope attached to Justin's neck had hung from a limb about a foot above him. The rope then led to another branch about five feet away where it was wrapped around two times and then tied into a knot.

Brandon borrowed a step ladder from a crime scene tech and inspected the knot where the rope was anchored. There were at least three areas where moss and bark had been rubbed away, exposing the meat of the tree underneath, as if someone had used the branch like a pulley to haul Justin's body into its current position. Even a grown man would have a hard time dragging Justin to this location, not to mention lifting his body off the ground.

Apparently, the murderer had killed Justin, slid the noose around his neck, and then pulled him up using the rope. The damaged tree bark was evidence it hadn't been easy.

Whoever had killed Justin was in a hurry, not very smart, or both. The head wound made it obvious this wasn't a suicide, but the scene was staged to make it appear to be. It could be the killer changed their mind. Murdering Justin, adding the bite mark to match Lauren's wounds—but then decided to make it appear to be a suicide at the last minute.

He met Lisa out by his SUV.

She said, "I figure he was killed by the rock or the shovel or both. But—"

"Just preliminary, I know."

"We'll see if it's only his blood or we find something else."

"The bite?" he asked.

"There's the possibility of saliva. At least a better chance than last time."

She had everything under control. He would expect nothing less. Brandon's eyes caught on her purple-tinted hair. Some people might think it was an attempt to appear younger. Lisa was probably in her mid-thirties. Let her color her hair any shade she wanted. There was something bold about it. A little quirky.

"We still on for tomorrow night?" she asked.

"Wouldn't miss it for the world."

Brandon contacted Justin's parents in Spokane, where the young man had grown up.

The boy's father had answered the phone and had been in shock just like every other parent he'd had to notify. Brandon only asked one question—any idea who would want to do this? Justin's father had no answer and for the time being Brandon didn't press the issue any further.

Brandon was back in town when Nolan called him.

"I have the girl," Nolan said. "The boy is here too."

"What boy?"

"Adam Cane."

"Where?" Brandon asked.

"At the aunt's home. Where Brooke is staying."

"I said bring her down to the station."

"She's too upset."

"You told her about Justin?"

"What was I supposed to do, lie?"

"Dammit, Nolan. I told you not to say anything."

Nolan was silent on the other end.

"How did she react?" Brandon asked.

"I don't know. She was crying. Wouldn't you be—"

"Just don't say another word to her. I'll be there in a minute."

The rambler wasn't far from the police station. He'd found the address in the notes he had taken that first night he'd interviewed Lauren's friends.

A stone walkway cut through neatly mowed grass. Matching hydrangeas hedged the steps leading to the front door, bees hovering and flitting about their blue blossoms.

It would be a good day for a picnic with Emma. If there weren't two murders to solve.

Brandon rang the bell. The door opened.

There, frowning back at him, was Olivia Baker, the mayor's Minister of Tourism.

"What the hell are you doing here?" Brandon asked. He looked over her shoulder, expecting to see Ted the reporter, too.

"I live here," she said.

"You what?"

"This is my house."

"I thought Brooke and Justin were staying with her aunt."

Olivia blinked at him. "I am her aunt."

Chapter 31

"I thought you knew," Olivia said.

All the times he'd discussed the case with the mayor when Olivia was present, she'd never once mentioned that she was Brooke's aunt.

"It looks to me like you went out of your way to hide your relationship to one of my suspects—"

"A suspect? Brooke isn't—"

"I decide who is a suspect. You stick to party planning or whatever the hell it is you do for the mayor."

"Brandon?"

Speak of the devil.

The mayor appeared behind Olivia. What was this, a frickin' party? Half the town was there, stepping all over his investigation.

"Did you know?" Brandon asked Mayor Kim.

She stared back at him quizzically.

Brandon continued, "That Brooke was Olivia's niece. That she was staying in this house."

"Not until today," she said. "But I'm sure this has nothing to do with the incidents you're investigating."

"What are you doing here?" Brandon asked.

"Olivia called me for support," Mayor Kim said, "when she learned her niece's boyfriend had been found dead."

And the only reason she knew that was because Nolan had opened his big mouth. Now, Brandon had lost his chance to see Brooke's—and Adam's—reactions to the news of Justin's death.

"I need to speak to Adam and Brooke," Brandon said.

"Come right in," Olivia said, not hiding the irritation in her voice.

She led Brandon to a den. Nolan stood next to a couch where Brooke and Adam were together, Adam's arm around her back.

Brandon made eye contact with Nolan.

"I'll take it from here," Brandon said.

"But—"

"You've done plenty today, Officer Nolan. Head to the station and do your write-up."

Nolan paused, hands on his belt. He nodded to the mayor and Olivia before leaving.

Brandon took the chair across from Brooke and Adam.

"I'm sorry about Justin," Brandon said.

Brooke sniffled and wiped her nose with a wad of tissue paper she had scrunched into a ball.

"He left last night..."

"Is it true he killed himself?" Adam asked.

"Is that what Officer Nolan told you?"

"He said you found him hanging." Adam's eyes landed on Brooke. "Doesn't that mean..."

"It could mean a lot of things," Brandon said. "Including murder."

Brooke glanced up at him. "You think someone did this to Justin?"

"Too soon to make any judgments—"

"I told you," Brooke said. "I told you."

She buried her head in her hands.

"Told him what, sweetie?" Olivia asked.

Brooke was silent for a long time.

"That woman Ruby. She threatened Lauren, threatened me and Justin," Brooke said. "She even chased us down the other day. And we had to go to the police department. But he wouldn't help us." She eyed Brandon accusingly.

"Is that true, Chief Mattson?" the mayor asked.

"Yes, Brooke and Justin made a complaint about Ruby."

"Then why isn't that woman in custody?" the mayor asked.

"If you had done your job," Olivia said. "Justin might still be alive."

"I'm going to let that slide, considering the situation here," Brandon said, eyeing Olivia. "But as far as I'm concerned, it would be a hell of a lot easier to do my job if I wasn't being lied to or deceived by the mayor's staff."

"How dare you—"

The mayor put a hand on Olivia's shoulder. "Let Chief Mattson talk."

Olivia huffed, breaking off eye contact with Brandon.

"Adam," Brandon said, "I need you to come down to the station with me."

Brooke leaned forward, the wad of tissue between both hands. "You don't think Adam did this?"

Adam rested his hand on her knee. "It's no big deal. I'll be fine."

Brandon stood.

"Glad to hear it. I'll need to talk to you too, Brooke."

"Wait, what?" Olivia interjected. "If you're accusing my niece—"

"At this point, I'm not accusing anyone."

Olivia planted herself in front of Brandon. "Brooke was with me last night, from the time I got off work until now."

Brandon stepped around Olivia. "And her friend Adam here, can you vouch for his whereabouts too?"

"He got here a couple of hours ago," Olivia said.

"Good to know." He motioned to Brooke and Adam. "Let's go. I'll try to make this as painless as possible."

One, or both, had information about Justin's death. And it seemed they'd suddenly become very close, Adam's arm around Brooke, his hand on her knee.

Alibi or not, something about their story didn't fit.

Brooke collapsed defiantly into the chair in the corner of the interview room.

Brandon read Brooke her rights and began recording.

"Tell me again where you were last night."

She crossed her arms. "My aunt already told you. I was at her house."

"When, exactly?"

"I came down here with Justin when you talked to us yesterday afternoon."

He had interviewed Justin and Brooke around 4:30 or 5:00.

"And then what?"

"We went back to my aunt's house."

"You didn't leave after that?"

"No."

"At what point did you realize Justin was missing?"

"This morning."

"And the last time you saw him?"

"I guess last night."

"You guess?" Brandon asked.

"My boyfriend just died, okay? I can't remember everything." She pulled out a tissue, her eyes welling with

246

tears. "Why are you asking me all of these questions? It's like you don't believe my aunt."

"I'm sure your Aunt Olivia is as honest as they come," Brandon said.

Brooke's gaze trailed away as if considering the comment.

When she didn't respond, Brandon asked, "Was Justin there when you went to bed last night?"

"No."

"And he never came home after that?"

Brooke sniffled. "I guess not."

"At some point, you didn't think that odd?"

"No. I mean, he'd go out sometimes, hang out with his buddies."

Justin wasn't from Forks.

"He had friends around here?"

"You act like I know everything about Justin," she said. "I was just his girlfriend, okay? Maybe he went up to Port Angeles."

"But he didn't, Brooke. We found him on the side of the road."

She slapped the table, the hard echo bouncing off the interview room walls. "I know that you freaking jerk. That's why he's dead. Because you let that whore Ruby kill him."

Brooke covered her face again, strands of her uncombed hair hanging over her hands.

Brandon leaned back in his chair, crossing his arms. "We don't have proof Ruby killed anyone. Unless you know something I don't."

"She's a freak. She wanted all of us dead—me, Lauren, Justin."

"What do you mean, she's a freak?"

Brooke considered him for a moment. "I don't know."

"You must have meant something by that."

Her eyes landed on the door. "Can I go now?"

"Not yet," Brandon said, crossing his arms. "Tell me about Justin and Lauren."

A flash of hatred slipped through her narrowed eyes. "What about them?"

"You knew they'd slept together."

She leaned away from him, sliding the strands of hair out of her face.

"That's not true."

"Has Justin cheated on you before?"

"Why does that matter?"

Because it could be motive for murder.

"How long have you known?" Brandon asked.

"I've had loser boyfriends before." Her eyes rose to meet Brandon's. "Most men do the same thing."

"Not most men, I hope."

She scoffed. "Because you're different, right?"

Brandon pointed a thumb at the door. "Did Adam believe Lauren and Justin were sleeping together?"

"Everyone knows Adam believed Lauren was cheating on him," she said.

"Adam told you Lauren was with Justin?"

"He said he suspected it. Like a couple of weeks ago."

"But yet you still went on the camping trip."

"I didn't believe him."

"And what about now? Do you believe Justin slept with Lauren?"

She glared back at him. "No, I don't."

"Okay, what time did Justin leave?"

"Like six or seven last night."

"And you were with your aunt the entire time. Didn't leave the house for even one moment?"

"I already said that."

"I appreciate your consistency," Brandon said.

"Thanks," she replied sincerely. The young woman's sarcasm detector was broken.

"Why would Justin purchase red spray paint?"

She took her time answering.

"I don't know."

"That doesn't surprise you?"

"Maybe he wanted to paint his truck."

Except he didn't.

"Okay. Thanks, Brooke. I'll be in touch."

Brandon stood, but Brooke stayed put.

"Yesterday you asked me about my relationship with Justin—you wouldn't tell me why. Is there something...do you have *proof* that Justin and Lauren slept together?"

"Did Justin tell you he'd slept with Lauren?" Brandon asked.

"No."

"Well then, let's just leave it at that for now."

"But I heard..."

"You heard what?"

"Nothing."

"Your aunt—Olivia. She told you something?"

Brandon had mentioned the DNA results to the mayor—that both Justin and Adam's semen had been found with Lauren's body. He'd informed the mayor about the results while Olivia was present.

"No," Brooke said, standing. "She hasn't told me anything."

Apparently, lying, or at least hiding the truth, was a family trait.

Brandon interviewed Adam next.

"We've been trying to find you for two days now," Brandon said.

"Yeah, a sheriff's deputy left a card on my door."

"And yet you didn't contact us?"

"I just got home when Brooke called and told me she couldn't get ahold of Justin."

"And you were concerned because Justin was such a good buddy?"

The enmity between Adam and Justin was one of the first things Brandon had noticed about Lauren's trio of friends.

"Most of the time, he acted like a d-bag, but that doesn't mean I killed him."

"I never said you killed him," Brandon said.

"You implied it," Adam said.

"Tell me again why you came down to visit Brooke instead of returning our calls."

"I wanted to support her."

"Where have you been the last couple of days?" Brandon asked.

"I went camping," Adam said.

"Where?"

"Olympic National Forest. Near the Deer Park campground."

Deer Park was up on the northern side of the Olympics, past Port Angeles. The middle of nowhere.

"Alone?" Brandon asked.

"Yes."

"So, no one has laid eyes on you for two days."

"I know it looks bad—"

"You let us decide what looks bad, okay?" Brandon said.

Adam nodded hesitantly.

"Why did you go camping with Lauren and her friends if you knew she was sleeping with Justin?"

"I didn't—"

"According to Brooke, you told her as much."

Adam's eyebrows wrinkled in confusion. "I didn't—"

"You didn't know Lauren and Justin were together?"

"No," he insisted. "I swear."

"Yet multiple people claim you were suspicious of Lauren cheating on you."

"Why would I go with them if I thought Justin was the one she was cheating on me with?"

Good question, but yet he still went camping with his girlfriend and the man she was sleeping with.

"What evidence do you have that Lauren slept with Justin?" Adam asked.

"We found semen."

"So? We had sex the night she died."

"But here's the problem, Adam. The semen was from you—and Justin."

Adam stared back at Brandon as if he'd just punched him in the gut. He seemed genuinely surprised.

"Do you believe Brooke knew about this?"

"Brooke? No, I mean, I don't think so. But why did she say I suspected Justin—"

"Good question."

"Maybe she misunderstood..."

"I'll be honest with you, Adam. You're a suspect. It doesn't help that you have no alibi for the last two days. And you told at least two people, your co-worker and Brooke, that you believed Lauren had been unfaithful."

251

"But I didn't kill her."

"Or Justin?"

He shook his head. "No."

"Anything else you want to tell me?" Brandon asked.

"I told you everything," Adam said.

Brandon thought back to the vampire poster in Adam's apartment, the day Brandon and Jackson visited him.

"You know anything about covens?" he asked.

"Like the one in town here?" Adam asked.

He considered the young man. How would Adam know about a coven in Forks? He hadn't recalled seeing his name on Vasile's list.

"Lauren told me about it. She said that woman who'd threatened her—"

"Ruby?"

"Yeah, that's her. Lauren said Ruby told her once that she'd better watch out, or she'd send her vampire crew after Lauren."

"When?"

"Like a month ago, something like that."

Another finger pointed at Ruby.

The case against Ruby—from her vitriol toward Lauren and Justin to her involvement in the vampire cult—continued to grow. But Brandon had to weed out what was real and what was a smokescreen. Adam could have fabricated the story about Ruby to get the focus off of himself.

Brandon needed to talk to Ruby before she had a chance to leave town.

He stood. "You're free to go. For now. No leaving the county without letting me know."

Adam searched Brandon's eyes.

"You're sure about the DNA? Justin and Lauren were together?"

"If by sure you mean only a one in a billion chance of being wrong? Yes, I'm sure."

Chapter 32

Brandon contacted Jackson. She was working the south side of town, not far from Ruby's property. He gave her Ruby's address and told her to meet him there.

Jackson had parked at the end of the gravel road that led to Ruby's place.

"You check if she's home yet?" Brandon asked.

"I figured I'd wait for you."

They made the trek down the road on foot, just as Brandon and Josiah had before.

Ruby wasn't home and her car was missing.

"Put out an APB. I want to talk to her ASAP."

"Got it," Jackson said. "I heard about the second murder. Any theories?"

"Lots, not to mention a good deal of finger-pointing."

Brandon described the details of Justin's death as they walked back toward the main road.

"This whole vampire thing," she said. "It could be a distraction."

"Might be," Brandon said. "But there's a reason the murderer is going to the trouble, and risk, of biting the victims. I'm hoping we get saliva off Justin's neck."

Just then, Ruby pulled onto the gravel lane. Her car slid to a stop. Ruby's wide, surprised eyes landed on Brandon.

She shifted into reverse and shot back onto the highway.

"Let's go," Brandon said. Jackson followed him in her Interceptor.

Brandon flipped his police lights and siren on. He accelerated until he hit 70. Half a minute later, he'd caught up to Ruby.

He slowed the SUV. Ruby kept her pace on the winding road at about 55, only 10 miles over the speed limit.

The two-lane road headed south into a forested area.

Brandon accelerated, sweeping past Ruby. He pulled in front of her. At the same time, Jackson crept up behind Ruby as Brandon decelerated, forcing Ruby to do the same.

Ruby veered into the other lane but quickly shot back to the right as a logging truck barreled by.

As she swerved back to her lane, Brandon tapped on the brakes again and forced Ruby to a crawl, pinned between Brandon and Jackson. Trapped, she brought the car to a halt.

Brandon leaped out of the SUV and unholstered his Glock, eyes on Ruby. Jackson made her way to the passenger side of Ruby's car, pistol drawn.

Ruby hadn't shown any predilection toward violence in the past, but she was desperate, and desperate people did stupid things.

"Hands where I can see them," Brandon said.

Ruby raised her arms as he approached. He opened the driver's door with one hand, pistol still trained on her.

"Out."

She stood and faced the car, her hands still up. She knew the routine.

Brandon holstered his pistol and lowered Ruby's hands behind her back so he could cuff her.

"I didn't do nothing wrong," Ruby said.

Brandon swiveled her around.

"You didn't notice the two police vehicles in your driveway?"

"Yeah. I just changed my mind about going home."

Brandon led her over to the shoulder of the road.

"And the flashing lights?" he asked.

"Didn't notice."

"Where you off to in such a hurry?"

Ruby scowled at him. "Away from you."

"You mind if we search your car?"

"Yes, I mind."

"I was asking to be nice," Brandon said. "I don't need your permission seeing as you attempted to elude a police officer."

He leaned down, scanning the contents of the car. "An open container, too. That's probable cause."

"Dammit," she said.

"You want to tell us what we might find in here?" Jackson asked.

"Is this where you promise me I'll get off easy if I cooperate? Because I don't believe you."

"Suit yourself," Brandon said. "Jackson, why don't you give our friend here a seat in the back of my vehicle."

"Am I under arrest?" Ruby asked.

"Not yet. Just detained."

He grabbed a pair of gloves from his SUV. Jackson did the same after securing Ruby in the back seat.

Brandon retrieved a half-empty can of Bud Light from the car and set it on the roof. He searched under the driver's seat and found a pipe and about a gram of weed. Marijuana was legal in Washington State, and he had no proof she'd been smoking it while driving.

He grabbed the keys out of the ignition and opened the trunk while Jackson continued to search the car's interior.

The problem with Ruby was she didn't know what was good for her. All they wanted was to discuss her relationship with Justin and Lauren, and to rule out any connection to the bite marks on the victims' necks.

Brandon scanned the mostly empty trunk. Nothing interesting. He peeled back the carpet, revealing a large bag full of pills.

And now Ruby was headed to jail for possession with intent to sell.

Brandon took the bag to Jackson. She'd crouched down inside the passenger door, her hand searching under the seat. She yanked out a wad of empty cigarette packs. "Nothing much yet."

"Lookie here," Brandon said, holding up the pills.

She looked up at him. "Wow, that was easy. And here I am on my hands and knees."

Jackson stood, eyeing the bag. "OxyContin?"

"Looks like it."

"You see anything else in here? Weapons? Dope?" Brandon asked.

"No, but does this mean anything to you?"

She held out a crumpled receipt. Brandon unfolded the paper. A receipt from the convenience store where Ruby worked. Dated June 10. 12:15 a.m.

"I think you outdid me, Jackson. By a mile."

"What is it?"

"A receipt for a six-pack of beer, same brand as Lauren purchased."

"Same night?"

"And same time."

Ruby was making it real hard for Brandon not to arrest her for the murder of Lauren Sandoval. The receipt, the coven, the grudge against Lauren.

"Get an evidence bag for this and the pills," he said. "I want fingerprints from this receipt."

"Lauren was in Ruby's car," Jackson said.

"After she bought the beer. And before she was killed."

Jackson pointed a finger at him. "You're right, Chief. I did outdo you. By *more* than a mile."

Brandon opened the SUV door and informed Ruby of her rights and that she was being arrested for the drug charges and the open container.

"Come on, man," Ruby said. "Those pills are mine. I have a prescription."

"The pills are the least of your worries," Brandon said. "Because right now, I have proof that Lauren Sandoval was in your vehicle the night she was murdered."

The blood drained from Ruby's face. She scrunched her eyes shut and shook her head. "I didn't kill her."

"But she was in your car."

"Yes, but—"

"We'll talk down at the station," he said, closing the door.

Jackson tucked the receipt and pills into evidence bags.

"You think she did it?" she asked.

"It's becoming pretty damn hard to disagree with everyone else who wants her to be the one who killed Lauren and Justin."

"You've been getting pressure to pin this on Ruby?"

"From Adam, Brooke, and Brooke's aunt, and probably the mayor too, if I asked her what she thought."

"I'll get her car towed."

258

"Straight to evidence," he said.

"I'll request a search for anything else related to the girl. Blood, hair, fingerprints."

"You got it."

This meant he would be home late. Again.

Brandon found the text Misty had sent him that first day he'd learned she was his neighbor. He called her and asked if she could keep an eye on Emma. She agreed and he was grateful for her help—despite Brandon rebuffing her advances. Not every woman would be so gracious.

Chapter 33

Back at the station, Brandon set a cup of water down in front of Ruby.

"Why you being so nice all of a sudden?" she asked.

He advised her of her rights again and asked her to sign a form indicating she understood. To Brandon's surprise, she did.

"I didn't kill that girl."

"What about Justin? You kill him?"

"Justin who?" Ruby asked.

"The young man you followed in your car the other day. Brooke and Justin."

"He's dead?" She slid her hand over her face. "Oh, my God. When? I was up in Port Angeles all yesterday. I got home late."

If that was an attempt at making up an alibi, she'd done a pretty crappy job. She'd basically admitted she was in the area around the time Justin died.

"We believe Justin was murdered last night."

"How?" she asked.

"Still under investigation," he said.

"I knew those girls were trouble," Ruby said. "The moment they started harassing me."

Brandon tapped his pen on the table. "Speaking of harassment. Adam, the deceased girl's boyfriend, claims you threatened her—"

"I never—"

"Hold on. You threatened to set your vampire friends on her."

"Vampire friends?" she laughed, hanging her arm over the back of the chair. "You believe that?"

"Does the name Vasile Anghel sound familiar?"

Ruby gasped, the air catching in her throat. She took a long drink of water and set the cup back down.

"You know I already know the answer," he said. "So let's cut the crap and you tell me the truth."

"Yes, I know him," she said.

"In what capacity?"

She let out a cynical laugh.

"You mean was I having sex with him?"

No, that's not what he meant, but if she wanted to go there. "Were you?"

"I'm not one of his little thirty-something vampire bunnies," she said with the resentment of a woman who's been spurned one too many times.

Vampire bunnies? So that's what Vasile got out of his goth-inspired costume parties.

"You are part of his coven?"

"Used to be," she said. "Until he found someone else, someone cheaper."

Since they weren't talking about sex, she must mean she was dealing to Vasile and his crew.

"But you were part of the coven?"

"Sure."

"You like the taste of blood?"

She bit her lip. "I won't deny I've tried it. Too expensive for me."

Brandon cringed. The question was meant to shock her. Instead, she'd surprised him.

"And the teeth, you have some of those too?"

"You mean the fangs? I guess. What do they have to do with anything?" Then, as if coming to a sudden

261

realization, she said, "Wait. You think I bit that girl. And the boy...was he bit too?"

"You tell me," Brandon said. "Where are these fangs you own?"

If they found the teeth used to bite Justin and Lauren, they'd be one step closer to finding the killer. Brandon guessed the bite marks on both victims would match the same set of teeth.

"Did you get the spit?" she asked.

"Huh?"

"The spit. There's always saliva from a bite mark. I saw it on one of those shows."

"Is that what you're worried about?"

"No, you dumbass, I'm hoping you find who actually did it. Was there spit or not?"

"Still waiting to find out. And by the way, I'm on your side here, Ruby. You're a lot of things, but a murderer?" Brandon spread his hands out. "Maybe. Maybe not."

"Screw you," she said.

"Speaking of saliva, are you willing to give a DNA sample?"

She blinked, opened her mouth to say something but then changed her mind.

"You see how bad this looks?" Brandon asked. "Lying about the girl in your car. Bite marks on the murder victims and you being part of some blood-sucking cult. Your hatred for both Lauren and Justin. Half the town wants you charged with murder."

"I didn't do it," she said.

"Are you going to give the sample or not?"

"I guess I don't have a choice."

"And Ruby, you never told me what happened to your vampire teeth."

She stared down at her hands.

"My fangs are missing," she said.

Ruby had done so many things wrong, it was almost as if she wanted him to charge her for the murders.

"Missing since when?"

"The night I gave the girl a ride. They were in a container on my front seat. I think she stole them."

"Why would she do that?"

Ruby tilted her head at him. "Hell if I know."

Brandon fetched the DNA kit and consent form, indicating the test was voluntary.

After securing Ruby's sample, Brandon leaned back in his chair. "Why was Lauren in your car the night she was murdered?"

"I picked her up on the road to the beach."

"How long after she left your store?" he asked.

"I don't know. Not long after."

"You'd just argued with her and we've established you couldn't stand each other."

Ruby crossed her arms. "So?"

"And you expect me to believe you played Good Samaritan to your worst enemy."

Ruby scoffed. "That girl was not my worst enemy."

"Okay. Then what happened?"

"I saw her walking on the side of the road, kind of swerving into the lane. I almost ran into her." She paused.

"And?" Brandon asked.

"I could have and you wouldn't have ever known."

"Your point?"

"It proves I didn't kill her," she said.

"No, it doesn't. And just to be clear, based on the history between you two and the video from the store, your car would be the first one I checked if we had found Lauren run over on the highway."

"Anyway," Ruby said, "she got in and she was so drunk I don't even think she knew who I was at first. She asked me to take her to the campground."

"Which one?"

"Second Beach," she said.

"That was on your way home?"

"No," Ruby said. "Just because I don't like people like her—"

"Like what?"

"Narcs. Snitches."

"Okay."

"It doesn't mean I wanted her to die. And who knows what those boys would have done to her."

"What boys?" Brandon asked.

"The contract workers from the hotel. The ones she left with," Ruby replied.

Those *boys* were 30-year-old men.

"Did she say anything when she was in your car?" he asked.

"Once she recognized me, she went on about how she didn't like me selling up in Port Angeles." Ruby paused. "I'm not confessing that I sell up there. Or anywhere. That's just what she said."

"Thanks for your candor," Brandon said with a hint of sarcasm.

"You don't have to be rude," Ruby said.

"My apologies. Continue."

"I told her to lay off. That got her quiet for a minute, and then she sort of fell asleep until I dropped her off."

"At the campground?"

"The parking lot there. She grabbed her beers and walked off. Didn't even close the door or say thank you or nothing."

"You didn't notice anyone else around?"

"No. And I went straight home and that was it until you came poking around accusing me of murder and all that."

"And you're sure you didn't go to the beach with her? Maybe drink a few beers?"

"Ha!" she said, "You think that little brat would share a beer with me?"

She had a point.

"You know anything about red spray paint?"

They had Justin on camera buying cans of paint. At the time, it seemed to point to Justin as somehow involved in the graffiti. But the last message had warned about someone dying. Because Justin was the next victim, that made it unlikely—but not impossible—that he'd given the warning.

Justin's purchase might be unrelated to the graffiti or the murder.

Her eyes widened. "You're not going to try to pin all that vampire graffiti bullshit on me, are you?"

"You have a problem with us searching your house?"

She considered her fingernails and the ragged remains of the pink polish that had once coated them. Brandon figured she was thinking about what the police might find in her home—especially drugs.

"Go ahead," she said.

"You willing to consent to that in writing?"

She didn't answer, her eyes shifting to the door. She was on the verge of asking for an attorney.

"Let me put it this way," Brandon said. "If we don't find anything connecting you to the murder of Justin or Lauren, that makes your case that much stronger."

"Okay."

Ruby signed a voluntary consent form, allowing the police to search her house for evidence related to the murders. She told him he could use the key from her keychain.

"Anyone else in the house?" Brandon asked.

She blinked at him. "I've been alone for years."

The words were steeped with regret. There was no point in asking her more about her personal life, for now. Bringing up old wounds might lead her to reconsider consenting to the search.

"Can I have a cigarette?" she asked.

Brandon grimaced. "Sorry, Ruby. No smoking in jail."

"Jail? I thought you were just questioning me."

"Remember that part where we placed you under arrest? For intent to sell and evading police?"

She glowered at him. "Fine. I want an attorney."

"Okay, but you're being held until the judge says you can leave."

Brandon opened the door.

"Wait," she said. "What about the murder? Do you think I did it?"

"Do I think you're capable? That you wanted to or at least thought about it? Sure."

"But I—"

Brandon held up a hand. "Wait until your attorney gets here."

He had Ruby fingerprinted. They contacted a court-appointed attorney contracted by the county to represent indigent defendants. He was there in less than an hour.

Ruby's attorney made it clear Ruby was done talking. He wasn't happy she'd already given a DNA sample, and when he learned she'd agreed to let Brandon search her house, he lost it.

To Brandon's surprise, Ruby didn't withdraw consent. He'd convinced her it was the only way to prove she was innocent of murder.

He hoped he was right, but there was just as much chance of Brandon and his team finding evidence that would send Ruby to prison for life.

Brandon called in Will and Jackson to help with the search. They were looking for teeth—fangs to be specific. Besides that, anything that might connect Ruby with the killings.

Ruby had no alibi for the time Justin was killed and it was a known fact that she didn't like the trio of friends who'd threatened her drug business. She'd even chased Brooke and Justin to the police station a day before his murder.

Now, she'd just confessed to lying about having Lauren in her car in the hours before her murder. And then there were the teeth. Ruby had even admitted to owning fangs like the ones used to bite Lauren and Justin.

It was 10:30 by the time they finished searching Ruby's place. They had found nothing of consequence. No fangs, no signs of struggle. Ruby kept a surprisingly neat and tidy home. The dishes were done, drying on the counter. No overflowing trash or piles of dirty clothes.

One frame photo showed a younger Ruby in the arms of what must have been a husband or boyfriend. There were photos of kids too, from age three or four to preteen. None past that point. That usually meant a severing of the relationship, either by choice or through state involvement.

The sparseness of Ruby's place made the search easier. Jackson discovered a bottle of pain pills which, ironically, were prescribed for Ruby.

Outside, Brandon searched the carport for rope matching the one used to hang Justin but found none.

They were walking away empty-handed, but that didn't get Ruby off the hook. Her motive and the evidence against her were solid. Even Jackson had said as much during the search, chaffing at the idea of holding off on charging her for Lauren's murder.

But Ruby wasn't the only suspect, and there was more work to do.

Tomorrow.

It was past eleven when he got home and found Emma asleep on the couch. Misty, bleary-eyed, leaned back in the recliner.

"Oh, hey," she said, sitting up.

"Thanks for coming over."

She stretched her arms. "Any time."

Misty stood, her eyes still half-closed.

"How'd it go?" he asked.

"Fine. Games, dinner, talking about boys," she said.

Boys? Emma didn't have a boyfriend, did she?

"How about you?" Misty asked.

"I'm going out of my way to prove one of my suspects is innocent, and I may be wasting my time."

Misty yawned, patting his chest. "You'll figure it out. Maybe she's guilty and you just need to get the proof."

"She?"

Misty knew he was talking about Ruby. Word of Ruby's involvement in the case had spread over the past several days.

"I'd better get going," she said.

"See you," he said.

"You, too." She stood on her tiptoes and pecked him on the lips, then shuffled out the door.

Hadn't he made it clear they couldn't be together?

If that were the case, why did he wish she were still there, that she'd given him a chance to respond, with more than a peck on the lips?

He shook his head. The case, the new job, this town was getting to him. He and Misty did not belong together. Not two decades ago and not now.

Not to mention, he had a date with Lisa Shipley.

Brandon watched Misty until she arrived safely on her own porch. He couldn't help but think, frazzled as her hair was, her walk like a wandering zombie, that she was just as beautiful as she'd been so long ago.

"Dad?"

"I'm home, sweetie. Come on. Off to bed for you."

Emma stared up at him with the vacant gaze of a sleepwalker.

"Let's go," he said, putting a hand under her arm.

"What happened with the case?" she asked.

"That doesn't matter."

"I want to know."

"Not now, Emma. I'm tired."

And hungry, and irritated.

"Fine," she said, pulling away from him. "Don't talk to me."

Brandon stifled a grin. If she'd seen his reaction, she would have been even more miffed. As it was, he wondered if she'd even remember the conversation come morning.

He opened the fridge and found a box of leftover pizza—only one slice left. There were a couple of beers too, but he'd be asleep in 10 minutes, so he let them be.

He devoured the pizza and headed for bed. It had been a long day. Another murder, a revelation that Olivia was Brooke's aunt, and growing evidence that Ruby was the killer he'd been searching for. His gut told him she wasn't. But intuition alone wouldn't bring a murderer to justice.

He thought back to the graffiti on the abandoned house. *More Will Die.*

If Ruby was the killer, she was in jail, for now. If she wasn't guilty, that meant the murderer was still out there, waiting to strike again.

Chapter 34

Brandon dropped Emma off at his dad's house on his way to the office. It was Sunday morning, and he'd planned on going to church with Emma and his dad. Brandon's dad attended the same Baptist church he'd gone to since Brandon was a kid.

The problem was, Brandon needed to wrap up the investigation.

Family was the reason he'd left the homicide department. He'd wanted regular hours and more time with Emma when she was with him.

He told her he'd try to make it to the 10:30 service. If not, he'd see them for lunch.

In moments like this, he wondered if taking the chief of police position had been a good idea. But he was here now and, despite his best efforts, was still dealing with murderers, drug dealers, and other lowlifes that inhabited society, be it in the city or this edge-of-the-continent backcountry.

Nolan and Josiah were huddled at the conference room table when Brandon arrived at the station. They'd just done shift briefing and were getting ready to head out for the day.

"We heard you made an arrest in the murder cases," Josiah said.

"Who told you that?" Brandon asked.

"He doesn't want to hear about rumors," Nolan said, shooting Josiah a warning.

"I'm dying to know," Brandon said. He'd learned from a former captain it was better to know the office gossip and address it head-on rather than wait for the fallout.

"You arrested Ruby," Josiah said. "Not to butt in or anything—"

"Josiah, if you have something to say about a case, I want you to speak up."

He couldn't say the same about Nolan.

"There's the vampire connection—she's part of that cult. And with the vampire bites..."

Josiah paused as if waiting for Brandon to interrupt.

"Go on," Brandon said.

"And she had it out for Lauren," Josiah said.

"Show him the tips we got," Nolan said, motioning to the desk behind Josiah.

Josiah twisted in his seat and picked up a piece of paper with handwritten notes on it. He handed it to Brandon.

There had been three phone calls. Two callers, both women, had information about Lauren's murder but were afraid to come forward. One of the women knew, "without a doubt," the killer was a member of the local vampire coven. The vampire bites proved it, the caller claimed. The third caller was male. He'd gotten straight to the point and mentioned Ruby by name.

"None of these people identified themselves?" Brandon asked.

"No—"

"Rumors, at best. At worst, they're trying to frame Ruby. And they aren't vampire bites. They're puncture wounds from a person wearing false teeth or fangs.

Whether that has some connection to the case, we don't know."

"What about motive?" Nolan said.

Brandon nodded. "Motive is important, but it doesn't prove anything. For every homicide, there might be four or five people who wished the victim dead. Of those, maybe two or three had the means and opportunity to commit murder."

"And that's Ruby—" Nolan started.

"And Brooke and Adam. Justin too, thanks to the unfortunate love triangle—"

"Justin's dead," Josiah said.

"I agree, it's probably the same killer. But don't assume that. It is possible Justin was involved in the first killing and a victim of the second."

Nolan shook his head. "It sounds like you don't want to charge Ruby. I mean, the girl was in her car. She has no alibi for Justin's murder."

The info about the car ride and the alibi was new, but it likely trickled down to Nolan through shift report. It wasn't the kind of information Brandon trusted in Nolan's hands. Still, he couldn't ask his department to hide information from Nolan without making it clear he was done with the recalcitrant officer.

"Like I said, we have more than one suspect here."

"How many don't have an alibi?" Nolan asked.

"On the night of Lauren's murder, they were all supposedly asleep. As for Justin's death, Brooke was at her aunt's during the time he was killed."

"That leaves Adam, Lauren's boyfriend," Josiah said.

"Having strong suspicions is a long way from charging someone with murder," Brandon said.

"So, you've had cases thrown out before?" Nolan asked.

"No, and the reason I didn't is because I know how to do my job. That means being careful, and not making a move until you're sure. Ruby's here on drug trafficking charges. For now."

Nolan stood. "I got to hit the streets." He eyed Brandon. "I still think she did it. And word is you know she did and just don't want to admit it."

Brandon hadn't shared his doubts about Ruby's innocence with anyone.

Except Misty.

Misty wouldn't share their private conversations with Nolan. Would she?

"Maybe you feel bad about not arresting her before Justin's murder," Nolan said.

"You know, you should be a therapist, as concerned as you are about my emotions," Brandon said.

With that, the conversation was over and Nolan left for his beat.

The comment about Brandon's doubts irked him. He'd confront Misty about that later. Brandon wasn't in a relationship with Misty—but it sure felt like it with as much trouble as she was causing him.

Brandon flipped on his computer monitor and stared at the stack of emails waiting for him. His cursor hovered over an email from Lisa Shipley. She'd sent it at six that morning.

He scanned the contents.

Justin hadn't died from hanging, her email explained, self-inflicted or otherwise. Not enough damage to the carotid artery.

That was consistent with what Brandon had noticed at the crime scene. The marks where the rope had worn away the tree's bark were evidence Justin had already been dead when his killer struggled to pull his body up to a hanging position.

He'd most likely died from head injuries caused by the shovel. Whoever had done this wanted to make sure he was dead.

They hadn't found any blood in Justin's truck. It was likely he'd been killed on-site.

It was good information, essentially ruling out suicide. But it didn't point to any one suspect. He kept reading. No saliva on the bite wound—it had been wiped clean.

Nothing was easy with this case.

He re-read the report and scrolled to the end.

Good news.

They'd found DNA on the beer cans he'd discovered on the sea stack. One profile was Lauren's. The other belonged to a woman. No one in the CODIS database.

A woman. Another strike against Ruby—if the murderer was the same person who'd shared the beers with Lauren.

Lauren's prints were on the cans and a partial print from another person. As far as the necklace Brandon had found at the scene, they'd obtained skin cells. DNA was pending.

Brandon closed his email and swiveled his chair to the whiteboard on the wall opposite his desk.

He began outlining the case.

A handful of people would have wanted Lauren dead. There was Adam, Lauren's jealous boyfriend. Brooke, whose boyfriend Lauren had been sleeping with. Justin, desperate to keep his fling with Lauren a secret. And

Ruby, the drug dealing vampire cult member who, were she honest, was probably happy to learn about Lauren's death.

None had a good alibi for the night of Lauren's murder.

Then again, it could be someone entirely disconnected from the case. Brandon thought back to Garrett Zornes, the tow truck driver that had given Lauren a ride to the convenience store. Or Doug Nevins and Derrick Green. They couldn't be ruled out, at least not for Lauren's murder. Doug Nevins had been in jail when Justin was murdered.

Lauren had most likely been shoved off the sea stack and dragged into the water. Before that, she'd had sex with Adam and Justin. Later, she'd had a few beers with someone. A woman, it seemed, now, based on the DNA evidence from the beer cans. Ruby had the Coors Light receipt in her car.

What was the connection between the two murders? The only physical similarity was the vampire teeth bite. Was there really a blood-crazed vampire killer on the loose in Forks? One of Vasile's followers? How was the graffiti connected to all of this?

In all the activity around Justin's death, he'd almost forgotten. They'd discovered the video evidence of Justin buying the spray paint up in Port Angeles.

Was Justin behind the vampire graffiti? Had he upset someone, possibly one of the cult members? Why paint the symbols to begin with?

For all the excitement around town, and in his department, about the vampire connection—especially as it involved Ruby—it was all too obvious.

A distraction.

He opened his phone and studied the photo of the most recent graffiti, the words *More Will Die* painted the day before Justin's death.

He had to admit, there was a connection there.

Whoever had killed Justin had tried to cover it up and had done a sloppy job.

Adam had no alibi. Neither did Ruby. Brooke was with her aunt, Olivia. What about the cans on the sea stack? Brooke had an alibi for Justin's murder, *not* for Lauren's.

As much as everyone wanted Ruby to be the one who'd done this, he wasn't ready to follow the easy conclusion that she was the guilty one.

He wished he could call his old partner, Bill Whitlock. They'd worked homicide together most of Brandon's career. Bill kept Brandon's head on straight, calling him out when it seemed some bias led Brandon to lean one way or another. Brandon had done the same for Bill a time or two. That's what partners did—called each other on their bullshit.

But Bill was somewhere down in Arizona getting a tan and enjoying a cold drink. He'd retired early after his father-in-law had left Bill and his wife a ton of money.

Brandon didn't have a partner. He was on his own. But he had a good team—with one exception. They'd solve this case with the tools they had.

His phone rang. It was the mayor. Against his better judgment, he answered.

"This is Mattson."

"Chief, if you have a few seconds—"

"I've got a lot going on, in case you haven't heard."

"I'll be waiting."

She disconnected before he could respond.

277

The mayor's door was open. He scanned the room. The mayor was alone, for once. He closed the door.

Mayor Kim stood as Brandon entered.

"Working on a Sunday?" she asked.

"I could ask the same of you," he replied.

"Now that we've agreed we're both overworked," she motioned toward the conference table. "Have a seat, Chief."

"I'll stand, thanks."

A flash of anger crossed her eyes.

"Suit yourself." The mayor sat on the edge of her desk, arms crossed. "We need to talk about the investigation," she said.

Brandon rested his hands on his duty belt. "If you're going to—"

She held a hand up. "I won't tell you how to do your job."

He didn't believe that, but he let her continue. Better to get this over with.

"The word is that Ruby Walker is the main suspect in the death of the two youngsters who were murdered."

"She's a suspect, not the main suspect."

"And who would that be?"

"Right now, there are a handful of people that had the means and desire to kill Lauren."

"And Justin?"

"If it's the same person, yes."

Brandon believed it was, but he was reluctant to share more information with the mayor. It wasn't so much that he didn't trust Mayor Kim, it was that he didn't trust her ability to keep whatever Brandon told her private.

"You're not considering that young man, Adam, are you?"

"Of course, I am."

"He seems like such a nice boy."

"Mayor, the world of homicide is full of examples of nice guys who were serial killers."

"That's different," she said.

"I got leads to follow today, mayor. Is there anything else?"

"Only that I'm getting reports of issues among the officers."

"Issues?"

"A loss of confidence," she said. "In your leadership."

"Reports from where?"

Most likely Nolan because he was sore with Brandon about being placed on unpaid leave after the shooting incident. And that Brandon had hired Jackson instead of his friend. And the noticeable level of disdain Brandon had for him. Come to think of it, Nolan had lots of reasons to be unhappy with Brandon.

None held any merit, though.

"The complaints are from within the department," she said.

"You mean Nolan?" Brandon asked.

She uncrossed her arms and stepped behind her desk.

"The person I talked to reported more than one officer is unhappy with the way things are going."

"It's Nolan, and he's lying," Brandon said. "And what exactly do my officers supposedly have a loss of confidence about?"

"This case, for one thing. The situation with Ruby—"

"I thought you weren't going to tell me how to do my job."

"You have a PR issue here."

Brandon shook his head.

"Hear me out," she said.

"Okay."

"Ruby Walker looks guilty of murder. The vampire connection with the teeth—"

"Nolan told you about that too?"

"If you don't figure this out soon, either charge Ruby with murder or find out who did this, you'll have an uprising on your hands."

An uprising? Really?

"This is a small town, Brandon. You know what that means. News travels fast and everyone has something to say about it. I can't have a chief of police no one trusts."

It wasn't the first time in his career he'd heard someone suggest politics was more important than the truth.

"I will continue to work on solving this murder. When you're ready to relieve me of my duties, let me know. In the meantime," he tipped his cap to her, "have a nice day, Mayor."

Chapter 35

It was a good thing Nolan was already out on patrol by the time Brandon got back to his office.

Brandon had been too easy on Nolan. He had a mind to take the lazy, disrespectful officer out to the parking lot and teach him a lesson. The mayor wanted to threaten Brandon with losing his job? She could have it.

He had a job to do, and that was to finish this murder investigation. He didn't have definitive proof that Ruby had killed either Justin or Lauren. Maybe she did, but if he planned on asking the prosecutor to move forward, he had to be sure.

When this case was over, he'd decide what to do next. Maybe he wasn't cut out to be chief of police in a small town full of rumors, hidden alliances, and petty jealousy. But he knew how to solve crimes, and that's what he would do.

Brandon spent the morning ignoring his phone and email, going over the case files again.

Lisa had said the DNA from the beer on the sea stack was from a woman, and the only woman whose DNA he didn't have yet was Brooke.

It wouldn't be easy, considering Brooke's connection with the mayor's Minister of Tourism, but Brandon would get her DNA even if it took a court order.

He checked the time. It was almost one. He'd told Emma and his dad he'd drop by for lunch.

Brandon climbed the steps to his dad's house. His father opened the door.

"You're late."

"It's barely one," Brandon said.

"One-fifteen. Most people eat lunch at noon."

His father shuffled aside, letting Brandon in.

Brandon found Emma in the kitchen washing dishes.

"Hey, Em."

"Hey," she said over her shoulder.

"Sorry I'm late."

"No big deal. We already ate."

Emma reached up to store a stack of plates away, then faced him.

"I'm getting used to you not being around."

"What?"

"Like yesterday, when you came home at like midnight," she said. "And you didn't show up to church this morning either."

"I called and said I'd be late. And I told you I might not be able to make it."

His dad sat down at the kitchen table. Brandon didn't want to have this conversation in front of him.

"We can talk about this later," Brandon said.

He glanced at his father.

"Don't mind me," his father said.

"I was worried about you," Emma said.

"Emma, I've been a cop for your entire life."

"And it's no big deal, right? Just like you told Mom."

"I was right, wasn't I? Nothing bad has happened yet."

"Yet. Did you know studies show police officers have a life expectancy ten to twenty years lower than the average person?"

"Where did you hear that?"

"Research, Dad. The National Bureau of Labor Statistics, the National Center for—"

"Okay, but this is Forks we're talking about here."

"What about that construction worker guy who shot at your officers? And there's been two murders. The graffiti says there will be more."

"That probably has nothing to do with the case, Em."

"Like that," she said. "You don't tell me anything about the case. Just let me sit and worry about you while I'm at home."

"I'm trying to protect you," he said.

"You think I can't handle it?"

"Well, yeah."

She shook her head. "See. You don't need me at all. I'm just supposed to stay locked up in my room all day—."

"Are you asking to go back to your mom's house?"

"I don't want to go back there," she said, crying now. "That's where Madison died. And if I leave you here, you're going to die too."

He wrapped his arms around Emma.

"I'm sorry, Em."

"I don't want you to get hurt."

"I won't. Not anytime soon."

"You can't promise that," she said.

He pulled back. "You're right. I can't. But I'm a pretty smart guy, and I've managed to do okay so far."

"Why can't we move back home?"

"This is my job now. And it's still safer than the city."

"But everyone hates you here."

Brandon stepped back. Why would she think that?

"It's in the paper." She pointed to the kitchen table.

Brandon's dad twisted his laptop so Brandon could see the local newspaper website.

"I was going to say something," his dad said, "but I didn't want to interrupt your Hallmark moment there."

Brandon picked up the laptop.

The lead headline read *New Chief Fumbling Murder Cases*, by Ted Nixon.

The article outlined the case against Ruby, with quotes from Olivia about how Brandon had supposedly manhandled Brooke and Adam while letting Ruby, the real culprit, go free. There was something else too—an anonymous source claiming Brandon knew he was wrong about Ruby but was too headstrong to admit it.

The same thing Nolan had said to Brandon that morning.

"Is all that true, about the vampire teeth and the Ruby woman giving the girl a ride right before she killed her?" Emma asked.

"Sort of."

"He makes a good case," his dad said. "She looks guilty as hell."

"The only reason Ted knows half of this is because Nolan leaked it."

"Is Nolan the one who used to date Misty?" Emma asked.

"Misty Brooks? That girl you dated forever?" his dad asked.

"Yes."

"She was a nice girl," his dad said. "Even your mom liked her. How'd you let that one get away?"

He knew exactly why Brandon and Misty hadn't stayed together.

"It doesn't matter," Brandon said. "None of this should be in the paper."

He was tired of the second-guessing, be it by the mayor, Nolan, the press—and now his family. Of all the people who could support him, his father should be one of them.

He ought to know better than to expect so much from Buzz Mattson.

"You say one of your officers leaked this, but no one cares about that," his dad said. "What they care about is that someone who looks like a murderer is getting away with it—"

"No one is getting away with anything," Brandon said. "And I don't need your advice on how to manage an investigation. If people would just mind their own damn business..."

His father glared back at him. "Eli never talked to me like that."

"Oh, hell. Here we go again. Let me tell you something. Eli was a great brother and all-around good guy. They even want to build a statue or monument or whatever to him. Great. But Eli never solved a murder case in his life."

"Don't talk ill of your brother," his dad said. "If your mom was here—"

"If Mom were here, you'd still be the same hard-ass you've always been. Hell, I'm surprised you don't blame me for her death too."

"It wouldn't hurt if you acted like you gave a damn about family."

"And if I hadn't ever left home, Eli wouldn't have got shot and Mom would still be alive, right?"

The room blurred behind the angry white specks that filled his vision. His father stared back at him, silent.

"I'll take that as your answer," Brandon said. "You know, if you thought about someone besides yourself for once in your life..." He'd said enough. "I've got to get back to work."

He gave Emma a quick hug and pecked her on the cheek. "I love you. I'll do my best to be home early."

"Okay."

"Brandon—" his father called out after him, but he'd already closed the front door.

Chapter 36

Brandon tugged on the door to the Forks Journal Extra.

Locked.

He'd heard that Ted ran the paper on his own, a sign he wasn't getting much advertising revenue. Going after Brandon with the stories about a department in disarray and an allegedly mishandled murder investigation was no doubt Ted's attempt to increase readership and, as a result, ad sales.

Sales or not, Ted was compromising Brandon's investigation. And the shots he'd taken at Brandon in his article had upset Emma. If he were honest, that was what had pissed him off the most.

He glanced up and noticed a Honda Civic approach the newspaper office. As the car came closer, Brandon could see it was Ted Nixon.

Ted's eyes widened and he sped up again, continuing down Forks Avenue.

Brandon hopped in the SUV and made a U-turn. He followed Ted as he swung right onto Calawah Way. Brandon flipped his lights on.

Ted pulled over.

Brandon approached the car. Ted rolled down the window.

"Good afternoon, officer."

"Cut the crap, Ted."

"Wait, don't tell me—I have a taillight out? No. Not that. I failed to use a turn signal, nope. Speeding—I wasn't doing that either."

Brandon pointed at Ted's rearview mirror. A collection of press badges and various backstage passes hung from the post.

"Your view is obstructed. You'll need to remove those."

Ted rolled his eyes.

"You need my ID, registration, insurance?" Ted said, handing them to Brandon.

Back in the Interceptor, Brandon checked Ted's driving record. The only mark against him was a speeding ticket—10 miles over the limit—from five years back.

He should give the reporter a ticket for the obstructed view. But that wasn't why he'd stopped Ted. He would give the man a warning, but one that had nothing to do with his driving.

He handed the papers back to Ted.

"No ticket?" Ted asked.

"Stop being a smart ass before I change my mind."

"Is that a threat, Chief? Should I record this conversation?"

"Record what you want," Brandon said, leaning down. "But know this. I don't appreciate being the target of a hit piece by some hack reporter."

"Nice one," Ted said. "But I gave you a chance to tell your side of the story."

"And when exactly did you do that?"

"Three or four times I asked you about the case and you refused to divulge any details."

"Because it's an active investigation."

"And back in the big city, you didn't share info with reporters?"

Those were professionals who knew when to keep their mouths shut.

"You know," Ted said. "The town doesn't trust you. Doesn't think you're doing your job. Letting Lauren Sandoval's killer get away with murder."

"And how much of that distrust is due to the crap you print?"

Ted cocked his head up at Brandon. "I tell it like I see it."

Brandon stood, his hand on Ted's car. "Well, Ted, here's how I see things. You can tell your friend Nolan that he's done being your mole in my department."

Ted's grin took a nosedive. He scowled at Brandon. "Who said anything about Nolan?"

"You did, by the look on your face just now."

"That doesn't prove anything."

"You've gone too far, Ted. That's the problem. You lost your only contact within the department and you probably just got him fired too."

Brandon planned to wait for Jackson before approaching Brooke about a DNA sample. He hoped the female officer's presence would help calm a potentially volatile situation.

Meanwhile, he would deal with Nolan. He asked one of the reserve officers to come in early and then called Nolan's cell and told him to report back to the station immediately.

Nolan stepped into Brandon's office.

"What's up, Chief? I have an hour left on my shift."

"Peterson will cover your area," Brandon said.

He considered Nolan carefully.

"I take it Ted contacted you," Brandon said.

Nolan's face reddened. "I...uh."

"Don't lie. It will only make it worse."

Nolan rested his thumbs on his belt. "I'm serious. I don't know what you're talking about."

"Ted told me everything," Brandon said. It was an old detective trick, but worth a try. A half-truth.

Nolan wouldn't budge. "Sorry, Chief. I don't—"

Brandon stood. "Place your pistol and badge on my desk."

"What?"

"You heard me. Do it."

Brandon's hand hovered near his own pistol. He didn't know Nolan well enough to trust the man, especially under pressure. He'd already shown, in the incident with Jackson and Doug Nevins, that he had trouble controlling his impulses.

Nolan released the magazine from his pistol and placed both on Brandon's desk.

"I don't understand."

"Your badge."

Nolan shook his head but placed the badge on the desk. Brandon locked both in his desk.

"Okay. I slipped Ted a few things about the case."

A few things? More than that. But what mattered was Nolan had just confessed to leaking sensitive information about a murder case.

"You told Ted I wasn't handling the case the right way."

Nolan shrugged his shoulders. "In my opinion—"

"Your opinion is not something that gets shared with the press. What you did amounts to insubordination."

"How was I to know he'd throw it on the front page?"

"Not only that, you shared confidential—"

"What, the bite marks? I thought that was public."

"Bull, Nolan. And you probably accused an innocent woman of murder."

"Ruby? Everyone knows she did it. Even you—"

"And telling Ted I supposedly had doubts about Ruby's innocence. Who told you that?"

Nolan's biceps twitched. "None of your business."

It had been Misty. What else had she shared with Nolan? Whatever it was, Nolan had passed the information along to Ted.

He wouldn't press Nolan any further about Misty. He didn't want to know what else she'd told Nolan about Brandon.

"Ruby hasn't been charged—"

"She should have been," Nolan said.

"And if she's not guilty, are you going to pay her attorney when she goes after the department?"

"You're firing me because I leaked a few details to the press? That wasn't any big deal until you got here."

"You're being fired for undermining my authority, for falsely accusing a citizen in the press, for releasing case information without permission," Brandon said. "Not to mention, you just got off unpaid leave for almost killing one of my officers."

"Jackson? That was her fault."

"Do you ever do anything wrong?" Brandon asked. "You haven't accepted responsibility for one thing I've mentioned."

Nolan shook his head again. "This is bull. You can't just take my job."

"Watch me."

"You'll hear from my attorney," Nolan said. "I've got a long list of complaints. I know you're pissed because you tried to steal my girlfriend—"

"Get the hell out of here," Brandon said.

A moment later, Sue walked into Brandon's office, a stack of papers in her hand.

"You all right, Chief?" she asked.

"You heard that, didn't you?"

She grimaced.

"I'm not going to lie."

"At least there's one of you that's honest."

Sue pressed her lips together. "You have a whole team of good people. Nolan, he wasn't one of them. In my opinion."

She dropped the papers on Brandon's desk. "Jackson's HR paperwork moving her to full-time."

"Thanks."

Sue paused at the door. "You did the right thing."

"Firing him?"

"Taking his gun. That guy's one bad traffic stop away from killing someone. Even the old chief thought that."

"Then why did he keep Nolan around?"

"Don't get me wrong, Chief Satler was a good man. But in the end, he was thinking more about fishing than anything else."

"I envy him."

"Hey," she said, tapping her finger on his desk. "Unlike us old folks, you got twenty years to go—at least. So, buck up. You haven't earned retirement yet."

He wasn't so sure about that.

"Alright, Sue. Thanks for the pep talk."

"Any time—as long as I'm on the clock."

Brandon signed Jackson's paperwork and wrote an email to HR, notifying them of Nolan's firing. That meant he had to hire yet another new officer. Technically, that meant Jackson was replacing Nolan, not Will.

He'd address that later. For now, he had an alleged loss of confidence in his leadership he needed to deal with.

An email from the mayor popped up on his screen. The subject line read: OUR MOONBEAM FESTIVAL IS RUINED.

Brandon didn't have time for the mayor's drama. He had enough going on within his own team. He hovered the cursor over the delete button. The phone rang.

He answered it.

"Have you seen the Forks Journal website?" the mayor asked.

"Yes."

"Not the piece about you, bad as that was. I mean the website."

"What about it?"

"It seems Ted contacted Tiffany Quick to ask her what she thought about the goings-on in Forks. He sent her a copy of the article."

"Okay."

"Now she's canceled her appearance at the Moonbeam Festival."

"I'm sorry mayor, but I'm dealing with other stuff here—"

"Chief Mattson, we have spent tens of thousands on advertising promising Tiffany Quick *in person*. This is a PR disaster."

With each word, her tone darkened, her voice growing louder.

Brandon held the phone away from his ear. "I don't know what to tell you."

"I blame this on you," she said.

"It's my fault you overpromised for your festival?"

There was a long pause, and he knew his words were a mistake.

"No," the mayor said, her words slow and even. "It is your fault, Brandon, that this case has not been solved. If you would just charge Ruby Walker like everyone wants—"

"Then I'd not be doing my job."

"Your job is to make people feel safe," she said. Her voice took on a softer tone. "Charging Ruby would reassure our citizens that Forks is safe and that the killer is behind bars. There's still a chance Tiffany Quick changes her mind."

"Mayor Kim, my job is not to make people *feel* safe, it's to make them safe. I can't do that if the killer is free."

"You know what, if you don't care about the economic health of this community—"

"Goodbye, mayor."

He hung up. Probably not the smartest thing to do, but had he stayed on the line, he'd tell the mayor what he really thought. That she was part of the problem. Her willingness to assign guilt to the most convenient suspect was the sort of thing that sent innocent people to jail and let killers go free.

He was running out of time to catch the real murderer.

If the mayor fired Brandon, it would be soon. Then, she would make sure Ruby went to prison for life—guilty or not. And the real killer would have gotten away with murder.

Chapter 37

Jackson and Will arrived at the station about a quarter to four. Josiah returned a little later to do shift briefing.

"Where's Nolan?" Josiah asked.

"Everyone in the conference room," Brandon said.

When they were all seated, he said, "I've let Nolan go."

Will whistled. "Wow."

"Why?" Jackson asked.

She was the last person Brandon thought would ask that question.

"Insubordination, leaking info to the press among other things."

"I take it you saw the headline in today's paper," Will said.

"Yes, but as I said, it's not just one thing. I know some of you have worked with Nolan for a long time. If you have any objections to my decision, speak your peace now. I won't tolerate this department working out our disagreements in the local paper."

Brandon considered Josiah. The young officer had, at times, seemed to be under the sway of Nolan's influence.

"Josiah?"

"I'm with you all the way, Chief. And, just so you know, I didn't talk to Ted—"

"But you knew it was going on?"

"Well..."

"We all knew about Nolan's antics," Will said.

"I'm not asking for my officers to spy on each other. But if someone is violating department policy, I need to hear about it."

"You're right," Will said, sliding a toothpick in his mouth. "We all let Nolan get out of hand."

Brandon appreciated Will's candor—and support.

"Alright, get back to work then," Brandon said.

"You got a minute?" Jackson asked.

She waited for Will and Josiah to leave.

"I processed your permanent hire paperwork," Brandon said.

"Thanks. But I have to know. You didn't fire Nolan because of me?"

"The shots fired incident was one of many reasons," Brandon said.

"Okay, but—"

"What are you worried about, Jackson?"

"I'm new here. And I'm a woman."

"Both true. What's that got to do with anything?"

"It's bad enough in the city, but in a place like this..." She looked up at him. "If my fellow officers think I had something to do with Nolan getting let go—"

"I just told them why, and it had nothing to do with you."

"If they believe you. And what about the community? People liked Nolan. What they said about you in the paper..."

"You think Ted will go after you because I fired Nolan?"

"Everyone knows Nolan had a problem with me. And Ted and Nolan were practically best buds."

"You don't need to worry about this. Nolan's firing is on me. I'll make it clear to anyone who will listen."

Sue knocked on the conference room door. Brandon waved her in.

"The sheriff is on the line," she said.

"*The* sheriff?"

"That's right, the big guy up in Port Angeles."

Brandon told Jackson to wait for him. He needed her assistance getting the DNA from Brooke.

He took the call in his office.

"How can I help you, Sheriff?"

"According to what I hear it sounds like you need a hell of a lot more help than I do," Sheriff Hart said. Despite the hint of humor in his voice, it was obvious he was there to talk business.

"You saw the paper?"

"Don't take it personally, Brandon. You're not the first officer targeted by that craphole of a newspaper. Hell, Chief Satler used to call me up threatening to run Ted out of town—"

"Really? I thought everyone loved Satler, even the paper."

"Nope. He was human, just like the rest of us."

"What are you calling me about, Sheriff?"

"It's related to the article, not because of it. Sounds like things are getting out of control—"

"You just said you didn't believe the paper."

"I've gotten calls from the community, the mayor—something about an annual festival being canceled."

"Apparently, the author changed her mind about visiting Forks."

"I even got a call from an officer. You'll know who he is, I'll guess, because you just fired him."

"Nolan."

"Right. He's filed a complaint," the sheriff said. "We'll deal with that later."

"I'm ready to discuss it when you are."

"Later. Let's talk about this murder case."

"Everyone wants it to be Ruby Walker. Maybe they're right, but I don't have a case yet. I can't let a suspect go to trial based on flimsy evidence."

"I spoke with the coroner," the sheriff said.

So, Hart did have his doubts about Brandon's work. He'd called Lisa Shipley to check up on him.

"And?" Brandon asked.

"She agrees with everything you're doing."

"Good to know," Brandon said, not hiding the hardness in his voice.

"It's not that I don't trust you."

"Could've fooled me," Brandon said.

"Are you a good homicide detective? I don't doubt it. I'm sure you could run circles around any of the detectives we have up here. But that's not my concern. It's the politics, Brandon. You got to take care of this case before it spirals out of control. If the mayor calls me again or you keep getting the kind of press I'm hearing about, I won't have much choice..."

Meaning, if the mayor didn't fire him, Hart would. Nothing like having two bosses—both with the authority to can you.

"Understood," Brandon said. "Anything else?"

"Solve these murders and, hey, try to be a little nicer to the mayor and her friends—including Ted."

"I can solve the murders. I'm not making any promises about Ted."

Brandon and Jackson rode to Olivia Baker's house together. It was nearly dinnertime, and he hoped this would go well. If Brooke agreed to the DNA test, the whole process would only take a few minutes.

Brandon didn't want a repeat of the night before where he'd come home late. He didn't like missing dinner with Emma and she was obviously still upset.

As they stepped out of the SUV, Brandon thought he spotted Ted's Civic down the street. The sun was at an angle, so it reflected off the windshield, making it impossible to see if there was anyone in the car.

"What is it?" Jackson asked.

"Nothing. Just wondering if we're being watched. By Ted."

"That article making you paranoid?" Jackson asked.

"It's not paranoia if it's true."

They climbed the steps to the house. The door swung open.

"We're having dinner," Olivia said curtly.

Good for you, Brandon thought. He wished he were having dinner now, too.

Then, he remembered—he was supposed to meet Lisa at seven. Brandon checked his watch. It was after five. And he'd told Emma he'd be home for dinner that evening. He couldn't be both places at the same time.

"We need to speak to Brooke," he said.

Olivia didn't budge.

"Ms. Baker," Jackson said. "We need to know if Brooke is here."

Olivia sighed. "Come in." She opened the screen door.

"Did you hear about Tiffany Quick?" Olivia asked Brandon. It was more of an accusation than a question.

299

"Yep. Where's Brooke?"

"In her room. I'll get her."

When Olivia had left, Brandon said, "I thought they were having dinner."

Jackson shrugged it off. "White lie."

"Hmm."

Brooke rounded the corner, her hair mussed as if she'd just woken up.

Brandon motioned to Jackson, indicating she should take the lead.

"Hi, Brooke, how are you feeling?"

Brooke glared suspiciously at the two officers in her aunt's living room.

"Um, fine."

"She's been sleeping a lot," Olivia said. "It's what you'd expect given what she's been through."

"I know it's been a hard week," Jackson said. "I can't imagine what it's been like for you."

"Yeah," Brooke said, lowering her head.

"So, why are you here?" Olivia asked.

"We have a few more questions for Brooke," Brandon said.

"I already told you everything I know," Brooke whined.

"You're just re-traumatizing her," Olivia said. "If your department listened to common sense—"

Brandon opened his mouth, but Jackson beat him to it.

"This won't take but a few moments," Jackson said. "And it could go a long way toward proving that you didn't have anything to do with any of this."

"How?" Brooke asked.

"We would like to obtain a DNA sample—"

300

"No way. You can't force her to do that," Olivia said.

They could get a warrant for Brooke's DNA if it came to that. He hoped it wouldn't.

"That's why we're asking nicely," Brandon said.

"Honey, you need to talk to an attorney," Olivia said. "This is all just a distraction from the real killer."

"Is this because of the bite marks?" Brooke asked.

"Yes, but—" Jackson started.

"You're right," Brandon said. He glanced at Jackson. "I guess, thanks to the newspaper, everyone knows about the bites."

"And there might be saliva on Justin's neck," Brooke said.

"Right," Brandon replied. In truth, they hadn't found saliva on Justin's bite mark.

"Don't do this," Olivia said.

"It sounds like you think your niece is guilty," Brandon said.

"That's not true at all. I just don't want her being framed by a cop who doesn't want to do his job."

It was a good thing Jackson was there. One, as a witness that Brandon hadn't responded inappropriately to Olivia's comments. And two, so he *wouldn't* respond inappropriately to her comments.

"We only want to clear your name so we can move on other suspects," Jackson said in a reassuring tone.

"Okay," Brooke said. "I don't have anything to hide."

A few minutes later, Brandon and Jackson escorted Brooke to the SUV and placed her in the back seat.

As they were leaving, Olivia held up her phone. She called out to Brandon. "I'm calling the mayor," Olivia said. "And the newspaper."

Brandon winked at her. "You do that. By the way, your friend Ted is down the street stalking your house. Save yourself the call."

He pointed to Ted's car a block away.

As they pulled away, Olivia eyed Ted's car up the street. Maybe she'd give him a piece of her mind for spying on *her*, the mayor's right-hand woman.

Brandon wished he could be there to hear it.

Chapter 38

Jackson noticed the reporters first.

"What's going on at the station?"

The news van's extendible satellite antenna was visible two blocks away. Were it a building, it would qualify as the tallest in town.

"Dammit," he said, pulling into the parking lot. "This is the last thing we need right now."

Brandon recognized the van's KIRO News logo. KIRO was one of the big three local stations in the Seattle area.

Brandon edged his SUV up to the automatic gate that led to the jail sally port. A camera crew approached. They were followed by a Black woman, neatly dressed but wearing a windbreaker over her business jacket. Brandon recognized her from his days working homicide in Seattle. He'd never talked to her directly, but she'd covered some of his partner's cases. Her name was Cherise McLaughlin.

"Sir, are you Chief Mattson?" Cherise asked as he drove past.

Brandon pulled through the gate, letting it slide shut so they were separated from the reporters. He told Jackson, "Take Brooke around back."

There was no reason to reveal who they were questioning. If Brooke was innocent, why expose her to the inevitable negative attention that came with being a suspect in a murder investigation?

Jackson jumped into the driver's seat while Brandon approached the news crew.

As much as he despised Ted, he'd had a point. By not addressing the media directly, he'd left them to their own imaginations.

"How can I help you?" he asked.

"Chief Mattson?"

"That's me."

"We'd like to get an update on the homicides here in Forks."

"Are you recording?" he asked.

"Not yet," Cherise said. "You willing to give us an interview? We received a tip you were en route with a suspect."

"You drove all the way out from Seattle for that?"

"We were coming out already. There's more on the way. We saw KOMO up in Port Angeles."

"Thanks for the heads up. Just curious. Who tipped you we were bringing someone in?" Brandon asked.

"Some local reporter."

"Hoping to get on your good side?"

"Probably. You ready to start recording?"

"Go," Brandon said. This wasn't his first time briefing the press on a homicide case.

But he wasn't ready for the first question she asked.

"What is your response to reports of a lack of confidence in your leadership?"

"I've addressed this with my staff, and I've been reassured that we are all on the same page."

He wasn't counting Nolan since the rogue officer wasn't part of the department any longer.

"What about those that say you aren't charging the real culprit in this case?" she asked.

"None of those people have over a decade working homicide. I do."

"You're relying upon your reputation as proof you're making the right decision?"

"You see, Cherise. That's the problem. I haven't made a decision yet. I won't until it's clear we have our person. The last thing we need, be it in Seattle or a small town like Forks, is to have citizens falsely accused, their lives ruined, while the real killer goes free."

"Thanks, Chief," Cherise said. "A couple of questions about the case?"

"You know I can't say much at this stage," he reminded her.

"Understood. Maybe just a summary."

Brandon outlined the basic facts of the case, mentioning only that Ruby was a suspect, but there were a few more leads they were following up on.

She handed him her card. "Let me know if anything changes? We'll be in the area."

"Will do," Brandon said, wishing Forks had reporters like Cherise. Instead, he was stuck with the likes of Ted Nixon.

Back in the station, Jackson had already finished with Brooke's DNA sample. He returned with Jackson to the interview room.

"You ready?" Brandon asked Brooke.

"I thought you had to ask me more questions," she said.

"I think we're good for now. Like the officer here said, you've been through enough."

She pressed her lips in an anemic smile. "How long will it take to prove my saliva isn't on the bite marks?"

"Days, maybe weeks," he said. "If we even get any saliva off Justin."

"Like someone might have wiped it off?"

"Exactly."

Jackson took the girl back to her aunt's house. Brandon and Jackson met up just outside of town.

"How'd it go?"

"Fine. The aunt was still complaining about police incompetence."

"Sorry I missed that," Brandon said. "Any news media there?"

"Not one."

"Alright. I'm late for dinner."

"Hey, Chief," Jackson said. "Back when we were first talking to Brooke and her aunt, Brooke asked if we were trying to find out if her saliva was on the victim's bite wounds."

"Right."

"And I was about to add that we could check against the cans you found."

"I know that's what you were about to tell her."

"I get it. You don't want her to know."

"We have to tell her something, and the bite marks are the most obvious. The beer cans, not so much. Never let a suspect know everything you know."

"Because if she was on the sea stack that night, she might have refused the DNA test."

"You know what, Jackson. I'd dub you lead detective," Brandon said.

"Really?"

"If there was such a thing in Forks."

"Wow. Thanks."

"Someday."

"Someday indeed. Have a good night, Chief."

Brandon started the truck's engine. The digital clock read 6:15. There was no way he'd make it to his date with Lisa.

He could ask his dad to take Emma home.

But Emma was right—he'd been home late more often than not the last few days. A first date with the local coroner wasn't a good enough reason to miss dinner again. He'd have to wait until things settled down.

Besides, he wasn't in the mood to ask his dad for anything after their confrontation at lunch. In fact, Brandon wasn't in the mood for anything but to see his daughter for a bit and forget about work for a while.

He pulled out his phone and typed a text to Lisa: *Can't make it. Work to do.*

Except he wasn't going to work. Why start out with a lie? He retyped the text: *Can't make it. Too much going on.*

That was the truth.

She responded 30 seconds later: *No problem. Take care.*

Emma came rushing out of her grandpa's house.

"It's about time," she said.

He studied her face. Was she upset again? She didn't seem to be.

"What?" she asked.

"Just thinking how much I love you," he said.

She punched him in the arm. "Stop being weird."

Brandon grinned. "Is it weird to say I love my daughter?"

He moved toward the SUV.

"Aren't you going to say goodbye to Grandpa?" Emma asked.

The thought hadn't crossed his mind. Was he really that disconnected from his father? Or just trying to avoid the fallout from the argument they'd had earlier in the day when he'd taken sides with Nolan and the others in town who wanted to railroad Ruby to jail without hard evidence. He read the newspaper too much, believed Ted more than his own son.

"Let's go," he said. She hopped in the truck. As Brandon drove away, he spotted his father's figure peering out the living room window.

Chapter 39

Brandon pulled onto the highway that led to town.

"You hungry?" he asked.

"Starving."

He'd planned on picking something up for dinner. Eventually, he'd get into the habit of making a list of meals and shopping in a more organized manner. The way Tori had. Cooking like a bachelor wouldn't fly, not with Emma here.

Shopping meant being in public. By now, everyone had read the article about Brandon and the department. He could face criticism just fine but right now he wanted to be with his daughter.

"We're going out," he said.

"Forks Diner?"

"How about Giuseppe's?"

"Where's that?"

"An Italian place up in Port Angeles. Maybe we can get a movie, too."

"Serious?"

"Do I look like I'm joking," he said, beaming.

"Okay," Emma said, "But what movie? I have to approve—"

"Whatever you want," he said. "As long as it doesn't involve a vampire love story."

"Gross," Emma said. "Who do you think I am? Grandpa?"

Emma ordered chicken parmigiana and to Brandon's surprise, she finished her meal—to the last noodle.

Brandon ordered a single-sized pepperoni and mushroom pizza. Giuseppe's had the best pizza in the county. As Brandon watched Emma finish her meal, his eyes rested on a table across the restaurant where Tori and he had sat when they'd stopped here on their first trip back from Forks as a couple. It was the day he'd introduced her to his parents for the first time.

His father had liked Tori right away. Brandon figured that was because they were both straight shooters. His dad because of his personality, Tori by necessity—she was a woman working as a trial lawyer in a sea of Armani-wearing sharks.

It had taken his mother a while longer, but once she overcame what she perceived as Tori's aloofness, she grew fond of her too.

"Dad?"

He shook away the memory. Emma had been speaking to him.

"Huh?"

"Are you listening?" she asked.

"Yeah."

She sighed. "Liar."

"Hey. Don't be disrespectful. I don't care how old you are."

She wiped her mouth with a napkin.

"I was saying, would you at least think about letting me stay here for the school year?"

"Emma—"

"What are your arguments against it?" she asked.

"For one, your mom—"

"What if she says it's okay?"

"And there's nothing here for you."

"Except my dad," she replied.

He shook his head. "Okay. Let me talk to your mom. But that means you'll be in Seattle all summer and here during the school year."

Hope flickered in her eyes. "Thank you!"

"After I talk to your mom."

If Tori didn't like the idea, it wouldn't work. Their divorce had been as amicable as possible, and he wasn't about to upset the balance they'd achieved so far. They couldn't go changing the parenting agreement every time their teenage daughter got in a fight with her mom.

But there was something else about the idea that bothered him.

"Em, earlier today when you mentioned Madison...it seems like you're still struggling with what happened."

She twisted her napkin in her hands. "I guess."

"I need to know the move out here isn't because you're trying to avoid being at school in Seattle."

Madison's car accident had occurred just a few blocks from Emma's high school.

She thought about it for a minute and then said, "No. I mean, yes it reminds me of her. But like my counselor, and you and mom said, I can't pretend it didn't happen."

"Right. But isn't changing schools just that—running away?"

"I know I talk about her a lot," Emma said. "But that's just my way of dealing with it. It's not a reason to freak out. Changing schools is moving on, not running away."

"But if you need to go back to counseling..."

"Then I would let you know."

"Promise?"

"Promise," she said.

He was grateful his daughter trusted him enough to share her hurts and fears with him. He would do his best to keep her trust—and that meant not panicking when she was brave enough to tell him what she was feeling.

Emma sat up in her seat. "Enough emo talk. The movie starts in twenty minutes."

He pulled out his wallet, but his phone rang. Misty's number splashed across the screen. He didn't answer.

"Who's that?" Emma asked.

"No one."

"Work?"

"No."

The server returned to take his card and while they were waiting, Emma asked, "Do you think that girl killed her boyfriend?"

"What girl?"

"Brooke. The one that invited me to the party."

He didn't want to discuss work with Emma but he remembered the conversation they'd had earlier about Brandon not trusting her. She wanted to feel more grown-up than she was. But she also wanted to be part of his life.

"To be honest, I don't know. Brooke was with her aunt the night Justin was murdered."

He could see the crank turning in her head.

"What night was he killed?" she asked.

"Friday."

Her eyes widened. "That's the night I went to her aunt's house to drop off Brooke's coat."

"You what?"

"Remember, she let me borrow her coat."

He did, and he'd told her he would take the coat back himself.

"And you returned it despite what I told you—"

"Okay, I'm sorry. But listen. No·one answered, so I left it on the porch, inside the front door. Misty went with me, so it's not like it wasn't safe."

That was the day Brandon had come home and Misty and Emma were talking on the porch. Why hadn't Misty mentioned their trip to Brooke's home?

"Did you knock?"

"Of course. The lights were off."

"I warned you not to get involved in the case, Emma."

She cast him an apologetic smile, but he could see the glimmer of excitement in her eyes, the thrill of the chase, knowing you had a clue that could lead to throwing the bad guys in jail.

"What time?" he asked.

"Before you came home."

"So maybe five or six?"

"I think so..."

"Was there a car in the driveway?" he asked.

"No."

Brooke's aunt, Olivia, had claimed Brooke was at home with her during the time Justin died—the same time Emma and Misty went to her home.

"You're sure?"

"Dad—"

"I believe you. It's just..."

"You sure you want to go to the movie?" She asked. "You look worried."

"No. We're going."

He'd told Emma they'd spend the evening together. He wouldn't break that promise no matter how hard it might be to keep his mind off the case—and the fact that Emma had just shattered Brooke's alibi.

The movie ran for almost two hours. With the romantic comedy plotline, cute dog, and small-town setting, it reminded Brandon of a Lifetime Channel flick he'd watched with Tori. He tried his best to laugh along with Emma. But his mind had latched onto what she'd said about Brooke. Had Olivia really lied about Brooke's alibi? If so, why?

Chapter 40

Brandon was out the door by 6:30 the next morning. The night before, Emma informed Brandon that his dad would be picking her up for a fishing trip sometime in the morning. He let her sleep.

He'd been up since before sunrise. Emma's information about Brooke's alibi was the break he needed.

They'd done the background checks on everyone. Brooke's only involvement with the police was the allegation of sexual assault against Justin. Justin had shrugged the accusation off as retaliation for cheating on her. If that was true, it showed Brooke was willing to go to great lengths to exact revenge on people who'd wronged her.

Emma's word—that she thought Brooke wasn't home the night of the murder—wasn't enough to move forward with charges. Little evidence connected Brooke to either of the murders. The case against Ruby was more compelling.

Brandon would follow up with Olivia regarding Brooke's supposed alibi.

First, he'd make one more trip up to the treatment center where Brooke had worked with Lauren and Justin. When Brandon had gone up to interview the methadone clinic staff with Jackson, they'd been focusing on Lauren, not her friends.

Monday morning traffic plodded along Forks Avenue. Trucks pulling boats headed for the river. Small clusters of tourists ambling to Forks Diner for a heavy dose of saturated fat and strong coffee.

A Moonbeam Festival sign still hung across the highway, announcing Tiffany Quick as the guest of honor. How would the mayor deal with the author's last-minute cancellation?

Not Brandon's problem, but he was sure to hear about it.

Brandon arrived at the clinic just as they were finishing their morning dosing. Brandon knew from his experience in King County that many clinics provided methadone at certain times of the day. Most were in the morning, allowing those picking up the daily dose to go to work or treatment after visiting the clinic.

He waited until the last person had left before approaching the dosing window.

The woman handing out the methadone wore a faded red and black flannel shirt and a denim blue headscarf. She had a teardrop tattoo just below her right eye.

"What's up?" she asked, eyeing him suspiciously.

"Hoping to speak with the supervisor," Brandon said.

"You're looking at her."

"You got a minute?"

"I didn't do it," she said with a guilty grin.

Brandon smiled back and the woman hacked out a smoker's laugh. "I'm just joshin' ya. You never know, what with old warrants."

"How long you been sober?" Brandon asked.

"Four years, six months."

"Nice."

"Let me lock up. I'll be out in a minute."

Brandon took a seat in the waiting area. About five minutes later, the woman came out, locking the door behind her.

"Let's go outside. I need a smoke."

Outside the clinic, the woman pulled out a pack of Pall Malls and lit one, blowing the smoke away from Brandon.

"I'm Brandon, by the way."

"Anita McElroy." She considered his uniform. "You here about one of our people? You know I can't share anything with you."

"Not a client. Brooke Whittaker."

Anita coughed.

"Sorry," she said. "Brooke?"

She took another long drag from the cigarette.

"Hard to forget her."

"Why?" Brandon asked.

"If she wasn't pissed because she thought her boyfriend was sleeping around, it was something else. You know, one of those people that seem to get their jollies being mad at everyone and everything."

It wasn't just Adam who had a jealous streak. And Brooke, it seemed, possessed a certain aggressiveness that Brandon hadn't noticed in Adam or Ruby.

"What did she do when she got mad?"

"I heard she beat up her boyfriend...what was his name?"

"Justin?"

"Yeah. Nice-looking kid. Don't know what he saw in her. Although I heard he liked to plant his stake wherever he could, if you get my drift."

She hacked out a laugh again.

"Justin wasn't a small kid," Brandon said.

317

"I hear you, but I've seen that girl take down other girls twice her size."

"You mean she used to get in fights a lot?"

"Brawls. Girls she thought were checking out her beau. I get it. You protect your claim on your old man, but that ain't no reason to start fights with every woman who passes by."

Not only aggressive, but violent.

"You saw her do this?"

"Hell yeah. More than once."

"No one called the police."

"No disrespect, officer," she said, eyeing his badge. "But we aren't too fond of your kind around here."

"I get it."

"That's why she got fired. Started a fight with one of the clients."

"Fired? She told me she quit."

Anita shook her head. "Nope. Does this have something to do with Lauren's death? I heard Justin might be in trouble—he hasn't been back to work—"

"Unfortunately, Justin passed away earlier this week."

Her eyes widened. "How?"

"That's what I'm trying to figure out."

"You think Brooke was involved?"

"Not yet, and I hope you'll keep this conversation between us. For now."

"Scout's honor," she said, forming her fingers into a mock salute. She extinguished her cigarette in an ashtray next to the clinic door.

"You know anything about Brooke's family? She has an aunt named Olivia."

"Never heard of her," Anita said. "I know her parents passed a while back. Boating accident."

318

"Did they have money?"

Brandon recalled what Lauren's mom had said about Brooke. What had she called her? A snotty rich girl?

"Brooke inherited a ton of cash before she started here. Life insurance or something like that. Partied it away, then the poor girl had to get a real job. She was working on her master's degree but dropped out."

She pulled her cell out of her back pocket. "Crap. I got a group to run."

Brandon handed her his card. "You've been very helpful, Anita. I may need you to make a formal statement."

"Ah hell. I don't want to go to court."

"We'll try to keep it from getting that far," he said.

"Promise?"

Brandon held up his hand. "Scout's honor."

"You know where to find me."

Brandon contacted Will and asked him to head to the aunt's home and pick up Brooke. He was to tell her they had a few questions for her and have her wait in the interview room.

He was just outside Port Angeles when Will called. "She's not there."

"And the aunt?"

"No car, no one answered the door."

"Alright. Keep an eye out for her."

"Will do."

Had he waited too long to bring Brooke in? Had she fled Forks and, if so, had Olivia helped her?

If Brooke was the murderer, that meant right now she was somewhere in his county, free to kill again.

319

Chapter 41

Brandon pulled into the police station parking lot and noticed two cars in front of the mayor's office. One was Mayor Kim's Range Rover. The other belonged to Olivia.

Inside, the door was open. Olivia sat in the chair across from the mayor's desk.

"Chief," the mayor said, noticing him.

Olivia glared at him. Her eyes were swollen. She held a crumpled tissue in her hand.

"Brooke is missing," she said in an accusatory tone.

"How long?" Brandon asked.

"She was gone when I woke up this morning. Her phone goes straight to voicemail." Olivia sniffled. "This is your fault."

The mayor stepped from behind her desk, put an arm around her. "Olivia..."

"Let her talk," Brandon said.

"This is like Justin and Lauren," Olivia said. "They were missing—and then they were killed."

"She has a point," the mayor said.

"If you would have arrested the right person—" Olivia started.

"You mean Ruby?"

"Of course."

"Ruby's been in jail on drug charges since before Brooke disappeared."

"Well, then. If you hadn't treated Brooke like a suspect, she might not have run away," Olivia said.

"You believe this too?" Brandon asked the mayor.

"It's all over the news," the mayor said. "About your department being in shambles, that there's a murderer in custody you refuse to charge."

"And if it's in the news, it must be true," Brandon said.

"It's not just that. The Moonbeam Festival will be a total flop because of this."

"I don't give a damn about your festival," Brandon said. "My job is to protect the citizens of this town. Even those accused of crimes."

Mayor Kim pointed a finger at him. "It's that exact attitude that concerns me. You're talking like a detective. Not a chief of police. I'm beginning to wonder if you're out of your league here, Brandon."

"I'm doing my job," he said. "As for you and your tourism minister or whatever fake name you've given her— all you've done is lie and step all over my case."

"I have not lied—"

"You knew Olivia was Brooke's aunt."

He stared her down, daring her to deny it.

"It's not lying to forgo telling someone an irrelevant fact."

She sounded just like the politician she was.

"Justin may have died because I received this information after Brooke killed a second person."

"Brooke didn't kill anyone," Olivia said.

"Yet, you think she's running?"

"That's not what I meant."

"I find it interesting that you're so worked up about a twenty-something girl who's only been gone for the better part of a morning. I'm asking you again, Olivia. You believe Brooke has a reason to run. Why?"

"Because..." Her shoulders sank. "I don't know."

"How about I try," Brandon said, taking a few steps forward. "Brooke doesn't have an alibi for the time Justin was murdered," he said.

Olivia's eyes widened.

"That's not true. I was with her."

"But I have at least two witnesses who said you weren't home that night."

"Who?"

Brandon would not call on his own daughter—or Misty—to testify to Brooke's lack of an alibi.

"That doesn't matter right now. Isn't it true you were gone most of the night?"

He didn't know how long she'd been out, but it was an educated guess.

"What night?" the mayor asked.

"Friday evening," Brandon said.

"Wasn't that the day you stayed over in Tacoma? At the communications conference? You were going to stay Friday night and return Saturday."

"I...yes but I came home instead."

"I thought you were at a hotel. I authorized the payment," Mayor Kim said.

"We can check the hotel records," Brandon said, pulling out his notebook.

She rested a hand on his arm as if to stop him from taking notes. "Okay. I wasn't there. But it doesn't mean anything."

"You gave Chief Mattson a false statement?" the mayor asked.

"Yes, but Brooke promised me she stayed home. She wouldn't lie about that."

"But you distrust her enough that you believe she's running now," Brandon said. "Why?"

"She said something about the DNA. The bite marks."

Brooke had offered the DNA willingly because she believed the police would limit the DNA-related aspects of the investigation to the bite mark. Brooke likely assumed that wiping the area clean would cover her tracks. She was right—they hadn't lifted any saliva from Justin or Lauren.

"What else was she worried about?"

She pleaded with the mayor. "I don't want Brooke to get in any more trouble—"

"Olivia, you're already in deep trouble yourself. Tell Brandon the truth."

"Okay. It wasn't just the teeth. Something about beer cans and you..." Her eyes settled on Brandon. "Brooke said you would frame her and claim you found her saliva on the beer cans where Lauren was killed."

That evidence wasn't public.

"You don't happen to be friends with Officer Nolan?" Brandon asked.

She didn't answer.

"How long has Brooke known?"

"Since yesterday. I thought it would calm her down. Officer Nolan said if they found the DNA on the cans it would prove it was Ruby..."

"Unless it wasn't Ruby," Brandon said. "What is Brooke driving?"

"She has an old Mercedes—"

"Define old."

"2006," she said.

"Color."

"Silver."

"Any idea where she might go?"

"No."

Brandon didn't believe that.

324

He thought of something else. He'd found more than beer cans at the sea stack.

Brandon pulled out his phone and showed Olivia the picture of the crescent moon necklace.

"Does this look familiar?"

She frowned. "I bought that for Brooke for her birthday last year. Why?"

"I discovered it at the scene of Lauren's death."

"Brandon," the mayor said. "You don't think—"

"Considering that everything discussed in this office leaks more than a raft full of holes, I won't say what I think."

"What are you going to do with Brooke?" Olivia asked.

"You can read about it in the papers," Brandon said.

Brandon was halfway across the parking lot when his phone rang. His dad's home number. He and Emma were supposed to be fishing.

"What happened?" Brandon asked. "Is Emma okay?"

"She's fine. But I need you to come over."

"I'm working a case right now," Brandon said.

"I know that. Just, get over here."

"Emma's fine?" Brandon asked.

"I already told you that." He hung up the phone.

He was headed out to the beaches and his dad's property was on the way. What could be so important that he had to drop everything and head to his house?

Brandon told dispatch to notify all officers in the county to be on the lookout for Brooke and her car. He contacted Sheriff Hart on his private cell and updated him on the situation. The sheriff would send someone out to keep an eye on Brooke's apartment in case she returned home.

Brandon pulled up to the house and his father appeared on the threshold.

"Where's Emma?" Brandon asked.

"She's in the garage organizing the fishing gear."

"I thought you'd be gone by now," Brandon said.

"I wanted a minute with you."

Brandon sighed, but walked up to the steps. His dad disappeared into the house, forcing Brandon to follow him.

He brought a cardboard box out of the kitchen.

"You should have this," he said.

He passed the box to Brandon. Inside were a pair of boots and some other items. They were Eli's.

"His badge is in there too."

"Why?"

"Eli was your brother. And you're the only surviving kin. Besides Emma."

He'd called him out here to give him Eli's old stuff?

"What about you?" Brandon asked.

"I've had this long enough."

Brandon stood there for an awkward moment. Taking in the living room, the fireplace, the scent of lavender. This is where he and Eli had fought, wrestled, hated, and loved each other as only brothers can. The box and its reminders of Eli brought back a flood of memories.

It was unsettling, feeling this way, this vulnerable, in front of his dad and in this house.

"Okay," Brandon said. "I'll figure out what to do with these."

He turned to leave, but his father touched his arm.

326

"Brandon, I'm sorry about yesterday."

"What?"

"Hell, I'm sorry about a lot of things, but to be specific. I didn't mean to tell you how to do your job."

Brandon met his father's gaze.

"I appreciate that."

"And as for everything else, the comparisons to Eli—"

"Dad, you don't—"

"Let me say my peace." He scratched his head, stared down at Brandon's feet. "I haven't always been fair, but I want you to know I loved you both the same. You and Eli."

Was his dad sick? Why the deathbed confession?

His dad continued. "If it makes you feel any better, you were always your mother's favorite."

It was his father's best attempt at a compliment.

"Are you okay?" Brandon asked.

His dad's eyes rose to Brandon. "What the hell is that supposed to mean?"

"It's just...why now?"

"I don't want us to be angry at each other."

This wasn't the confrontation-loving Buzz Mattson he'd grown up with. He wasn't sure how to react to this softer version of his father.

"Maybe it's my granddaughter's influence. Making me soft."

Brandon smiled. "Yes, daughters do have that effect."

"Anyway, I just want you to know, screw everyone who doesn't think you're doing your job."

Brandon smiled. "Thanks, Dad."

He paused. "And I'm sorry for what I said. You know about you blaming me—"

"No need for that," his dad said. "Just...be careful," he glanced at the front door. "There's a murderer out there."

Chapter 42

The lot at Second Beach was full of cars, but none were Brooke's. After a couple of hours of searching the west county area, he headed back to town. He'd checked in with the unmarked car watching Brooke's apartment. No sign of her.

Forks was on the main highway between Port Angeles and Aberdeen. You either went north or south or stayed put. To the west was the ocean and to the east the Olympic Mountains. Brooke didn't seem the type to rough it in the wilderness. She'd have to come out of hiding, eventually.

If Brooke was the killer, was she done exacting her revenge? What about Adam? He was still a suspect. The bite marks indicated Brooke hoped to make it appear Justin was the victim of a vampire-obsessed killer. What if she did the same to Adam?

It was after five when Brandon got home. He called Emma, and she said they were done fishing but had gone down to Aberdeen for dinner. They wouldn't be home until late. Brandon was on his own.

He made himself eggs and toast and pulled out his notepad, flipping through until he got to Adam's number.

"Hello?" Adam answered.

"Brandon Mattson with the Forks Police Department."

"Hey."

"When's the last time you heard from Brooke?"

"Um...I was down there yesterday, hanging out with her."

"Nothing since then? Not even a text or phone call?"

He paused. "No."

"You're sure?" Brandon asked.

When Adam didn't reply, Brandon said, "Son, either you were involved in this murder or you're hiding something. Either way, you're in trouble. This is your chance to come clean."

"She said Ruby killed Justin. Something about the bite marks. Ruby has fangs and Brooke is going to prove it."

They hadn't found any fangs in the search of Ruby's home.

"When?"

"Today, I think. She said no one would be paying attention—"

"Did she tell you how she would prove Ruby was guilty?"

There was another pause and an intake of breath. "No."

He was lying, and if it came to it, Brandon would take the young man into custody.

"Adam, why would Brooke tell you this?"

"I don't know. I mean, she knew I was freaked about going to jail. I'm the number one suspect, right?"

"Did you kill Lauren?" Brandon asked.

"No."

"Justin?"

"No way," Adam said.

"Do you know who did?"

"If I did, I'd tell you. I mean, I don't want to go to jail for what someone else did."

"Neither does anyone else," Brandon said, thinking of Ruby.

What was Brooke's plan? Was she innocent, desperate to find a way to prove she hadn't killed Lauren and Justin? Or was she targeting Ruby—hoping to frame her for a crime Ruby hadn't committed?

There was a knock at his front door.

"Thanks for the information, Adam. We'll be in touch."

Brandon cracked the door open.

"You got a minute?" Misty asked.

He stepped back, letting her in. "Just a few. I've got to get down to the station."

"I need to apologize for the other night," she said.

"You mean—"

"The kiss," she said, holding onto his hand. "I shouldn't have done that."

Branded pulled back.

"What's wrong?" she asked.

What was wrong was that she kept giving him reasons not to trust her.

"The other day, I mentioned my doubts about Ruby's innocence."

"You did?"

He hated it when people played dumb.

"You told Nolan."

She squinted at him. "I...I mean—"

"Please don't," he said. "I know it's true. What I don't know is what other information you've shared. About me, about Emma."

"I wouldn't do that."

"Really?"

"Okay, I might have mentioned to Nolan what you said about Ruby Walker. That you wondered if she was guilty. Other stuff...I don't know."

331

All the time they'd spent together over the last several days. The time she'd spent with Emma...

"Is that why you fired Nolan?" she asked. "Because he talked to the newspaper?"

"I'm not going to discuss Nolan or anything to do with my department."

She moved closer, her hand on his chest. He swept it aside.

"You'd better go."

"I'm sorry, Brandon. I didn't know."

"And when you said you were taking a break from Nolan—but you were passing along information about me?"

"It wasn't like that."

There was something else.

"And before you go dragging my daughter to a suspect's home—"

"What are you talking about?"

"You and Emma went to Brooke's home to return her coat. Without telling me."

"I thought you'd be upset," she said.

"So, you hid the truth?"

Now Brandon wondered—had Misty known Brooke was Olivia's niece all this time?

He decided it didn't matter. He was done.

"Brandon—"

He waved her off. "I've heard it before. Remember, twenty years ago? You lied then too."

"That was different," she said.

He considered telling her he was dating someone else—Lisa Shipley. But that wasn't close to the truth.

"Goodbye, Misty."

Misty turned and left without another word. Brandon closed the door behind her.

He cursed, punting an empty moving box across the living room.

He'd been stupid—for trusting Misty, letting her back into his life. What made him believe she would change?

It was moments like this when he wished Tori were there. Despite their differences, she was someone he could trust no matter what the circumstances. But it wasn't like he could call her and complain about how his ex had duped him, again.

He considered calling Tori anyway but thought better of it. Then he considered texting Lisa to set up a new time to meet.

The time wasn't right. After he wrapped up the case. If she was still interested.

He grabbed his keys and headed back to the station. He had an idea how Brooke might try to frame Ruby. His plan for catching her, if it worked, would require help.

Chapter 43

Brandon found Will at the station filing his reports for the day.

"Any plans after work?" Brandon asked.

"A glass of Jameson and my recliner. I plan to fall asleep watching the Mariners lose."

"Sounds boring," Brandon said.

"That's the point—"

"I need your help solving a murder. Or two."

Will sighed. "Did I mention I'm too old for this?"

"We'll take my truck."

"Undercover work?"

"Exactly."

Brandon headed to the end of the dirt road, several hundred feet past Ruby's property. He pulled into an opening in the woods, a plot used by illegal dumpers to toss everything from mattresses to couches and washing machines.

"Explain again why I'm missing my dinner?" Will asked as they walked back down the road to Ruby's place.

"Brooke told Adam she could prove Ruby killed Justin and Lauren. Tonight."

"Tonight when?"

"Don't know. That's why we're getting here early."

Will shook his head. "Why do I get the feeling this will take a while?"

"Because," Brandon said, "you're a seasoned veteran."

"Seasoned is right. I remember the first time I pulled you over for speeding."

"And I begged you for a warning, but you still gave me a ticket. My dad was so pissed at me."

"I was trying to teach you a lesson."

"Huh," Brandon grunted.

"It must have worked. You turned out alright."

Brandon often forgot how much he'd idolized Will when he was a kid. It was his memories of the kindly yet hard-assed cop that had partially influenced his decision to enter the force.

Ruby's mobile home was edged into a nook in a stand of alder and fir.

The porch lights were off, the inside of the house shadowed too. It was twilight, and the moon had risen just above the treetops.

Brandon pulled out the key he had taken from Ruby's belongings at the jail.

"You sure you're not wasting my time on inadmissible evidence?" Will asked.

"She gave me the okay to do this."

"How the hell did you convince her to do that?"

"I told her if my plan worked, we would have the person who killed Lauren and Justin. Meaning she wouldn't have to worry about a murder charge."

Ruby's attorney had insisted Brandon release Ruby as part of the deal. But he'd already charged her with possession with intent. It was better for Ruby if she were locked up until the murder investigation was complete—for her own safety and to prevent any further accusations against her.

"You sure are stuck on proving she didn't do this, but if Ruby were in your shoes, she wouldn't be trying this hard."

335

"I'm getting to the truth. That's what matters."

They stepped into the mobile home. The acrid stench of smoke and Pine-Sol slapped them across the face like a whiff of smelling salts.

"Stinks like an old folks' home. Back when there weren't any rules about smoking inside," Will said.

"Brooke will try to prove the bite marks are from a pair of fangs Ruby owns," Brandon said.

"But we never found fangs here during the search."

"Right."

Will eyed Brandon. "Then what the hell are we doing standing here in the dark?"

"I think Brooke stole them from Lauren—who'd already taken them from Ruby the night Ruby gave her a ride. Ruby said they were missing from her car. They'd been in a container on the seat next to her—"

Brandon froze. He'd heard something. A moment later, lights swept across the living room wall.

"Come on," Brandon said. At the end of the hallway, there was one room to the left, another to the right. Both doors were closed.

Brandon pointed right. "In there, make yourself invisible. Don't do anything until you see what she's up to."

Brandon entered the room on the left. A mattress lay on the floor, but there were no sheets, and, as Brandon recalled from the earlier search, the closet was empty too. The window on the far side of the room faced the driveway.

As the vehicle pulled onto Ruby's property, its headlights went dark.

A car door clicked shut. Whoever it was, they were trying to be quiet and were taking their time, scoping out the scene.

He crept to the window.

The waxing moon was nearly full. A feeble glow seeped in through indigo curtains. Brandon reached for the curtains but just then heard footsteps approaching the house.

He slid back, waiting.

A moment later, there was a knock at the front door. Three quick taps.

It could be someone legitimate, or one of Ruby's customers hoping to score some pills.

Two more taps.

Then, the front steps creaked.

A shadow passed by the window.

They were headed for the back of the house.

Was it a woman who had passed by? It was impossible to tell through the dark window dressings.

The other entrance was a back door off the kitchen.

He could end this now, bust them for breaking and entering. But that wasn't the point. They were here to catch Brooke planting evidence in an attempt to pin the murders on Ruby.

He'd wait for her next move.

Whoever it was, they were taking their time, probably trying the windows first.

A sharp crack of glass shattered the silence. There was a rolling thud on the kitchen floor—like they'd thrown a large rock through the kitchen door window.

The back door scraped open, followed by the shuffling of feet scattering glass across the linoleum.

Brandon squeezed behind the door but left it open, shielding himself from view.

Footsteps creaked down the hallway.

The steps paused. Brandon held his breath and pressed himself against the wall.

He peered through the crack in the door.

Was it Brooke?

If she saw him now, she would bolt, and with that, they'd lose any chance of finding out exactly what her plan was.

The door to Ruby's room scraped across the carpet.

Hopefully, Will had hidden. Brandon recalled there was a closet to the right as you entered the room. The bed was on the left.

A drawer slid open. Papers shuffled.

"Alright, don't move," Will commanded.

Brandon bolted from behind the door and rushed into the bedroom, unholstering his pistol.

The figure rushed at Will.

Will grunted in pain. The suspect twisted to Brandon, then froze.

Brandon's pistol and flashlight were aimed at the rage-twisted face of Olivia Baker.

Olivia dropped the knife.

"Show me your hands," Brandon said.

Olivia obeyed.

"Face the bed and put your arms behind your back."

Brandon cuffed her and set her on the bed.

"You all right, Will?" Brandon asked, eyeing the knife.

"Just a nick," Will said.

Brandon flipped the light on.

A wicked slice ran up Will's left arm, blood seeping through his sleeve and down his bicep.

"A couple of inches to the left and—" Brandon said.

"Yeah. My wife's gonna be pissed. At you."

Brandon called for a medic to take care of Will. Then, he contacted dispatch to get officers on-scene.

"Tell me what happened," Brandon said to Will.

"I was in the closet, heard the glass. She headed right for the nightstand and dropped a container in. That's when I called out."

Brandon checked the still-open drawer where there was a pair of vampire fangs in a zip lock bag.

As right as he'd been about the teeth—that they'd be returned to frame Ruby—he was just as wrong about who'd be the one to set her up.

"Brooke had nothing to do with this," Olivia said. "It was all my idea."

"So, you're admitting to killing Lauren and Justin?"

Olivia stared at his feet. "Yes."

Brandon didn't believe her. Nothing connected Olivia to Lauren's death. Justin's murder—possibly.

"Where is Brooke?" Brandon asked.

She refused to make eye contact.

"Olivia—"

"I said I don't know. Just take me to prison or whatever you're going to do with me."

He held on to Olivia's arm and pulled her to her feet. "Let's go."

They left through the front door and were halfway to Olivia's car. Sirens pierced the air, medics responding to Brandon's call.

The passenger door flew open. A figure emerged in the dim light.

Olivia tried to tug free of Brandon's grip. "Brooke! Run!"

Brandon let go of Olivia and unholstered his pistol.

Brooke lunged into the car but quickly reemerged holding a handgun.

Brandon trained his weapon on her.

"Drop the weapon and don't take another step."

Brooke froze, the pistol still at her side.

"Drop it, Brooke."

Brandon's trigger finger twitched.

"Now!"

She let the gun slip from her hands.

Brandon exhaled. No one else would have to die.

"On the ground, Brooke. Will, you got Olivia?"

"I'll call for transport, Chief."

Chapter 44

Brandon insisted Will get checked out at the hospital. He did, but not until making a barrage of comments like I don't need a doctor and, if you really cared, you'd let me go home and eat my dinner and, I'm no sissy—I've been doing this longer than you've been alive.

Brandon called Jackson in to help interview the two women.

Olivia stuck to her story—she'd committed the murders of both Lauren and Justin. Her professed motive was revenge on the duo for cheating on her niece. Brandon was sure she was involved in Justin's death—or at least the cover-up. But was she capable of murder? Or just protecting Brooke from a lifetime in prison?

They interviewed Brooke next. Gone was the young woman's sad, lost-my-best-friend demeanor. Now, she wore an expression of defiance, even hatred.

"You thought you could frame Ruby for the murders you committed," Brandon said. "Is that right?"

Brooke tapped her fingers on the table. Brandon wasn't buying the weak attempt at appearing unconcerned.

"We caught your aunt Olivia planting the fangs you used on Justin and Lauren."

"That doesn't prove anything," Brooke said. She stared up at the camera in the corner of the room.

"And when I get the DNA back from the beer cans you shared with Lauren? And your necklace—did that come off when you shoved Lauren, your best friend, to her death?"

Brooke glanced at the door, but she wasn't going anywhere for a very long time.

"And your prints from the rope. The shovel, too. You left evidence everywhere."

It was a guess, but one he'd bet money on. The chaotic nature of the crime scene—the shovel, the hurried attempt to make Justin's murder look like a suicide—it spoke of someone in a hurry. Someone who wouldn't think to wear gloves.

"Maybe we can tell you what we think," Jackson said, her voice quiet and calm in contrast to Brandon's.

As a detective, Brandon wasn't always the bad cop, but he'd found himself irritated by Brooke's defiant attitude. It didn't help that she'd invited Emma to a party where there were drinking and drugs. He was happy to let Jackson have a crack at her.

"You learned Justin was cheating—"

"Learned?" Brooke scoffed. "Like it was a new thing? Yeah, I knew he'd messed around on me before."

"But you thought he'd changed," Jackson said.

"He did. For a while."

"And then?"

"Lauren was cheating on Adam."

"How did you find out?" Brandon asked.

"Adam told me. It didn't take long to figure out it was with Justin."

"She was your friend. That must have hurt," Jackson said.

"I trusted her. Every other slut in Port Angeles wanted a piece of Justin. But Lauren, she wasn't supposed to be like that."

"How long had you known?" Brandon asked.

"Right before the camping trip. I mean, I thought maybe it wasn't true, that Adam was just messing with my head. But then that night, we were all partying and Lauren and Justin were flirting like I wasn't even freaking there."

"But you went to your tent?"

"Justin did too, acted like he was passed out, so I fell asleep. Until he got up. I heard him and Lauren talking, and they took off together. That's when I knew Adam was right."

"And then what?" Brandon asked.

"Justin came back later, and I knew what happened. I was going to tell that bitch what I thought of her, but she was gone."

"Did you confront Justin?"

"No. He just went to sleep, and I waited for her. Later, she showed up with the beer, all happy like nothing had happened. She said, let's go out to the rock, so I did."

"You were hurt, mad at her because she'd betrayed you."

"Hell yes," Brooke said, her voice more intense now. "Do you know what it's like to have someone cheat on you? With your best friend?"

Jackson didn't answer.

"What happened at the sea stack?" Brandon asked.

"We drank a few. Lauren showed me the teeth she'd stolen from Ruby. Everything was a big joke to Lauren. I got more and more pissed the longer we sat there."

How many homicide cases had he been involved in over the years where the difference between life and death was a matter of being in the wrong place at the wrong time?

343

If Lauren hadn't gone into town, hadn't returned with more beer, and hadn't gone out to the sea stack—she might still be alive, despite Brooke's rage.

"You confronted her about what she did with Justin?" Jackson asked.

"I told her I knew what she did. I thought she would deny it, but that bitch said, yeah, sorry. I couldn't help myself."

Behind the tears forming in Brooke's eyes, there burned a fierce hatred for Lauren.

"And then?" Brandon asked.

"I slapped her. Not that hard. I would have left after that, but she hit me."

Would Brooke claim self-defense? Too much about this case that pointed toward premeditated murder.

"And you had to defend yourself?" Jackson asked. Normally, Brandon would object to Jackson feeding Brooke a statement that gave her an out. But the evidence for murder, at the very least a cover-up, was so strong, he stayed silent.

"Right. We fought and then she was gone. Off the side of the rock."

"So, you were fighting and she fell off?" Jackson asked. "Are you sure you didn't shove her? You were angry—"

"She fell. I already told you that."

"And then you tried to help her?" Jackson asked.

"I climbed down to check on her. She didn't say anything."

Brooke sank her head in her hands.

"How did you get her into the water?" Brandon asked.

Her gaze was fixed on the table. "Justin helped me."

Brandon thought back to one of his interviews with Justin. The kid had been most concerned about Brooke

344

leaving him because of his tryst with Lauren. Despite his infidelity, he was willing to participate in covering up a murder just to keep Brooke happy.

"Okay," Brandon said, practicing his best good-cop voice. "We really appreciate your honesty."

Brooke's vacant eyes searched Brandon's face. "Am I going to go to jail for the rest of my life?"

If I have anything to do with it, yes.

"That's up to the judge and jury. But I can tell you that the more truthful you are with us, the better it will be for you. If Justin helped you get rid of Lauren's body, he must have known what happened at the rock."

"I told him it was an accident," she said. "Because it was."

"Then why kill Justin?" Brandon asked, hoping the quick question would elicit an unpracticed, honest answer.

"Because he was weak," she said as if it was the most obvious thing in the world. "He freaked out, wanted to confess what he'd done, that he'd helped me. He thought you would find out what we did."

"You killed Justin because you believed he'd snitch on you?" Jackson asked.

"I know what he was thinking. He'd leave me to rot in jail for murder and he'd make a deal with the cops."

She was probably right.

More importantly, she'd confessed to killing Justin. Cold-blooded, premeditated murder. But some things didn't fit.

"The spray paint?" Brandon asked.

"That was Justin's idea. He thought it would scare people, make them think it was one of those vampire freaks who killed Lauren."

"And the teeth?"

345

"I took the fangs from Lauren after she died. I don't know. It was just an idea."

"You bit Lauren and Justin to throw us off," Brandon said. "So we'd assume Ruby was the murderer."

She shrugged. "It worked. For a while."

"How did you kill Justin?" Brandon asked.

"I told him we had to bury the teeth. I still had them and if the cops found out, we'd both be busted."

"But he was going to come to us anyway," Brandon said.

"He was thinking about it."

"So you killed him."

"We brought a shovel from my aunt's house. He turned his back on me and I hit him a couple of times with the shovel. I came back later with the rope."

"How'd you get Justin's body up in the tree?"

Strong as Brooke was, Brandon doubted she'd done it alone. In fact, he'd figured Adam must have helped her simply because of the effort involved in hauling a young man of Justin's size.

"Don't forget," Brandon reminded her. "We'll have prints from anyone who handled that rope."

"I called my aunt Olivia, freaking out."

"She wasn't there when you killed Justin?"

"No."

"But she helped you lift his body up in the tree," Brandon said.

Brooke shrugged. "Yeah."

"And planting the teeth in Ruby's house?"

"That was my idea."

Brandon wasn't sure if she was covering for her aunt or not, but it didn't matter whose idea it was. He had a long list of crimes with which to charge Olivia, too.

Brandon waited in his office while Jackson took Brooke back to her cell.

It gave Brandon a chance to review the case one more time. They'd caught the killer. But he'd learned over the years that, even in success, there was often a lesson to be learned.

He'd considered all of Lauren's friends—including Brooke—suspects from the start. Had he missed something, some clue that could have identified Brooke as the killer before Justin's death?

He reminded himself that he was working against Brooke and Justin—both were complicit in the cover-up around Lauren's death. Plus Olivia, who had a direct line to the mayor.

He wondered now—what would have been different had Justin gone for help when Brooke told him what she'd done?

He'd never know because Brooke, Justin, and even Olivia, had chosen deceit over the truth. It was a universal law of human interaction—the easy way out always made things so much harder in the end.

Jackson dropped into the chair across from Brandon's desk.

"Thanks for your help in there," Brandon said.

"We make a good team," she said.

"Yeah, too bad there's only one chief position."

"I'll settle for lead detective."

"I'll talk to the mayor about the budget. You never know. We may have saved her Moonbeam Festival. She won't be happy about her Minister of Tourism, though. Either way, I'm glad you're here."

347

"You know," she said, "It's hard to believe what people will do, all for a relationship. Even a bad one. I mean, Brooke could have left Justin and found someone else. Same for Adam, Lauren—all of them."

"People do what people do," Brandon said.

She looked askance at him. "You want to interpret that for me?"

"We all have our patterns, our way of being. Maybe because we figure we're not good enough, that we don't deserve better. So we stay in the same bad relationships, over and over, until something breaks."

Jackson stood. "Well, it's a good thing that for most of us *breaking* doesn't mean hurling our friends off a cliff."

"Yes," Brandon said, "that is a good thing."

Chapter 45

Brandon checked in with his dad and asked if Emma could stay the night at his house. He agreed, and Brandon spent the rest of the evening piecing together the evidence and writing up a confession for Brooke to sign.

He'd contact the prosecutor and, if he guessed right, Brooke would spend at least two decades in the women's state penitentiary. Olivia's case was more complicated, but they'd be pressing charges.

A knock at his front door woke Brandon. He rolled over and checked his phone. Seven-thirty in the morning.

He pulled a shirt on and opened the door.

Misty. Again.

"Did I wake you?"

"No."

"I only have a minute," she said as if he'd been the one who'd come to her front door. At first, he thought she'd been crying, but then realized she wasn't wearing any makeup.

"I'm here to say goodbye," she said.

"You're leaving?"

"I was offered a promotion. Down in Aberdeen."

She'd mentioned the possibility of moving for work. Aberdeen was almost two hours south of Forks.

"Well," Brandon said, still holding the door. "Congratulations."

Misty glanced back toward her house for a moment before turning to Brandon.

"Tell Emma I'll miss her."

His stomach dropped. Emma would be upset about Misty leaving. Then again, Emma didn't know about Misty spilling information to Nolan.

"I'll let her know," he said.

"I'll miss you too," she said.

Was she trying to make him feel bad for spurning her advances?

It almost worked.

Then, he remembered what she'd done, how she'd shared his doubts about the case with Nolan, and how those had ended up in the newspaper.

It was more likely the result of her ignorance than any ill will toward Brandon. But one thing was clear, she was still close to Nolan, an officer Brandon had fired. There would be a legal battle around his dismissal.

He didn't trust her, couldn't trust her after everything they'd been through—20 years ago and the last two weeks.

It was for the best that she was leaving. For now.

"Do you forgive me, Brandon?"

He wondered if she meant for what she'd done in the distant past, or the last week.

"Yes," he said.

She slid the door open and Brandon let go of the handle. She tugged on his shirt, pulling him closer.

"Good," she said, pecking him on the lips.

Then, she was gone, crossing the street with that confident sway that was both infuriating and captivating all at once. He should say something, let her know she couldn't do that to him. She didn't own him...

Let her go, he told himself. You did it before and you can do it again.

He closed the door, made himself an omelet and coffee, and called Tori.

For the next hour, he updated Tori on everything that had happened over the last few days. How Emma had helped solve the case and how he and Will had captured Brooke and Adam.

Tori had been trying to get ahold of Brandon after learning about Justin's death on the Seattle news. He reassured her Emma was safe, but Tori wasn't happy now that she'd learned about Emma's involvement.

It was strangely comforting, unloading his troubles on Tori. She'd been his best friend for most of his adult life. She got Brandon in a way Misty never would. It was one of the tragedies of the divorce—they'd gotten along better apart than when they were together. He hoped it stayed that way—for Emma's sake, and his.

In the morning, Brandon got dressed and dropped by Will's house. He'd been stitched up at the hospital and sent home after a couple of hours. He was in good spirits, although Brandon had had a hard time making it past Will's wife after she answered the door.

She'd made it clear she wasn't happy about Brandon taking an officer "Will's age" out on a dangerous call.

When she'd finally left Will and Brandon alone, Brandon said, "I should know better than asking you this here, but with Nolan gone—"

"Are you seriously going to ask me to put off retirement again?"

Brandon had asked Will to stick around through the transition and until his replacement was hired. Technically, that had happened. Jackson would take Will's position.

Nolan would likely appeal his termination, and the union would no doubt back him. But based on the

351

evidence against Nolan, from the 'shots fired' situation with Jackson to his admitted leaking info to the press, Brandon was pretty sure he'd remain just that—terminated.

"I'm still down one officer."

"Yeah, sounds like a problem," he said. "Your problem."

"I need someone like you on the team, Will."

"*Like* me?"

"Your experience with the town, your—"

"Ah, cut the crap. I'll give you six months, not more. I've already made reservations for Christmas in Maui."

"Thanks, Will."

"I'm on desk duty for at least two weeks. Understood?"

"Sounds fair," Brandon said.

"And, uh, if I were you, I'd get out of here before my wife returns. Wait 'til she hears I'm staying on the force..."

Brandon hightailed it back to his SUV, a wide smile on his face. As much as he wanted to believe he could do this on his own, he could use Will's leadership in the office. Even though they didn't always agree on everything, Will supported Brandon, and support was exactly what he would need in the coming weeks.

Chapter 46

Brandon held a press conference later that day. Overnight, just about every television and radio news station from Seattle had descended on Forks. News rigs packed the police station parking lot. Except for the satellite antennas atop each vehicle, it could have been a food truck convention.

Ted showed up for the conference too, but his voice wasn't to be heard over the questions of the savvier—and more diplomatic—big-city reporters.

Brandon let them know he'd obtained a signed confession from Brooke. He held back on some other details. He saved the mayor some heartburn—for the time being—by not mentioning her staff's involvement in the coverup. The point was that the murderer was in custody. The graffiti and all the hype around the vampire culture had been a distraction.

The town was safe again.

The day after the news conference, the Forks Journal Extra included a page-two story about the department solving the local murder of two young out-of-towners. *Page two*—right next to a story about a former officer appealing his "unfair termination" from the Forks Police Department.

The front-page headline? The mayor had heard from Tiffany Quick, author of the beloved *Moonbeam Darklove* series. Now that the murder case was solved, she had deemed Forks safe after all.

Brandon and the mayor had a heart-to-heart conversation about her over-involvement in the case. She'd apologized and promised to stay clear of police business. He wished he could believe her. To Brandon's surprise, she didn't seem too upset about losing her Minister of Tourism.

"Nothing I can't handle myself," she'd insisted. "Save the taxpayers some money."

In other words, the Moonbeam Festival would continue as planned and all was well with the world again.

Tuesday afternoon, Brandon was in the office working through his notes on the case when he decided he couldn't wait to call Lisa any longer. He needed an update on the lab results. And he wanted to offer an apology for standing her up Sunday night.

"I was just about to call you," Lisa said. "Brooke's DNA was on two of the beer cans you found out at the beach. We have her prints on the shovel. Her aunt's too."

"You've given the prosecutor plenty to work with in case Brooke rescinds her confession."

"What's going to happen to Ruby? From what I read in the local news, everyone was ready to toss her in prison."

"She'll be arraigned and released on bail, pending the drug charges."

"You did the right thing," Lisa said. "It would have been easy to charge her for Lauren's murder, considering the early evidence."

Despite his dislike for Ruby—personally and because of her profession—he'd let the court know how she'd let them use her house to catch the murderer. Meanwhile, he'd warned Ruby that the minute she tried to sell anything in his jurisdiction, her next stay in jail would be for much longer than her recent experience.

"We couldn't have done it without your work on this case," Brandon said. "I mean it."

"Just doing my job. Consistent, reliable me. So reliable, maybe I'm boring."

He knew where she was going.

"That's not why I stood you up on Sunday."

He could hear the smile in her voice. "Prove it," she said.

"Okay—"

"Don't make promises you can't keep."

"Never," he said, smiling now too. "Give me this week to clear things up around here. Then we'll set something up. I'll be there come hell or high water."

"I'll be waiting."

Brandon had just hung up when Sue appeared at his door.

"She's a nice young lady," Sue said.

Brandon leaned back in his chair. "You listening in on my calls, Sue?"

She crossed her arms. "Why would you accuse me of something like that? I was out here in the hallway waiting. I could have been rude and interrupted—"

"Okay, I get it," Brandon said. "What do you need?"

"Do I have to have a reason to talk to my boss?"

"You want an honest answer?" Brandon said.

Sue cracked a smile. "I just need you to sign off on my leave. I'm on vacation next week."

"Again?"

"Hey, you been here as long as me, you accrue vacation. Not my fault you young folk haven't earned it yet."

"Are you doing anything fun?"

"Preparing food for about a thousand people—it's for a huge gathering of several tribal nations, friends of our Tribe. You should come."

"Are you inviting me?"

"Don't act so daft. Of course, I am."

"I'll be there. Just give me the info."

Sue paused in the doorway. "One more thing, Chief."

"Yeah?"

"You've done good so far. Just remember, folks around here don't do well with outsiders."

"Except I'm from here," Brandon said.

"You left. It takes a while for people to get over that. Anyway, I'm glad you're here."

"Me too," Brandon said.

Sunday morning, Brandon and Emma finally made it to church together. His dad was there too. For the moment, he let himself enjoy the sense of completion. His department had solved two murders—as a team. He had a long way to go toward being good at his job. He had the homicide stuff down. Being chief, that was another thing altogether.

After the service, the town gathered at Tillicum Park for the unveiling of Eli's memorial.

It was a cool June afternoon, the stingy sun offering scant warmth despite a cloudless sky.

Brandon, Emma, and Brandon's father were seated in the front row of chairs set out for the crowd. For most of the town, it was standing room only. Brandon spotted Jackson and her family, Will and his wife. All the other officers in his department were present and in uniform.

There were speeches by two city council members, reciting Eli's work as an officer, how much he'd meant to Forks.

Then, the mayor swept aside a black cloth covering the bust of Eli. Below Eli's smiling face the inscription read *Eli Mattson died protecting his hometown of Forks, WA. Always a hero.*

Sheriff Hart delivered a brief but heartfelt speech about the few times he'd met Eli and the pain of losing a loved one in the line of duty.

Brandon's father trembled, the convulsions of a man fighting a losing battle with his own grief. He turned to Brandon. "Promise me you'll catch them. The people that killed Eli."

Eli's case had gone cold despite being an unsolved murder of a fellow officer.

That hadn't sat well with Brandon.

Now he could do something about it.

He might be chief of police, but Brandon wasn't done being a detective—not yet. He still had at least one more case to solve.

He locked eyes with his father.

"I will," he said. "You have my word."

THE END

Thank You

Thank you for reading *Eventide*. If you have a second, please leave a review on Amazon. I read each one and appreciate your time. Please know it makes a difference!

Keep reading for a free sample of *Dark Forest—A Brandon Mattson Mystery Book 2*.

Go to richardryker.com and sign up to receive updates on new releases, offers for free books, and more. I promise not to bother you with a ton of emails! Join now and you'll receive two free short stories. The first features Brandon and Tori (in their younger years) working together to thwart a vengeful kidnapper. The second story, *Special Delivery*, takes place after *Death Cap*. To avoid spoilers, I strongly suggest waiting to read that one until after you've finished the fourth book in the series.

The idea behind *Eventide* is one that's been on my to-do list for years. A previous job took me to the real Forks, WA every few months and I was able to get to know some of the "locals" there. I hadn't read the popular YA vampire love series that put the town on the map, but during my visits I was struck by the number of tourists who flocked to Forks to take in the sights and buy handfuls of vampire-themed trinkets. My wife had read the series and, she'll reluctantly admit, stood in line for opening night so many years ago.

Despite my general familiarity with the area, all of the characters are fictional and I had to change some aspects of the town to make the story work. As a dad who both enjoyed and survived parenting during the teen years, writing Brandon's relationship with his daughter was a highlight of working on *Eventide*.

Writing is a passion I hope to continue to pursue for many years. I'm currently working full time, so I find time to write before work in the morning and on my lunch break (often in the front seat of my car!). I hope to share my characters and their stories with as many people as possible. The best way for me to do that is to get more reviews on Amazon. Would you consider leaving a review on Amazon? I appreciate your effort, even if it is just a couple of sentences. (Okay—I'll stop pestering you now...)

If you were dissatisfied or found errors, please send me an email. I'm always interested in feedback: richard@richardryker.com

Sample Chapter: Dark Forest (Brandon Mattson Mysteries Book 2)

Brandon stood on the edge of the boundless wilderness that was the Olympic National Forest. He cocked his head, listening as the rumble and growl of chainsaws ripped through the silence. He had a hunch the poachers were over a ridge just south of the forest service road where he stood now.

An October chill had settled over the coastal forest as the sun made a quick descent behind a scowling swirl of storm clouds brewing over the Pacific. In just a few short weeks, autumn winds would ravage the Olympic Mountains. The breeze bending the tips of the evergreens was the calm before the storm.

He fetched his rifle from the SUV and headed for the poachers.

Brandon crossed into the woods, waist-high in sword ferns and huckleberry, the wet instantly soaking his pants. He trudged forward, maneuvering around a thicket of fledgling maple. The green shoots snapped under his boots.

As he peaked the ridge, he surveyed the ravine below.

The chainsaws choked silent and Brandon fell to a crouch.

He was outnumbered and most likely outgunned. It could take anywhere between 20 and 40 minutes for help to reach him this far into the wilderness.

A man shouted, "We're done for today."

"We can carry more than this," a younger voice replied.

"You're not as strong as you think you are," the first man said. "Besides, I need a drink."

"You always need a drink."

"Shut up, boy, or I'll make you haul every damn piece out of here yourself."

Brandon sat up, scanning the scene.

The maple grove lay in a level area about a third of the way down the slope.

Following a tip that a band of local timber thieves had targeted the grove, Brandon had traveled the unpaved track five miles up a steady incline. This group of poachers, his informant claimed, had come across a grove of big leaf maples with the rare figured pattern that could earn thousands of dollars for a few hours of work.

There were two types of figured maple—flame and quilted. The rippled quilted maple, found primarily in the Pacific Northwest, was prized for use in everything from high-end musical instruments to gun stocks. Companies like Gibson could sell figured-maple guitars for upwards of ten thousand dollars each.

As chief of police of Forks, WA, Brandon was responsible for a department that covered a wide area across the western end of Clallam County. This particular acreage didn't fall within his authority. But the stakes were too high to worry about jurisdiction. He wasn't there to round up just any timber poachers.

He was there to catch his brother's killers.

A year before Brandon's return to Forks to take the chief of police position, his brother had been murdered during a routine traffic stop. The killers, Brandon believed, were tied to a local timber poaching operation. Despite Eli's longtime service in law enforcement, the detectives up in Port Angeles hadn't done due diligence on the case—at least that was Brandon's opinion. As a former homicide detective, he figured his opinion mattered.

Brandon had set out to hunt down, arrest, and interrogate every last poacher in the region until he solved Eli's murder.

If he helped save a few trees in the meantime, so be it. This was public land, after all, and poaching timber was a felony.

The underbrush behind him shifted with a rustle.

He wasn't alone.

Brandon swung around, cursing himself. He knew better than to let his guard down. He swiveled the barrel of the rifle, searching for the source.

About 20 feet away, a raccoon stood on its hind legs, combing through a thicket of wilted berries, the last of the season. Spotting Brandon, it hunched down, slinking back into the undergrowth.

Only a raccoon. But there were larger and more dangerous mammals in the forest. He tapped his belt, making sure he'd remembered his bear spray.

He returned his attention to the maple grove.

A flicker of neon yellow glinted off one of the men's coats as they faded into the trees, heading back toward the service road entrance.

Evening hovered over the forest as Brandon reached his Police Interceptor SUV. He headed back toward the highway, the whole time scanning the woods to the right for any sign of the men. When he passed their truck—he'd seen it on the way up—he rounded the next bend in the road and pulled out of sight.

He rolled his window down and waited.

Fifteen minutes later, Ursa Major had crept above the mountains to the east as night tucked the last glimpse of sunlight into the horizon.

Had they headed the other direction? Brandon had scouted the area for weeks. There was no other way out.

He tilted his head at the crackle of tires over gravel.

Headlights swept over the treetops as the truck rounded the bend. Brandon had parked several feet off the road, but even now the truck's beams glinted off the SUV's reflectors. The truck skidded to a stop.

They'd spotted him.

The truck backed up, brights landing on Brandon.

Squinting under the glare, he pointed his spotlight at the vehicle and switched it on. The truck didn't budge.

Brandon started the engine and flipped on the light bar. He stuck it in drive and lurched forward, aiming to block the road.

Gravel flew as the driver floored the truck, narrowly missing the SUV. Brandon pulled onto the road behind them.

Then Brandon remembered—he'd left the service gate open.

"Dammit."

He called for backup. A deputy to block the entrance to the forest road near milepost 215 on Highway 101. Involving other law enforcement would make things messy. People would ask questions. But he couldn't risk losing the poachers and any leads they might offer.

The SUV swayed and rumbled over the uneven road. Up ahead, the truck slowed before navigating through a deep gash in the road.

Brandon slowed too, guiding the SUV through the ditch.

His targets had already gained more ground.

He checked with dispatch. A deputy was on the way.

Brandon swerved around a bend, headlights illuminating the eyes of a possum stooped at the edge of the track.

Another curve in the road and they began the final descent to the highway.

A hundred yards ahead, a semi sped by on Highway 101, its lights cutting through the gloaming. They had almost reached the main road.

The poachers floored it as they neared the bottom of the hill. The amber reflectors of a forest service gate lit up the path ahead.

It was shut.

The truck's brake lights flared as it twisted sideways, sliding to a halt inches from the gate. Brandon shoved his boot on the brake. The SUV careened toward the truck.

His push bumper came to a rest against the driver's door.

Brandon threw his door open, rifle pointed at the truck.

"Out of the vehicle!"

The passenger door creaked open.

The two timber thieves flew out of the truck.

Brandon dashed after them. Both men leaped over the gate.

"Sheriff's office!" a voice shouted from the highway.

One of the men froze, raising his hands.

The other veered toward the forest to Brandon's right.

"Stop!" Brandon shouted.

Brandon was only a few steps behind. The man twisted and, seeing Brandon's rifle, he obeyed.

"Hands where I can see them. Nice and high."

"We weren't doing anything," the man said as Brandon cuffed him.

"Except evading police, poaching timber on public lands—"

"You can't prove that."

Brandon gripped the man's shoulder and led him to the pickup. He popped the tailgate and unhooked three bungee cords holding a frayed blue tarp in place. He yanked the tarp free and focused his flashlight on the truck bed, revealing at least a dozen cuts of high-value figured maple.

"Is that proof enough?" Brandon asked.

Brandon settled the man into his Interceptor and headed for the sheriff's deputy. He'd already cuffed and stuffed the second man.

"You're that police chief from down in Forks," the deputy said.

"Brandon Mattson," he replied. "Thanks for the help."

"I was just up the highway," the deputy said. "I figured seeing the gate shut would scare them enough to stop."

"Good thinking," Brandon said.

If they hadn't braked before slamming into the gate's massive metal bars, their chances of survival would've been slim to none. Forest service gates only opened inward.

"Thompson," the deputy said, shaking Brandon's hand. "What are you doing all the way up here?"

"Following up on a local situation," Brandon said. "Maple thieves. I tracked them up here."

The deputy regarded Brandon. It was obvious he didn't believe him.

It didn't matter. Brandon worked for the sheriff, and he outranked the deputy.

"What do you need me to do?" the deputy asked.

"Call for a tow truck. I'll take these two to Forks."

"You sure you don't want me to transport them up to Port Angeles? This isn't your area—"

"Don't worry about it," Brandon said, ending the discussion.

The deputy hiked up his utility belt, thought about it for a second, and said, "Okay, Chief."

Deputy Thompson, Brandon sensed, wasn't the kind of guy to keep a secret from his superiors. Eventually, Brandon would hear from the sheriff about his out-of-jurisdiction forays. Sheriff Hart had already made it clear he didn't like Brandon second-guessing the detectives assigned to Eli's homicide. The case was off-limits to Brandon. When the sheriff found out about Brandon's involvement, it wouldn't bode well for him.

It was a price he was willing to pay. Brandon had a murder to solve and it was time to find out what these two men knew about Eli's killers...

The story continues in *Dark Forest: A Chief Mattson Mystery (Book 2)*